"YOU MAKE ME FEEL ALIVE AGAIN, MAGGIE.

"You make me feel like there's a reason to get up every morning and nothing to fear about going to bed every night. Sometimes I dream about you, and sometimes I just feel you there with me."

"Scott, I can't. I haven't let go of Mark yet." She held up her left hand and studied her engagement ring and wedding ring. "If you and I, if we . . ." She took a deep breath, then started over. "If we made love, I'd feel like I was betraying him."

He let out a ragged breath and hugged her close. "Oh Maggie, what a pair we are. This hasn't been easy on me either, you know. I find myself torn between the joy of falling in love with you and the guilt of forgetting how I felt about Annie."

Maggie's eyes widened. *Falling in love.* She felt a shaft of panic race up her spine . . .

Halfway to Paradise

NEESA HART

AVON BOOKS ◆ NEW YORK

This is a work of fiction. Names, characters, places, and incidents either are the product of the author's imagination or are used fictitiously. Any resemblance to actual events, locales, organizations, or persons, living or dead, is entirely coincidental and beyond the intent of either the author or the publisher.

AVON BOOKS, INC.
1350 Avenue of the Americas
New York, New York 10019

Copyright © 1999 by Moneesa Hart
Inside cover author photo by James Stephenson/Chrysalis Studios
Published by arrangement with the author
Library of Congress Catalog Card Number: 98-93787
ISBN: 0-380-80156-6
www.avonbooks.com/romance

First Avon Books Printing: April 1999

AVON TRADEMARK REG. U.S. PAT. OFF. AND IN OTHER COUNTRIES, MARCA REGISTRADA, HECHO EN U.S.A.

Printed in the U.S.A.

WCD   10 9 8 7 6 5 4 3 2 1

To Stobie Piel—a great writer and even better friend. My life is enriched for knowing you.

To the fathers and mothers; sons and daughters; husbands and wives; sweethearts and friends whose loved ones keep watch over our nation's freedom. Thank you for your courage.

And to that mother and daughter whose triumph I witnessed one morning in the Northwest Airlines terminal at Reagan National Airport. I never knew your names, but I never forgot your story. I'm so glad you were able to tell him, "Welcome Home."

Acknowledgments

The author would like to thank U.S. Marine Corporal Jerry Filner of the Public Affairs Office in Quantico, Virginia; Joyce Flaherty for finding a new home for this book; Lucia Macro for loving it as much as I do; Leanne Banks for invaluable and optimistic advice; Chris McElvey for information on the design and bidding procedure for major resort properties; and Spencer Tracy for inspiring Max.

One

Maggie had never felt more isolated than she did standing near Gate 19 in the crush of the 7:00 A.M. crowd at the Dallas/Fort Worth airport.

The terminal had a dense, air-conditioned feel, despite the slight cooling of the normally stifling outdoor temperature. A late-November mist shrouded the airport in a glove of dismal fog. The beginnings of the holiday crowds paced among duffel bags and backpacks. Hundreds of business travelers, made anxious by the weather and ensuing delayed flights and congested traffic, huddled over laptop computers, cellular phones, and morning papers. The unmistakable scent of polystyrene and disinfectant contrasted with the smell of stale cigars and cheap cigarettes.

She was surrounded by people. And she'd never been so alone.

Maggie set her briefcase on the concrete floor. She sank down onto one of the padded benches, her gaze drawn, involuntarily, to the drama unfolding at Gate 19.

A young woman, no more than twenty-four or -five, stood near the gate, clutching the fingers of her

1

small daughter with one hand, and a tiny American flag with the other. It was a familiar scene. Mother and daughter, clad in matching red, white, and blue shirts, and holding American flags and yellow ribbons, could only be waiting for a serviceman, husband and father, returning from assignment. The woman's tension, and the eager, unsettled movements of her child, suggested that this homecoming probably followed months, perhaps even a year or more, of separation and worry.

Maggie had witnessed dozens such homecomings dozens of times. She had even participated when her own husband had been among the returning heroes. She knew the tension of the final moments before the plane landed. She knew the rush of joy and relief, accompanied by uninhibited tears. She knew the feel of her husband's arms, warm, secure, safe, after months of tear-soaked pillows and anxiety-driven fatigue.

Feelings she would never know again. Maggie felt like a hard, relentless band had clenched around her throat, and tears threatened to flood over the pathetic resistance of her eyelids. She swallowed, unable to tear her eyes from the mother and child. Their excitement was palpable. All around her, Maggie felt passengers begin to abandon their isolated existence, setting aside tempers and frustrations, to step into the growing circle of warmth near Gate 19.

The young mother paused, only briefly taking her eyes from the closed door at the gate, to adjust a yellow bow in her daughter's strawberry blond hair. And then the waiting resumed.

The young woman clutched her child's hand, while an airline employee spoke in low, calming tones, gently doing his best to hold the two of them behind the white line on the floor. It seemed an eternity before the door finally opened.

Mother and daughter leaned forward, flags held high, necks straining, their toes as close to the forbidding white line as possible. The child began to fidget. She pulled anxiously on her mother's hand, and when passengers finally began to stream through the massive door, she let out an excited squeal that immediately summoned the attention of the other passengers in the terminal. No one moved. To Maggie, the events seemed to unfold in slow motion.

One by one, weary travelers, laden with garment bags and carry-on luggage, streamed through Gate 19. Every eye in the southwest end of the Dallas/Fort Worth airport remained riveted on the door. Seconds became minutes, minutes dragged together, time slugged forward with the alacrity of Southern molasses, and the young woman and her daughter strained against the confining line as they eagerly searched among the disembarking passengers for a glimpse, a first look at their returning hero. Maggie felt the first tear spill over her lower lashes.

Finally, when it seemed there couldn't be room on the plane for even one more passenger, when the burgeoning crowd had grown so large, and the wait had dragged on so long, a young Marine, resplendent, handsome, full of life, wearing his dress uniform, stepped through Gate 19. Mother and daughter flew forward, no airline regulation, or white line, or barrier on earth able to restrain them. The young Marine dropped his duffel bag and lifted his daughter in the air, pausing only to wrap his other arm around his crying wife.

The passengers in the terminal broke into spontaneous applause, peppered with cheers of "welcome home," and an occasional muffled sniffle.

Maggie's focus blurred as tears filled her eyes, and pain filled her heart. Unable to watch any longer, knowing there would never be another scene in another airport with another Marine who held her close and promised all would be well, she grabbed her briefcase and ran for her flight.

Scott Bishop stretched his long legs as he wiggled his toes inside his worn boots. He leaned his head back against the padded rest of seat 3A. The hard rain that pelted the small window of the aircraft suggested yet another delay. His 5:00 A.M. flight had already been canceled, because of hazardous runway conditions. The only remaining seat on the seven o'clock flight was in first-class. At least, he thought, flexing his shoulders, he wasn't crammed in a center seat back in coach. With his six-foot, five-inch frame, flying coach was always a challenge. With any luck, the added space and a quiet and uneventful flight to Boston's Logan Airport would allow him to catch up on his sleep.

Any thoughts of a few quiet hours were quickly dashed when he caught sight of the young woman making her way down the aisle. At the combination of her tear-filled eyes and an expression so mournful, so tragic it spoke of volumes of pain and sorrow, Scott felt his insides clench into a hard ball. He had felt the same hopeless anguish he now saw in the young woman's face. He recognized that particular kind of pain, even from a distance. Even in the face of a stranger.

As she slipped past the stewardess, her chocolate brown eyes darted briefly across the seat numbers. Scott saw the tiny lines around her full mouth, the telltale crease in her forehead, and had to restrain an irrational impulse to reach out and take her hand, offering comfort.

She stopped at his row. He had the briefest glimpse of whitened knuckles clutching the handle of a burgundy briefcase, before she mumbled an apology beneath her breath, then slipped past him. She dropped into the window seat. Brushing a long wave of pale blond hair behind her ear, she began searching through her briefcase while tears spilled down her face and dripped onto the burgundy leather. Scott slipped his hand into his back pocket and pulled out a clean white handkerchief. He extended it to her without comment.

She glanced up, startled, before her fingers closed on the soft cotton. "Thank you," she mumbled, wiping her eyes.

Scott nodded briefly. "My pleasure."

She sniffled, pausing to blow her nose. "I must look like an idiot." She hiccuped once, her breathing still punctuated by an occasional sob.

Scott felt another twinge of sympathy. "No, you don't. I've felt about that miserable in my life. There's nothing idiotic about it."

She met his gaze again. Scott was struck by the notion that her eyes were the softest brown he'd ever seen. "I . . ." she paused, wiping her cheeks again, "Thank you. For being so kind."

Scott hesitated only slightly before summoning the stewardess. There was no point in pretending he wasn't already involved in this woman's problem. He couldn't possibly ignore her distress during the long flight to Boston.

The stewardess had been watching them, keenly interested in the small scene. At Scott's gesture, she hastened over to his side. "Is there anything you need, sir?" Her eyes darted to the crying woman in the window seat. "Anything I can do?"

Scott nodded. "I'd like two aspirin and a glass of water." He squeezed his seat mate's elbow. "Unless you'd prefer wine?"

She shook her head. "No, no. Water is fine."

Scott gave the stewardess a brief look. "And aspirin." She hurried away, to return within minutes with a small packet and a glass of ice water. Scott thanked her as he tore open the packet. He shook the two white tablets onto his hand, and offered them to the young woman at his side. "Here ya' go. This should help."

She accepted the pills and swallowed them with a long sip of water. Leaning her head back against the seat, she gave him a grateful, if tremulous, shadow of a smile. "Thank you. You're being very kind about this."

Scott studied her in the dim, artificial light. When he'd lost Annie, he'd felt the same empty, clawing grief he saw in the velvet brown of this woman's gaze. The memories were still too fresh for him simply to ignore that kind of hurt in a fellow human being. "Let's just say I recognize the symptoms."

She tipped her head and sniffled. "I'm sure an hysterical seat mate isn't your idea of an ideal seven A.M. flight."

He shrugged. "Is there any such thing as an ideal seven A.M. flight?"

That won a small, tentative smile. "I guess not."

Scott wiped his hands on his thighs. She looked even more vulnerable when she smiled. He felt like his heart had dropped to the bottom of his boots. "My name is Scott Bishop," he said. "And I'd say you're a long way from hysterical."

She waved the handkerchief at him. "Not so long, I don't think. Are you always so chivalrous, Mr. Bishop?"

"Only to ladies on the verge of hysteria." He gave her a conspiratorial wink. "I find it helps turn the tide in a more favorable direction"—he indicated his shoulder—"and saves me money on dry cleaning bills. Handkerchiefs are less expensive to clean than suits."

She sniffed. "This time, you might be right." She held out her slim hand. "My name is Maggie Connell. It's nice to meet you."

He briefly shook the hand she offered. He liked the firm, slender feel of her handshake. "I'm glad I could be of assistance."

"I'm not usually so emotional, it was just . . ." she trailed off as her voice slightly wavered on a fresh flood of tears.

Something about the entreaty in her eyes, or perhaps it was the curve of her mouth, a curve he suspected would be more comfortable laughing than it was with the tiny lines of fatigue pulling at the corners, beckoned to him, made him want to talk to this utter, vulnerable stranger about the answering ache in his own heart, the one he'd grown so adept at hiding beneath a ready smile and a quick wit. "You don't have to explain anything, Maggie Connell," he said softly.

The plane had begun to fill more steadily, and Scott shifted closer to Maggie when a passenger brushed past him with a large garment bag. He caught the faintest scent of her light perfume and fought the urge to lift her hair and find its source. "Although," he said, dragging his thoughts back where they belonged, "I'd be glad to listen if you'd like to talk about it."

She gave him a curious look. "Are you willing to risk the very real possibility that I might dissolve into tears all over again?"

Scott nodded. "I'm a brave man. I feel compelled to warn you, though, that I've given you my last handkerchief."

Maggie dabbed at her eyes once more. "I . . . it was the scene in the airport, with that young Marine lieutenant. I suppose you didn't see it?"

He shook his head. "I boarded early."

She swallowed. "His family was meeting him at the plane and I . . ." Scott waited while she fought back a fresh surge of tears. "It triggered a lot of memories for me."

His gaze slid to the third finger of her left hand. "Did you lose your husband?"

Two tears spilled over her spiky lashes as she nodded. "Yes. Mark was a captain in the Marine Corps. He died in a training exercise in Saudi Arabia about a year ago."

Scott felt something inside his heart, the heart he thought had turned to stone long ago, tighten into a hard fist. "A year ago?" he asked.

Maggie nodded. "He was killed December twenty-third."

His breath came out in a long whoosh, powered by

some spring of longing deep inside his being. "I lost my wife to cancer last year," he said quietly. "December twenty-first."

Maggie reached out and touched his arm in an offer of comfort that seemed compulsive. "I'm so sorry. I—I'm sure you loved her very much."

How many times in the months following Annie's death had he heard trite, if well-meaning, offers of sympathy and advice? How many times had he listened to condolences with a heart too numb, and a spirit too exhausted to do more than shrink back into its own dark corner of sorrow? A hundred? A thousand? Yet no one, not in the days or weeks or months since Annie died, had ever so knowingly put their finger on the source of his pain like this virtual stranger in seat 3B. "I did," he said.

"I know," she whispered.

Scott felt suddenly drained, like a ship cast adrift by a dying breeze. His memories of Annie rushed in with the force of a great winter wind and consumed every space, every facet of his emotional and mental energy. "Would you like to tell me about your husband?" he asked. He wondered if his voice sounded odd to Maggie.

She paused. "It's an ordinary story. It's only extraordinary to me. He was a pilot, and he died when his helicopter went down over Saudi Arabia."

Scott shook his head. "That's not what I meant. I don't want to know how he died. I want to know how he lived."

Maggie's gaze registered her surprise. She studied him for a minute. Then a whisper of a smile touched her lips. "I would like very much to tell you that, Mr. Bishop."

Scott tipped his head back and closed his eyes. The sound of her voice was like a warm breeze, and he found comfort in it. "Start at the beginning," he said.

The aircraft engines roared to life. The plane began a slow taxi away from the gate. Even through the din, he was sure he heard Maggie's soft sigh. "The first time I met Mark," she said, "I was sitting on the porch swing outside my dorm, and he was walking to class, eating an apple."

There were times when Mark Connell really hated being a ghost. As he watched his seven-year-old son Ryan prepare for a penalty shot that would be the winning point in his peewee league hockey game, he decided it was definitely one of those times. Across the empty expanse of ice, he met Ryan's gaze and admitted to himself that only his son's willing acceptance of his father's otherworldly existence made the whole thing bearable. He smiled at Ryan, then skated across the ice to join him beside the puck.

With arms that ached to hold, and hands that ached to touch, Mark skated next to Ryan as he circled the puck. Ryan looked at him with a bright grin. The bruise on his eye was already starting to purple. Mark knew he'd soon be sporting the full effect of the illegal hit that had earned him the penalty shot. Mark winked at him.

The fact that only Ryan could see or hear him had long since ceased to bother Mark. Instead of agonizing over what he couldn't seem to change, he'd concentrated his efforts on building a relationship, no matter how strange, no matter how different, with his son. Besides, he thought, glancing at Ryan's coach where he stood tensely gripping the boards, none of the other dads got to offer on-ice coaching. That was a privilege reserved for fathers of the more invisible variety.

With a slight smile, Mark leaned forward and braced his hands on his knees. "Are you ready, son?"

Ryan turned his gaze to the goalie. He gave Mark a brief, no-nonsense nod. "Ready," he said beneath his breath.

"Have you been practicing that lift shot?"

Ryan nodded again.

On instinct, Mark reached out, wanting to give a reassuring squeeze to Ryan's shoulder, but his fingers, devoid of substance, met only the cool air of the ice rink. He forced back the disappointment. "All right," he said. "Give it your best shot, and remember, no matter how it turns out, I'm proud of you, Ryan."

Ryan pulled his protective mask over his small face. His gloved fingers clenched and unclenched on the grips of his stick. As Mark had instructed him, he circled twice around the puck before he started his charge on goal.

Mark watched from his spot at center ice. His shoulders shifted slightly with each of Ryan's movements. When Ryan neared the goal, Mark clenched his hands together and leaned forward in anticipation. He knew the instant that Ryan released the puck from his stick that it would sail past the goalie's left shoulder and lodge in the net.

The small crowd went wild when the shot registered on the scoreboard. Mark threw his hands up in the air with a loud whoop. He could not have been more exultant had Ryan just won the Stanley Cup. Ryan pivoted to an abrupt stop on the ice. He met Mark's gaze across the frozen expanse. His grin was broader than before, his eyes sparkled, a flush had settled in his cheeks. Mark gave him a victory salute.

For an instant, Ryan ignored the clamor of his teammates, who were now pouring onto the ice. He lowered his head and began skating toward Mark, picking up speed as he crossed the ice. Mark waited, anticipating. When Ryan drew within a yard of Mark's spot on the ice, he scrunched his little body into a tight ball and skated directly through Mark's image.

For the barest of seconds, Mark felt the slight touch of their souls, as fleeting and tender as a fluff of down on a summer breeze. He closed his eyes, savored, then willed himself to Maggie.

Seconds later, he settled back in the comfortable first-class seat across from Maggie's row on the plane. He pulled a Granny Smith apple from his pocket and took a bite. It took him several moments to realize that the attractive young woman with light brown hair and pixielike eyes in the seat next to him was staring at him. Disconcerted, he stared back. When her gaze didn't flinch, he threw a quick glance over his shoulder. He was relieved to find she was actually focused on the view from the aircraft window.

He returned his gaze to Maggie. She'd been crying, he realized. He decided to move closer so he could eavesdrop on her conversation with the tall, blond stranger—the stranger who was sitting far too close to Maggie for Mark's peace of mind.

He moved to lever himself out of his seat, then stopped, shocked, when his hand encountered the very real, very warm flesh of the young woman next to him, and his foot made sound contact with her shin.

"Ow!" She rubbed her leg and glared at him in temperamental protest.

Mark jerked back his hand, and stared at her. "Can you see me?" he asked.

She smiled at him, a slight, enigmatic smile. "Ever since you dropped into that seat." She extended her hand. "My name's Annie. Annie Bishop. I guess you're Mark."

Mark wiped the apple juice from his lips with the sleeve of his faded Marine Corps sweatshirt. "How do you know that?"

Annie inclined her head toward Maggie. "That's my husband, Scott. Your wife has been telling him about you for the last half hour."

Mark blinked. When he opened his eyes, she was still beside him. "Can you—I mean, are you—"

"A ghost?"

Mark nodded. She shrugged and tucked her feet beneath her long, gauzy skirt. "I guess, although, I stopped thinking about it a long time ago. No one can see me. No one can hear me. I can't do anything. I just follow Scott around."

Mark looked across the row again and studied the view of Maggie bent close in conversation with Scott Bishop. "Maggie can't see me either." He stopped and glanced back at Annie. "But Ryan can."

"I suspected that," Annie said.

Mark frowned at her. "What do you mean?"

"Your wife mentioned that your son claims he talks to you. She believes he's having trouble accepting your death." She made a small gesture with her hands. "I wondered if perhaps you were like me. Here, but not here."

"I didn't know there were others," Mark said. He

pushed up the sleeves of his sweatshirt. "You're the first one I've ever seen."

She nodded. "Me too."

Mark closed his eyes for a minute. "I can't imagine what it must be like for you. Ryan is the only thing that makes this tolerable for me."

Her gaze turned wistful. "He sounds like a wonderful boy."

Mark's eyes opened again, and he nodded. "Yeah. He's seven and a half. Smart as a whip, too, and the absolute spitting image of Maggie." He watched Maggie's animated expression for a few seconds. "When Ryan was born, I couldn't believe how much I loved that little guy. When Maggie handed him to me the first time in the hospital, it was like my whole inside exploded."

"Do you think Maggie's right? Is he having trouble accepting that you're gone?"

Mark nodded. "I've tried to explain to him that I'm not real. He knows he can't touch me, but he knows he can see me and hear me. It's a lot for a kid to take in. What hurts the most is how sad he is. He was never like that," Mark said. "One of the things that makes Ryan easy to love is the way he smiles at you."

Annie threaded her fingers through her hair. "Perhaps he needs you so much, he's willed you to be visible to him."

Mark frowned and studied the slender young woman next to him. After nearly a year of his solitary existence, a year made tolerable only by the comforting, if odd, reality of his relationship with Ryan, he wasn't sure what to make of this new development, or her probing questions. "Do you think," he asked cautiously, barely daring to voice the question that nagged him almost daily, "that we'll ever get out of here?"

Annie looked over her shoulder and studied Scott. "I don't know. I guess I almost started to believe this is what happens when you die. You're just stuck here."

Mark's gaze strayed back to Maggie's profile. She was laughing, ever so slightly, at something Scott Bishop was telling her. Mark watched as she tucked a strand of pale blond hair behind her ear and smiled at Scott. He remembered those smiles. What the hell was she doing passing them around? "The worst part is being with Maggie, and not being with her all at the same time."

Annie's eyelashes fluttered briefly. "Did you have a chance to say good-bye?"

"No. I left for Saudi Arabia in August. I was supposed to be back the fifteenth of January. Maggie even promised to stall Christmas." He smiled sadly. "We never even thought about the fact that I wouldn't come back. It was supposed to be a routine training mission. Not coming back wasn't an option. What about you and Scott?"

"We said good-bye. I had to make Scott say good-bye. I was afraid he'd hold on forever if he didn't."

Mark studied her. "How did you—go?"

"Cancer." She rocked back and forth slightly, swinging her legs over the side of the seat. "I was diagnosed a year before I died, though, so I had time to prepare Scott."

Mark glanced back at Maggie. "Nothing could have prepared Maggie."

"What about you?"

The question took him by surprise. "What about me?"

"Were you prepared?"

"To die, you mean?"

Annie nodded. Mark thought the question over. "No," he said. "You never think about dying. You just fly each mission, go on each tour, do what you're supposed to do. I guess it's always there, in the back of your mind, but you never think about it."

Annie smoothed a hand over the hem of her pink sweater. "Missing Scott is the hardest part. I know how much he hurts sometimes. It makes me feel bad."

"I know. Maggie is having a rough time. She's trying so hard." He felt his chest constrict as he watched her pull a picture of Ryan out of her briefcase to show to Scott. "She really wants to move on. Sometimes I feel guilty for hanging around Ryan, like I'm keeping him from recovering or something."

"Why don't you leave?" she asked, her voice quiet.

"That would be like dying all over again."

Annie's breath came out on a long sigh. She looked once at Scott, then back at Mark. She pulled at a string on her sweater, and unraveled part of the hem. "Do you think maybe this is what was supposed to happen all along?"

"What?" he asked, not sure he liked the grave note in her voice. He stuffed his apple core into the seat pouch in front of him, then crossed his long, jeans-clad legs. He was glad Maggie was flying first-class this trip. He hated it when she flew coach and his knees were crammed up under his chin.

"This," she said. She indicated Scott and Maggie over her shoulder. "Do you think this is what we're supposed to be doing?" At his confused look, she leaned over to place a slim hand on his forearm. The contact felt odd. He could tell by the way she was staring at her fingers against his skin that she was thinking it, too. "I haven't touched anyone in so long."

"Neither have I. What do you mean we're supposed to be doing this? Doing what?"

She met his gaze. "I can't help but wonder if we're here," she glanced over her shoulder, "with them, for a reason."

Mark leaned back in his seat. "Do you think we're supposed to do something?"

"I hope so," she said. "I really, really hope so."

Two

"*I* hope so," *Maggie said, in answer to Scott's wistful* question about the timeliness of their flight. She glanced at her watch. "I was supposed to fly out last night, but between the weather and the airline strike, so many flights were canceled, that this was the first one I could get. Ryan had a hockey game this morning, and I missed it."

Scott nodded. "I was supposed to be on the five A.M. flight. That's how I ended up in first-class."

"I hope Ryan won't be too upset. It was such an odd time for a game, but we had that big ice storm last week. That's why his Saturday game got canceled. I guess they figured it would be all right since the kids were already off for the holiday."

"I'm sure he'll understand. How old did you say he was? Seven?"

Maggie felt drained. She could scarcely believe she'd spent the last hour and a half talking so openly with this stranger. Something in his voice, in the way he'd told her about his wife drew her to him more closely than she'd ever felt drawn to all the expensive therapists and well-meaning friends who had sur-

rounded her after Mark's death. For the first time
since she'd boarded the plane in such a panic, she
took a good look at the man who'd been so kind to
her.

He was tall, well over six feet she estimated judging
by the way his long, denim-clad legs stretched in front
of him to disappear under the seat. Casually attired
in well-worn jeans and a soft flannel shirt, he looked
completely at his ease with the charged emotional
atmosphere their conversation had created. His sandy
brown hair was slightly long, falling to just below his
collar, but it had been his eyes that had drawn her,
giving her the courage to trust him with the pain of
losing Mark. His eyes were a clear hazel that deepened to a smoky green when he talked about his late
wife.

She realized that those eyes were still watching her
intently, waiting for her to continue. "He's seven,"
she said, smiling, as a mental picture of Ryan popped
into her head. "He's really a super kid."

"It must be hard on you, raising him on your own."

"Sometimes. It's like having a piece of Mark,
though. Something he left behind. It's been tough on
Ryan, and I've been taking him to the counselor at
our church. He still can't seem to accept that Mark is
gone. He insists that he can see him." She looked at
him, sensing a shift in his mood. "You and Annie
didn't have children, did you?"

He shook his head. A lock of his hair brushed his
forehead. She just barely resisted the urge to smooth
it back into place. "It's my biggest regret. There never
seemed to be enough time, or enough money. We had
agreed to wait." He made a small sound in the back

of his throat. "I had no idea we couldn't afford the luxury."

"Would you like to tell me about Annie?" she asked.

Scott exhaled a long breath. Maggie heard the regret, the loneliness in the soft whisper of air. "Annie." Her name sounded more like a sigh. "Annie was the love of my life. I'd known her since we were kids, and even when I was too-tall and too-skinny and too-serious, Annie used to talk to me for hours about my plans to be an architect. I think I fell in love with her when I was twelve. I told her I wanted to build things, so she bought me an Erector set for Christmas that year."

Maggie smiled. "And are you an architect?"

"Yes." He sounded wistful. "That's why I'm going to Massachusetts, as a matter of fact. I'm a partner with Hertson and Hubbard in Dallas, and we're bidding on the Cape Hope project."

Maggie drew a quick breath. "You're bidding on Cape Hope?"

He nodded. "It's my project all the way. If we get the bid, I think I'll finally have enough recognition as a designer to start my own firm."

"Did I happen to mention why I was in Dallas?" she asked.

"Please don't tell me you're an architect, and that you were sent to sabotage my plans." He flashed her a brief smile. "It would ruin what I hope will become a perfectly decent friendship."

"Nothing so dramatic." Maggie decided she liked the way Scott's eyes reflected the sun from the tiny aircraft window. "I'm an interior decorator. I was at the Dallas design show picking up ideas for my own bid on the Cape Hope project."

Scott looked intrigued. His long fingers flexed on his knees. "Really?"

She nodded, encouraged. "Yes. Ryan and I live in Cape Hope, and when the planning commission announced the project, I jumped at the chance to bid on it."

"Have you ever handled something this big before?"

She shook her head. "I started my company, By Design, after Mark—with the money from his life insurance. So far, I've been doing smaller projects—homes, offices, that kind of thing. I'm counting on Cape Hope to make my business solvent. Mark left us very secure, and the money isn't really the issue, but I needed to do this for me. I needed to feel like I was someone apart from his widow. My own person."

"I can understand that. It must have been hard being a military wife and an extension of his career, then having to adjust to being on your own."

Hard hadn't been the word. Impossible. Insurmountable. Devastating. "Mark was stationed out of Cherry Point in North Carolina. After he died, I just couldn't stay there. I needed to start over. That's why Ryan and I moved to Cape Hope."

"How did you pick Massachusetts?"

"I had a great aunt who lived in Cape Hope until she died about six years ago. She left me her house in her will, and it seemed the perfect place for me to take Ryan. I had studied interior design when I was in college. So I decided that would be the best way for me to start doing something on my own for a change."

"I imagine the hours work out well for you since you have Ryan to take care of."

"Oh, yes. I can do most of my site work and bidding while Ryan's in school, and then do my designing at night out of my home. I wouldn't want to be away from him, especially now when everything is different and things are so hard."

"But your business is struggling?"

She groaned. "I didn't know how competitive the field was. I guess I was just naive, but there are a couple of very large, very established firms in Cape Hope and in Boston. I think I've done well in carving out my own niche, but it's still been tough. I've lost a couple of key bids on office suites in the last two months because the companies didn't think I had enough experience."

Scott studied her. "Are you worried that might be an issue with the resort project?"

She shook her head. "I think my plans are so different, that it's going to be strictly a matter of taste. It'll just depend on what the developers want. In both the previous cases, I was working within preconceived ideas. Those companies already knew what they wanted. With Cape Hope, at least for the interior project, the developers threw open the gates for us. We could draw up any type of plans, any colors, any themes we wanted. I have a great vision for this project, and I'm really proud of the work I've done on it. Now it's just a matter of waiting out the developers' decision."

Scott rubbed his chin between his thumb and forefinger. "It was largely the same with the structural bids. We weren't really given any guidelines. That's what drew me to the project to begin with. I normally wouldn't have bid on something so far away from Dallas, but I was attracted to the creative control. If I can win this bid, it will be a major boost for my career."

Maggie shifted in her seat, feeling a familiar rush of excitement as she talked about the Cape Hope project. "Would it be completely beyond the pale if I asked what your plans for the structure entailed? I mean, I don't want to intrude on your artistic territory, but I would like to know, just out of curiosity."

"No, no it wouldn't be a problem at all." He gave her a wry smile. "Unless, of course, you're a cleverly disguised mole for Cassiter and Claus."

Maggie recognized the name of the Boston architectural firm. She laughed. "I think if Lyle Cassiter was going to send someone after your plans, he could have done a lot better than a half-hysterical female."

Scott looked dubious. "Maybe. In any case, I was going to suggest that if you'd feel comfortable with it, I'd like to look at your designs. Maybe I could give you some input from a structural perspective."

"Would you do that?"

He looked sheepish. "Especially if you were willing to look at the plans I've drawn and let me know what you think about the aesthetics."

Maggie felt the tingle of excitement spread over her scalp and warm her skin. She refused to believe it had anything to do with spending more time with Scott Bishop, enjoying the way he smiled easily and listened intently. Her memories of Mark were still too fresh, too painful, too vivid. No, it had to be the notion that Scott Bishop clearly took her seriously as a professional in her field, a respect she knew was hard-earned. "I'd be glad to," she said.

"I've got one more site inspection to do before I can complete my plans. Right now all I have are sketches."

"Is that why you're on your way to Massachusetts now?"

"Yes. I'll be traveling up to Cape Hope today, and I'll have until Friday to make my final calculations and surveys. I've got to have my preliminary plans into the planning commission by a week from Friday."

Maggie nodded. "The interior concepts are due then, too. That's why I decided to do the Dallas show instead of waiting until the Boston show came up in the spring. I needed the input now."

"If you want, well, maybe we could get together in the next day or so and look at the plans."

Maggie looked at him in amazement. He looked embarrassed, abashed even, at the suggestion. She felt a buoyancy in her spirit that hadn't been there before. "That would be great."

"I, uh, I have these tickets." He pulled the hockey tickets out of his pocket. "My boss gave them to me as kind of a good-luck present."

Maggie looked at the tickets. There were four of them. "These are tickets to the Bruins game."

"Yeah. You said Ryan liked hockey. I thought, well, maybe we could go—the three of us."

"Ryan would be your friend for life."

"Can't ask for more than that."

"Are you sure you don't want to use these for a client or something?"

"I don't think Steve expected me to fly any of my clients in from Dallas. I think he was sort of hoping I'd find a date."

A date. Maggie couldn't even remen...
time the word had entered her vocabulary.
sure?"

"Sure, I'm sure. I'd love to take you and Ry...n to the game."

"We'd love to go." She paused and met his gaze, inwardly marveling at the aplomb with which she managed to accept his casual invitation. She hadn't thought, hadn't even considered the possibility of starting a friendship, or anything else for that matter, with a man since Mark's death. She'd met several people in Cape Hope she counted as friends, but despite their encouragement for her to get out more, she'd found the idea distasteful. Until she'd met Scott Bishop. "I'm sure Ryan will be ecstatic." She handed him the tickets. "I don't get to do things like this with him as often as I'd like."

Scott rubbed his palms on his thighs. "I'm sure it's been difficult for the little guy. In a way, I was almost glad Annie and I didn't have children. I wouldn't have wanted to put them through this. The grief, I mean."

"I know. Ryan was always such a happy child, but, well, I'm just not sure I've been able to give him what he needs to deal with the situation. Nothing has been able to shake his assertions that he can see and hear Mark. I want to believe it's just a phase, like an imaginary friend, but I'm not sure." She tipped her head and studied the man in the seat next to her, thinking that in the three hours it had taken them to reach Boston, she'd grown to know him better than she did many of the people she'd known for years. "Besides"—she waved the white handkerchief at him— "the least I can do after you've been so kind, is show you around Boston. What better place to start than a Bruins game?"

The seat-belt sign blinked overhead as the plane began its descent into Logan Airport. Scott fastened his seat belt before meeting her gaze again. "All right then. If you'll give me the address, I'll take a cab over."

Maggie buckled her own seat belt. "You don't rent a car while you're in town?"

He looked aghast. "And drive in Boston? Are you kidding?"

She laughed. "It's not really so bad. Not once you get used to it."

"That's easy for you to say. I'm used to driving in Dallas, where the city's on a grid pattern and folks obey traffic laws."

Maggie paused, thoroughly enjoying the warm look he gave her. Something cold in her heart, something that had been frozen since the day Mark's commanding officer had called and told her about the accident, responded to that warmth like a flower daring to peek at the spring sun through lingering snows of late winter. And it felt good.

It felt good to smile, and be warm, and share some of the nagging pain that had clawed at her heart for a long, relentless year. She smiled at him, wanting to share some of that warmth with her new friend. "Well, as long as you're going my way, at least let me give you a ride. What kind of host would I be if I let you risk your life in a Boston cab?"

"Are you sure it won't be out of your way?"

"In Cape Hope?" she asked. "Where a drive across town takes ten minutes on a bad day? How could it possibly be out of my way?"

"I won't be taking up too much of your time?"

"No. It won't take more than an extra fifteen minutes tops."

He relented with a slight grin. "I'd appreciate it then. I used a cab last time I was here, and I'm still recovering from the gray hairs."

The plane bounced when it touched the ground before settling to a smooth stop. Maggie set her briefcase on her lap and waited while the plane taxied to the gate. "Well then, Mr. Bishop, it will be my pleasure to see you safely escorted to Cape Hope." Maggie paused. She didn't feel as though she could simply ignore the fact that they'd shared such a charged conversation. It seemed somehow unfair to leave him with the impression that she'd so readily dismissed his kindness. "And I—if I didn't say it before, thank you for listening, for being so nice."

Scott smiled at her. "I think I needed to listen, Maggie. You helped me, too, whether you know it or not. I'm glad things worked out like this."

She tried to ignore her sudden awkwardness. "I'm glad, too."

Passengers began to make their way down the crowded aisle of the plane. Scott paused to smile at Maggie, then stood up to retrieve his bag from the luggage rack. "You know something, Maggie?" he said, dropping his black cashmere overcoat onto the seat, before he lifted down his suitcase.

"What?" She looked up at him.

He put his bag down on the floor, and picked up his coat. "If I didn't know any better, I'd think Annie planned this whole thing."

Maggie tipped her head and studied him. "What do you mean?"

He fixed her with a serious look, his gaze intense. "It might sound crazy to you, but I can't get over the feeling Annie would be mighty pleased with herself about now. I haven't been able to talk much about this before, and I have to say it felt good to get it off my chest." His smile was fleeting. "I wouldn't put it past her to be sitting up in Heaven right now, grinning at me."

Annie smiled. She rubbed her hands on the sleeves of her pink sweater, wishing she could kiss Scott. He was such a fine man. The best she'd ever known, and despite the way he always insisted that she'd taken pity on him when he was an awkward teenager, she knew better. Scott had been good to her. Better than anyone in her whole life, and the hardest part about dying had been leaving him behind.

She looked at Mark Connell. When the plane landed, he'd stood to stretch his legs. His head had disappeared into the overhead compartment. She tugged on his sweatshirt until he leaned down, bringing his head back into view. "I think they're getting along very well."

He frowned. "What makes you think that?"

Annie studied him. "What are you so cross about?"

He sighed and dropped back down into the seat. He propped his elbows on his knees to bury his face in his hands. "I hadn't heard Maggie talk about this before. It kind of worries me. I'm worried about her, and I'm worried about Ryan." He shook his head. "Maggie's the kind of woman who should have half a dozen kids running around. Anybody with that much love to give shouldn't be wasting it."

Annie hesitated before reaching over to run her fingers over Mark's back. "Maybe that's it, Mark."

He raised his head and looked at her. "What is?"

Annie let her gaze wander back to where Scott was helping Maggie into her coat. "Maybe that's why we're here. Maybe they can't say good-bye to us until we say good-bye to them."

"Now hold on just one minute. You're not thinking of some harebrained plan to match the two of them up, are you?"

"Why not?"

"Because, because," he waved his hand in Scott's direction, "he's all wrong for her. That's why."

She wet her lips with the tip of her tongue, then held out her hand to Mark. She should have known he'd be stubborn about it. Evidently, dead men weren't all that different from live ones. "Look," she said. "Look at my fingers."

Mark stared at her hand. "You're see-through. Sort of."

Annie nodded. "I'm fading. I noticed it when I first got on the plane with Scott. It's as if I'm disappearing. I'm starting to lose some of my memories, too. I don't feel like I'm quite real anymore."

Mark spread his own hands out in front of him. He stared at them. "Mine are still intact."

From the corner of her eyes, she saw Scott and Maggie start to exit the aircraft. Annie stood, motioning for Mark to follow her from the plane. "Maybe Maggie is still holding on too tight."

Mark's gaze shot to Maggie's back as she made her way off the plane with Scott. "That's ridiculous."

"I don't think so. Why else would we be here like this? And what about Ryan? Don't you remember what Maggie said about how much trouble Ryan was having accepting your death?"

Mark let out a long, ragged breath. "I'm telling you right now, Annie, the solution to this is not to pair off your husband and my wife. It won't work."

"Stop acting like a jealous male."

"I am a jealous male."

"Well, grow up, then. What if this is their last chance?" Annie picked her way through the crowd. She followed Scott and Maggie through the airport, periodically checking to see if Mark was still behind her. "I know this is hard, Mark. I mean"—she felt her voice catch—"it's easier for me. I just have Scott to worry about. You have Maggie *and* Ryan."

Mark looked at her in alarm. He reached over to wrap an arm around her shoulders. He didn't bother to steer around the luggage conveyors, he just walked straight through. "You're not going to start to cry are you?"

She almost smiled at the frantic note in his voice. She reached up to wipe away what should have been tears, only to find ice crystals instead. She held out her fingers to Mark. "Look. No tears," she said. "Nothing to panic over."

"Thank God."

"I'll bet Maggie was most attracted to your sensitive nature," she quipped, a remarkable accomplishment given the circumstances.

He shot her a dry look. Scott and Maggie had exited the airport. They were working their way toward the parking deck. Annie picked up the pace, pulling Mark along with her. "Just be glad I can't cry real tears. We'd be looking for buckets soon."

He looked contrite. "I'm sorry, Annie, I wasn't trying to be a jerk." A dimple appeared in his cheek. "Sometimes it just comes naturally to me."

She drew a deep, shaky breath. "Will you promise me something, Mark?"

"Will it keep you from crying?"

"Probably. For a little while, anyway."

He nodded. "Then absolutely. Anything."

"Will you promise that you'll do whatever you can to help Maggie and Ryan? I don't know why all this is happening, and I don't understand it any better than you do." She let her gaze wander to the parking lot where Maggie was unlocking the back of her Ford Bronco. Annie had to fight a fresh surge of tears. "But I can't stand to see Scott hurt so much." She wiped two more icy tears away from her cheeks. "I can't even have a good solid cry to get it out of my system."

She could tell by the expression on his face that he was going to relent, at least a little. "We're in this together, Annie. I don't know why, and I don't know for how long, but for some reason, we're stuck with this situation. I'll do what I can to help Maggie."

Annie rubbed her face against his soft sweatshirt. She thought of Scott, of his kind eyes and kinder heart, and of how much she wanted to see him laugh again, how much she wanted to see him happy. She sniffled again. "Let's go catch up to those two and see if we can figure out what's going on," she said.

Mark smiled at her. Together, they watched as Maggie and Scott climbed into Maggie's Bronco. Mark lifted Annie into the backseat, then slid in next to her. He shook his head at the faint grinding noise when Maggie pushed the gearshift into reverse. He shot Annie a wry look. "I never could teach her how to drive a stick."

Annie laughed. "Scott couldn't teach me either. I couldn't ever remember how to shift down."

"She loses things, too," he said as Maggie approached the toll plaza. "Watch this. I'll bet you a quarter she has a monthly pass for that toll plaza, and she won't be able to find it." Maggie started digging in the glove compartment. Annie stifled a giggle. Maggie had to finally accept the two-dollar toll from Scott with an offer to pay him back. Mark shook his head again. "Just wait until we have to watch her find her car keys. It'll take twenty minutes."

Annie laughed, feeling more lighthearted in the face of Mark's banter. "That's nothing. Scott has no sense of direction. I guarantee he'll get lost in his hotel trying to find his room."

Mark smiled at her. "And you think these two would make a great couple? Maggie can't find anything she owns, and Scott can't find himself."

They lapsed into silence for a while, listening to Maggie and Scott discuss the Cape Hope project. When Maggie dropped Scott off at his hotel, with a promise to call him about arrangements for the hockey game the following evening, Mark and Annie climbed down from the Bronco. They followed Scott into the Holiday Inn just to see how long it would take him to find his room. Mark laughed when Scott wandered around on the third floor for fifteen minutes trying to find Room 327. "Is he always that bad?"

Annie nodded. "Always. He was twenty minutes late for our wedding because he got lost on the way to the church."

"Maggie didn't wear her veil because she couldn't find it," he said with a slow smile. "She'll be home soon. I want to go with her, OK?"

Annie nodded.

"Will you be all right?"

She smiled, then kissed his cheek. "I'll be fine. Tell Ryan I can't wait to meet him. I wonder ... do you think he'll be able to see me?"

"I hope so," he said, and disappeared.

Annie followed Scott into his room. She wished he'd flip on the television so she could watch something while he unpacked. He didn't though. He sank down on the bed and buried his head in his hands. Annie wanted desperately to touch him. She sat down next to him, and stroked her fingers over the contour of his head, wishing she could feel the crisp waves twined around her fingers.

His big shoulders shuddered once, and Annie felt it all the way to her toes. "Oh, Scott," she whispered, even as she felt the cold sting of ice on her face, "don't do this."

Three

"Don't do this, Maggie," Maggie told herself as she wiped a tear off her face. She turned into the driveway of the small Victorian-Era house she and Ryan now called home. She took several deep breaths until she felt she had pulled her emotions at least somewhat under control. With a heavy sigh, she climbed out of the Bronco to make her way through the snow to the front door. She opened it with a resolved push.

"Ryan?" Maggie called, dropping her keys on the hall table and setting her bag on the floor. "Honey? I'm home."

Ryan came barreling out of the kitchen and threw his arms around her legs. "Mom!"

She smiled and ruffled his hair. "Did you miss me?"

Ryan tipped his head back and grinned at her, showing the gap where his two front teeth had once been, and the unmistakable bluish bruise of a black eye. "I scored two goals in my hockey game today," he announced.

"Two goals?" Maggie said, duly impressed. She rubbed her thumb over his bruised eye. She satisfied herself it was more show than substance. "Is this what you have to show for it?"

"Yeah. Tommy Willis hooked me with his stick, and Coach Bullard was really mad, but I got to take the penalty shot, and we won. Isn't it cool?"

Maggie rolled her eyes, satisfied that there was no permanent damage. "Yeah. Cool. Did Mrs. Sophy take care of it?" she asked, referring to the neighbor who'd stayed with Ryan while Maggie had been in Dallas.

"Dad checked it out at the ice. He said it was no big deal. A real, first-class shiner."

Maggie sighed. "Ryan, honey, we've talked about this before. Daddy's gone."

"Mom, he was right there. He even told me how to make the shot."

She decided she was too tired to argue, and knew from experience it was a losing battle anyway. "Why don't we just talk about it later, all right?"

He looked like he wanted to argue. "He was there."

Maggie ignored his mumbled protest. She shrugged out of her coat. "Did Mrs. Sophy put anything on your eye?"

"Yeah. She gave me this huge piece of steak. It was really cool. It didn't hurt hardly at all. Mrs. Soph made me a chocolate cake 'cause I scored two goals. Can we go out for pizza since you weren't here last night?" Ryan disentangled himself from her legs.

Maggie handed her coat to him. "Will you put that away for me while I go thank Mrs. Sophy for staying with you?"

"OK, but can we go out for pizza?"

Maggie tweaked his stomach, eliciting a delighted squeal. "Yes, we can go out for pizza." She gave his behind a playful swat. "Now go hang my coat up."

"OK, Mom."

Ryan was halfway down the hall when Maggie turned toward the kitchen. She found Edith Sophy, an apron tied around her ample waist, washing dishes. What had to be the world's most delectable-looking chocolate cake sat half-eaten on the counter. "Hello, Edith."

Edith Sophy had the kindest eyes Maggie had ever seen. A sudden memory of hazel eyes, flecked with gold, intruded on the thought, and Maggie felt a warm tingle on her skin. She smiled at Edith Sophy and took a plate from the cupboard.

"Well, hello there," Edith said, drying her hands on a dish towel. "I'm glad you made it back before the storm sets in."

"Storm?" Maggie found a knife in the silverware drawer and cut herself a piece of the cake.

Edith nodded, handing Maggie a fork. "We're expecting more snow starting tomorrow night. Looks like we'll have a white Thanksgiving this year." She reached up and patted her salt-and-pepper hair.

Maggie took a bite of the cake, letting the dark chocolate roll on her tongue. "Mmmm. This is sinful, Edith."

Edith smiled. "Ryan was so proud of himself. I wish you could have been here."

"I wish so, too." She swallowed another bite of cake and shot a quick glance out the kitchen window. "I was going to take Ryan shopping with me tomorrow to buy the stuff for dinner on Thursday. Maybe we'd better do it today instead." She paused and studied Edith. "Did you have any problems?"

Edith shook her head. "No. Just the usual. He says

his dad played a big role at the game this morning."

Maggie sighed. "I know. I'll have to have a talk with him about it tonight. We'll have plenty of time while we're shopping."

Edith draped the dish towel over the end of the stove and reached around to untie her apron. "Are you sure you won't reconsider and join us for Thanksgiving dinner, Maggie? All the kids and grandkids are coming, and we'd love to have you and Ryan with us. It might do him some good to be around other children."

Maggie shook her head and took another bite of the cake. "It's very kind of you to offer, Edith, but I think Ryan and I need to do this alone."

"How about tomorrow night, then? You could come just for supper."

"Can't. We're going out."

Edith raised her eyebrows. "Out?"

"Yes. We've been invited to the Bruins game."

"In Boston?" she said. The way Edith stressed the word, she might as well have asked Maggie if they were going to the moon.

"Yes."

"Is this a business associate?" Edith asked. She wasn't even trying to pretend not to pry.

Maggie shook her head. "No. It's a friend."

"Lord, child. It's like pulling teeth with you. What are the vital statistics?"

Maggie laughed. "I don't know them yet. He's just this very nice man I met on the plane today. He's in town on business—bidding on the Cape Hope project, in fact. He's alone, had the tickets, and asked if Ryan and I wanted to go."

"Oh, really?"

Maggie brandished her fork. "Really."

"This is a pleasant turn of events."

"I guess so."

Edith pursed her lips. "You say you met the man today?"

Maggie laughed at the badly disguised curiosity in Edith's tone. "Don't worry, Edith. I don't think he's a masher. He's an architect from Dallas, and, as I said, he's bidding on the Cape Hope project. We agreed to review each other's designs, and he asked me if Ryan and I would like to go to the game." She licked the frosting from her fork. "Did I tell you this is very good cake?"

Edith ignored the comment about the cake. She reached over to pat Maggie's arm. "I think that's wonderful. It's high time you started getting on with things. A young woman like you has no business being alone."

Maggie paused, the fork still pressed between her lips, and looked at Edith. She slowly removed the fork and set it on the edge of the plate. "It isn't as if I haven't been doing anything with my life," she said, sounding defensive and hating it.

"You've done a lot, Maggie. More than a lot of women would have the strength to do under your circumstances, but I'm not talking about your business or your financial security. I'm talking about you personally. You shouldn't be alone, and neither should Ryan. I know he's got his friends at school, and his teammates, but maybe he wouldn't be so dependent on his fantasies about his father if he had another male role model."

Maggie was spared a retort when Ryan came running through the swinging door. "When are we leaving?" he asked, leaping up onto a chair next to Maggie and plunging his fingers into the remains of her piece of cake. "Dad's in the living room, and he wants to know if he can go along."

Maggie frowned. "Ryan, one more mention of your father and we're not going. Do you understand?"

"But—"

"I mean it."

He nodded slowly. He looked hurt. "OK." He stuffed his fingers into his mouth to lick the chocolate.

Edith gave him a censorious look that didn't quite reach her eyes. "You eat that cake, and you won't have room for pizza." Ryan favored her with a toothless grin.

Edith smiled at Maggie. She opened one of the cabinets and hung the apron on a hook. She tapped her finger on the door before she gave Maggie a thoughtful look. "How long did you say this fellow was in town, Maggie?"

"I don't know. Several days I guess."

"Then why don't you invite him over for Thanksgiving dinner?"

Maggie stared at her. "Because," she blurted out, "because I couldn't. It's too . . . personal."

"Ask who?" Ryan said.

Edith ignored him. "You said yourself he was alone in town. It'd be the decent thing to do, Maggie."

"Then why don't you ask him?"

"Ask who?" Ryan tried again.

Edith gave Maggie a knowing smirk. "Because I'm not the one who took up with the man on the airplane."

"Mom." Ryan was starting to sound insistent.

"Just a minute, honey." Maggie continued to stare

at Edith. "I can't just invite the man over for Thanksgiving dinner. I don't even know him."

"You're going all the way into Boston to see a
hockey game with him, and you can't even share a
turkey at your own table."

Ryan tugged at her sleeve. "What hockey game?"

Maggie shook her head. "I don't know, Edith. I'll
have to think it over."

"You do that."

"What hockey game?"

"The Bruins game," Maggie told Ryan.

"Wow! Are we going to that? I thought you said
the tickets cost too much. Wow!" he said again. He
was staring at Maggie as if she'd just sprouted wings
out of her head.

Maggie frowned at Edith. "Do you really think I
should?"

"I certainly do. If nothing else, you can see how
things go tomorrow, and then decide."

"I guess that would be all right."

Ryan pulled on her sleeve again. "Where are our
seats, Mom? Are we close to the ice?"

Edith shook her head. She brushed her finger over
Ryan's bruised eye. "Not too close, I hope. You could
get hit with a puck."

"This is so cool," he said. "I bet Coach Bullard is
playing. Can I call Franklin and tell him? Can we take
Franklin, too, Mom? Can we?"

Maggie rolled her eyes at Edith. "Great."

Edith laughed. "Now if you need anything for
Thursday, Maggie, you just let me know."

"I will."

Edith gave her a knowing look. "And remember
what I said, even if it is none of my business."

"I *will*," Maggie insisted.

Edith's nod was brief. "All right then. I'll leave you two to do your shopping. Palmer's has turkey on sale, by the way, and Kroger has the best buy on fresh cranberries."

Maggie smiled. "Palmer's and Kroger. I got it."

"Now don't forget what I said about putting your turkey in the oven overnight." Edith picked up her purse. "And if you decide to make pumpkin pie, use the deep-dish crusts, or you'll have a mess in your oven."

Maggie nodded. "Overnight. Deep-dish."

Edith pulled her keys out of her purse. "And enjoy yourself, Maggie. You've earned it."

"Thanks for watching Ryan, Edith."

Edith shook her head in Ryan's direction. He had a dark smudge of chocolate on his cheek. "He wasn't any trouble. He's a good boy that one."

Ryan grinned at her. Maggie prodded his shoulder. "Tell Mrs. Sophy 'thank you' for the cake."

Ryan swallowed the bite in his mouth and nodded. "Thanks, Mrs. Soph," he said, using his preferred shorter version of the older woman's name.

Edith smiled at him. "You're welcome, young man. And the next time Tommy Willis hooks you with his stick," she said, grabbing her purse in both hands, "give him an elbow in the ribs for me." She made a jabbing motion with her elbow, and Ryan giggled.

Maggie smiled at her. "Thanks again, Edith. I always feel good knowing you're here with him. Tell Roy I said 'hello.'"

"I'll do that. And you call me on Thursday if you have anything to report." Edith shot Ryan a speculative look. "Or if you want me to pick up Ryan so he can play with my grandsons. I'll understand if you want the house to yourself for a while."

Maggie's jaw dropped open. "Edith!"

Edith chuckled and walked out of the kitchen. Ryan shot Maggie a curious look. "What's she talking about, Mom?"

"Nonsense," Maggie said, reaching for a paper towel. She wet it and grabbed one of Ryan's chocolate-covered hands.

"Can we take Franklin to the game, Mom?"

"No. We can't."

"But why?"

"Because I don't have tickets. We're going with a"— she paused—"with a friend."

"What friend?"

"A new friend."

"The guy whose coming for Thanksgiving?"

"I don't know if he's coming for Thanksgiving or not."

"Why not?"

Maggie finished cleaning the chocolate off his face. She dropped the wet paper towel into the wastebasket. Things were so simple for Ryan. "Because I haven't asked him, for one thing."

"Are you gonna?"

"I don't know."

He frowned. "But if he's taking us to the game, don't you think it'd be nice of us to let him eat here?"

"Do you think so?"

Ryan nodded. "Yeah. Can I at least call Franklin and tell him we're going?"

"Yes, you may."

"Cool." He started to squirm off his stool.

"Wait a minute, Ry, have you got any homework?"

He shook his head. "Mrs. Mitchell said we would spend our first day back just going over our math stuff and spend the rest of the day reading books and junk."

Maggie wiped his other hand. "Well, it's just after twelve. What do you say you call Franklin, then you and I go grocery shopping. We'll buy everything we need for Thursday—"

"Are we going to have a turkey?"

"Yes."

"And stuffing?"

"Yes."

"Are you going to make that sweet-potato stuff? The kind Dad likes?"

Maggie felt a brief twinge. Mark had loved her sweet-potato casserole. It had been his favorite part of holiday meals. Something in her balked at making it when he wasn't going to be there to enjoy it. "Do you want me to?"

Ryan nodded. "Yeah, with extra nuts on top."

She relented with a soft sigh of regret. "All right. Sweet-potato casserole with extra nuts." She tweaked his nose. "Just for you."

Ryan grinned at her. "Cool."

"Now, go put your shoes on and call Franklin. We should leave before the stores get too crowded."

"And then we're going out for pizza?"

"And then we're going out for pizza."

Ryan leapt down from his chair and raced out of the kitchen, moving, as usual, at a full run. Maggie scooped up her plate and silverware and carried them to the sink. As she rinsed them, her gaze fell on the picture of Mark and Ryan she kept on the windowsill. She picked it up, feeling a fresh surge of tears.

The two of them had gone fishing the summer before Mark had left for Saudi Arabia, and in the picture, Ryan was proudly holding a trout almost as big as he was, and Mark was holding what looked like a glorified goldfish. Ryan was grinning from ear to ear, and Mark was looking at Ryan with something as close to adoration as Maggie had ever seen. She sniffled and put the picture back down.

And thought of Scott Bishop and his kind eyes and his sad smile and his big heart. She attacked the smeared chocolate on the plate with renewed vigor. Perhaps Edith was right. Maybe she had spent too much time concentrating on the external circumstances of her life and not enough time working on the inside. Her gaze strayed to the picture and she wondered if Mark was going to have sweet-potato casserole for Thanksgiving.

When she heard the doorbell ring the following evening, Maggie checked her reflection in the mirror one more time. She felt ridiculous, like a sixteen-year-old preparing for the prom.

"I'll get it, Mom," she heard Ryan yell from his room. He'd been ready for an hour.

She wrinkled her nose at her reflection. As usual, she cursed the especially dry winter air that made her fine hair so flighty. In North Carolina, the humidity had always made it limp. It seemed there was no pleasing it.

"He's here, Mom," Ryan yelled from the foyer.

Maggie took a deep breath. She saw him standing in the door of her foyer as soon as she reached the landing. "Hi."

He glanced up. His smile was as warm, as kind as she remembered. "Hi."

"Would you like to come in for a while?" she asked, continuing down the stairs. "I don't think we have to leave just yet."

"We'll be late," Ryan protested.

"We have plenty of time, Ryan," she assured him. "Did you introduce yourself to Mr. Bishop?"

Ryan stuck out his hand. "Hi. I'm Ryan."

Scott gave his hand a firm shake. "I'm Scott."

Mark Connell leaned back against the doorframe and studied Scott Bishop. Maggie was leading him into the living room. Mark didn't like the way the guy was studying her back as she walked. He knew masculine appreciation when he saw it.

"Well," Annie asked, tweaking Mark's ribs, "do you think this is going to work?"

Mark frowned. "I don't know why you're so hellbent on getting Maggie fixed up with this guy. I said she needed to get over my death; I didn't say she needed marrying off."

Annie shook her head and gave him a disgusted look. "Men. You're all alike. This is some territorial thing for you, isn't it?"

"Don't be ridiculous." Mark shoved away from the doorframe and stalked across the room toward Scott. "He's too tall for her."

"He's only an inch taller than you are," Annie said.

"He's got blond hair."

"So?"

"So Maggie doesn't like men with blond hair."

Annie's smile was smug. "She seems to like Scott well enough."

Mark rolled his eyes. "Doesn't this bother you? Even a little?"

She blinked. "What?"

"Him. Her. Them."

Annie smiled a knowing smile and crossed the room, laying her hand on Mark's forearm. "I want Scott to be happy again, Mark. I think he needs Maggie to make that happen."

"There's no good reason why I should go along with this," he said, watching Scott examine the pictures on the wall. "I've had a whole day to think about this, and the more I think, the dumber it sounds. The only guarantee I've got that it's going to work is the promise of some half-invisible ghost." He looked at Annie's cloudy fingers where they still rested on his arm.

She gave his forearm a tight squeeze before she released it. "You know I'm right, Mark. I was sure of it when I walked in the door with Scott. I could tell by the way you were looking at Maggie."

"Look. I gave this a lot of thought yesterday and today. I've been talking to Ryan, listening to Maggie." He shrugged. "I think I changed—" Mark lost his train of thought when he saw the way Ryan was watching him. And Annie. "Uh-oh."

Annie gave him a sharp look. "What?"

Mark indicated Ryan with a brief nod of his head. "He can see you."

"Do you think so?"

"I'm sure of it."

"Then why hasn't he said anything?"

"He's careful about discussing me in front of Maggie. She gets upset." He winked at Ryan. "But he can see you, all right."

"Oh," She stood up and smoothed a hand over her pink sweater. "How do I look?"

Mark raised an eyebrow. "Like a ghost."

Maggie felt Ryan pulling on the arm of her sweater. She broke off her conversation with Scott about the Cape Hope project. "What, honey?"

"Who's the lady?"

Maggie frowned. "What lady?"

Ryan pointed at Annie. "That lady."

Maggie's gaze turned to alarm. "Ryan, there is no lady."

"Sure there is." He walked over and stared at Annie. "Right here."

Annie smiled at him. "Hello, Ryan. I'm Annie."

He tipped his head to the side. "Hi, Annie."

Maggie gasped. "Ryan! That's not funny. I told you about Mr. Bishop's wife so you'd know why he's here with us. I want you to apologize right now."

Ryan looked at Mark, then back at Annie. "Oh," he mumbled. He turned miserable eyes to Maggie. "I'm sorry."

He ran out of the room, and Mark dropped into a large wingback chair. "Oh, boy."

Annie nodded. "Oh, boy."

Maggie looked at Scott and frowned. "I'm sorry, I—I don't know what to say. I'm not sure what that was all about."

Scott rubbed his hand over his chest. "I think its about a kid who's having a tough time dealing with the loss of his dad. It's OK, Maggie."

"Sometimes I just don't know what to do for him."

Scott looked at the kitchen door. "He's probably more sane than the rest of us."

*   *   *

By the time they were in the car, on the way to Boston, Maggie was a nervous wreck. Ryan seemed to have forgotten the bizarre incident, as had Scott, but anxiety niggled at Maggie. She should never have agreed to the date. It was too much. It was too soon. It was too real. She should have known she wouldn't be able to handle it. Already, her palms were so clammy, she was afraid they'd slide off the steering wheel.

It didn't help matters any that Scott looked even more handsome than she remembered. She had secretly hoped that her tears on the plane had muddled her vision, and that Scott Bishop wasn't as alarmingly attractive as she'd thought. That hope had been handily demolished. He was wearing well-worn jeans, a blue-and-green flannel shirt that made his eyes sparkle, and a roomy navy wool jacket. Maggie's stomach had fluttered when she'd seen him smiling at her from the foyer of her house.

In the distance, she could see the Boston skyline. Ryan began pointing out buildings to Scott. Maggie was so absorbed in her own thoughts, she didn't notice Scott's hand reaching for hers until she felt the pressure of his gloved fingers. She nearly jumped through the windshield. When she slammed on the brakes, Scott gave her a curious look.

"Sorry," she mumbled. "I thought I saw something in the road."

Ryan indicated a group of buildings and bridges on the left. "That's the harbor," he said.

Scott asked Ryan about one of the ships, earning another litany of description. As they neared the stadium, Ryan's nonstop chatter turned, inevitably, to the matter at hand. Maggie eased her way through the city streets, idly listening as Ryan rattled off statistics about the Boston Bruins.

Occasionally, Scott would slide a glance in her direction, but he appeared to be content to listen to Ryan while he continued to hold Maggie's hand. When he started to rub his thumb on her palm, her mouth went dry as dust. Maggie firmly instructed herself to get a grip. As they neared the stadium, Maggie used the excuse of the traffic to free her hand from his grasp. Her relief was short-lived, however. Scott asked Ryan a question about the "sticking" rule, then settled his hand on Maggie's knee.

She headed for The FleetCenter.

"There's the stadium, Mom," Ryan said, pointing to the enormous coliseum-type structure that housed the Bruins and the Celtics.

"You ever been here before?" Scott asked him.

"Sure. Lot's of times. Coach brings us."

"Coach?"

Maggie cleared her throat. "Chuck Bullard is Ryan's hockey coach. He's also a forward for the Boston Bruins."

"I've never seen a game here, though," Ryan said. "The tickets cost too much."

Maggie concentrated on the traffic. She hoped Scott couldn't see her discomfort.

"Well, then, we all got lucky," Scott said. "I've never seen a hockey game either."

"Never?" Ryan asked. Scott might as well have told him he'd never been to a grocery store.

"Not even on television."

"Wow."

"Hockey's not very popular in Texas," Scott said.

Maggie thought he sounded embarrassed. "They play more football and baseball there, Ryan."

"Oh."

Scott flashed Maggie a grateful smile. "Thanks. I was beginning to feel like a foreigner."

"Mom," Ryan said, "can we buy a program so I can show Scott all the players?"

"I guess," she said.

"And a soft pretzel?"

She turned into the parking garage. "Sure."

"And a jersey?"

Maggie gave Ryan a dry look. "Don't push your luck."

"But, Mom—"

"I said 'no,' Ryan."

He flopped back against the seat. "I told Franklin that we'd get him a puck."

Maggie pulled into a parking space. "Well, then, I guess you'll just have to catch one."

"Can't we buy one?"

"No, Ryan." She gave him a sharp look.

Scott was studying her in the dim, fluorescent lighting. She fought the urge to meet his gaze. "Don't forget your coat," she told Ryan, as he climbed down from the Bronco.

He grabbed the jacket off the seat. Scott reached for Maggie's arm, delaying her when she would have gotten out of the car. "Maggie, is something wrong?"

"Wrong?"

"You seem, I don't know, tense."

"Nothing's wrong."

He held her gaze for several long seconds. Ryan dragged her door open. "Come on, Mom. I want to see where our seats are."

"You're sure," Scott said.

Maggie let Ryan pull her from the car. "Of course," she told Scott, then slammed the car door. He let himself out on his side of the Bronco. Maggie made Ryan wait until Scott rounded the vehicle.

Scott tried again. "Maggie—"

She felt like a fool. They were two responsible adults, and she was acting like a first-class idiot. She stopped. Ryan gave her hand a sharp tug. "Wait a minute," she told him. She met Scott's gaze. In the hazy lighting of the parking deck, his eyes looked like amber crystal. "I'm sorry. I . . . it's just that this—" she muttered beneath her breath in frustration. "I haven't done this in a long time." She wondered if Scott would think she was talking about the hockey game.

His smile told her that he didn't. "You haven't been on a date since Mark. Have you?"

She shook her head. "No."

Scott reached for her hand. He looked so relieved, Maggie almost laughed. "Good," he said. "I haven't been on one since Annie. We'll just have to muddle through. I think I forgot all the rules."

"Mom." Ryan pulled at her hand again. "I want to find our seats."

"Ryan." The look she gave him momentarily stilled his protests. She glanced back at Scott. "I'm sorry I'm so edgy."

He squeezed her hand. "You're not the only one. I've got to be a complete idiot to bring a woman and her kid to a sporting event I know nothing about. A guy's ego, and all."

Ryan pointed to the elevator bank. "Look, Mom. It's Sergei Polokov," he said, sounding awed.

Maggie recognized the Bruins defenseman from the

distance. He was entering through the players' door. "Sure is." She gave Scott a conspiratorial look. "By the end of the evening, you'll be an expert. Ryan's going to talk your ear off."

She let Ryan lead the way into the stadium complex. They found their seats at rinkside center ice. "Your boss sure knows how to pick 'em," Maggie said.

Scott stuffed his gloves into the pockets of his jacket. "He's a big fan," Scott said. "He used to live in Boston."

She sank into her seat. The tension she'd felt from the moment Scott had arrived on her doorstep had finally dissipated with her confession in the parking deck. She still felt odd, and out of place, but it helped knowing he wasn't entirely comfortable either. Fortunately, Ryan's excitement had an unexpected side benefit. His continuous commentary on everything from the color of the stadium seats to the new display on the digital scoreboard eliminated the need for conversation.

By the time the game began, Maggie was feeling almost completely at ease. Ryan sat between her and Scott, giving Scott detailed analysis of the action on the ice. As expected, the play between the Bruins and the New York Rangers was fast-paced and aggressive. It kept Ryan fully occupied. Maggie used the time to concentrate on what she was going to do about Scott Bishop and his presence in her life.

"Yikes!" Annie hopped out of the way as a Bruins defenseman bore down on her.

Mark laughed. "He can't hurt you, Annie."

"That doesn't mean I want to be run over." She

picked her way gingerly across the ice. "It also doesn't mean I can't fall and break my neck out here." She gave Mark an acid look. "Why are we standing in the middle of the ice?" From the corner of her eye, she saw the Rangers center level the Bruins defenseman. "Serves you right," she muttered as the man skidded past her, facedown on the ice.

"I had no idea you were so vindictive," Mark said.

"I'm not vindictive." She screeched, and brought her hands to her face as two more players skated through her image. "I just think you could have found a better place for us."

He indicated the sellout crowd with a sweep of his arm. "The game's sold out. These are the best seats in the house."

"I don't care about the game." She pointed to Scott and Maggie. "I want to be over there."

"There's nowhere to sit over there."

"We can't hear what they're saying"—she side-stepped a fallen player—"from over here."

"We don't need to hear what they're saying."

"You're not cooperating."

He pointed to Maggie. "Look. Maggie's not saying anything. Ryan's doing all the talking, and I'll bet you ten to one he's telling your husband more than the guy ever wants to know about hockey."

Annie had to dodge a flying puck. Mark didn't even flinch as the black missile sailed through his forehead. "I'd laugh if you got knocked unconscious."

He shook his head. "No you wouldn't. Without me, you couldn't get off the ice."

"I could, too."

"Please," he said. He removed his hand from her

elbow. She wobbled. "You can barely stand up."

"It's slippery."

"It's ice. Of course it's slippery."

"Smart aleck."

"Look," he said. He pointed toward the Bruins goal. "Don't you want me to explain what's going on?"

"If we were with Scott and Maggie, Ryan would be explaining what's going on."

"He'd also be distracted."

"Can't he see us out here?"

Mark shrugged. "Sure. He envies us, too. We've got the best seats in the house."

"So why isn't he distracted if we're over here, and he would be if we were over there?" she asked. She knew she sounded even more confused than she actually was.

"Because, he won't feel like he has to talk to us," Mark said. "This way, he can concentrate on the game."

Annie ducked as a hockey stick flew over her head. "We aren't here so Ryan can concentrate on the game, you know. We're here to help Scott and Maggie."

"Annie," Mark said, sounding exasperated, "if Ryan concentrates on the game, Maggie won't have to concentrate on him. If she doesn't have to concentrate on him, she can concentrate on"—he paused perceptibly—"other stuff."

"Oh." Comprehension dawned. "Oh." Annie beamed at Mark. "You are helping."

"I'm helping. Now will you shut up and let me explain what's going on?"

Annie stepped over a spot of blood on the ice. "I know what's going on." She pointed to a fight that had broken out behind the Bruins goal. "They're trying to kill each other."

Four

The Bruins won five goals to three. Ryan was so worn-out from the excitement, and the late hour, that he fell asleep almost before he managed to climb into the backseat of the Bronco. Maggie buckled him in. "That's it," she told Scott. "He's catatonic." She tossed Scott the keys. "Would you mind driving back?" she asked.

He looked at her in surprise. "Driving?" It wasn't the thought of driving that made him nervous. It was the thought of getting lost. He hadn't bothered to pay much attention when Maggie had driven them to the stadium, thinking she would drive on the way back, as well. The thought of confessing his deplorable sense of direction to Maggie made him feel squeamish. He'd swallowed enough male pride for one night with his self-confessed ignorance about the game. He balked at the idea of telling her he couldn't find his way out of a paper bag.

He fingered the keys. It couldn't be so hard, he reminded himself. Cape Hope was north of Boston. As long as he stayed on the interstate and followed the signs, how bad could it get?

"Don't worry," Maggie was assuring him. "We're right on the expressway. You won't hit any traffic."

He remembered their conversation on the plane. He'd told her he didn't rent a car because of the traffic. "Sure," he said, pulling open the passenger-side door for her. "I'll be glad to drive."

"Thanks for doing this. I'm beat."

He chanted "north on the expressway" like a mantra all the way around to his side of the car. He had to adjust the seat to accommodate his height. He finally climbed in, then favored Maggie with a look of supreme confidence. If he pulled this off, he was going to nominate himself for an Academy Award. "North on the expressway, right?" he said, hoping he sounded cavalier.

She rested her head back against the seat with a slight yawn. "North then west. You can't miss it."

He could miss it. He could miss a skyscraper in the middle of west Texas. If he wasn't careful, he could miss the nose on the end of his face. "Right." He threw the car into reverse, then eased out of the parking space.

Maggie was asleep before he exited the parking garage.

He knew he was in trouble when he saw the freeway sign to Providence. Rhode Island. He reassured himself with the notion that Massachusetts, unlike Texas, was such a small state, that it was common to see road signs indicating out-of-state locales.

Until he passed the WELCOME TO RHODE ISLAND sign. Scott shot a quick glance at Maggie. She was sleeping like the dead. Ryan was softly snoring in the backseat. Scott seriously considered his chances of getting them out of the mess he'd created without Maggie knowing. He wondered if he could sneak into her house and set all the clocks back by two, maybe three hours, before she woke up.

Resolutely, he pulled off the interstate. "Maggie," he prodded her arm. "Maggie, wake up."

"Hmmm."

Not very promising. "Maggie," he tried again. "We're lost. Wake up."

Her eyelids drifted open. "Lost?"

"Yeah."

"Where are we?"

He paused. "Providence."

Several seconds of silence elapsed before Maggie sat bolt upright in the seat. "Providence? Rhode Island?"

"I guess."

She looked around. "What time is it?"

"Uh," he checked his watch. "After two."

"In the morning?"

"Well, it's dark outside. It's either morning, or it's the world's longest-lasting solar eclipse."

Maggie gave him a blank stare. He could tell by the glazed look in her eyes that she still wasn't fully awake. "Solar eclipse?"

"Earth to Maggie," he said, deliberately making his voice sound hollow.

She blinked. "Solar—" the joke finally made sense. Maggie dropped back against the seat with a choked laugh. "How on earth did we end up in Providence?"

"Are you mad?"

"Is this anything like running out of gas on your way home from the prom?"

Scott shook his head. "No. It's more like forgetting to get gas in the first place."

"Providence," she repeated. She sounded incredulous.

Scott wished she would stop saying it. "Yeah. If you just point me in the right direction, I'll get us back on the road. You can go back to sleep."

"Scott, Providence is almost an hour south of Boston."

"I know."

"But we left the stadium at just after eleven. If you took a wrong turn on the freeway, why is it so late?"

"I think I got here by way of Des Moines."

"Des—" Maggie started to giggle. She pressed her gloved hand to her mouth, but it didn't help.

Scott squirmed. "It's not that funny."

"Scott, what happened?"

"You gave the keys to your car to a man with no sense of direction," he said. He figured he probably sounded surly, but couldn't help it. He didn't like it that Maggie was laughing at him.

"Just how bad is your sense of direction?" she asked.

"In my apartment in Texas, I have a sign on the wall that tells me which way to turn when I come out of the bathroom."

Her giggle turned into a full-fledged laugh. In spite of himself, or maybe because of it, Scott laughed, too. He was surprised to find how much he liked laughing with Maggie. "Stop laughing." He gave her a playful poke in the ribs. "You'll irreparably damage my ego."

"Sorry." She wiped a hand over her face. "I'm sorry."

"Are you going to get us out of here, or not?"

"Do you want me to drive?"

He shook his head. "I'll drive. Just stay awake and

talk to me this time. We might end up in San Francisco if you don't."

"I've never been to San Francisco."

"I have. It's foggy. You can't see a damn thing."

"I'll bet you got lost a lot."

"Every time I walked out the front door. Now how do we get out of here, Captain?"

Maggie laughed again. "All right. Turn around and head north." At his pointed look, she indicated the direction with her finger. "That way. I'll talk you through this."

"Thanks."

"Don't mention it. I want to make sure Ryan is home in time for school next Monday."

The drive didn't take nearly as long as Scott had feared. Or perhaps it only seemed shorter because Maggie kept up a steady stream of conversation. They talked about their childhoods, told funny stories about their courtships, laughed at each other's jokes, enjoyed each other's company. Scott felt better than he had in a long time.

Sometime on the long trip, Maggie's hand found its way into his, where it rested comfortably. He liked the feel of her fingers entwined with his, and wished they weren't both wearing gloves.

She was telling him a story about Ryan when he pulled into her driveway. "We're here," she said. She sounded surprised.

"We're here." He wished they weren't. He wasn't ready to give up the closeness of the car. In the moonlight, Maggie's hair looked like spun silver. Despite her baggy purple jacket, he had a vivid recollection of the way her dark red sweater hugged her figure. It made his fingers twitch.

Resolutely, he dragged his thoughts back to her hair. He wondered if it was as soft as it looked. Unable to resist, he touched it with his gloved fingers. "You have beautiful hair, Maggie."

Her eyes widened. Scott was suddenly aware of everything about her. He smelled her faint perfume. He could distinguish it from the scent of her shampoo. He felt the rhythm of her breathing, saw the uncertainty in her gaze. Reluctantly, he lowered his hand. "Thank you for going with me tonight," he said. She continued to stare at him. "I had a good time." He wanted to ask her out again, wanted it badly, but something in the startled way she was watching him made him hesitate.

"Scott, I—"

"Yes?"

"Would you help me carry Ryan inside?"

He had momentarily forgotten about the child sleeping in the back of the car. He seized the fragile excuse to spend even ten more minutes in the warm cocoon of Maggie's company like a lifeline. "Of course."

Scott climbed out of the Bronco, then reached inside to lift Ryan's sleeping body. "I'll carry him," he said. "Why don't you unlock the door."

It took Maggie mere minutes to get Ryan settled in his bed. Scott had already called a cab by the time she returned to the foyer. Maggie stood at the top of the landing for several long seconds, watching him. He was staring out the window, his features lit by the moonlight. She had removed her shoes in Ryan's room, so she padded silently down the carpet.

He started when she touched his shoulder. "Scott?"

He turned abruptly. "I didn't hear you," he said. "Is Ryan in bed?"

Maggie nodded. Almost against her will, she laid her open palm on his jacket. "Scott, I—we had a good time. Ryan really enjoyed himself."

"What about you, Maggie? Did you enjoy yourself?"

"Except for getting lost," she quipped, uncomfortable with the mounting tension between them. She was having trouble keeping her gaze off the firm contours of his mouth.

"Be honest, Maggie," Scott said.

She met his gaze. "Yes. I had a good time."

He breathed a sigh of relief. "Can I see you again?"

"I . . . all right."

"Ah, Maggie," he jerked his hands from his pockets to pull her into his arms. When his mouth found hers in a ravenous kiss, she melted into him. The kiss was hot, hungry. Maggie wrapped her arms around his neck even as she forced aside lingering doubts. This was right. Being with him was right.

At the sound of a horn in the distance, Scott raised his head. She gasped at the sudden lack of contact. "My cab's here," he said. "When can I see you again?"

Maggie shivered. When? She tried to lock on to a date, and found the edges of her concentration dimmed. "When?" she repeated.

The horn sounded again. "I'm not leaving until you tell me," Scott said.

"Thanksgiving," she said.

"Thanksgiving?" he sounded confused.

"It's the day after tomorrow."

He nodded. His arms were still wrapped around

her. Maggie twined her fingers into the hair at his nape. "I know when it is," he said. "I planned this trip on purpose. I didn't want to spend the holiday in Dallas. My family wanted me to come, but I didn't think I could take it."

"Ryan and I will be alone here. Why don't you join us?" She didn't have time to consider the wisdom of the invitation, or the odd sensation that she was somehow doing something wrong. Scott's hands were rubbing her back through her wool sweater, and she only knew that she couldn't let him leave without first ensuring that she'd see him again.

Scott hesitated only briefly before he responded. "As long as you're sure I won't be intruding."

She shook her head. "The truth is, I'd appreciate the company. I wasn't really looking forward to the holiday anyway, but I felt like it was important for Ryan's sake to try and restore some semblance of normalcy to our routine." Maggie leaned her head against Scott's chest. She ignored the sound of the taxi horn.

Scott waved at the driver through the window, signaling him to wait. "I don't know, Maggie. It's kind of a family thing."

"Ryan's had a tough time with all this," Maggie continued, "and I know Christmas is going to be very hard on him. I thought we might try and do a dry run at Thanksgiving, just to see." She wondered if he'd accept. He seemed wary, as if he, too, knew that the invitation was more than just another date. She was asking him to share a part of her life.

Scott tipped her chin up with his thumb. "What time should I be here?"

*   *   *

When Scott rang Maggie's doorbell on Thursday morning, he was thankful for the biting cold. It froze the sweat on his palms. He still wasn't sure it had been wise to agree to share Thanksgiving dinner with her and Ryan. He was even less sure it had been wise to agree to do it at her house, in the center of her life, rather than in someplace more neutral. He was still reeling from the effects of their date two nights ago. There was a connection between him and Maggie Connell that made him feel like the world had tilted off its axis. He didn't know what it was, but it scared the life out of him.

In the thirty-six hours since he'd seen Maggie, he'd had a nagging, persistent feeling of misery coupled with the strongest sensation of Annie's presence he'd felt since the days just following her death. It had thrown him mentally off-balance, and he wasn't sure he was up to handling what could prove to be an explosively emotional situation. Worse yet, he hadn't had the courage to call her yesterday, and he had no idea if she was as disturbed as he.

The door swung open. Scott stared at Maggie for a few seconds before he thought to say anything. "Hi."

She studied him warily. "Hi." Maggie stepped aside and motioned for him to come into the house.

He paused to brush the snow off his shoulders. "I'm sorry I'm a little early. The cab didn't get here this fast the other night. The guy must have taken a shortcut."

Maggie shook her head. "I guess you wouldn't know, would you?" she joked, in obvious reference to his lack of directional aptitude.

Scott choked out a slight laugh. "Guess not."

She motioned him inside. "Don't worry about it. In

fact, I was just going to try and start a fire in the living room. As long as you're here, you might as well make yourself useful."

He sniffed appreciatively at the combination of scents wafting from the back of the house. "Something smells really good."

She held out her hands for his coat. "It's the sweet-potato casserole that Ryan insisted we had to have."

He paused, feeling awkward. Maggie was nervously smoothing an invisible wrinkle off the sleeve of his cashmere coat. He reached over and touched her hand. "Maggie?"

She looked up. "Yes?"

"I'm sorry I didn't call you yesterday. I should have." She looked so appealing, standing there with an apron looped over her neck and tied around her slim waist. Her blue sweater made her eyes look even clearer than he remembered, and the glimpse of jeans-clad legs beneath the apron hinted at the long, shapely limbs he hadn't been able to stop fantasizing about. He swallowed.

She shrugged. "Why would you think that? I did wonder if you'd come, when you didn't call to confirm, I mean, but there was no reason for you to feel obligated to—"

"Maggie," he said, cutting off her protest. "It was rude. I should have called. I just needed—I needed some distance." He spread his hands out in front of him. "It's hard to explain."

She sighed. "I understand, Scott." She met his gaze. "I was kind of undone by the whole thing myself." She juggled his coat onto her other arm. "I'm really glad you came."

Scott almost sagged in relief. "So am I." He

dropped a brief kiss on her forehead. "Now, which way is the fireplace?"

She waved a hand to her left. "In the living room. If you need anything, I'll be in the kitchen."

Scott made his way into the living room. He took his time building the fire while he studied the room around him. There hadn't been much time the night of the hockey game.

It was comfortable and unpretentious, with an understated elegance that reminded him of Maggie. Mostly deep blues and soft pinks, its warmth was accented, not diminished, by the homey touches of a hockey stick jutting out from the umbrella stand and the scattered pictures strewn across the mantel.

He lit the kindling and waited, blowing gently until the fire seemed to catch. He stood and examined the pictures. He hadn't had time to really examine them the other night.

Most were of Ryan. His face was a miniature copy of Maggie's. There was a formal shot of him, probably a school picture, and another of his tiny body swallowed up in hockey gear. Scott chuckled at another picture where he was covered in mud, holding a squirming cat beneath his arm.

He stopped short when he came to the picture of a Marine captain in dress uniform. Mark. Scott looked closely at the blue eyes, the determined face, the dark hair, and wondered how long before Mark's death the picture had been taken.

Mark pointed at Scott. "Why is he staring at my picture like that?" he asked Annie.

"Sizing up the competition," she said.

"That's not funny."

"It wasn't supposed to be."

"Look, I don't think this—" he lost his train of thought when he saw Maggie walk into the room carrying a plate of cookies and a coffeepot. "Dinner will be ready in about an hour," she told Scott as she set her burden on the coffee table. "I made these yesterday, and I thought you might like some coffee. I have soda and tea if you'd rather."

"Coffee is fine," Scott said, still staring at the picture of Mark.

"I see you got the fire started."

Scott turned from his inspection of the mantel to smile at Maggie. At the sight of that smile, Mark felt something uncomfortable shift around in the pit of his stomach.

Scott strolled over to the couch and sat down next to Maggie. "Maggie," he said, reaching for her hand.

Mark stepped forward, but Annie restrained him with a hand on his shoulder.

"Yes?" Maggie said, pouring a cup of coffee.

Scott leaned back on the couch to stare up at the ceiling. "Nothing. You'll think I'm nuts."

Maggie handed him his cup. "Depends on what you have to say."

Scott took a sip of his coffee. "Yesterday"—he paused—"why I didn't call you."

Maggie picked up her own cup. "It's because of Annie, isn't it?"

Scott stared at her. "Why do you think that?"

"Because," Maggie said, "ever since the other night, I've had the strangest feeling that Mark was here, watching me." Annie's fingers tightened on Mark's shoulder. Maggie continued to watch Scott. "You've felt the same way about Annie, haven't you?"

Annie gasped. Scott thumped his cup down on the table. "Yes. God. I thought I was going crazy."

Maggie shook her head. "I felt it, too. Maybe it was the discussion we had on the plane. That was the first time I've really talked about Mark with anyone since the weeks following the funeral."

Mark started pacing the room. "What the hell?" he said, meeting Annie's gaze. "This has never happened before. At least, not that I know of."

Annie shook her head. "I don't think it's happened to Scott either."

"What if"—Mark looked back at Maggie and Scott—"what if they are subconsciously aware of us?"

Annie frowned. "What do you mean?"

"What if we really are here? What if they can hear us, see us, and they just don't know about it?"

"Why wouldn't they have noticed before?" Annie said, crossing the room to sit next to Scott. She ran her fingers over the moss green of his sweater.

Mark shrugged. "There are two of us now. Maybe it's like, increased activity or something."

"You watch too much television," Annie said.

Mark stalked over to the couch. He braced his hands on the curved back, leaned down, and stared right into Scott's face. Scott didn't blink. Mark looked at Annie. "Something is going on here."

Scott released a long breath. He smiled at Maggie before Annie had a chance to respond to Mark's challenge. "Well," Scott said, "at least that's settled. I'm glad I'm not the only one hearing things that go bump in the night."

Maggie shook her head. "I've heard a few of those myself lately."

"See," Mark told Annie. "They can hear us."

"It's just an expression." She waved a hand in his direction. "Shut up for a minute, I want to listen."

"That's eavesdropping."

"It is not."

Scott swallowed a bite of sugar cookie. He leaned back on the couch. "Maggie, I think it's more than just the plane."

"You do?"

"Yeah. I think there's something going on between us, and we both know where it's headed."

"Maybe you're right."

"I know I'm right. You can't tell me you haven't thought about it, what it was like," he said, referring to the kiss.

He knew from the look in her eyes that she had thought about it as much as he had. "I don't think we should discuss this right now." Before he could interrupt, she hastened to add, "I don't want Ryan to hear us talking about it."

Scott could certainly see the wisdom in that. He felt better knowing she wasn't simply trying to avoid the issue. "Where is Ryan?" he asked.

Maggie put her cup down on the coffee table. "He's in the kitchen watching the rolls rise. He thinks they're breathing." She looked over her shoulder toward the swinging door. "Ryan! Ryan, honey, come here a minute."

"Hold on, Mom!" Ryan's voice came from behind the door.

"Right now," she said. "Come say hello."

"What about the rolls?" Ryan called.

"They'll still be breathing when you get back. Come out here."

Ryan crashed open the door and ran into the room.

He skidded to a stop in front of Scott. "Hi, Scott."

Scott nodded and stuck out his hand. "Hey, bud."

"Did you know we're having sweet-potato casserole?"

"Your mom told me."

"Then can we build a snowman, right?"

"This afternoon," Scott said.

Ryan beamed at him. "It has to be a really big one. With a hat, and a broom."

"Can't have a snowman without those," Scott concurred.

"Cool," Ryan said. "How long do you think it will last?"

Scott met Maggie's gaze over Ryan's head. "A very long time," he said.

Five

*E*xcept for Ryan's polite inquiry as to whether he should set the table for three or five, the rest of the afternoon passed without incident. Maggie was relieved when the meal was finally over, and Ryan seemed ready for a nap, despite his protests to the contrary. Under the guise of letting him listen to music in his room, Maggie took him upstairs. She handed Scott her design book before she left the living room. "Here are my plans for Cape Hope," she told him. "I'll be back down in a minute."

Once upstairs, she tucked Ryan in, then bent down to kiss his forehead.

"When can me and Scott build our snowman?" he asked.

"After you wake up."

"But I'm not tired."

"I know." She snapped off the light. The room was dark except for the weak sunlight fighting its way through Ryan's shades.

"Mom?" he said, visibly stifling a yawn.

"What?"

"Why don't you think I can see Annie and Dad?"

71

Maggie closed her eyes briefly. When she opened them again, Ryan was watching her intently. "I know you think you see them, Ryan, but I want you to stop talking about it in front of Scott."

"But I really see her, Mom," he said, looking toward the corner of the room. "She's standing right over there."

Maggie sat down on the side of the bed. "I know she's real to you, Ryan, just like Daddy."

"No," he said, staring at the corner. "She's different than Dad. She's kind of see-through."

Maggie stroked the side of his face. "Oh, Ryan."

"She's wearing a pink sweater and a pink skirt, and she's got brown hair. It's real short, too."

Maggie tucked the blankets closer around his slender shoulders. "Just try to remember what we talked about, OK?"

Ryan turned onto his side and met her gaze. "I know. She isn't real. I just think so."

Maggie felt a twinge of regret at his mournful tone. She brushed a lock of blond hair off his forehead. "She's real to you, Ryan. Just like Daddy. That's real enough for me. I just think it's hard for Scott when you talk about her. So let's keep it between us. Deal?"

He smiled at her. "OK, Mom." The last was lost in a massive yawn.

"I love you."

He mumbled something that might have been "I love you, too," but Maggie couldn't be entirely sure.

Scott was waiting for her on the sofa, idly flipping through the sketches she'd handed him. He looked up with a smile. "Is he asleep?"

Maggie nodded. "Out like a light." He looked at ease, right, seated on her couch. The sleeves of his burgundy-chambray shirt were rolled back to expose strong forearms dusted with light hair and freckles. His long, jeans-clad legs were stretched out in front of him as he examined her designs, and, somehow, impossibly, his masculine presence seemed to belong in the Victorian decor, and among the laces and bows and baskets of her home. She sat down on the couch, indicating the sketches with a wave of her hand. "What do you think?"

"These are amazing, Maggie. I mean, really amazing."

She looked at him, skeptical. "Do you think so, or are you just trying to make me feel better?"

He shook his head and pointed to a sketch. "I love this. The whole design is wonderful. I don't think there's another resort in the country that can come close to this type of concept."

She breathed a sigh of relief. "I wanted to do something different. I had the idea to emulate the Newport Beach properties when I was driving through Martha's Vineyard with Ryan one day. I don't think people will come to Cape Hope for a traditional beach vacation. We don't have the weather, for one thing, and the atmosphere is different for another. It's a more sedate, traditional kind of place. I sort of think of the Vanderbilts out for a Sunday afternoon stroll on the beach."

Scott turned to another sketch. "I especially like what you've done with the dining room. Guests get the atmosphere of an elegant formal dinner without the demands of a full dinner party. These six-seat tables and alcoves are brilliant."

"Thank you."

Scott put the sketches down on the coffee table. "I

think you've got something really special here. Do you have any idea what else is being proposed?"

She shrugged. "There are at least three firms that I know of who are bidding on the project. I think my stiffest competition is Irene Fussman."

"From New York?"

"Do you know her?"

Scott snorted. "We call her Fussman the Dragon Lady."

Maggie laughed. "You obviously know her."

"My partners and I have worked with her on a couple of hotel chains we did. Mainly Parker and Stylton lines. She's a nightmare."

"I think her proposals are more traditional. The typical resort-type thing. It will just depend on how the planning commission decides to proceed." She gave him a meaningful look. "And what structural design they go with."

Scott grinned at her and reached for the plastic tube by his knee. "This will blow your mind."

"You're pretty sure of yourself."

He laughed and shook his head. "Not the designs, the concept. Go ahead. Take a peek."

Maggie pulled the plans from the tube and spread them out on the coffee table. "Oh, Scott."

"Do you like it?"

The exquisitely detailed Victorian-Era mansion enchanted her. She flipped through the designs, stopping to admire the landscaping and the elegant layout for the spacious first-floor ballrooms and restaurants. "This is wonderful."

"It fits kind of nicely with your sketches. Don't you think?"

Maggie ran a finger along the outline of a garden

terrace. "It will be perfect. Just perfect. The developers have to go for this. It's so right."

"I don't know. There are two very competitive firms bidding against me. I think there may be a few others, but I consider Jason Challow and Fred Derring to be my biggest competition."

Maggie frowned. She looked at another drawing. "Everything Jason Challow designs looks like a glorified bar of soap. Did you see that hotel he did in Las Vegas."

Scott laughed. "The Billings Grand?"

"Yeah. All it needed was IVORY emblazoned on the side. He's really into those bubble buildings. I think he's seriously aspiring to design the first US space colony."

"Come on, Maggie, Jason is a very respected architect."

"If you like soap."

"What about Fred?"

She glanced at Scott. "His designs are nice, very artistic. I really like the plaza building he did in New York, but I think they'd be out of place in Cape Hope. I just can't see a huge steel-and-glass monstrosity looming over the skyline." She looked back at his drawings. "This, on the other hand, this *is* Cape Hope."

He slid closer to her on the sofa. "You wouldn't be just the least bit biased, would you?"

Maggie smiled at him. "Would you mind if I were?"

Scott shook his head and pressed a kiss to her temple. "No. I don't think I'd mind at all."

Maggie's heart skipped a beat. She stared at Scott for several long seconds. Her stomach had that now-familiar fluttery sensation again. "Scott?"

"Yeah, Maggie?" His breath fanned across her cheek, and something inside her quivered.

She swallowed. "Do you think—do you think Mark and Annie are watching us right now?"

Scott shrugged. "I don't know. Why do you ask?"

She ran the tip of her tongue along her upper lip to moisten it. Scott's gaze followed the small movement. "Because I'd really like for you to kiss me, and I can almost guarantee that Mark wouldn't like it if you did."

"Hey!" Mark pulled at Annie's hands. She'd clamped them over his eyes seconds after Maggie asked Scott to kiss her. "Cut that out. Let go."

"No." She hung on.

"I want to see this. Your husband is kissing my wife."

"Your wife asked my husband to kiss her."

Mark tugged on her wrists. Annie jumped on his back and hung on. Mark growled at her. "This is not what I had in mind."

Annie's laugh was smug. "It's exactly what I had in mind. If I let go, do you promise to behave?"

"What am I going to do? Drive my fist through his body? I can't touch him, remember?"

"I don't want to risk it."

Mark grunted. "Fine. I promise I won't overreact."

Annie lowered herself to the floor and took her hands off his eyes. "I don't know why this is bugging you so much. He kissed her the other night."

"Not like that, he didn't. Look at that. He's got his tongue—" Mark bit off a curse. "It's not right." Scott had levered Maggie back on the sofa just enough so her head tipped back. Her hands were twined in his hair, and he cradled her face between his palms. Mark took an angry step forward. Annie placed herself between him and the sofa, pressing her hands to his chest. "You promised."

Mark pointed at Scott. "I didn't know it was *that* kind of kiss. He's only known her for three days, for God's sake. What's he doing kissing her like that?"

Annie looked over her shoulder. "She doesn't seem to mind."

"Well, I mind." He took another step.

Annie's feet slid on the hardwood floor until they connected with the carpet. "I think we should go for a walk or something. It's not nice to eavesdrop."

"We aren't eavesdropping. There's no conversation going on. I don't hear anything. Do *you* hear anything?"

Annie pushed at his chest. "Stop it, Mark. Just stop it. I think we should leave them alone."

"Leave them alone? Are you out of your mind? I'm not going to leave them alone."

"She's not your wife anymore, Mark."

Mark froze and stared at Annie. His stomach twisted. He looked quickly at Maggie and Scott. "She's not, is she?" His voice sounded hoarse to his own ears.

Annie shook her head. She wrapped her arms around his waist. "She's not."

Mark shuddered. "Just tell me one thing, Annie, and then I'll go anywhere you want."

She tipped her head back and looked at him. "OK. What do you want to know?"

"On a scale of one to ten, how good a kisser is he?"

Annie looked over her shoulder before returning

her gaze to Mark. "He's an eleven. Definitely an eleven."

Scott slid his mouth over Maggie's, suddenly ravenous for her and the easy way she turned into his embrace. Her lips were full and moist. When he dipped his tongue into her mouth, the lingering taste of coffee and whipped cream assaulted his senses. He groaned. It had been so long. So damned long.

Maggie sighed and wrapped her arms around his neck. "Oh, Scott." She felt herself sinking into a dark, wonderful cloud.

He hadn't even realized until that moment how much he had craved the warmth, the comfort of touch. Since Annie's death, he had hidden himself, protected himself, but Maggie, Maggie dared him to step outside and see the world again. He deepened the kiss, driving his tongue into her mouth and withdrawing, only to taste her again. He was fast losing control and there wasn't a damned thing he could do about it. He was barely aware of her gasp when he slid his hand under the waistband of her sweater and splayed his fingers on her back.

Maggie felt her nerve endings come alive under the scalding touch of Scott's fingers. She clung to him, clutched at him. She pushed aside every conscious thought, and willed herself to concentrate only on the feel of his mouth, his hands on her body.

She was as soft and as warm as he had imagined, only more so. The scent of her light perfume and the feel of her body pressed into his melded with the heady taste of her to wash through him with the subtlety of a tidal wave. He nipped at her lower lip, groaning in response when she responded by twining her tongue with his.

Scott felt a rush of white-hot desire pool in his loins. He grabbed Maggie's hands and put them on his chest. "Touch me, Maggie," he whispered. "Please."

Maggie drew in a quick breath. She could feel his heat through the fabric of his shirt. Her fingers fluttered. Her heartbeat accelerated. She moved her hands to the white buttons and started working them free. Scott groaned sharply, then buried his mouth on hers once more.

Maggie worked loose four buttons before she slipped her hands inside his shirt. She twined her fingers in the crisp hair on his chest. Scott murmured an encouragement against her lips before he tore his mouth free to rub it along the curve of her jaw. When his lips found the sensitive hollow beneath her ear, Maggie arched into him with a soft cry.

Something inside her exploded. Scott slid one large hand along her rib cage. He caressed her fevered skin with the callused tips of his fingers. His hand brushed the sensitive underside of her breast, and caressed her through the lace of her bra. Unleashed, free, Maggie flexed her fingers against the smooth skin of his chest, then nipped at his lower lip.

Scott let her plunder the recesses of his mouth. He drank in the feel of her hot tongue as it tripped along the edge of his teeth. When the pain in his lungs reminded him to breathe, he reluctantly lifted his head to meet her gaze. "Wow."

She flushed, slowly withdrawing her hands from his shirt. "Wow back."

Scott brushed one thumb over the full curve of her lower lip, while his other hand flexed against her

breast. "You taste good, Maggie. Really, really good."
Maggie moved away from him. Reluctantly, he let his
hand fall away. He allowed the small separation, but
reached for her hand. He wasn't about to let her re-
treat to the opposite end of the sofa. Her lips were
still swollen and moist from his kiss. He just barely
resisted the urge to push her back into the couch and
pick up where they'd stopped.

Maggie's fingers trembled in his hand. She tucked
a strand of hair behind her ear. "Scott, I—I hope you
don't think I—" She broke off the sentence, visibly
flustered.

Scott leveled his gaze at her. "It's been a long time
for me, too."

"What I mean is, I hope you don't think I'm always
so, so, forward. I've never actually asked a man to
kiss me before."

"I've never been asked. Unless of course you count
Mary Jean Monroe in the fourth grade, and I'd kind
of like to forget that. I don't remember it as being a
very pleasurable experience. I think you're the first."

She groaned. "Oh God."

Scott laughed and pulled her back into his arms.
"Maggie, relax. I don't think you're some kind of
loose woman just because of a kiss."

"It's just been so long since . . . since I touched anyone like that. So long since I've been held. Ever since
the other night, I couldn't stop thinking about it. I just
didn't think it would get so out of control."

He gave her a quick squeeze. "It did, didn't it?" He
felt absurdly pleased. "It wasn't any less powerful for
me, if it makes you feel better. I'm not exactly in the
habit of kissing women I've just met."

"I'm glad." Her voice was quiet, hesitant.

Scott tipped his head and studied the look in her eyes. "I'm glad, too. I don't want you to think this is a habit for me."

"I don't."

He arched his neck so he could rub his lips over the curve of her eyebrow. "However, it could become a habit." He kissed her again. "Easily."

Maggie smiled against his mouth, evidently reassured. She pressed her lips closer to his. It took seconds for the kiss to flare hot and urgent once more. Maggie sucked at his tongue and he thought that maybe, just maybe, he went a little bit insane.

He was almost sure of it when he heard the unmistakable first notes of "Rockin' Robin."

"Mark!" Annie shot Mark a censorious look as Bobby Day's bird noises filled Ryan's bedroom. "You're going to get Ryan in trouble."

Mark grinned at Ryan. "He's not in trouble. Turn it up, son."

Ryan laughed and reached for the volume knob on his portable stereo. "Let's dance, Dad. Let's dance." Ryan bounded out of bed to stand next to his father. He flipped up the collar of his shirt.

Annie shook her head. "He's supposed to be taking a nap."

"I'm not tired. I'm not. Come on, Dad."

Mark paused only briefly before he reached for a toy microphone on Ryan's dresser. He flipped it from hand to hand before joining Bobby Day's voice on the chorus. Ryan laughed in delight, playing his imaginary guitar with a finesse that Annie secretly thought even Axl Rose would envy. At the beginning of the second verse, Mark and Ryan started to dance.

In spite of herself, Annie couldn't help but laugh at the rhythmic gyrations that were part Elvis Presley, part John Travolta and part Fred Astaire.

The song ended, and Ryan was still laughing hysterically when the first strains of "The Great Pretender" filled the room.

"Ryan!" Maggie's voice came from downstairs. It held a note of warning.

Maggie stared at the ceiling as she waited for a response. Scott was nuzzling her neck. She felt her pulse flutter beneath the warm pressure of his lips on the base of her throat. She gasped. "The Great Pretender" faded, and Ryan yelled, "Yeah, Mom?"

"You're supposed to be sleeping," she said. Scott nipped her earlobe.

"I am sleeping," he yelled back. Scott lifted his head and smiled at Maggie.

Maggie rolled her eyes. "Why is the music on?"

Scott chuckled. "Maybe he knows I'm down here necking with his mom."

"Be quiet." Maggie thumped the back of his head with her finger. "Ryan?" she called again.

"Dad wanted to hear 'Rockin' Robin.'"

Maggie groaned. "Well, tell Dad he can listen to it another time. Shut off the stereo."

The music stopped, and there was a brief shuffling before the house grew quiet again. Maggie shifted away from Scott with an apologetic smile. "I'm sorry. I guess the holidays have been harder on him than I thought they'd be."

Scott ran his thumb over the curve of her cheek. Then he reached for his drafts of the Cape Hope project. He began rolling them into a tube. "Don't apologize, Maggie. I know when a mood's been broken. It's OK."

She held the plastic container while he slid the plans into it. "I'm sorry about that thing with Annie, too. I told him before you got here the other night about your wife. I thought it would help him understand. I had no idea he'd imagine her like he imagines Mark."

"Maggie." Scott put the tube down on the coffee table. He turned to study her. "Stop apologizing to me. Ryan's a kid. He's having a tough time. I understand that."

"I should have prepared him better. There was no excuse for—"

"Stop. When did you get it into your head that Ryan's imagination makes you a bad mother."

"It's been so hard, Scott. His teachers, his coach, even people at the church keep telling me how he thinks Mark is real."

"What do you think?"

"I think Ryan knows Mark is dead. He seems very aware of that. He just—likes to talk to him."

"Didn't you have an imaginary friend when you were a kid?"

"Yes, but it was someone really imaginary. I made her up. She didn't exist and then die."

Scott shrugged. "So. I don't think there's a manual or something on which imaginary friends are OK and which ones aren't."

Maggie managed a slight smile. "Still, I'm worried."

"You're a mother. You're supposed to be worried. That's what mothers do." He squeezed her knee. "Just trust your instincts, Maggie. He's a great kid."

She nodded. "He is. He really is."

Scott kissed her lightly on the cheek before he stood up. "I think I'd better get going." He shot a quick glance out the window. "This snow is getting pretty bad. Do me a favor and tell Ryan we'll build the snowman next time?"

Maggie suppressed a sigh of regret. Things were moving very quickly with Scott, and despite her urge to ask him to stay a while longer, she thought better of it. She needed time to think things through. She stood up and handed him the plastic tube. "No problem," she said.

"There will be a next time?"

"Of course," she said, without hesitation. "I'm really glad you came today."

He smiled at her. "I am, too."

"Will I see you again before you go back to Dallas?" She could have kicked herself. She felt like she was whining.

He walked with her to the front door. "No. I'm taking an early flight out of Logan tomorrow." He waited until Maggie retrieved his coat from the hall closet. "But I'll be back on Tuesday."

She held out his coat. After he shrugged into it, Maggie settled the collar into place. "Well," she said, biting back a sigh of disappointment, "I hope you have a safe trip."

Scott pulled her into his arms with a slight laugh. "Ah, Maggie, you're so delightfully transparent."

She fixed her gaze on the gold-crested button of his overcoat. "What's that supposed to mean?"

Scott tipped her chin up with his finger. "It means I'm tickled to death that you're disappointed I'll be gone, and of course I'll call you on Tuesday—probably before."

She ignored the embarrassed blush she felt rising on her face. "I've got a meeting Tuesday morning, but I'll be here all afternoon."

He gave her a leisurely kiss. "I'll see you around two?" he asked, lifting his head.

"Perfect."

Maggie spent the rest of the afternoon cleaning the kitchen, and thinking about Scott Bishop. Ryan had finally fallen asleep. The house had grown quiet as the afternoon shadows lengthened, the stillness punctuated only by the whisper of snow against the windows.

As she stacked dishes in the dishwasher, a clear image of laughter in Scott's hazel eyes demanded her attention. It had been a long time since she'd enjoyed laughter, the real from-the-inside kind. It felt good. It felt very, very good. Her gaze strayed to the picture of Mark and Ryan she kept on the windowsill. She could no longer deny the pangs of guilt, the eerie feeling that somehow, Mark knew she'd met this man. That she was attracted to him. And that he didn't like it.

Maggie stared at the picture. "Oh, Mark, what am I supposed to do?"

Mark smacked his fist down on the kitchen table in frustration. "Damn it, Maggie, how the hell should I know?"

Six

*S*cott *rubbed his eyes with his thumb and forefinger.*
He glanced at the small alarm clock in his hotel room.
It was already after eleven o'clock. If he hoped to
catch his 6:00 A.M. flight the next morning, he'd better
call it a night. He stretched his arms, working the
kinks out of his back. He dropped his pencil on the
desk.

When he'd returned from Maggie's that afternoon,
he'd spent most of the evening redrafting part of his
proposal. He'd seen something in her interior designs
that had intrigued him, and he was delighted to find
it fit perfectly in his new vision for the bedrooms of
the Cape Hope project.

Half a dozen times he'd tried to convince himself
that he was having trouble concentrating because he
didn't have proper drafting tools. But it hadn't
worked. He'd known from the minute he stepped into
the snowy afternoon outside Maggie's house that he
was sinking. Fast.

Scott leaned back in his chair. He stared out the
window at the lights of Cape Hope. And thought of
Maggie. Since Annie's death, really since her illness

the year before, he had managed to find solace in his work. During the long, anxious months leading up to Annie's passing, he had relied on the simplicity of his drawings to maintain his sanity. The result had been a blissful numbing effect that had dulled the edges of his grief, and kept the haunting memories at bay. Until now.

Maggie Connell with her chocolate brown eyes, and bewitching smile, had touched some part of him he'd tried desperately to ignore. When he was with her, he felt almost complete again, like she restored his missing piece. It didn't help matters any that he got aroused just looking at her. He felt a stirring in his lower body and shifted in his chair with a low groan. Evidently, he didn't need to look. Just thinking about her was enough. It was starting to scare the hell out of him.

He reached for his briefcase. Inside, he found the picture of Annie he'd taken on their last vacation together. She was smiling at him. She had always smiled at him. Annie had made him feel ten feet tall. Maggie touched some new part of him, something he wasn't sure he liked. Annie made him feel like a giant. Maggie made him feel like a man. Scott put the picture down and stared at it. "I feel like I'm losing you, Annie."

Annie wiped away a frozen tear. She sat on the bed cross-legged and watched him, just as she had all evening. "You'll never lose me, Scott. You just need to let go."

He slipped the picture back in his briefcase before he stood. He loosened the knot on his robe. He brushed his teeth, checked the setting on the alarm clock, switched the lights out, then climbed into the king-size bed. Still uneasy. Still unsettled. He stared at the ceiling for several long minutes before he switched the light back on. He reached for the phone.

"Hello." Maggie sounded sleepy.

He felt guilty for calling her so late. "Maggie? Were you asleep?"

He heard her yawn. "Scott?"

"Yeah. I'm sorry if I woke you." He leaned back against the pillows.

"You didn't. I was lying in bed reading."

He waited several seconds. Now that he had her on the phone he felt like a fool. What had he been thinking calling her in the middle of the night?

"Scott?" she prompted.

"Yeah?"

"Did you want something?"

He closed his eyes. He wanted something all right. Something he didn't have any damned business wanting, and something he sure as hell wasn't going to tell her about. "I just wanted to talk to you. I couldn't sleep."

He heard her shift in the bed. "I couldn't either," she admitted.

"I've never felt like this, Maggie. It's like I'm breaking up inside."

"I know."

He threaded his fingers into his hair. "You feel the same way, don't you?"

"Yes."

He paused. The clock on his bedside table clicked when another minute rolled by. "What do you think we ought to do about it?"

"I don't think there's anything we can do. I haven't, I can't—" She stopped.

Scott waited several seconds. "What were you going to say?"

"It's not important. What time did you say your flight was in the morning?"

He ignored her change in subject. "Please, Maggie." He heard her move the phone to her other ear. There was something incredibly erotic about talking to Maggie and lying in bed, knowing she was lying in bed, too. "Talk to me," he prompted.

"It's just that I . . . I haven't been with a man since Mark. It feels strange. Good strange, but strange."

"Yeah. I know."

"Do you remember this morning, when you told me you'd had such a strong sense of Annie's presence the past few days?"

"Yes."

"It's been the same for me. It's almost like I think Mark is watching. I'm not sure yet what he thinks."

"Does it matter what he thinks?" Scott asked, surprised at the question.

"I don't know," she said frankly. "I'm not sure."

"Maggie, I really want to see you when I get back from Dallas."

"I want to see you, too."

"Things are moving very fast."

"I know."

He bent one knee so he could rest his foot flat on the bed. "Do you mind?"

"I'm not sure. Can't we just make it up as we go along?"

Scott felt a wave of relief pour through him. "I'd like that. I don't want to scare you away, but I'm not sure I can control what's going on here."

"Me either."

He released the breath he hadn't known he was holding. "I'm sorry I called so late. I just wanted to talk to you before I went to sleep."

"I'm glad you did."

He waited, not ready to end the connection. "Maggie?"

"Um-hmm?"

"Would you be offended if I asked you what you sleep in?"

There was a slight pause. "Do you want to know?"

"Just in case I dream about you. I want to make sure I get it right."

"I sleep in a Bruins jersey. Number twenty-seven."

The picture flashed in his mind and he instantly regretted asking. The image of Maggie covered only by a thigh-length black-and-gold hockey jersey was far more devastating than any combination of silk or lace or satin or lack thereof he could have possibly concocted on his own. He'd have been better off not knowing.

"Scott?"

"Yeah?"

"Is something wrong?"

It occurred to him that the curve of her buttocks would be visible beneath the hem of the jersey. It made him hard. "No, why?" He wondered if his voice sounded hoarse to her.

"You groaned."

"I did?"

"Yes. Are you sorry you asked what I sleep in?"

"Yes and no," he said, forcibly pushing the thought from his head.

"What did you think I slept in?"

"Maggie, are you trying to give me erotic dreams?"

She gasped. "Can I?"

His laugh was short, humorless. "Would it surprise you to know that I can almost guarantee it?"

She laughed, and by contrast to his, it had a warm, smoky ring to it. "This feels, well, naughty. Like the time I was thirteen and I sneaked the phone in my room to call David Wanger in the middle of the night."

"Did he ask you what you slept in?"

"No. I think he asked if he could copy my homework."

Scott felt some of the tension drain out of his body. "I'm going to miss you, Maggie."

"I'm going to miss you, too. This is good-bye, I guess."

He paused, searching for words. "If it's all right with you, can we just say good night? Annie never liked to say good-bye. She said it was too final. I don't think I realized until right now that she sort of got me into the habit."

"All right, but don't I get to know what you sleep in?"

"No. We're not going to talk about beds or bedrooms or bedclothes or sheets or blankets or pillows or anything else related to this subject ever again."

"That's awfully limiting."

"I don't think I can take it otherwise. Next time I call you in the middle of the night, I'm asking for your math homework."

Maggie laughed. "All right. I guess I'll just have to use my imagination."

"Maggie," he warned.

She didn't give him a chance to chastise her further. "Good night, Scott."

He smiled. "Good night, Maggie."

*   *   *

"Hi, Mom!" On Tuesday afternoon, Ryan crashed through the door, dumped his book bag down on the sofa, and grinned at Maggie. "Guess what?"

She looked up from her desk. "What?"

He crossed the room to stand next to her. "Billy Cooper got in this huge fight at school today."

Maggie set down her pencil. She ruffled his hair with her fingers. "What got Billy Cooper so riled up?"

Ryan started to giggle when she tickled him under the chin. He squirmed away. "Franklin said we're going to beat Billy's team at the game tonight."

"Oh. It was a hockey brawl."

"Yeah. Isn't it cool?"

Maggie nodded obediently. In Ryan's world, "cool" was the penultimate experience. "Uh-huh. Cool." She rubbed her thumb over his eye where the dark bruise still showed from his encounter with Tommy Willis's hockey stick the week before. "Do you have any homework to do before the game tonight?"

He nodded. "Yeah. I have to find a picture of the president in the newspaper or a magazine, and cut it out, and write what he's doing."

"We have to leave for the rink in about two hours. If you do that right now, we'll have time to eat first."

"OK, Mom." Ryan bounded for the stairs, and Maggie watched him with a slight shake of her head. Since Thanksgiving, Ryan had not even mentioned Mark or Annie. He had helped Maggie shovel snow that Friday morning and spent most of Saturday playing with Edith Sophy's grandchildren. Maggie had been relieved.

She closed her design book. She slipped it into her desk drawer, pleased with the progress she'd made on her work. The final designs were due to the developers' office by Friday, and she was almost finished doing her color palettes, one of the last steps before she completed the project.

With a will of its own, her gaze slid to the calendar on her desk. Today was the first of December. Tuesday. Scott.

Maggie frowned at the date. Scott had not called her since he'd left Cape Hope and returned to Dallas. By Sunday afternoon, she'd begun to suspect that he was having second thoughts. Given time and distance, he'd decided their relationship was moving too quickly. She should be relieved. She'd decided the same thing.

Why, then, was her stomach tied in knots and her nerves frayed at the thought that he was supposed to have arrived back in town that afternoon at two o'clock? It was 3:12, and there was no sign of him. Maggie slammed the calendar shut, then stalked into the kitchen. She barely knew the man, and he had her running around in circles already. A dozen times she'd considered the fact that she knew only the barest of information about him. They had not been together much, and almost never alone, yet something about Scott's warm personality and open vulnerability drew her like a fly to honey.

A vision of hazel eyes and attractively rumpled sand blond hair popped into her head. She reached for a mug, filled it with milk, then popped it into the microwave. "Ryan?" she called.

"What?"

"Do you want some cocoa?"

"Yeah."

Maggie rolled her eyes. Manners were a new concept to him. "Yes, what?"

"Uh, please," he yelled back.

She had already filled his mug. She slid it into the microwave with her own and waited for them to heat. Scott's face still lingered in her memory. She used the time to reflect on it. She liked the way he smiled at her. She liked the way his eyes crinkled at the corners when he laughed. She liked the way his lips had felt when . . . The microwave buzzed, and Maggie nearly jumped through the ceiling. "It's ready," she called.

Maggie carried both mugs to the table. She sat in a wedge of sunlight from the kitchen window, where she could stare out at the snow while she stirred chocolate syrup into Ryan's mug. He came barreling through the kitchen door clutching a magazine.

He thrust the magazine in front of her. "Is this him?"

Maggie looked at the picture of the president. "That's he," she said. "Get the scissors out of the drawer."

He retrieved them. He climbed into his chair, then went to work on the magazine. Maggie cradled her mug in both hands and watched him. "What else happened at school today?"

He glanced up. "Nothing. Just the fight."

"Did you learn anything?"

He shook his head. "No."

Maggie studied him in speculation. Ryan was hiding something. He generally talked her ear off when he got home from school. He liked school, usually, and Maggie had long since discerned that he had a crush of sorts on his teacher. "Ryan?"

He put down the scissors and studied the picture. "It's nothing, Mom."

"Did something happen?"

He started to squirm. "Some of the kids were teasing me because I was talking to Dad in the bathroom, and they heard me."

"Oh, Ryan."

"He was there, Mom. He was."

Maggie set down her mug and reached for his hand. "Ryan, your father is dead. He's not here."

"Not here here," he said. "Here."

"Do you think maybe we should make another appointment and go see Dr. Jericho at the church?"

"I don't want to."

"Maybe it would help if you—"

Ryan's face puckered into an anguished mask. "No. I don't want to talk to Dr. Jericho. I won't talk about it anymore. I won't. I promise."

Maggie slid her chair back. She motioned for him to come sit on her lap. He hesitated only briefly before he slipped out of his chair and crossed to her. Maggie hugged him close. "I don't want you to stop talking about it, Ryan. It's not bad that you talk to Daddy. I know you miss him."

Ryan laid his cheek against her chest and she felt him sob. "Do you miss him?"

"Yes."

"Do you ever talk to him?"

Maggie nodded. "Sometimes."

Ryan raised his tear-streaked face and looked at her in surprise. "Really?"

She nodded again. "Really. I can't see him like you can, though." She brushed a lock of hair off his heated face. She remembered how strongly she'd felt Mark's presence in the days before Thanksgiving. "Maybe I just don't know how to look for him," she said.

Ryan was quiet for a long while. "Mom?"

"Hmmm?"

"Are we gonna have Christmas this year?"

She felt a twinge of guilt. "What do you mean?"

"I mean, are we gonna have a tree and stuff?"

This was the conversation she'd been dreading. Before Mark had left, she'd promised him she'd hold Christmas until he returned. She and Ryan had planned to wait until Mark got back before they opened their presents. Maggie had even refused to light the Christmas tree, assuring Ryan that they'd do it as soon as Mark walked in the door.

Of all the things she'd had to deal with since Mark's death, this was the one she knew she couldn't handle. She'd bought Ryan Christmas presents, of course, but she knew she'd never get through decorating the house. She especially knew she couldn't handle a tree. "We're going to give gifts," she hedged, in answer to his question.

"I want a tree like always."

"Honey"—she shifted him on her lap—"I think maybe we should wait until next year to get a tree."

"Why?"

"Because it's a new house, and everything is all packed away. It would be hard to find all the ornaments." She felt rotten for not telling him the truth, but she was too close to tears.

"We could make ornaments. We don't need a lot."

"Ryan, I just don't think we need to have a tree this year."

"Dad wants a tree," he said quietly.

She hugged him, feeling selfish. She thought back

to Thanksgiving, to how sure she'd been that Mark's presence was in the house. Why hadn't it occurred to her that Ryan would feel it just as intensely? What if he'd pictured Mark in his mind's eye in order to explain the odd sensation of his presence in the house. "What's he wearing when you talk to him?"

Ryan wiped one eye with his fist. "Jeans and a sweatshirt."

Maggie smiled. It had been Mark's uniform of choice when he was around the house. It seemed normal for Ryan to picture him that way. "The blue sweatshirt with the Marine Corps emblem on the front?"

Ryan nodded. "Yeah."

"You know what, Ryan?"

"What?"

"I wish I could see him sometimes. I'd like to know how he's doing."

Ryan laid his cheek back against her shoulder. A shudder wracked his small body. "Mom?"

"Uh-huh?"

Ryan pointed to the corner of the kitchen. "He's over there."

She was saved a retort by the ringing of the doorbell.

Scott waited a few seconds, then rang the bell again when no one answered Maggie's door. The door was flung open. He stared into blank space for several moments before he thought to look down. Ryan was staring at him. "Hi, Ryan."

"Hi." Ryan craned his neck and tried to see behind Scott. "Did you bring Annie?"

Scott stepped into the foyer. "I don't know. Did I?"

Ryan was still looking at the porch. "Hi, Annie."

Scott started to unbutton his coat. Maggie walked into the foyer with a smile on her face that made his heart skip a beat. "Hi," she said, crossing to him. She placed her hands over his. "I was afraid you wouldn't make it."

He grinned at her. "You were afraid I wasn't coming."

Maggie blushed. "Maybe."

He shook his head, and continued unbuttoning his coat. "You're a rotten liar, Maggie. I had to change planes in DC, and my flight got delayed on the ground. I'm sorry I'm so late."

She looked at Ryan. "Honey, shut the door."

He stepped aside, probably, Scott thought, to let the imaginary Annie into the house, before closing the heavy wooden door. "You'd better go and finish your homework," Maggie told him. "We're going to have to eat early to make your game at six."

"OK, Mom." He ran out of the room to disappear into the kitchen. He left the door swinging behind him.

Scott thought about the propriety of the situation, seriously contemplated taking time to ask Maggie how she had been since he'd left, and then decided against it. He pulled her into his arms and kissed her instead. His skin and lips were cool from the weather. The feel of her warm, cocoa-flavored mouth moving under his intoxicated him. "Ah, Maggie," he said, before slanting his mouth over hers to deepen the kiss.

She threaded her fingers through the hair at his nape as she pressed against him. Scott nipped at her lower lip with his teeth, then reluctantly lifted his head. He reached up to brush the moisture off her mouth with his thumb. "Hi," he said, his smile lazy.

She smiled back. "Hi, yourself. I missed you."

"I missed you, too." He threw his head back for an instant. "You have no idea how I missed you. I was going to call you while I was in Dallas, but I was killing myself trying to get everything done and get back here. How have you been?"

Maggie stepped away from him. She helped him remove his coat. "All right. I've made a lot of progress on my designs. I feel really good about them."

He waited while she hung his coat in the closet. "Good. I have my final meeting with the developers on Thursday, and then I've got to get the drafts finalized by close of business Friday."

Maggie nodded. "Me too. In fact, I think that meeting Thursday is for all parties involved. I'm supposed to be there, too."

"Maybe we'll get a sneak preview of Jason Challow's latest variation on the soap theme."

Maggie laughed. "With any luck, you and Irene Fussman can talk about old times."

Scott let out a tortured groan, but not without acknowledging that it felt good, really good, to laugh with Maggie again. As good as he remembered. Maybe better. He brushed a hand over her shoulder. "Maggie," he said, lowering his head until his lips were just a fraction of an inch from hers.

"Hmmm?"

"Did I tell you I missed you?"

She nodded. "Once."

"Will it be all right if I tell you again?"

"I'd be disappointed if you didn't."

Scott kissed her again. He waited until some of the desperation he felt passed before he lifted his head.

"Sorry," he said with a rueful smile. "I didn't mean to be all over you as soon as I got here."

Maggie took a deep breath. She grabbed his hand. "Come on." She began leading him toward the kitchen. "I've got to get dinner started. You can sit in here and talk to me about it while I do."

He followed her through the swinging door. "I'll help you cook," he volunteered.

Ryan looked up from the table. "You can cook?" he asked, clearly skeptical.

Scott shrugged. "Sort of. I'm great with fish sticks. I do a mean chicken noodle soup, and I've even been known to successfully execute brownies. Although there was the time I forgot the eggs and they came out like chocolate glue."

"Ooooh!" Ryan made a face.

Maggie pushed Scott down in a chair. "You can peel vegetables. I'll handle the rest."

Scott shrugged and dropped down in the chair, deciding he liked the feel of Maggie's kitchen. He especially liked the feel of sitting in her house, talking to her, listening to her idle chatter with Ryan. It felt warm. It felt like a home. He accepted the bag of carrots and the carrot peeler she gave him. He pulled the trash can between his legs to catch the peels.

Ryan tossed a demolished magazine in the trash can. He picked up two pictures from the kitchen table. "I'm done, Mom."

She looked over her shoulder. "Did you find a good picture of the president?"

"Yeah. He's giving a speech to some guys." He held it up before showing her the other one. "This one is Carson Lipter."

"You didn't tell me you were supposed to find a picture of the Bruins center."

Ryan's grin was sheepish. "This one's for me."

"I wouldn't have guessed. All right. Go upstairs and glue that picture of the president on a piece of paper so you can write your sentence about it. Then you need to change and come on back downstairs. We'll eat in about twenty minutes."

He raced out of the room. Maggie set a bowl of salad down on the table in front of Scott. "You can slice those into here when you're done peeling them. How do you like your hamburgers?"

"Medium." He nodded his head in the direction of the swinging door. It was still creaking in Ryan's wake. "Does he ever walk anywhere?"

She shook her head. "Never. And you should see him on the ice—" she stopped. "I didn't think to tell you earlier. Ryan's got a hockey game tonight, so I won't be home until eight or so."

"Great. I'd love to see him play. What time's the game?"

Maggie frowned. "You want to go?"

Scott thought of the three hockey games he'd watched on television during the last week hoping to catch a glimpse of a Bruins jersey. "Sure. I'd love to go."

Maggie looked dubious. "But you must be exhausted."

"Don't worry about it. I want to go." She still looked skeptical, and in truth, a little panicky. "Really."

"You don't have to," Maggie hedged. She was starting to look really nervous.

"I know. I have a perfectly decent hotel room ten minutes across town."

Maggie studied him a few more seconds before heading for the refrigerator. "I'm sure this is not your idea of a great evening." She held up a bottle of salad dressing. "Is ranch OK?"

"It's fine."

"Here. Catch." She floated it to him.

He set it down on the table with a *plunk*. "Look, about this hockey game—" he said.

"I told you you didn't have to go."

"I want to go, Maggie. I just don't want to be in your way."

She placed four frozen hamburgers on a broiler pan and cast him a quick glance. "What's that supposed to mean?"

He plucked a carrot from the salad bowl, and popped it into his mouth. "How well do you know these people, and are they going to think it's weird that you're there with me?"

She nearly dropped the pan. "What?"

He could tell by the strangled sound in her voice that he'd hit the mark. "I thought so."

She slid the pan into the oven. She shut the door partway before turning around. "What are you talking about?"

Scott stood up and walked across the kitchen. He pinned her against the counter by placing his hands on either side of her hips. "Maggie, things are moving fast for me, too. Don't think they aren't."

"I don't."

"But these people are your friends. I'm sure you know most of the parents from Ryan's hockey team."

She nodded. "Most of them."

"If you're not comfortable answering questions about me, just say so. I'll understand."

Maggie stared at him for several seconds. Finally, she wrapped her arms around his waist and hugged. "I was beginning to think maybe you were having second thoughts," she said.

"When I didn't call you?" he guessed. She nodded. "Maybe I was," he confessed.

"Me too."

"It's been hard, Maggie. Missing Annie, wanting you, not knowing if I should want you, not knowing if you want me in return. What I'm feeling is very complicated, and I don't think I could do a very good job of telling you about it even if I tried."

She tipped her head back to look at him. "I feel the same way. I feel, well, guilty almost. Like maybe Mark wouldn't approve of this."

"You said that before, and I asked you if it mattered."

She nodded. "I know. It's just that he's so real to Ryan. It's like he's a ghost, and Ryan talks to him."

Scott pushed her hair off her face. "Ryan was talking to Annie when you came into the foyer earlier."

"Oh, Scott, I'm sorry."

He shook his head. "It doesn't bother me. Not really. Hell, I wish I could talk to her."

Maggie nodded. "I was just thinking that about Mark this afternoon. Ryan got teased at school today because some of his friends overheard him talking to Mark."

"Poor little guy."

"It's so real to him, almost as if he's conjured him up. I was thinking about how I felt last week. Remember I told you how much I'd sensed Mark's presence?"

Scott nodded. "I told you the same thing about Annie."

"That's right. Well, what if it's the same for Ryan, only his imagination conjures them up?"

Scott shrugged. "It's possible I guess."

Maggie laid her cheek against his shirt again. "Scott?"

"Yeah?"

"What if they're real?"

"Mark and Annie?"

"Yes."

Scott looked around the room. "Then I'd say we're in for a pretty rough ride," he said, running a soothing hand down her spine.

Annie shot Mark a sideways glance and frowned. "This isn't working."

Mark leaned back in his kitchen chair. He continued to watch Scott stroke Maggie's back. He snorted. "It looks like it's working to me."

"Stop being jealous."

Mark met her gaze. "Stop being jealous? How the hell am I supposed to stop being jealous when that guy has his hands all over my wife?"

"She's not your wife anymore, Mark. I think you're going to have to get over that, or this is going to be a disaster."

"Or a rough ride," he said, echoing Scott's comment.

"Come on. What have you got against Scott?"

"I don't like him touching Maggie."

"Besides that," Annie said, not bothering to add

that it wasn't easy for her to watch either.

Mark's expression stayed stubbornly disgruntled. "Nothing, I suppose."

Annie reached over and squeezed his hand. "Don't you want her to be happy?"

"Of course."

"Then why are you fighting this so hard?"

He looked back at Scott and Maggie. "Because it hurts," he said.

Annie felt tears scorch the backs of her eyes. "I know."

Mark didn't seem to hear her. "Do you know I take showers with her sometimes, just to pretend I can still touch her, that she's still mine?"

Annie nodded. "Yes."

"I sit by her bed and watch her sleep until it hurts so much I have to leave the room." Annie kept quiet and waited for him to continue. "Every time she cries I fall apart a little bit inside." He looked at Annie. "I hate this."

Annie studied him for several long seconds before she held up her hand. "Look. Look at my hand."

Mark frowned. "You're fading. So what?"

"So I wasn't fading in Dallas."

"What do you mean?"

"When we got back to Dallas, I wasn't fading. I was as solid as you are."

"What's that supposed to mean?"

"I think Scott needs Maggie to let go of me," Annie said.

"So?"

"So I think Maggie can't let of go of you until you let go, too."

Mark's frown deepened. "That doesn't make any sense."

Annie moved from her chair to stand in front of him so that she blocked his view of Maggie and Scott. "It makes a lot of sense, Mark. You can't keep holding on to Maggie. You're hurting her."

"How can I be hurting her when she can't see me? I'm not even real to her."

"You're real enough. Come on, Mark. Look me in the eye and tell me she didn't cry one single time while I was gone with Scott."

"Well, sure she did, but Maggie's just like that. She cries all the time."

Annie looked over her shoulder, then back at Mark. "I don't think so. I think Maggie's feeling a lot more fragile than usual right now, and that you're tearing her to pieces."

Seven

"I'm going to rip his head off." *Maggie jumped up and* started stalking toward the ice.

Scott grabbed her hand to pull her back into her seat. "Maggie, calm down."

"Calm down?" she said, outraged. "Did you see that? Did you see what that kid did to Ryan? He rode him right into the dasher boards." She pointed an angry finger in the direction of the ice. "And there was no call." She glared at the referee, and shouted, "Where's the call?"

"Take it easy, Maggie. Ryan's all right."

She glared at him. "Only because of all those pads." She returned her attention to the ice. She watched as Ryan collided with an opponent.

Her friend, Lily Webb, looked past Maggie's intense profile at Scott. "Don't even bother to try and calm her down," Lily said. "She's always been like that."

Scott laughed. "I'd just like to keep her from killing anyone."

Lily momentarily returned her attention to the ice. "Good shot, Franklin," she encouraged when her son's shot flew just shy of the goal.

Maggie watched Ryan take control of the puck. She felt her insides clench as he brought it out from behind the goal. "Come on, Ryan," she yelled. He executed the shot with near flawless precision, sneaking it right through the corner and into the net. The goal light flashed on. Maggie felt a surge of adrenaline. She grabbed Scott's arm and whooped. "Did you see that? Did you see that? That was great!"

Scott grinned at her. "Almost perfect."

"What the hell do you mean almost?" She felt an irrational surge of anger.

"He really should have centered it more."

"What?" She poked his chest. "Shows what you know, you big—" She stopped when Scott started to laugh.

"Maggie, I'm just yanking your chain. It was a great shot."

She relented a little, warmed by the teasing light in his eyes. "It was, wasn't it?" She barely noticed the buzzer sounding the end of the first period. She was distracted by Lily's tug on her arm.

The look Lily gave her was very insistent. "Come on, Maggie, it's the end of the period. Come to the rest room with me."

Maggie shook her head. "I don't need—"

"I want you to go with me," Lily said, her gaze flashing momentarily to Scott. "I need to talk to you."

Maggie gave in. Lily Webb had been one of the first friends she'd made in Cape Hope. Her vivacious personality and giving spirit had been a great comfort to Maggie in the months following Mark's death. She was short and slightly plump, and had the blackest hair Maggie had ever seen. Her husband adored her, as did everyone else who knew her, and it had taken

Maggie only a few minutes to fall completely under her spell. Despite the fact that she knew Lily's trip to the ladies' room would undoubtedly end in what amounted to a rehash of the Spanish Inquisition, Maggie couldn't deny her.

Lily wasted no time. She tugged Maggie through the rest-room door and impaled her with an eager look. "So?"

Maggie shrugged. She turned to inspect her reflection in the mirror. She brushed at a smudge on her cheek. "So what?"

Lily snorted. "Don't play smart with me, Ms. Connell. So where did you find Adonis, and what are you doing with him?"

Maggie laughed as she turned around to face Lily. "I'm not doing anything with him."

"Why the hell not?" Lily looked appalled.

"For heaven's sake, Lily, we're just friends."

"Whose fault is that?" Lily pursed her red lips into a knowing smirk.

"You're making a really big deal out of nothing."

Lily looked at herself in the mirror. She brushed a curl off her forehead. It immediately fell back. She ignored it, and pulled on another. "Honey, I'd know that look in a man's eyes anywhere, anytime. That man does *not* want to be your friend."

"We just met, Lily. It would be highly inappropriate for us to be more than friends." Maggie didn't think it would be wise to discuss the heated kisses, or rapidly escalating passion, between her and Scott. Lily would undoubtedly draw the wrong conclusion.

"What do you mean it would be inappropriate? What, have you got some kind of rule book or something?"

Maggie hedged. "Something like that."

Lily shot her a skeptical look. "You listen to me, Maggie-mine, that man's a prize. An A-1 prize. Don't you dare put him off because you're hung up about propriety." She paused, looking thoughtful. "Maybe Ryan should come home with us tonight. He and Franklin can have a slumber party."

"Get a grip, Lil."

She seemed not to hear. "If you're not attracted, that's one thing, but if you've got some cockamamy Southern idea about being genteel, forget it."

Maggie shook her head, laughing. "That's what I like about you, Lily. I can always count on your opinion."

The humor faded from Lily's eyes. "Maggie," she said, her voice softer, "I'm just worried about you. He seems really nice. Don't get scared on me and bail out. You need to take some control in your life."

Maggie nodded. "He is nice. He's very nice. He's almost too nice. I'm starting to think maybe he's a serial killer or something. You know how they always say on those cheesy TV shows how nice they are, how no one suspects they're keeping dead bodies in the cellar."

It was Lily's turn to laugh. She quickly glanced at her watch. "The second period starts in four minutes. Tell me everything."

By the time they returned to their seats, Maggie had filled Lily in on how she'd met Scott. She'd even gone so far as to tell her that there was definitely a certain passion between them. She was good and sorry for revealing it when they reached their seat to find Scott and Lily's husband Tom deep in conversation.

Lily flashed Scott a brilliant smile. "So, Scott, Maggie tells me you're an architect."

Scott waited for Maggie to sit down before he nodded at Lily. "That's right. I'm bidding on Cape Hope."

Lily took her seat between Maggie and Tom. She scooted so close to Maggie, she nearly forced her onto Scott's lap. Maggie shot her a quelling glance. Lily ignored it. "Well, isn't that a pleasant coincidence. I mean, you and Maggie working on the same project."

Maggie felt herself cringe at the telling glance she received from Scott. She pointed to the ice. "Look," she said, determined to change the subject. "The period's starting."

Scott's gaze lingered on her face a few more seconds before he turned to watch the game. By the middle of the third period, Maggie was so tense from Lily's constant prodding on one side, and Scott's intense gaze on the other, she nearly pulled her hair out in frustration. The game was tied. Maggie twisted her hands in her sweatshirt, and tried to ignore the knot in the pit of her stomach.

Ryan had the puck. "Come on, Ry," she shouted, watching him charge on goal. He passed to Franklin seconds before an opposing defenseman leveled him. Ryan sprawled on the ice, spinning twice before he bounced off the dasher boards.

It was Scott's turn to shout at the referee. "Hey! Hey, where's the call? He almost took his head off!"

Lily looked at Maggie and grinned, a smug, knowing smile that made Maggie squirm. She had the uncomfortable feeling that she was blushing.

The game finally ended in a tie. Maggie felt her breathing start to return to normal. Scott smiled at her, and it went erratic all over again. "That was great," he said. "You were right about those kids being little devils on the ice."

Maggie nodded. Lily leaned beyond Maggie. She stuck out her hand to Scott. "It was nice meeting you, Scott."

He took her hand. "It was nice meeting you." His gaze slid to Tom. "You too, Tom."

Tom nodded briefly, pausing to study Scott, his gaze wandering to where Scott's left hand rested casually on Maggie's shoulder. "I hope you have success with Cape Hope. Maybe we'll see you around."

"I hope so, too."

Lily studiously avoided Maggie's attempts to make eye contact. "If you're going to be in town for a while," she told Scott, "you and Maggie should come to dinner." She paused as she tapped her lower lip. "Ryan and Franklin are such good friends, I'm sure they'd enjoy the time together."

"We'll do that," Scott said.

Maggie exhaled a long breath. "Lily—"

Lily turned, her expression tabby-cat sly, and looked at Maggie. "Yeees?"

Maggie glared at her. "I'm not sure how long Scott will be in Cape Hope. He's on a business trip."

"Well, then," Lily said, "maybe Ryan should come home with us tonight. I'll be glad to get him off to school in the morning."

Maggie groaned. She buried her face in her hands. Scott laughed. "It's all right, Lily, I think we can handle Ryan. We will take you up on that dinner offer, though."

Lily beamed at him. "I'm looking forward to it."

She waved as Tom tugged on her hand, guiding her out of the bleacher seats.

Scott squeezed Maggie's shoulder. "What's wrong, Mag?"

She looked up. "Aren't you the least bit concerned that Lily just automatically assumed that we wanted to be alone tonight?"

A smile tugged at his lips. "Are you?"

"Well, of course I'm concerned. Lily is one of my best friends, but I don't necessarily want her to think I'd just fall into bed with you." She looked around to ensure no one was listening. "That is what she thought, you know?"

He looked appalled. "No!"

At his mock outrage, Maggie poked him in the ribs. "It's not funny."

"Come on, Maggie, loosen up. I'm sure she was just trying to help. Besides"—he lowered his lips to the curve of her ear—"I was half-tempted to let her have Ryan for the night."

Maggie felt a heated flush race up her skin and bury itself in the roots of her hair. She coughed. Should she tell him she had been more than half-tempted, or try to bluff her way through? When she met his intense gaze, her embarrassment fled. She was suddenly oblivious to the lingering crowd, the damp smell of the ice rink mingled with popcorn and beer. Instead, she noticed the spicy scent of his aftershave. She noticed the way his eyes gleamed and the shine in his hair under the glare of the fluorescent lights. She noticed the cleft in his chin, and the firm contours of his mouth. And she reached out to trace a finger over the full curve of his lower lip. "So was I," she said in a soft whisper. "I didn't want her to think it, but so was I."

Scott's gaze turned heated. He visibly swallowed, grabbing her hand in his to press a brief kiss into the palm. "Maggie, I—"

"Hey, Maggie!"

It took a minute to absorb the intrusion. The voice came from her left. Maggie blinked. She tore her gaze from Scott's.

"Maggie!"

She finally identified the voice. Chuck Bullard, Ryan's coach and the leading point scorer for the Boston Bruins, was signaling to her. She gave him a bright, welcoming smile, then waved him over. "Hi, Chuck."

He climbed over the side of the dasher boards. He started up the bleachers toward them. "Maggie, have you got a minute?"

She nodded. "We're waiting for Ry to change."

Chuck stopped in front of them and leaned over to kiss her cheek. "How have you been?"

"Good." She turned to Scott. "Chuck, this is Scott Bishop, a colleague of mine. Scott, this is Chuck Bullard from the Boston Bruins."

Chuck laughed, and stuck out his hand. "Not tonight, I'm not. Tonight I'm Coach Bullard. Nice to meet you."

Scott draped an arm over Maggie's shoulders before shaking Chuck's hand. "Nice to meet you, too," he drawled.

Maggie gave him a speculative look before turning back to Chuck. "What's the trouble, Chuck?"

He stuffed his hands in the pockets of his coaching jacket. "I'm worried about Ryan."

Scott studied Bullard through half-closed eyes. The man was handsome, he supposed, in a rugged sort of way. He had dark curling hair and a broad smile that Scott thought showed a remarkable number of teeth for a professional hockey player. He didn't like the way the man was looking at Maggie. And he sure as hell didn't like the way she'd introduced him to Chuck Bullard as her "colleague." What the hell kind of statement was that? And why was Maggie looking at Ryan's coach with that soft look in her eyes?

"What about Ryan?" Maggie asked.

Chuck's expression conveyed his concern. "Did he tell you about the father/son game next Saturday?"

"No," Maggie said, clearly surprised.

"I didn't think so."

"I didn't think to ask him because it's usually not until after the New Year—right?"

Chuck nodded. "We moved it up this year. It was becoming too difficult to cram into the training schedule."

Maggie looked at Scott. "Every year, Chuck organizes a father/son game for the team. He tries to get some of the Bruins to referee. A few even play."

"It's a charity thing," Chuck said. "The proceeds go to the Boston Literacy Council."

Maggie gave Chuck an adoring look that made Scott's toes curl. "This is so good of you, Chuck."

He shifted on his feet. "It's nothing, Maggie. Really."

"Don't be so modest," she said. She looked at Scott. "Chuck didn't learn to read until he was twenty-one. He's the Boston area spokesman for the Literacy Council."

"That's great," Scott said, admitting a reluctant admiration.

Chuck cleared his throat. "Anyway, I really want Ryan to play. I think he's hedging on me because of his dad."

"It's been worse lately," Maggie said.

"I know. I talked with him after practice Saturday. He said he forgot to ask you about the father/son game."

Scott could see the internal struggle on Maggie's face. "He's just feeling so awkward," she said. "It's hard for him."

Chuck put his foot on one of the bleacher seats, and leaned forward. "You know I've got extra guys from the Bruins who want to play, Maggie. I'm already lining up Bill Turson and Sergei Polokov with two of my kids. Not all the dads can skate, you know?"

"I know."

"I'll get Ryan a partner. Hell, I've been putting pressure on Lipter to play for three years now. I think this might be just what Carson needs to convince him."

Maggie smiled. "Carson Lipter. You really know where to hit a guy, don't you, Chuck?"

"I know Ryan really looks up to Carson. I don't want Ryan not to play just because his dad can't play with him."

"I'll talk to him. That's the best I can do."

"Do you think it would help if I talked to Carson?"

Maggie hesitated. "I don't know. I think Ryan would still feel—different. Like he had a substitute dad instead of the real thing."

Scott saw Ryan emerge from the locker room and

look around. He waved at him. "There he is," Scott said.

Ryan smiled, and bounded up the bleachers toward them. "Hi, Coach. Hi, Mom. Hi, Scott. Did you see me cream into the boards? Wasn't it awesome?"

Maggie groaned. Chuck ruffled Ryan's hair. "You're supposed to stay on your feet, Ry, not kiss the boards."

Ryan shrugged. "It was cool. It didn't hurt or nothing."

"Ryan," Maggie said, "Chuck and I were just discussing the father/son game. Why didn't you tell me about it?"

Ryan's face fell. "I forgot."

Maggie sat down so her face was at eye level with his. "Chuck said he'd get you a partner if you wanted to play. He thinks he can even get Carson Lipter."

"I don't want to," Ryan said, his eyes starting to cloud over.

Chuck put a hand on his shoulder. "You won't be the only one there with a Bruins partner, Ry. You know I'm assigning Polokov and Turson to Teddy and Buck."

"I know."

Maggie pushed a lock of hair off his small forehead. "But you still don't want to play?"

Ryan shook his head. "I don't want a partner. I want Dad."

Maggie turned anguished eyes to Chuck. Chuck looked uncomfortable. Scott straddled a bleacher and sat down in front of Ryan. "What if I play with you?"

Ryan tipped his head and studied him. "Why would you? You're not my dad."

Scott shook his head. "No, I'm not. But I'm your friend, right?"

Ryan looked unsure. "Yeah. I guess."

"So friends help each other out. You need a partner. I'm your friend. Seems pretty obvious to me."

"I don't know." Ryan shrugged.

Scott nudged his chin up. "Come on, Ryan. I want to. Honest."

"But you don't know how to play hockey."

"So you'll teach me." He stuck out his hand. "Do we have a deal?"

Ryan hesitated only briefly before he shook Scott's hand. "Deal."

Scott was vividly aware that Maggie was looking at him with that same soft look she'd given Chuck Bullard earlier. He felt it all the way to the roots of his hair. He smiled at Ryan. "Well, now that we have that settled, what do you say we go out for dessert?"

"Cool." Ryan looked at Maggie. He seemed to have recovered with childlike swiftness. "Can we go to Tom Foolery?"

Maggie nodded. "I think we can swing that." She looked at Chuck. "Thanks, Chuck. I really appreciate everything you're doing."

Chuck shrugged. "He's a great kid, Mag. I like working with him." He held up his hand and looked at Ryan. "High five, Bruiser?"

Ryan smacked his hand. "High five, Coach."

"I'll see you later, Maggie," Chuck said, before he looked at Scott. "I appreciate your willingness to do this." He paused and looked thoughtful. "You can skate, can't you?"

Scott nodded. "Of course," he said, and prayed to God he could learn before the game.

*   *   *

Mark frowned as he watched Scott and Maggie leave the ice rink with Ryan. "I'll bet he's never played hockey in his life."

Annie shook her head. "He hasn't."

"Then that was pretty damn dumb of him to volunteer to play. He's going to look like a fool."

Annie studied the back of Scott's head. "He did it for Ryan."

"He did not."

"Yes, he did," she argued. "He did it because he knew it was important to Ryan."

Mark snorted. "Shows what you know. He did it because he thinks Maggie is hot for Chuck Bullard."

Annie shot him a withering look. "You are the most unromantic man I have ever known."

"I'm practical. I saw the way Maggie was looking at Bullard. She thinks the guy walks on water. Scott felt jealous, so he volunteered to play. He's going to feel like a moron when he gets on the ice."

Annie glared at him. "Drop dead, Connell."

He grinned at her. "You're too late, Babe. I've already got it covered."

HALFWAY TO PARADISE   119

Eight

*S*cott's smile of greeting faded when he saw the harried look on Maggie's face the following afternoon. He'd agreed to meet her at her house for lunch, but one look at the worry lines around her eyes told him things were not going well.

"Hey there," he said.

Maggie managed a weak smile. "Hi. I almost forgot you were coming."

"Should I be insulted?"

She shook her head. "Come on in. I'm sorry I'm such a grouch."

He paused to brush the snow off his shoulders. "Anything I can help with?"

"No. I'm just really feeling pressured to get my sketches done by Thursday. I decided to make a few changes. It put me behind again."

"Look"—he shrugged out of his coat—"you've never done a bid like this before, have you?"

"No."

"You don't have to submit an exact product. Hell, half of it will change after a structural design is determined. They're just looking for style."

Maggie took his coat to hang it in the hall closet. "I don't have a style."

She sounded so miserable that Scott had to laugh. "Maggie, it can't be that bad."

"I'm just drowning in work, and I don't feel like I have enough time to finish it."

"OK, look. Why don't we just forget about lunch? I'll make us a couple of sandwiches, and you can work straight through."

She stared at him. "You'd do that?"

"Even I can handle peanut butter and jelly."

"No, no, I meant, you don't mind? What about your day?"

Scott studied her, thoughtful. She seemed genuinely amazed that he was willing to give up something as mundane as a lunch date. "What about it? I came to spend the day with you. That's what we're doing."

"But Ryan will be home around two-thirty. I'll have to help him do his homework."

"Geez, Maggie, I'm not a complete idiot. I think I can help a seven-year-old deal with his homework. Just go work. If we don't hear from you by dinner, we'll come check your pulse."

Maggie hesitated. "Are you sure?"

"Sure. Don't worry about it."

"But—"

Scott put his hands on her shoulders. He turned her toward the stairs and gave a gentle shove. "Go."

"All right, but—"

He leaned against the banister and smiled at her. "You know, it's no wonder you don't get anything done. You talk too much."

Maggie stared at him a moment longer, then pressed a quick kiss to his forehead before she ran up the stairs. Scott stood in the foyer for a long time, staring out the window, wondering. Maggie had seemed surprised, stunned even, by his offer to give her some much needed peace and quiet. It made him wonder how Maggie had ended up so unsure of herself—and it made him determined to do something about it.

Two and a half hours later he cocked the phone against his shoulder as he walked to the front door to answer the doorbell. "OK, Kristen," he told his secretary, "tell Bill I'll talk to him about it tomorrow." He swung the door open. Ryan stared at him. "OK," Scott said into the receiver, "you know where to find me." He placed the receiver back in the cradle, then smiled at Ryan. "Hiya, sport."

Ryan dropped his Batman backpack into a corner of the hallway. He gave Scott a curious look. "Hi. What are you doing here?"

Scott dangled the phone in his left hand. He took Ryan's coat with his right. "Your mom's upstairs working. I told her I'd wait for you."

"What's she doing?" Ryan stuffed his mittens into the sleeves of his coat.

"Drawings and stuff for the Cape Hope project. How was your day?"

Ryan shrugged. "It was OK." He leaned to the side to look beyond Scott into the living room.

Scott smiled at the small wave Ryan gave the couch. "You waving at Annie?"

The boy's look was wary. "Yeah."

"Tell her I said 'hi.' "

"Do you really believe I can see her?"

"I think you believe you can. That works for me."

Ryan studied him for a minute. "Are you really going to skate with me in the father/son game next week?''

It took Scott a few seconds to adjust to the lightning-fast change of subject. "I said I would, didn't I?"

"Do you know how to skate?"

"We have ice in Dallas."

"Dad's a great skater. He grew up in Michigan and used to play hockey like me."

"He must be pretty good then."

"Are you going to marry my mom?"

Scott coughed. "We haven't talked about it."

"I don't want you to."

Scott paused. "I'll tell you what. Why don't you and I go into the kitchen and talk it over? I'll see if I can find us something to eat."

"You're not going to make brownies, are you?"

Scott remembered telling the story about his eggless brownies and laughed. "No. I think I can probably find an apple or something."

"Mom peels the skin off for me."

"Then it's time you learned to eat apples like a man, kiddo. Come with me."

Ryan dashed ahead of Scott to crash through the swinging door. He climbed up on one of the stools, and told Scott where to find glasses and napkins. Scott handed him an unpeeled apple.

"I can't eat this," Ryan said.

"It's just a peel, Ryan. It's not bad for you. Just take a bite."

"I can't."

"Why not?"

Ryan gave him a disgusted look. He curled back

his lips and pointed to the space where his teeth had once been. "No teeth."

Scott laughed. "That does present a problem, doesn't it." He took the apple, sliced it into wedges, then set it down in front of Ryan. "How's that?"

He grinned at him. "OK. Do you like the peel?"

"Yeah. It tastes different than the apple."

Ryan shoved a wedge into his mouth. He chewed, his expression thoughtful. Scott watched him. "What do you think?" he asked.

Ryan nodded. "Good."

"OK. So you want to talk about your mom?"

Ryan wiped his mouth with the back of his sleeve. "Yeah. Are you going to marry her?"

"I don't know," Scott replied. "You said you didn't want me to."

"Dad wouldn't like it." Ryan shoved another wedge of apple in his mouth.

"Did you ask him?"

"No."

"Then how do you know?"

"He just wouldn't."

Scott looked around the kitchen. "Is he here now?"

Ryan shook his head. "He's in the den talking to Annie."

"I see." Scott paused. "What if I decided to marry your mom? How do you feel about it?"

"Dad wouldn't like it."

"But what about you?"

Ryan frowned. "I don't know. You're OK, I guess. You're not Dad."

"No. I'm not your dad."

Ryan spun an apple wedge on the counter, and stared at it. "Do you want to be?"

Scott took a deep breath. "Ryan, I'd never try and take the place of your father. I'd also never try to take your mom away from you. I might ask you to share her with me, but I wouldn't take her away."

Ryan raised stricken eyes to Scott's. "She cries a lot."

"I know."

"She never used to cry."

"It hurt your mom real bad when your dad died."

"Me too." His mouth started to tremble.

Scott walked around the counter to sit next to Ryan. "Do you want to tell me about it?"

Ryan shook his head. He was staring at his apple wedges. Scott ruffled his blond hair. "It's OK if you cry, Ryan. I cried when Annie died. I still do every now and then."

He raised tear-filled eyes to Scott. "I don't like to cry."

"Me either."

"Do you do it anyway?"

"Sometimes. Sometimes when I'm real sad."

"Like now?"

"Like now."

A tear slid down Ryan's face. "I don't think Dad ever cried."

Scott managed a slight smile. He picked Ryan up, and sat him on his lap. Ryan's slender arms wrapped around his neck. "I think he probably did, sport. I know he wouldn't mind if you did."

Ryan started to sob. Scott rocked him back and forth as he turned his gaze to the window. Snow-laden clouds had turned the sky a misty gray. Scott was starting to wonder if the sun ever shone in Cape Hope.

As Ryan's hot tears flooded the front of his shirt, Scott thought about Maggie, about the way she'd cried on the plane the day he'd met her. She was suffering so much, holding on to her memories of Mark so tightly, that Scott was beginning to wonder if there was any chance at all for them. He didn't know what he could do to ease her burden other than listen and wait. What he did know was that his heart was becoming increasingly linked to the happiness of this family. Their grief was his grief. Their pain, his pain. Their healing, his healing.

He hugged Ryan close to his chest, and waited.

Mark clenched his fingers into a fist and stormed into the living room.

"Mark?" Annie followed him. "Are you all right?"

The look he gave her tore her heart out. "I can't take this."

"Oh, Mark." She wrapped her arms around his waist. "I'm so sorry. I'm so sorry you had to hear that."

Mark wrapped his arms around Annie. "I feel rotten."

She gave him a tight squeeze. "We're doing the right thing. I know we are."

"I'm afraid I might break into pieces before this is over."

Annie met his gaze. She laid her hand on his cheek. "I'll hold you together if you'll do the same for me."

He hesitated. She thought he was going to refuse. Finally, he exhaled a long, tired breath. "Deal."

Fifteen minutes later, Ryan's tears were completely spent. Scott marveled at the resiliency of youth. The only traces of his outburst were the lingering redness around his eyes and the occasional catch in his voice.

When the worst of his tears had passed, he'd pulled away from Scott. He had been embarrassed, unsure.

Scott had poured him a glass of milk.

Ryan seemed to accept the gesture as an offer of masculine comfort. He wiped his nose on his sleeve before picking up the glass.

Scott took another bite of his apple. "So," he said, deciding to pursue a more neutral topic, "tell me about this father/son hockey game. What are the rules?"

Ryan plunked his glass down on the table. His serious expression was lightened by his milk mustache. "The dads' team only gets three players on the ice at a time. We get to play with six."

"Sounds fair," Scott said.

"You have to use short sticks, too. The rest is the same as a regular game. The dads fall a lot."

That, Scott thought, was a good thing. "How many of the Bruins play?"

"Last year, it was just Coach Bullard and Mr. Polokov. But this year, it's gonna be awesome 'cause Coach says he might get Carson Lipter to play."

"That's what I hear."

"Carson Lipter is the greatest hockey player in the world," Ryan assured him.

"So how come you turned down the chance to have Carson Lipter partner you, Ryan?"

He looked away. "I don't know."

"Come on, Ryan, we agreed to be friends, right?"

"I guess."

"So can't you tell me?"

Ryan met his gaze again. "I wanted Coach to do it."

Scott considered that for a minute. "Coach Bullard?"

"Yeah."

"Why?"

Ryan squirmed. "Mom likes him."

Revelation dawned. Scott smiled. "Ah."

"She likes you, too," Ryan said.

"I hope so."

Ryan toyed with a piece of his apple. "I think she likes you better."

"I guess I hope that's true as well."

Ryan seemed to hesitate. "Is that why you agreed to skate with me on Saturday?"

Scott shook his head. "No. I did that because I like you."

Ryan tipped his head to the side. His gaze was suspicious. "Do you really know how to skate?"

"I told you that we have ice in Dallas."

"Yeah, I guess. We have a frozen pond in the back. Did you know that?"

"No. I didn't."

"Maybe if Mom finishes working, we can go skating after dinner."

Scott swallowed. "Maybe we can." Dear Lord but he hoped Maggie would put a stop to that idea. He reassured himself with the knowledge that he didn't have skates.

Ryan shrugged. He seemed to be finished with the conversation. "I have to do my homework now. Can I do it in here?"

"Sure. Do you need help?"

"No."

"All right. How about if I go in the living room and work on some stuff? If you need me, I'll be in there."

"OK."

Scott threw away his apple core as he walked into the living room. He'd gotten himself into one hell of a mess with this hockey game. He'd never ice-skated before, and hadn't even roller-skated since he was a child. There was a very real possibility that he was going to make an utter fool of himself, but it had been the look on Ryan's face that had done him in. In many ways, the kid was having an even harder time than Maggie in adjusting to his father's death. Ryan's insistence that he could see Mark, talk to him, and worse yet, that Mark talked back, was evidence of that.

Scott dropped down on the couch and picked up the phone. No matter how much he wanted to believe he'd win the Cape Hope project, he couldn't simply ignore his existing clients in Texas.

An hour later, Scott hung up the phone. He rubbed his eyes with his thumb and forefinger. It had been an exhausting day. It didn't help matters any that his clients were frustrated by his long absences. A noise from the kitchen caught his attention, and Scott realized with a growing sense of dread that Ryan was still in there. Did it take second-graders an hour to do their homework?

He remembered the night he'd accompanied Ryan and Maggie to Ryan's hockey game. Hadn't his homework consisted of writing a sentence about a picture he'd found in the newspaper? Scott stared at the swinging door. This could be bad.

He walked across the room to nudge open the door. The sight that greeted him made him slide it shut and cast a quick, anxious glance at the stairs. There was no noise from Maggie's room, and with any luck, she was still immersed in her sketches. He cracked open the door again.

Ryan had dragged what appeared to be every mixing bowl in the house out of the cabinets. They were strewn across the counter. A few littered the floor. Broken eggshells and globs of yolk and egg white covered the kitchen table. A whirring sound drew Scott's attention to the mixer, where something that looked like paste, and probably tasted worse, was being flung against the walls. An overturned canister had left a white, sticky wave of sugar flowing onto the floor, and everywhere, *everywhere*, a cloud of white flour dust hung like fog in the room.

Scott had to scan the room twice before he located Ryan, standing on a barstool, the bag of flour clutched in his hands, aiming for a large mixing bowl. "This is bad," Scott mumbled. "This is really bad."

Ryan looked up. His face was covered with flour. He smiled at Scott. "Hi."

"Hi."

"I'm making cookies for Mom. I couldn't find chocolate chips, so I'm using Cocoa Puffs. You think it'll be OK?"

"This is really, really bad," Scott said.

Ryan's brow puckered. "What?"

Scott shook his head. "Nothing."

"You don't look so good."

Scott waved his hand in front of his face to clear a puff of flour dust. "Maybe it's the flour."

"I tried not to make a mess." He looked down at the bowl. "A lot of it spilled."

Scott took a deep breath. He looked back at the

kitchen door. He had visions of Maggie finding the kitchen in this condition and going ballistic. He wondered if she'd believe they'd been hit by a tornado while she was working. The evidence was certainly damning enough. "Maybe," he said, scanning the room, "maybe we should try to clean up a little bit and then finish the cookies."

"I want them to be done when Mom comes downstairs."

"Maybe we'll have time to do both. I don't think your mom would want to find the kitchen messy. How about you?"

Ryan thought it over. "I guess not."

"So what do you say you put down the flour and we try to get this place straightened up a little?"

Ryan plunked the flour bag down on the counter. Another white cloud billowed forth. "OK. What do you want me to do?"

Scott unbuttoned the cuffs of his shirt and started to roll his sleeves back. "Let's start with the flour."

Maggie put the finishing touches on a valance design and put her pencil down. She clasped her hands together above her head to stretch the cramped muscles in her shoulders and back. The clock on the bedside table said it was just after four-thirty. She squinted at the weak light through her window. She hadn't even realized she'd been working so long.

Ryan's giggle carried up the stairs. Maggie smiled as she stretched once more. Scott must still be with him. It felt good, and right, and comfortable to know that Scott was taking care of Ryan. It would be easy to get used to that.

Maggie's gaze moved to the picture of Mark on her

desk. She wondered if it was her imagination or if his smile wasn't quite as bright as she remembered.

Another giggle, followed by a deeper, masculine laugh caught her attention. Maggie put aside the troubling thoughts and concentrated on the pleasant aroma in the air. She identified it as the mingled scents of brewed coffee and baked cookies. The picture of Scott and Ryan alone in her kitchen was enough to lure her out of her reverie.

When she entered the kitchen, Scott's back was to her, and all she could see beyond his shoulder was Ryan's face, covered in white icing. She recognized his look of intense concentration by the sight of his pink tongue poked between his teeth. "Hi," Maggie said.

"Shh." Scott waved a hand behind his back. Ryan shot her a panicked look.

Maggie raised her eyebrows as she eased forward. "What are you working on?"

Scott didn't look around. "Al-most done." He drawled out each syllable with slow precision.

Maggie peered over his shoulder. Her eyes widened. Scott was placing an icing-coated rectangular sugar cookie on top of a structure that looked amazingly like a cross between the Leaning Tower of Pisa and the Empire State Building. Ryan grinned at her. "Isn't it cool, Mom?"

Scott set the final cookie in place, then leaned back from the tower with a look of boyish glee. "Done."

"Wow!" Ryan stared at the tower.

Maggie couldn't prevent her lips from twitching with an amused smile. "That's quite impressive," she told Scott.

He beamed at her. "The best I've ever done. I've

never been able to get one over four layers high before. Now I know I didn't take all those classes in
structural design for nothing."

"This is so cool." Ryan peered at Maggie through
the latticework of the cookie tower.

"When did you two decide to do this?" Maggie
asked.

Ryan looked at Scott. Maggie didn't miss the conspiratorial glance that passed between them. Scott met
her gaze. "We thought we'd give you a chance to get
some work done this afternoon. Right, Ry?"

Ryan nodded. "Right."

"So," Scott said, awkwardly changing the subject,
"did you?"

Maggie looked around the kitchen. Nothing appeared to be amiss. "Did I what?"

"Get some work done."

"Yes. I'm almost finished with my sketches." She
regarded Scott through narrowed eyes. "Is there anything I should know?"

From the corner of her eye, she saw the panicky
look on Ryan's face. Scott shook his head. "No, nothing. Oh wait," he said, clearing his throat, "Lily
called. She wanted to know if we'd like to have dinner
at her house tonight. I said it was OK as far as I knew,
but I'd have to check with you first."

Maggie hesitated. She wasn't really up to Lily's
questions. "I don't know."

"Come on, Maggie. It'll be fun."

Fun, she thought. Fun like hurricanes and earth-
quakes and tornadoes were fun. Scott was licking the
icing off his finger, looking at her expectantly. She
remembered that he'd given up his afternoon for her.
Guilt prompted her to shrug. "I guess it will be all

right. What time are we supposed to be there?"

"Seven."

Ryan jumped down from his seat. "I gotta go finish my homework."

"Hold it." Maggie caught him by the shoulder. "Wash that icing off your face first."

Ryan shuffled his feet. He looked anxiously at Scott. "I'll do it upstairs," he said.

"What's wrong with here?"

He took two steps toward the door. "Nothing. I just want to do it upstairs."

Maggie shook her head. "Here."

"Uh, Maggie," Scott said, his expression turning sheepish.

She looked from Scott to Ryan and back again. "What is going on?"

"It's about the sink," Scott said.

"The sink?"

"Yeah. I was going to fix it after we finished the tower."

"It's not his fault, Mom."

"What's not?"

Scott edged around Maggie and backed toward the sink. "Now before you look, I think you should know it's really not that bad."

Ryan tugged on Maggie's hand. "He didn't know we don't have a bis . . . a dis . . ."

"Disposal," Scott helpfully supplied.

"A disposal," Ryan echoed.

"You clogged the sink?"

"Sort of," Scott said.

Maggie raised her eyebrows. "So big deal. We'll just dump some Dranó in there."

"Uh . . ." Scott took another step backward. "I think

maybe you should help Ryan with his homework, and let me handle this."

"What is with you?" Maggie advanced toward the sink.

"Mom, don't. Don't look." Ryan pulled on her hand.

"It's just a clog," she said. "Good Lord, you'd think you two had burned the house down or something."

Scott winced. Maggie stared at him. "What's going on?"

Scott gave Ryan an apologetic look before he stepped away from the sink. Maggie hesitated, then stepped forward. Her eyes widened. The sink was half-full of a sticky white sludge. Eggshells floated among burnt shards of indistiguishable origin. She stuck a finger into the white goo. "What is this?"

"Sugar," Scott said.

"Flour," Ryan answered simultaneously.

"Sugar or flour?"

Scott looked over her shoulder at the mess in the sink. "Both."

"What are those burnt things?" She pointed to an indistinguishable charred lump.

Ryan slipped beneath her arm to peer into the sink. "Cocoa Puff cookies."

"Oh." Maggie pulled a film-coated glass out of the sink. "Did anything get broken."

"Uh," Scott said, trying to pry her away from the sink. "Nothing big."

"Nothing big?"

Ryan grinned at her. "Just the blue bowl. The one you said you don't like 'cause it's too heavy."

"Just the blue bowl?"

"Yeah," Ryan continued, "and we burned a hole in one of the cookie sheets."

Maggie had to swallow a giggle at Scott's stricken expression. "How did you manage that?"

"Oh, it was really cool," Ryan said. "Scott put the cookie sheet down on the burner and it melted all the way through. It got slimy and everything."

"I think," Maggie said, "that I will go upstairs and take a shower. If Lily is expecting us at seven, I'd better get dressed."

Ryan stared at her. "You aren't mad."

She shook her head. "No."

"Really?"

"Really."

Scott rolled his eyes in relief. "Thanks, Maggie."

"I have a feeling," she told him, "that I'm very glad I didn't come down here earlier."

Scott nodded. "Yeah. You are. If you go take that shower, Ryan and I can finish cleaning up. The sugar cookies should be out of the oven by the time you come back down."

"What?" she said. "We get to actually eat them? Aren't you planning another structural masterpiece?"

Scott grinned at her. "One a day's my limit. I don't like to overstretch my creative capacity."

Nine

Scott leaned back in his chair in Lily Webb's kitchen. Maggie had seemed relaxed enough that afternoon, had even pitched in to help finish cleaning the kitchen, but almost the instant they'd set foot in the Webbs' house, she'd been tense, anxious. He could see it in the tight lines of her face. Experimentally, he draped his arm across the back of her chair.

She jumped. Lily didn't seem to notice. "So tell me, Scott," she was saying, "how are the plans coming for the Cape Hope project?"

"Good," he said, pulling his gaze from Maggie. "I finalized them this morning. I've just got a few details to work out, and I'm ready to submit them. The way I understand it, Max Wedgins should make a preliminary decision in the next two weeks." He brushed his hand over Maggie's shoulder. She shifted away from him.

"What about you, Maggie?" Lily asked. "Do you feel like you have a real shot at this?"

"I hope so." She slid to the edge of her seat. "You know I need this project."

Lily nodded. Her husband, Tom, returned to the

table from the kitchen sink to finish clearing the
dishes. "Why don't we go into the living room?" he
suggested. "It would be a lot more comfortable."

Lily swatted his behind. "Are you trying to get out
of doing the rest of the dishes?"

Tom grinned at her. "You were always wise to me."

Lily looked at Scott and Maggie. "You just can't
find good help anymore. Why don't you two go on
into the living room? Tom and I will be there in a
minute."

"You just want to have your wicked way with me,"
Tom said.

"Can't blame a girl for trying," Lily shot back.

Scott laughed as he pushed his chair back. "Come
on, Maggie, I know how to take a hint."

Maggie gave Lily a panicked look. "I'll help you
with the dishes. You shouldn't have to do them by
yourself."

Lily raised her eyebrows. "Who said anything
about doing the dishes?"

Maggie blushed. Scott tugged on her hand. "I think
I saw a wad of mistletoe out here somewhere. Let's
see if we can find it."

Maggie's gaze flew to his. "Scott."

"Go on," Lily urged. She picked up a dish towel.
"We'll be right there."

Scott guided Maggie through the kitchen to the living room before she could protest. He slid the kitchen
door shut. "Why are you so tense?"

"I'm not tense." Maggie moved away from him.

"Maggie."

She walked to the piano, where she stopped to
study the array of pictures. "I'm not tense."

"You've been tight as a rubber band ever since we

walked in here. What's wrong with you?"

"Nothing."

"Come on, Maggie." Scott walked up behind her. He placed his hands on her waist. She started. "You don't normally tense up every time I touch you."

Maggie evaded his embrace. "I don't think it's appropriate in front of my friends. That's all."

"What's not appropriate?"

"This." She looked anxiously at the door. "You and me."

"Could you be a little more clear? I'm afraid you lost me."

Maggie frowned. "I don't think it's appropriate for you to have your hands all over me in front of my friends. Is that clear enough?"

Scott blinked. "My hands—for crying out loud, Maggie, I don't have my hands all over you."

"Oh, no? What was that bit at dinner with the rolls? You practically fed me one for God's sake."

"Geez, Maggie. I only wanted half the roll. I gave you the other half. It's no big deal."

"It was a big deal to me."

Scott took a deep breath. "What's really bothering you?"

She looked at the kitchen door. "It's Lily and Tom. They think . . . You made them think we're a couple."

"Aren't we?"

"Not like that."

"Then what kind of couple are we?"

"Just not that kind." She turned back to the piano. "I don't want to talk about it right now. Ryan's downstairs playing with Franklin, and I don't want him to hear us arguing."

"Maggie—"

"Not now."

Scott frowned at her for several seconds. She was one complicated woman. "I think I deserve an answer."

"I don't have an answer. Why am I supposed to have an answer?"

"Because, everything was fine this afternoon until we got over here. What is wrong with Lily and Tom seeing us together?"

Maggie shrugged. "It just bothers me."

"Why?"

She spun on her heel to stare at him. "It just does. Isn't that enough for you?"

He shook his head. "I don't think so."

"So what do you want?"

"I want to know why the thought that your friends might think you're attracted to me has you climbing through the roof."

"It isn't like that."

"Then what is it like?"

Maggie blew a lock of hair off her forehead with an angry puff of air. "I'm just not comfortable with this. What are they going to think if they know I'm involved with someone so soon after Mark's death?"

Scott stared at her. "It's been a year, Maggie. It's not like he died last week." He regretted the words the moment he'd said them.

Maggie looked stricken. "It feels like he did."

Scott reached for her. "Oh, Maggie." He pulled her into his arms. "I'm not trying to rush you into anything. You know that, don't you?"

"I'm just so confused. I . . ."

He rubbed his hand down her back. "What?"

"This afternoon. Why did you do that for me?"

"Do what?"

"You gave up your whole day for me. Why?"

So, Scott thought, *we're back to this.* "Why wouldn't I? You needed the time. I was in a position to help you." When Maggie didn't say anything, Scott gave her a tight squeeze. "Talk to me, Maggie."

She curled her fingers into his shirtfront. "Mark wouldn't have."

Scott felt his heartbeat accelerate. "Wouldn't have what?"

"He wouldn't have done that for me."

"Why not?"

Maggie shuddered. "I don't know."

"I think you do."

She tipped her head back to meet his gaze. Her eyes were sad, hurting. Scott's heart missed a beat. Maggie drew a deep breath. "I don't think he would have thought that what I was doing was important."

Scott framed her face with his hands. "But you know it's important."

"I . . ." she trailed off.

"Go ahead. It's all right."

A flash of guilt flared in her eyes. "I resented him for that. I still do."

Scott exhaled a long breath. "It's OK, Maggie."

"But he's dead."

"Honey, listen to me. I know you loved Mark very much. I know it was incredibly painful for you when he died. But nobody said it wasn't all right for you to be angry at him."

Maggie's lips trembled. "I didn't want to come here tonight. I was afraid to face Lily and Tom with you."

"Why?"

"Because I was afraid they might think I was being unfaithful to Mark's memory."

"Is that the truth? The honest-to-God truth?"

"What do you mean?"

"Are you sure it's not because it's easier for you to pretend what's happening between us isn't important if you can hide it? If no one knows, it doesn't make it real."

She started to shake her head, then looked away. "I'm sorry. I'm acting like a fool."

Scott tipped her chin up with his thumb. "You're hurting, Maggie. Nobody said you had to make every decision right the first time."

"I'm sorry," she mumbled again.

Scott decided he couldn't wait any longer to kiss her. It was meant to be a quiet kiss, the comforting type, but no sooner did his lips meet hers than he felt the familiar rush of blood in his head. His body tightened, his pulse accelerated, his toes curled inside his shoes. "Ah, Maggie," he whispered, and pulled her close against him, "I need you."

She leaned into his embrace. Scott didn't need any further encouragement. He rubbed his lips over hers in a slow, hungry caress. Maggie's arms stole around his neck to hold him close to her. A groan tore from his throat.

A cough sounded in the doorway. Scott reluctantly raised his head. "Uh"—Lily pointed to the stairwell—"the mistletoe's that way."

"I guess they made do without," Tom drawled.

Maggie blushed crimson. She buried her face against Scott's shirt. He laughed. "Guess we did," he said. "Are the dishes all done?"

Lily studied Maggie with a calculating look. "We

could always wash the silverware again if you, ah, wanted a few more minutes."

Maggie poked Scott in the chest. "We're done."

"Could have fooled me," Tom said.

Lily jabbed him in the ribs with her elbow. "Shut up, Tom."

"Yeah, Tom," Maggie said, stepping away from Scott. She ran her hand through her hair. "Quit while you're ahead."

Two days later, Maggie adjusted the hem of her skirt as she shifted in her chair in Pete Sherban's conference room. Pete was one of the top investors in the Cape Hope development project. He had called this Thursday meeting for all the bidders. Maggie stole a surreptitious glance at her watch while she idly listened to Pete explain the bid and selection process, and wondered why Scott was running late. She hadn't seen him since their dinner at Lily's. She was still uncomfortable, and unsure, at the way their relationship was proceeding.

She had been forced to admit the truth when he'd suggested that she didn't want people to know about their relationship. She *had* been trying to pretend it didn't matter. The last two days had taught her the folly in that line of reasoning. Everything about Scott Bishop mattered.

It mattered what he wore. It mattered where he was. It mattered what he said or didn't say to her. She had begun to think she was acting like a teenager again. It had taken every ounce of willpower she possessed not to call his hotel the previous night.

He'd told her when they'd left Lily's that he wouldn't see her again until this meeting. She knew, of course, that he had work to do, but still, it hadn't helped any that he hadn't called. She was beginning to feel like the universe had been permanently turned inside out.

As if she'd conjured him up with her concentration, the door to the conference room opened and Scott glided into the room with Irene Fussman. Maggie frowned. What was he doing with her? Scott met her gaze across the conference table as he slipped into his seat. There was nothing in the warm look he gave her to suggest that anything was amiss.

"Glad you could make it, Irene, Bishop," Pete said, pausing to let them get settled. "I was just finishing my summary on the selection process."

Scott nodded. "I'm sorry we interrupted you."

Maggie lifted an eyebrow. Scott's apology insinuated that he and Irene had arrived together, not as a matter of coincidence, but as a matter of choice. She felt like an idiot for jumping to conclusions, especially when Scott had told her how he felt about Irene. It was the other woman's cool sophistication that got to Maggie. Her elegant suit, her meticulously coifed hair, her impossibly perfect fingernails, made Maggie feel like a country cousin trying to make her way in the big city. Forcibly, she turned her attention back to Pete. But her thoughts kept straying across the table.

"And that does it," Pete was saying. "Does anyone have any questions?"

Irene shifted forward in her seat. Maggie watched as Scott's eyes rested briefly on the other woman's profile, then returned to Pete Sherban. "What about cost estimates?" Irene said. "I can't do an interior estimate until I know the complete scope of the project."

Pete nodded. "We know that, Irene. Maxwell

Wedgins is the developer for this project. He's got very specific ways of doing things. We're just trying to accommodate him."

A look of irritation flashed on Irene's flawless features. "This is highly unusual. How can I possibly do a comprehensive bid if I don't know what Wedgins wants?"

Pete looked uncomfortable. "I think that's the whole idea, Irene. Max wants you to be creative. He wants to know what you want. Not tell you what he wants."

"Well, we can't read his mind," Jason Challow said. "If this project weren't so big, I'd never have agreed to bid on it."

Carl Fortwell, Pete Sherban's partner, shot Jason a wry look. "No one's twisting your arm, Jason. I'm sure any of your competitors would be glad to see you pull your plans."

There was a general murmur from the small group in the conference room. Jason gave Carl a bitter look. Maggie lifted her pen to get Pete's attention. "I have a question, Pete."

"Shoot, Maggie."

"Is Wedgins looking for conceptual ideas only, or does he want something more concrete?"

Irene's lips turned down at the corner. "Your inexperience is showing, Maggie. I realize By Design has never handled a project this large, but you should know that preliminary bids are always limited to conceptuals. You can't possibly give the man room layouts and color charts if you don't know what the structural design is going to be."

Maggie just resisted the urge to squirm under Irene's barely veiled attack. Carl frowned. "Actually," he said, "that's an excellent question. I spoke with Max about the specific challenges of this project last night. I think he'd like to see as much as you feel you can give him, Maggie."

Pete Sherban pulled on the knot of his tie, as if suddenly finding it too confining. Irene slanted him a dark look. She leaned back in her chair, an unpleasant scowl on her red lips. Maggie just barely caught Carl Fortwell's sly smile. It made her feel better.

Pete cleared his throat. "Anyone else?" When no one moved, Pete nodded. "OK, then. That covers it. Make sure you pick the addendum to the bidding packet on the way out. We'll expect to see plans by close of business tomorrow. Max has agreed to review everything by the end of next week."

Maggie scooped up her briefcase and rose, intent on bolting for the door before Scott had a chance to intercept her. She simply wasn't ready to deal with him yet.

"Maggie."

She was relieved to hear Carl Fortwell call her name. She liked Carl enormously. Had, in fact, first met him because his grandson played on Ryan's hockey team. Carl was tall, very distinguished, in his late sixties, and scared the hell out of almost every one. Every one except Maggie. He had reminded her so much of her own father, she'd immediately seen beyond his austere bearing and poker-faced expressions to find a heart of gold. She smiled at him, making her way in his direction. "Hi, Carl."

He tipped his head in acknowledgment, his version of a smile. "I didn't have a chance to tell you before, but I'm really glad you're bidding on this project."

"I am, too. If nothing else, I could use the experience of a bid this size."

Carl frowned beyond her shoulder. Maggie knew he was looking at Irene. "Don't let anything that woman says get under your skin. She's a class-A bitch." He returned his gaze to Maggie. "And I didn't say I'm glad you're bidding because I think you need the experience. I meant I'm glad because I think Max is really going to like your style."

Maggie raised her eyebrows. "I didn't know you were familiar with my work, Carl."

"I do my homework. It's what makes me good at my job. Just go with your instincts and don't let anybody talk you out of it."

Maggie shifted her briefcase to her other hand. "Just how much do you know about Max Wedgins?"

Carl regarded her with a shrewd stare. "I know there are rumors about Max. He's an odd sort. No doubt about it. But you almost have to be odd to make the kind of money Max has just following his nose."

"Have you ever met him?"

Carl shook his head. "No. I've talked to him on the phone once or twice, but he deals mostly with Pete. He's a recluse, almost never seen in public. I've heard stories that range from wild expensive parties with lots of women, to reenactments of sea battles using minimodels and remote-controlled equipment on a private lake on his estate. Last time I heard, Max was having twenty-seven miles of railroad track laid inside his house. No one knows why."

"Aren't you a little worried about your investment?"

Carl made a small sound in the back of his throat.

"Maggie, the guy predicted the personal-computing boom and made a fortune off it, he was one of the first investors to turn an enormous profit off of real estate, and somehow, he avoided losing his shirt when the market went belly up in the late eighties. He owns a cruise line, a major-league sports franchise, a television network, a baseball diamond, a Broadway production company, a telecommunications conglomerate, one of the leading software producers in the world, a toy manufacturer, a gold mine, and, I hear, although this is the only thing that's not in his portfolio, that he's got an aviary filled with rare and exotic birds that would rival any sanctuary on the face of the planet."

Carl paused and straightened the knot of his tie. "If Max Wedgins says Cape Hope is worth three-point-four billion, it is. It's the closest guarantee you can get in this business."

A movement to her left caught Maggie's attention. She frowned when she saw Scott tip his head closer to Irene, as if to catch some soft-spoken comment. She forcibly pulled her conversation back to Carl. "Then what makes you think Wedgins will be interested in my work?"

"He's unorthodox."

"Weird," Maggie said.

Carl's frown didn't quite reach his eyes. "Different. If you submit something unusual, the kind of thing I know you can put together, I think Max will go for it. Especially if he's confronted with two or three more traditional scenarios."

Maggie felt better than she had all morning. "I appreciate the tip. I hope I'm not going to disappoint you."

He nodded briefly. "You won't. I've seen what you can do. I think you're going to blow Max Wedgins right through the roof of his seventeen-million-dollar house." Pete Sherban was signaling for his attention, and Carl said a quick good-bye before easing his way through the lingering crowd toward his partner. Maggie studied Carl's retreating form a few seconds before she turned to leave. And collided with Scott Bishop.

He flashed her a brilliant smile that made her teeth grind. "Hey there," he said. "Where are you going in such a hurry?"

"Out," she snapped.

His smile faded a bit. "I thought we were going to lunch."

"Why don't you take Irene to lunch?" Maggie said, brushing past him. She had time to register his befuddled expression before she marched toward the door. She heard the jealous note in her own voice and hated it. Between the scene she'd made at Lily's, and now this, she was turning into a lunatic.

"Maggie"—Scott's fingers closed on her elbow—"what the hell are you talking about?"

She walked through the reception area of Sherban Imports, and stopped at the elevator bank. "The two of you looked cozy enough this morning. Maybe you'd enjoy a little change of scenery. I'm sure Irene would enjoy the chance to pick your brain on the project a little."

Scott frowned at her. "Cozy"—his eyes widened—"Maggie, you don't think—"

"Think what?" she said, punching the elevator button a second time.

Scott grinned at her. "You do. You're jealous."

"I am not. Why on earth should I be jealous?"

"You tell me," he said. The elevator doors glided open and Scott stepped aside to let Maggie enter first.

"Oh, forget it," she said. She walked into the elevator. She opened her purse and started digging for her keys.

Scott followed her inside. He waited until the door shut before he wrapped a hand behind her head and gave her a hard, thorough kiss. "You're adorable, Ms. Connell," he said when he lifted his head.

She frowned at him. "What did you do that for?" Her hand was still buried inside her purse. She flexed her fingers, feeling her way along the bottom. "Where the hell are my keys?"

Scott's smile was lazy. "I did it because you looked all prickly and flustered, and it turned me on."

Maggie felt herself blush. "I am not flustered." She zipped the compartment of her purse shut with a muttered oath, then started searching in the other side.

"Oh no?" he said.

"No." She shoved her wallet to the side as she continued to scrounge through the contents.

He pointed to her briefcase, where her keys were linked to the handle. "Then how come you're having so much trouble finding those?"

Maggie glared at him as she grabbed the keys. "Oh, shut up."

Scott laughed. "Maggie, how could you possibly think I was interested in Irene Fussman?" He shivered. "Just the thought makes my skin crawl. The woman has as much warmth as a boa constrictor. I can just imagine her in bed with—"

"*Shut up*, Scott."

The elevator glided to a stop. Maggie stepped out, feeling foolish and embarrassed. "I haven't seen or heard from you for two days. Then the two of you arrived together, late," she said. She knew she sounded defensive, but didn't see any help for it. "What was I supposed to think?"

"How about that I got turned around on my way to the building. I got lost, got here late, and ran into Irene in the foyer?"

Maggie retrieved her coat from the coat check. She shrugged into it. She tucked her scarf around her neck, then waited while Scott pulled on his cashmere overcoat. "I'm sorry. I'm just tired. And stressed. And it bugged me."

Scott's gaze narrowed. "How late were you up last night working on your designs?"

She hedged. "I don't know. Late, I guess."

"How late?"

Maggie met his gaze. "Four-thirty."

Scott frowned. He grabbed her elbow, ushering her toward the door. "Geez, Maggie. You're going to drop dead if you keep that pace. They're just preliminaries."

"I know. It's just that I want them to be perfect."

He pushed open the door and let her precede him into the frigid afternoon air. "Jackrabbits it's cold." Scott flipped up the collar of his coat before linking his gloved fingers through hers. He set a brisk pace down the street.

"Where are you going?" she asked.

He gave her a hopeful look. "Downtown?"

Maggie shook her head. "This way." She pointed in the opposite direction.

With a shrug, Scott turned, then started toward the

downtown area. "You're really worried about this bid, aren't you?" he asked.

Maggie paused. "Yes. I suppose I am."

"Is it that important to your business?" He met her gaze while he waited for a crossing light to change. "I didn't know you were having that much trouble."

She shook her head. When the light changed, they stepped into the street. "It's not the money. Not really. I'm doing all right with the business just doing homes and offices and smaller things. It's the idea that I can do this."

Scott pushed open the door of a small restaurant, then hurried inside with her. "Of course you can do it." He looked at the hostess. "Two, please. Nonsmoking."

"There'll be a ten-minute wait," the young woman said.

Scott nodded. "Fine." He looked back at Maggie. "Now, what are you talking about?"

Maggie slowly unwrapped her scarf. "I've never done anything this big. Not on my own."

"Are you talking about the designs or the business?"

She rewarded his insight with a small smile while she stuffed her gloves into the pockets of her coat. "The business. I married Mark when I was twenty-one years old. I've never proven to myself that I can make it on my own. I really want this bid, Scott. I need it."

Scott opened his mouth to respond when a blast of cold air caught his attention. His gaze slid to the door. When Maggie saw his eyebrows lift in surprise, she slowly turned her head. Her eyes widened when she saw Pete Sherban enter the cozy interior of the restaurant with Irene Fussman hanging on his arm.

Annie's gaze narrowed on Irene. "I don't like this," she told Mark.

He frowned. "Me either. If Sherban's one of the key investors on this project, what's he doing cozied up with that bitch?"

"What do you think we should do?" Annie glanced at Maggie. She was frowning at Pete Sherban.

Mark didn't take his eyes off Pete and Irene. "I think we should stick real close to them."

Maggie studied Pete across the dim expanse of the restaurant foyer. "What's he doing?"

Scott's gaze narrowed on Pete and Irene. "I don't know."

"That's really odd for the two of them to be together. People could say it jeopardizes Pete's objectivity for the bidding process."

"People could," Scott agreed.

Maggie pressed her hand against her throat. "You don't think . . ."

"I don't know what I think."

"Bishop," Scott jumped when the restaurant hostess called his name, "party of two."

Maggie looked quickly at Pete Sherban. He appeared to be engrossed in his conversation with Irene, who was stroking his arm with long, red-tipped fingernails. It reminded Maggie of a cat preparing to scratch the stuffing out of a piece of furniture.

Neither of them seemed to have noticed her or Scott. Maggie followed Scott to a partially secluded table, breathing a sigh of relief when she realized they would be almost completely hidden from view.

She accepted a menu from the hostess as she slipped into the booth. She peeked over the top at Scott. "What do you think they're doing here?"

He glanced back toward the foyer. "Who knows? Maybe Irene's working on another project for him."

"But you don't think so?"

"I think it's damned convenient that she's bidding on a multimillion-dollar deal, and she's stuck to Pete Sherban like white on rice." He lowered his menu, his expression thoughtful. "How well do you know Pete Sherban?"

"Hardly at all," Maggie admitted. "I do know Carl Fortwell, though, and he hardly seems the type to be in business with a man who'd do something so shady."

"Maybe Carl doesn't know."

"He's pretty shrewd." Maggie leaned her chin on her hand. "In fact, I'd say he's very shrewd. Besides, do you think Irene and Pete would be here, in a place so public, if they were really conducting business under the table?"

Scott snorted. "Under the sheets is more like it."

"Scott!"

He frowned. "Sorry, Maggie. I shouldn't have said that."

She took a sip of water and slowly replaced her glass. "But really. Don't you think this is a little obvious?"

Scott folded his menu, then laid it down on the table. "It's been my experience that boardroom affairs are usually conducted in public. I think it must add to the thrill. What good would a woman like Irene be to a geezer like Pete Sherban if he didn't have the chance to show off a little? It's a male thing."

"What's her excuse?"

Scott smiled. "Your claws are showing, Maggie."

"Sorry," she mumbled. "But you've got to wonder. I mean, Pete can't possibly think Irene is attracted to him."

His smile turned into a laugh. "Men are capable of convincing themselves of a lot of things, especially after they reach middle age."

Maggie leaned forward so she could study Pete and Irene through the protective foliage of a large fern. Irene was draped against his side like a well-worn overcoat, and a seductive smile was plastered on her lips. Pete appeared to be enthralled. "What do you think we should do?"

"How much do you know about Max Wedgins?" Scott asked.

Maggie looked at him in surprise. "The developer? Nothing. Nobody knows anything. There are plenty of rumors about how reclusive he is. I think he lives just outside Boston, and I've heard rumors that his house is a throwback to the Tower of London, but I've never actually met the man. I don't think anyone has. Maybe not even Pete and Carl. He's weird. Real weird."

Scott stroked his chin. His forehead furrowed in concentration. "I wonder how Wedgins would respond if he knew one of the guys he was counting on for advice and guidance in this Cape Hope project was thinking with his sex drive."

"Now, Scott, we don't know that."

"No, but it's damned suspicious."

Maggie wet her lips. "I guess, but I just, well I hesitate to do anything based on what could be a perfectly friendly lunch appointment. It isn't as if we actually saw them doing anything, or that we know Pete's not capable of separating one from the other."

"You really are naive, aren't you?"

Maggie felt stung. "I don't consider trying to find the good in people naive. I consider it nice."

Scott frowned. "I'm sorry. I'm acting like a jerk. This just really puts a burr under my saddle."

She smiled at the Western idiom. "And dust in your boots?"

He looked baffled. "Dust in my—Oh. That's supposed to be funny."

"Yeah."

"You're making fun of my Westernism."

"It's just good-natured teasing. I didn't know you were so touchy."

His smile was slow, but finally came. "I'm not. I guess I'm just determined to be in a bad mood. I have to leave tomorrow after I put my plans in, and I'm feeling the pressure."

Maggie reached over and laced her fingers through his. "Maybe we should just forget we saw Pete and Irene today."

Scott frowned. "Yeah. Maybe."

But Maggie didn't believe for a minute that he was convinced.

"All right." Mark ducked around the corner of the Carson Hotel. He signaled Annie to follow him. "The coast is clear."

She frowned. "What do you mean the coast is clear? No one can see us. Remember?"

"Shh." Mark felt an odd tension, as if something were not quite right about their presence in the hotel.

Annie's irreverent disregard for the circumstances was eating at him. "I can't explain it to you, Annie. I just know something is wrong."

"You mean besides the fact that we're sneaking around trying to catch Pete Sherban and that Irene woman in the act."

Mark stopped by Room 716. He shook his head. "I don't know. I feel like we've got to do this. What if Sherban is wielding influence with Wedgins on the bid process? That could hurt Maggie."

"What if it's none of our business?"

Mark flexed his shoulders, willing away some of the tension. "How can it not be our business? If Sherban is trying to hurt Maggie, you'd better damn well believe it's my business."

"I just don't feel right about this, Mark. I mean, what are we going to do if we find out it's true?"

"I haven't gotten that far," he admitted. "I'm not sure. All I know is, Irene Fussman checked into this hotel this afternoon, and I'd bet the ranch that Pete Sherban is going to join her."

Annie sighed. "She's from out of town, Mark. It's perfectly normal for her to be staying in a hotel."

"I know."

"But you think there's something going on?"

"Didn't you see enough at lunch today to make you suspicious?"

Annie waited until a young couple, seemingly oblivious to their presence, passed by. "This feels weird. It was hard, I mean really, really hard to leave Scott. I feel like part of me is missing."

Mark hesitated. He had felt the same way when he'd finally left Maggie's home and met Annie at the hotel. There had been a persistent nagging pain in his midsection ever since he'd stepped out the door. "I felt it, too."

Her eyes widened. "Why didn't you tell me?"

"I think this is more important."

Annie held out her hands and stared at them. "Look at me. I'm really starting to disappear now." She rubbed her hands together. "My skin is tingling, like it's dry or something."

Mark cast a quick look down the hall before returning his gaze to Annie. He paused, then pulled his sweatshirt up so she could see his midriff. "Look."

Annie's eyes widened. "Mark." She reached out a tentative hand and touched the place where the hallway carpet was clearly visible through the previous substance of his torso. "What's happening?"

He shrugged. "Same thing that's happening to you, I guess."

"But why there?"

"I don't know. I'm as new at this as you are."

She managed a slight smile. "Of course you are. That was a dumb question."

"It started this afternoon. I've felt kind of funny all day. All I know is, I have this sense of urgency, like we've got to hurry up and get this over with. I can't explain it, and I don't understand it, but I've got the strongest feeling that if we don't do something about Pete Sherban, it could ruin everything."

Annie leaned against the wall. She stared at the elevator doors. "All right. We'll wait a little while longer, but I'm exhausted. I think it takes more energy to keep myself away from Scott."

Mark laid his arm across her shoulders. "I know. I'm not sure how much longer . . ." He trailed off when the elevator doors slid open and Pete Sherban, looking guilty as hell, hurried down the hall toward Room 716. "I'll be damned."

Annie sucked in a sharp breath when Irene, wearing a smile as red and seductive as her negligee, opened the door and let Pete inside. "This is disgusting," she said.

Mark grabbed her hand, then pulled her through the wall. "Come on."

Annie yelped. "Mark!" They were inside the room. "For God's sake! I don't want to watch."

Mark was staring intently at the sight of Pete Sherban's pudgy hands anchoring Irene's slender form against him in a torrid embrace. "We have to. I need to know if this is your basic extramarital fling, or if Petey here is influence peddling."

Annie covered her eyes with her hands. "This is gross."

Mark narrowed his gaze on Irene. Her long red nails were threaded in Pete's thinning hair. He was sucking on her earlobe, and she was watching the mirror with a look that had "victory" written all over it. "Wait in the bathroom," Mark said.

"What?" Annie looked up, only to turn her back when she saw Pete roughly palm Irene's full breast.

Mark pointed to the door. "The bathroom. Wait in there. I'll come get you when it's over."

She frowned at him. "I'll still be able to hear."

"Then wait in the hall," he said, exasperated. "We don't have another choice, Annie."

She looked over her shoulder at Pete and Irene. "The bathroom," she said with a heavy sigh. "I'll wait in the bathroom. Just hurry." She looked quickly at Pete and Irene. "This is so gross."

Annie disappeared through the bathroom door.

Mark turned his full attention to the groping couple. He was more certain than ever that Pete Sherban was selling Maggie, and the other bidders, out for a quick roll in the hay with Irene Fussman. All he needed was something to prove it. He sat down in a chair, ignoring a twinge of revulsion, and watched as Pete and Irene carried out their carnal drama in Room 716.

Twenty minutes later, Mark rolled his eyes. He resumed his now well-practiced pacing of the floor. How much more of this was he going to have to endure? Pete Sherban had already climaxed twice, and except for the brief flashes of annoyance Mark had seen cross Irene's features, he still had no indication that Pete was peddling influence with Max Wedgins in exchange for sexual favors from Irene.

Pete was pumping into Irene for the third time, having been made hard and ready by the antics of her full red mouth. Mark waited while the bed rocked and the floor squeaked and Irene moaned in Pete's ear until, finally, Pete collapsed on top of her with a guttural oath. Irene scored her nails down his hair-covered back. "You're hot, baby," she whispered.

"Damn, you're good," he said, rolling off her. He threw an arm over his eyes.

She rolled to her side to reach for a pack of cigarettes on the nightstand. Pete accepted the lighter from her, flipping it open. Irene took a long draw on the cigarette, and the ember flared bright in the dim light. "You do it for me, Pete. I told you."

He grunted as he rolled his arm back to look at her. "You're the kinkiest woman, Irene. I don't think you need me to do it for you."

Abruptly, Irene stubbed out the cigarette in the

crystal ashtray by the bed. She turned to Pete with a look so distressed, so anxious, Mark wanted to vomit. "That's not true," she whined as she pouted and laid her hand on his chest. "I can't believe you said that."

"Now, Irene—"

"You think I'm loose, don't you?"

"I'm not an idiot, Irene. I've heard things."

"They're lies, Pete." She pressed her naked body into his. "How could you defame what we have by saying I'd behave like this with anyone else?"

He snorted. "What we have is great sex."

She covered her mouth with her hand. Her eyes filled with tears so convincing even Mark was impressed. Pete sat up and reached for her. "Now, damn it, Irene, don't cry."

"Don't cry? Don't cry? How could you say that, think that?"

Mark caught the calculating look Irene gave the mirror while she held Pete's face against her neck. Pete ran his hand down her back. "Irene, baby, now stop that. You know that's not what I meant."

"It was," she said, sounding miserable.

"No it wasn't. I just meant I can't see what a sexy woman like you would want with a middle-aged flabby guy like me."

Mark wondered if Irene would point out that Pete had passed middle age about two decades before. She didn't. She sniffed delicately and pulled on his hair until he met her gaze. "Oh, Peter, how can you think that? You know I love you. I love you because you take care of me." She wiggled against him. "No one's ever taken care of me like you."

"Irene—"

She shook her head and moved away from him to

climb out of bed. Mark watched as she walked to the window. He'd have bet a fortune she knew exactly how the moonlight seeped in through the sheer curtains and highlighted the curves of her body. She glanced quickly over her shoulder, and gave Pete a siren's smile. "It's because of Max Wedgins, isn't it?"

Mark stiffened. Pete sat up in the bed. "It doesn't have anything to do with Max."

She leaned against the window, giving Pete an excellent view of high, firm breasts and flaring hips. "It does. I never asked you to use your influence with Max. I wanted to get the bid on my own. You were the one who went to him, Pete, and now you think the only reason I—" She paused, choking back a dramatic sob. "You think that's all I want from you."

Pete tossed the covers aside. He lumbered off the bed, then crossed the room to her. She turned her back to him, but Pete wrapped his arms around her waist from behind. "That's not true, Babe. I don't think that."

"I want you to call Wedgins right now, and tell him I'm not going to bid."

"Now, Irene—"

"I mean it. I won't have you thinking that I—"

Mark could see Pete's hands, reflected in the window, roaming over Irene's body. They came up and squeezed her breasts. "I don't want you to do that, baby," Pete said. "You deserve that bid. That's why I talked to Max."

Irene dropped her head back on his shoulder. "Do you really mean that?"

Pete slid one hand down her belly. He cupped the nest of curls at the apex of her thighs and hauled her back against him. "You don't think I'd let sex, no matter how hot it is, cloud my judgment, do you?"

Mark snorted. Irene reached up a hand and caressed Pete's face. "You're too good a businessman for that, lover."

"That's exactly right," Pete said. He bent his head to nuzzle her neck. "And I don't want to hear any more shit about your pulling your bid. Max is already expecting your designs."

Irene rubbed her buttocks against his crotch. "You don't have to, Peter."

"I want to," he said, pressing her closer. "I didn't mean to make you think otherwise." He nipped her earlobe. "I'm just not very good at expressing myself with you."

Irene smiled a victorious smile at her reflection in the window before turning in his arms. She pressed a steamy, openmouthed kiss to his lips, sucking at his lower lip as she drew away. "I know one thing you're good at expressing," she said, and dropped to her knees in front of him.

Mark swore in disgust. He stalked into the bathroom. He found Annie, seated on the floor, her knees drawn up under her chin, her eyes closed, her fingers stuck in her ears, singing "Take Me Out to the Ball Game" off-key and at the top of her lungs. He smiled as he tapped her on the head. She stopped singing. Her eyes flew open. "Time to go," he said.

She pulled her fingers from her ears. "What?"

"Time to go."

She scrambled to her feet. "Thank goodness." She paused to frown at the noises coming from the bedroom. "Did you get what you wanted?"

Mark nodded. "Pete's definitely wheeling and dealing with Wedgins to get Irene the bid."

"I hope she's worth it."

"Well, I have to admit I've never seen a woman who—"

Annie slapped a hand over his mouth. "For crying out loud, Mark, I don't want to know the details. I just want to get out of here."

He pulled her hand away. "As you wish." He tossed her over his shoulder, then stepped through the wall into the corridor.

Annie slapped his back. "Put me down, you big bully."

Mark dropped her feet to the floor with an exaggerated sigh. "Some people are never satisfied."

Annie glowered at him while she straightened her clothes. "All right, so now you know Irene's not competing on a level playing field. What do you think you're going to do about it?"

Mark took her hand. He started toward the stairwell. "That's the tricky part. I'm not sure what we can do."

"What about Ryan?"

"What about him?"

"What if he called that Carl guy and tipped him off?"

Mark looked at her, stunned. "I'm not going to tell Ryan that Irene Fussman and Pete Sherban are having an affair."

Annie frowned. "Do you think I'm a complete idiot? Of course you aren't."

"Then what do you think I should do?"

"Maggie seemed to know Carl fairly well at that meeting."

Mark nodded. "His grandson plays on Ryan's hockey team."

"Well, there you go."

"There I go what?"

"Have Ryan call Carl for some hockey reason. I don't know—the father/son game maybe. He can sell him a ticket or something."

"And in the middle of the conversation, my seven-year-old can just happen to mention that maybe Carl should pay closer attention to the sexual behavior of his partner?"

Annie looked stung. "I didn't mean that."

Mark let out a ragged breath. "I know. I'm acting like an asshole. I'm sorry. I'm exhausted," he said, by way of explanation.

She nodded. "Me too. I can't remember the last time I was this tired."

"I think being away from Maggie and Ryan is draining my energy. My concentration is shot."

"Maybe we should just go home and talk about it in the morning."

"Good idea. I think you're right about Ryan. He's the only one we can communicate with, so somehow he's going to have to tip off Carl. I just don't want to get him involved in this."

Annie reached up and smoothed the crease from his forehead. "Don't worry. We'll think of something."

Ten

Maggie propped her slippered feet on the coffee table.
She sank back against her couch. It had been a long
and exhausting day, but despite her bone-deep fatigue, she had been unable to sleep. She took a sip of
her cocoa.

The moon was bright, and she shut her eyes, allow-
ing herself to ponder the strange feeling of unease that
had plagued her all evening. Ryan had been edgy,
upset when Scott had picked her up for dinner that
evening. They'd dropped him at Lily's, but even the
promise of Franklin's companionship had done little
to calm him down. Lily confessed that Ryan had spent
most of the evening curled up in front of the television, looking miserable. Maggie hadn't been able to
get any answers out of him except for a mumbled
explanation about missing his father, before he'd finally settled into an exhausted sleep.

It hadn't helped matters any that Scott had been
tense as well. Maggie's nerves were stripped raw by
the time he kissed her good-bye and told her he'd be
back from Dallas the following Tuesday. She'd been
almost relieved that the evening was finally over.

She studied the silhouette of snow-laden evergreens outside her window. In the silver moonlight, the trees looked enchanted. What, she wondered, had soured her mood so completely? She was stressed, she knew, about submitting her plans the next day, but the meeting had gone well that morning, and except for that small business with Pete and Irene at the restaurant, she had enjoyed a pleasurable afternoon showing Scott around Cape Hope.

It hadn't been until later, just before they left for dinner, that her mood had begun to deteriorate. She'd had an inexplicable uneasy feeling all evening, and despite Scott's reassurances to the contrary, she was certain he had suffered the effects. Maggie took another sip of her cocoa, followed by several deep, calming breaths.

She was concentrating so hard, she barely heard the knock on her door. Maggie tipped her head and listened. She had nearly convinced herself it was a trick of the wind, when the knock sounded again. She was certain it was Scott.

She pulled the door open to find him shivering in the snow. "Scott!" She grabbed his hand to drag him into the house, so she could shut the door behind him. "What are you doing here? Where's your coat?"

He shook his head. "I had to see you, Maggie." He rubbed his upper arms for warmth. "I know it's late, but I got to the hotel, and I couldn't sleep."

"Me either," she said. "Come on in. I'll make you some cocoa."

"Don't go to any trouble."

"I won't. I had already heated the milk." She pointed to her mug on the coffee table.

Scott's gaze slipped past the mug to the empty fireplace. "There's a chill in here. Do you mind if I start a fire?"

She waved her hand in the direction of the living room. "Go ahead. I was too tired to bother. I'll just get your cocoa and join you in a minute."

Five minutes later, Maggie sat down beside him on the sofa. She handed him a mug. He'd built a robust fire, and the orange glow cast eerie shadows on his handsome face. Maggie shivered. "Here you go."

Scott wrapped his long fingers around the mug. "Thanks, Maggie. I—I'm sorry it's so late. I shouldn't have come."

"It's all right." She picked up her mug. "I told you I couldn't sleep either."

Scott swallowed some of his cocoa. "Maggie," he paused, "about tonight—"

She held up her hand. "You don't have to say anything, Scott. I felt it, too. That's why I couldn't sleep."

"I don't know what's wrong with me. I'm so"—he searched for a word—"tense."

"Edgy," Maggie supplied at the same instant.

Scott's smile was rueful. "You noticed."

"You weren't the only one. Ryan was climbing the walls when we picked him up at Lily's, and I'd be lying if I told you I wasn't out of sorts myself."

"What do you think's going on?"

"I don't know. Full moon, high tides, cosmic forces." She shrugged. "Maybe it was just the stress of that meeting today."

Scott set his mug down on the table. He pried hers loose from her fingers, then set it down as well. Taking both her hands in his, he met her gaze. "Maggie, something's going on here, and I don't know what it is, or why it's happening, but I do know that I need to be with you tonight. Even if we just sit here and talk, I can't spend another minute alone in my hotel."

"I don't want to be alone either."

Scott tugged on her hands until she moved into his embrace. "I want you," he said, "I want you in a way I've never wanted another woman in my life. Not even Annie."

She looked at him, startled. "Scott—"

"Don't say anything," he said. "I know it's too soon for you. I shouldn't be saying this." He ran his hand down her spine. "I swear I'd never push you into anything. But you make me feel alive again, Maggie. I used to think I died when Annie did. Like there was nothing left of me. You make me feel like there's a reason to get up every morning and nothing to fear about going to bed every night. Sometimes, I dream about you, and sometimes I just feel you, there with me." He grumbled something beneath his breath. "This sounds like crap. I know it does."

Maggie shook her head. "No it doesn't."

"I can't explain it. I'm confused and frustrated, and then tonight—oh hell."

Maggie laid her head against his chest. She listened to the heavy, even rhythm of his heart. He was warm and solid, and she wrapped her arms around his waist and hung on. "Scott?"

"Yeah?"

"I can't sleep with you."

"I know."

She waited. "Are you angry?" she asked when he didn't say anything else.

"No."

"Do you want to know why?"

"It's too soon for you," he said.

She shook her head. "That's not the reason."

Scott tipped her chin up. He stared at her. "It's not?"

"No. I'm not going to deny that I want to," she said. "That wouldn't be fair."

Scott's eyes darkened. "Maggie?" His voice sounded hoarse.

"I want to," she said. "I want to a lot."

"Maggie what are you saying?"

She took a deep breath. "I haven't let go of Mark yet. I still feel married to him." She held up her left hand, and studied her engagement ring and wedding band. "If you and I, if we—" She took a deep breath, then started over. "If we made love, I'd feel like I was betraying him," she explained, feeling more than a little foolish. She wondered if Scott would think she was crazy.

Scott let out a ragged breath and hugged her close. "Oh, Maggie, what a pair we are."

"Scott, I—"

He pressed a finger to her lips and shook his head. "You don't have to say anything. I know what you're feeling."

"You do?"

He nodded. "This hasn't been easy on me either, you know. I find myself torn between the joy of falling in love with you, and the guilt of forgetting how I felt about Annie."

Her eyes widened. She felt a shaft of panic race up her spine, and in that instant, she put a name to the feeling that had been clawing at her all evening. It was fear. "Falling in love?"

He chuckled. "You can't tell me you didn't know. The signs were all over the place."

Maggie was having trouble breathing. He couldn't love her. He just couldn't. "I guess I didn't want to think about it."

He brushed her hair off her face. "I didn't either. There was a time when I could see Annie's face as clear as a picture. Now, I'm not so sure. Sometimes, I can't see her at all for thinking about you."

"Scott," she said, feeling her throat constrict, "this isn't right. You can't fall in love with me."

"The way I see it, you don't have much say in the matter." He tugged on a lock of her hair.

Maggie pushed his hand away. "I mean it," she said. "You can't."

His eyes narrowed. "What are you afraid of, Maggie?"

She hesitated. "I'm not afraid."

"You are. I can see it in your eyes. You have the most expressive eyes I've ever seen. Have I told you that before?"

"I'm serious."

"So am I. You're scared out of your mind."

"I'm not scared, I'm cautious."

"Cautious of what?"

"Of this. Of us. Of you," she admitted.

Scott stared at her. "Me? I'd never hurt you. You know I wouldn't."

"You can't guarantee that. No one can. Mark didn't want to hurt me either, but he did. He died and left me alone to raise Ryan. How can a person hurt you more than that?"

"Oh, Maggie. Honey, you can't be afraid to love someone just because they might leave you someday."

"I can't go through that again. I can't."

He cradled her face in his hands. "Sweetheart, listen to me. When I lost Annie, I wanted to die right along with her. I couldn't imagine living without her to share my life. I loved her so much, it was all I could do to get up in the morning for months after she was gone."

Maggie sucked in a tight breath. "Sometimes, I still feel that way," she said.

"But being with you has changed that," Scott said. "It's a good change, but a hurting change all at the same time. I had numbed everything after Annie's death. I couldn't face the pain, so I ignored it. You've put the edge back on my feelings. You don't let me forget."

Maggie felt the impact of his words like a blow to her midsection. How could he be feeling what she was feeling? "It's like that for me, too," she admitted. "Do you remember when I told you I'd stayed up too late working on my plans last night?"

"Yes."

"That wasn't entirely true. I did work on them, but only because I couldn't stop crying long enough to go to sleep. I haven't done that since the month or so after Mark died."

"Maggie, I'm sorry."

"Sometimes it's so bad, I can't stand it. I don't know what I'll do if I fall in love with you, Scott. I don't think I'll live through it."

Scott ran his thumb over the curve of her cheek. The pad was rough and warm, and Maggie shivered. "We can make it together," he said.

"That's not all." She was driven now. Driven by a need to tell him everything, to put into words the feelings that had been clawing at her almost from the moment she'd met him. "This"—she curled her fingers into the flannel of his shirt—"this passion between us. I've never felt anything like this. It's like an inferno." He stared at her. "I think it's consuming me."

A ragged groan sounded in his throat. He dropped his head back against the sofa. "I'm on fire for you," he confessed, and ran his hand along the soft, worn fabric of her sweatshirt until he found the hem. He slid his hand beneath it to splay his fingers on the bare skin of her lower back. "Your skin feels like hot satin. Just thinking about you makes me ache." He moved against her, and Maggie felt the evidence of his words. "I want you so much it makes me tremble inside."

She was the one who was trembling. "I can't, Scott. I'm not ready. I don't think I'll ever be ready."

"I'm not going to rush you. I said I wouldn't."

Maggie swallowed, then plunged ahead. "And what about your bid on the Cape Hope project?"

"What about it?"

"What if you don't get it?"

Scott shrugged. "I'd still have my position in Dallas."

"I'm here," Maggie said, wondering if she sounded as forlorn as she felt.

Scott sighed. "We'd work it out, Maggie."

"How?"

"Well, I was thinking, I have some excellent connections with design firms in Dallas. I could get you on as an associate."

Maggie shook her head. "I don't want to be an associate."

"Maggie, honey, be reasonable. You said yourself

that By Design was struggling. Do you really want to run your own business, or do you want the freedom to design?"

"I'm just starting to feel like Ryan and I have a new life here. I don't want to uproot him again."

"OK, OK. I don't claim to have all the answers. Hell, I don't even think I have half the answers. We don't know yet what's going to happen with Cape Hope."

"But—"

He gave her a quick squeeze to interrupt her. "If there's one thing I learned about life during Annie's illness it was not to dwell too much on the future. I want to be with you, Maggie. We'll find a way to work it out."

"What if we can't?"

"We will. I knew it tonight. I've never felt as uneasy or on edge as I did this evening. It was as if . . . as if everything that had become familiar to me in the months following Annie's death was suddenly stripped away. I felt vulnerable, exposed."

She stared at him in surprise. "Alone," she said.

"Completely."

Maggie moved one hand to his shoulder and clung to him. "What's happening to us?"

"I don't know, but I need to hold you tonight, Maggie. I can't be alone."

"Neither can I," she admitted, and knew it was true. She needed the feel of Scott's warmth, of his solid strength. "I'm still afraid," she said.

"So am I." His voice was so soft, she barely heard him.

And then the wind whistled beneath the eaves of the old house, and the fire danced as a cool draft played across the room. Maggie clung to Scott, aware of a slow sense of calm that was seeping into her disquieted soul. The wind moved through the open vents in the attic, humming its way through the house in a low, mournful cry. Maggie felt a stillness, a sense of well-being. Scott relaxed beneath her, his tight grip relaxing, his breathing slowing to a leisurely cadence.

Maggie rubbed her face against his shirt. She shivered, suddenly aware of a completeness, a rightness in his being there.

"Cold?" he asked.

She shook her head. "Not really."

He seemed not to hear. "That draft is really bad. You should have that fixed."

Maggie drew in a deep breath. She felt at peace for the first time in hours. "I've always liked the way the wind whistles under the eaves," she said. "It reminds me of Mark. He used to say if anything every happened to him, I'd hear him in the wind."

Scott stiffened. "What?" His voice sounded strangled.

"He was a pilot, remember? He said if anything should happen, I'd always know he was watching over us because I'd hear him every time I heard the wind."

"Annie used to say that."

Maggie looked at Scott in surprise. He was staring at the trees out the window, watching intently as the brisk December breeze blew clumps of snow from their laden boughs. "She did?" Maggie asked.

Scott nodded. "It was from a poem she liked. I think it was called 'They Softly Walk.' "

Maggie looked at him, amazed. "It's by Hugh Robert Orr. Mark liked it, too."

"Mark liked poetry?" Scott asked.

Maggie laughed softly. "Only when he thought I'd be impressed. He found the poem in a book, and wrote it in a letter for me the day before he left on his first mission. I used to pull that letter out and read it over and over in the days following Mark's death. I ended up memorizing the poem. It goes:

> They are not gone who pass
> Beyond the clasp of hand.
> They have put off their shoes
> Softly to walk within the wind,
> Each day, our thought-led paths
>   of memory.

Her voice faded, lost in the whistle of the winter breeze. Scott wrapped his arms closer around her. "Within the wind," he quietly repeated.

Maggie met his gaze. "Do you think they're up there?" she asked, pointing to the ceiling.

Scott paused. "Have you felt the difference in this house since the wind picked up?"

She nodded. "I thought it was you—having you here I mean."

He tipped his head and listened to the quiet, gentle blowing. "Somehow," he whispered. "I don't think so."

Annie leaned back in her chair in Maggie's living room. She looked at Mark. After they'd left the hotel, they'd found themselves in Maggie's living room, watching, listening to Maggie's conversation with Scott. Mark's expression told Annie that he was struggling. She got out of her chair and went to him.

Kneeling in front of him, she took his hands in hers. She waited until he tore his gaze from Maggie and Scott to look her in the eye. "Mark," she said, "this is good. This is what we want."

"I know."

"You agreed to help them."

"I *know*."

She squeezed his hands. "Why don't we go upstairs for a while?"

He shook his head. "I'm too exhausted to move. I told you being away from Maggie and Ryan was wearing me down. Don't you feel the same way?"

Annie paused only briefly before she nodded. It had been exhausting for her to remain separate from Scott for so long. "Yes. I feel the same way."

Mark shifted his hands and laced his fingers through hers. "Annie, do you think—"

"Yes?"

"Could we just sit here for a while? Together." He nodded his head toward Scott and Maggie. "Like them."

Annie slipped into his lap with a slight smile. She wrapped her arms around his waist. "I think I'd like that."

Eleven

Scott awoke, *vaguely aware of an unfamiliar stiffness* in his shoulders and legs. He flexed his muscles, only to find himself pinned down by a weight so warm, so soft, it reminded him of waking up with . . . His eyes popped open. He was staring at the ceiling of Maggie's living room. A brief glance at Maggie's head, tucked securely against the curve of his neck, brought memories of the previous evening rushing back to him.

The first weak rays of dawn cast a pink hue on the room. Scott lifted a hand gently to stroke the soft disarray of Maggie's hair. She sighed and shifted against him. Memories of the previous night flooded in. He closed his eyes, recalling the long hours of shared sorrow; the tender, comforting promises; the warmth of companionship. There had been no hint of the passion that normally surged between them. Instead, it had been a time of one soul meeting another to share a common burden.

But now, as the falling snow whispered against the windows, and the dawn settled a warm glow on Maggie's sleeping features, Scott felt his body respond with a rush of desire so strong, so intense, he feared he might explode. He drew a deep breath as he gently shifted Maggie to his side. A stab of white-hot passion rushed through him when her thigh brushed his groin.

Determined, he stretched out a hand to lift the top off the glass candy dish on the coffee table. He picked up two peppermints. He popped one into his mouth, before sliding down on the sofa so that Maggie's body was aligned with his. "Maggie," he whispered, pressing the other peppermint against her lips. "Honey, wake up."

Her eyes drifted open. She parted her lips just enough for him to slide the candy into her mouth. He smiled at her bemused expression. It took several moments for her eyes to clear. As recognition and recollection dawned, Scott leaned down and rubbed his mouth against hers in a half kiss that made the blood rush to his head. "Good morning," he whispered.

Maggie's eyes widened. "I—good morning."

Scott decided not to give her time to adjust to her surroundings. He took her lips in a hot kiss full of all the rife hunger he'd told her about during the night. To his delight, Maggie moaned and pressed into him. "God, Maggie," he said, then slanted his mouth over hers.

Her fingers threaded into his hair, rubbing over his scalp in haphazard abandon. Scott groaned. He wrapped his arms around her, pulling her full against him. He felt desire, wild and hot and uncontrollable, racing through his blood with the force of a stampede. His tongue delved into her mouth, and he knew a moment of dizzying passion when her fingers clenched in his hair.

On fire, Scott slid one leg between hers. He moved
a hand to the bottom of her sweatshirt. He was consumed by a need for the feel of her flesh, warm and
alive and real. She immediately began tugging at the
buttons of his flannel shirt, pulling them free as she
sucked at his tongue. Finally, she wrenched the shirt
open and yanked his tee shirt from his waistband. Her
cool fingers slid up his chest at the exact instant he
worked her sweatshirt up and spread his fingers on
her back. The sensation of skin against skin was devastating. Scott tore his mouth from hers as a ragged
groan ripped from his lips.

His body was hard, throbbing. He ran his lips along
the curve of her jaw. He reveled in the raspy sound
of her uneven breathing fanning across his ears. Fear-
ing spontaneous combustion, he moved his thigh between hers, and when her hipbone pushed into his
groin he nearly went insane. Still half-asleep, Maggie
kissed him with an ardor and abandon that made his
head swim. He could feel his pulse pounding a reck-
less rhythm as the blood roared in his ears, and his
lungs squeezed from lack of air.

Maggie fought back a wave of reality and clung to
him. It felt so good, so incredibly good. Mark had
known, always known, exactly how and where to
touch her, but with Scott, the exploration was a mutual experience. He shuddered when she brushed her
fingers over his ribs. She moaned when he dipped his
tongue into the whorl of her ear.

Reality that it was her house, and her couch, and
that her son was sleeping upstairs began to intrude.
Maggie thrust it aside. She skimmed her fingers over
the smooth contours of his chest. She threaded them
in the crisp hairs that covered his warm skin. Scott

was worrying her earlobe with his teeth. Maggie gasped when he found the sensitive spot just beneath it. She felt him smile against her skin.

"Are you sensitive here?" he asked.

"Yes." Her voice was a breathy hiss. "Yes."

Scott nuzzled the pulse point, and she felt her insides quiver. His strong, muscled thigh was trapped between her legs. She shifted on it, hoping to relieve some of the throbbing ache spreading through her lower body. Her thigh slid across his hardened length. Scott's body jerked in reaction. Maggie felt a brief smile tug at her lips. "Are you sensitive here?" she asked.

He growled something in her ear before reclaiming her lips for another heart-stopping kiss. Maggie moved her hands over his ribs, his back, the firm planes of his shoulders, clinging, clutching at the pleasure he offered. If only she could forget . . . she pushed the thought aside. There was this and him and now, and she wouldn't dwell on what had been or what would be. "No," she gasped, sucking on his lower lip when he moved to end the kiss. "Not yet."

He moved one hand to her breast, cupped it, tested its weight, rubbed his callused thumb over the tip of her nipple. "Maggie," he rasped, his voice a harsh whisper, "Maggie, I can't take this."

She arched into his hand, pushing her breast against his palm. Her loins ached, and her heart raced, and her head pounded with the heady wonderful feel of him pressing down on her. "Please," she said, rubbing her mouth over his. "Please, don't stop."

"Honey." Scott's fingers flexed into her breast. Maggie leaned into his palm. "Darlin', I'm going to explode in a second."

She bit down on his lower lip. "So long," she said. "So long. Please."

Scott sucked in a harsh breath and brought his mouth down hard on hers once more. He was losing control. Any thought of resisting what Maggie offered was quickly shredding into a pile of tatters. She wanted it. He wanted it. He moved his thigh between her legs, then groaned when he felt the moist heat of her. There was no reason, no sense in denying themselves any longer.

Ruthlessly, he pushed aside Maggie's objections of the night before. He refused to dwell on her fears, her anxiety. Her breasts were tight and full against his hands, her skin smooth as silk. He rubbed his palm in slow circles on her breasts. When she moaned and clasped his thigh between both of hers, he felt a rush of desire so strong it stole his breath. No, there was no reason.

Maggie arched against him, and twined her fingers into Scott's hair. Her voice was a breathy whisper against his face when she said, "Mark."

He froze.

That was a damn good reason.

Maggie seemed not to notice his sudden stillness. She clutched at his head as she ran her tongue along the line of his teeth. Scott took several deep breaths before reaching up to disentangle her hand from his hair. "Maggie," he said, his voice a hollow rasp. He felt all the passion in his body drain away. "Honey, look at me."

She shook her head. Her lips were swollen, her skin flushed, and for an instant Scott was tempted to ignore what had happened. "Open your eyes, darlin'."

She shuddered once. Her eyes slowly drifted open,

and she met his gaze. He watched the play of emotions on her face. Slowly, he withdrew his hand from beneath her sweatshirt, then lifted it to brush her hair off her forehead. Maggie stared at him. "Scott," she said.

He felt a surge of jealousy as he rolled away from her and sat up on the couch. "That's right. Scott. I don't want you to forget it either."

She reached for him, laid her hand on his forearm. He flinched and drew away. "Scott," she said, her voice a plea, "I didn't mean—"

"Didn't mean what, Maggie?" he asked. She visibly cringed. He bit back a quiet oath of self-loathing. He pulled her gently against him. "I was the one who promised not to push," he said. He held out his hand so they could both see it tremble. "And here I was all over you while I knew you were half-asleep."

Maggie shuddered. "I didn't mean to say that, Scott. I knew who you were."

He hugged her once before setting her away from him. "Maybe it was for the best. Maybe you knew I was getting to the point of no return."

"So was I," she whispered.

He tucked his tee shirt into his pants, then started to button his shirt. "So maybe you knew that would do the trick. God. You probably think every time I get you on that sofa I'm going to attack you or something."

Maggie wrapped her arms around her waist and rocked back and forth a few times. "Scott, I—"

He shook his head. He leaned over to kiss her lightly. "Forget it, Maggie. I've got plans to submit and a plane to catch. You've got to get Ryan off to school, and, well, whatever else you normally do in

the mornings. We'll just talk about it when I get back
from Dallas. Okay?"

She hesitated. "Scott—"

"Not now. I can't right now."

"Are you angry?"

"No."

"Then what—"

He moved quickly to cover her mouth with his
hand. "It's been a rocky night. I need some time. All
right?" Her eyes searched his. He gave her a gentle
shake. "Say yes."

She nodded. Scott dropped his hand, "OK. Now, I
need to use your phone to call a cab."

Maggie shook her head. "That's ridiculous. I'm going to take Ryan to school at eight, then go by Carl's
and drop off my proposal. Why don't we just swing
by your hotel then, and we'll go over to Carl's office
together?"

He paused, not sure he was ready to experience
something as normal as a morning routine with Maggie and Ryan. He saw the uncertain look in her eyes,
and it swayed him. She was still insecure about what
had happened. "All right," he said with a slight
shrug. He dropped back onto the couch. "What do
you think we should do until Ryan wakes up?"

Maggie smiled. "If we start looking for my car keys
now, we won't be late when it's time to leave."

Mark gritted his teeth. He resumed his pacing of
the living room. Annie laughed. "You look like a lion
stalking your prey," she said.

He glared at her, jabbing an angry finger in Scott's
direction. "He deliberately took advantage of her.
Maggie's always disoriented when she wakes up."

"He didn't know that," Annie pointed out.

"Oh, he knew. Believe me, he knew."

"Mark, you're overreacting."

"I am not overreacting. Will you stop saying that?"

"They're going to sleep together, you know."

"Not if I have anything to say about it."

"You don't. So quit acting like a child."

Mark dropped down into his chair with a huff. "Doesn't this bother you at all? My God!" He jerked a hand in the direction of the sofa. "How can you sit there and glibly inform me that they're going to end up in bed together!"

"Of course it bothers me," she snapped, her patience wearing thin. Despite what Mark seemed to think, it wasn't any easier on her to see Maggie and Scott together. When Scott had told Maggie during the previous night that he'd never felt with Annie the way he felt with her, Annie had wanted to curl up in a corner and weep. The fact that she couldn't—could no longer even weep normally—had only made the situation worse. "It hurts more than you can possibly imagine."

Mark's head snapped up. He stared at her. "Damn," he swore softly. "I'm a first-class idiot."

"Pretty close," she said, miserable.

Mark got out of his chair and crossed to her. "I should have paid more attention. I've been so busy wanting to tear his throat out, I never even thought about what this was doing to you."

"Well, it hurts. It hurts me just as much as it hurts you." She knew she sounded petulant and frankly didn't care.

Mark exhaled a long breath. "I'm sorry, Annie. I'm really sorry."

"Forget it."

He shook his head. "No. I won't forget it. I think we should just get out of here for a while." He glanced over his shoulder. "Leave them alone."

"I thought you didn't want to leave them alone."

"I don't," he confessed with a half smile. "But I don't want to watch either." He tugged on her hand. "Come on. You haven't lived until you've seen Ryan get up in the morning."

Annie reluctantly agreed, and was forced to admit five minutes later that there was something rather amazing about the experience of watching Ryan Connell wake up. They found him, turned bottom to top in his bed, his feet resting against the headboard. His mouth was open and his blond hair stood up in unruly tufts. Annie smiled at Mark. "Which side of the family did he get this from?"

Mark grinned. "Mine. Maggie used to complain that as soon as we got in bed, I'd put my elbows and feet on her side and kept all the good stuff on my side."

Annie laughed. "Some fun you were."

His expression turned to mock outrage. "I'll have you know, Miss-Know-It-All, that I was a lot of fun. Ask Maggie."

She snorted. "No thanks."

Mark flashed her a smile before leaning over Ryan. "Ryan," he said, "buddy. It's time to get up."

Ryan grumbled beneath his breath as he rolled over. His arm sprawled out and smacked the bedpost. Mark winced. "He'll have a bruise for that one."

"He can add it to his black eye and that enormous scrape on his shin."

Mark ignored her. "Come on, Ryan. Wake up, son."

Ryan rubbed a fisted hand in his eyes. "Don't want to."

"Too bad," Mark said. "Mom'll be up here soon banging on your door."

Ryan opened his eyes. The morning light made him squint. He stared at Mark for a few seconds. "Dad?"

"Were you expecting someone else, maybe?"

Ryan sat up in bed. "Dad! Where were you last night?"

Mark glanced briefly at Annie. "I had some stuff I had to do. Did you miss me?"

Ryan nodded. The cowlick in his hair bobbed back and forth. "I thought you were gone."

"I wasn't gone. I promised I'd tell you if I'm leaving for good."

"Do you promise?" Ryan looked at Annie. "You have to make him promise."

Ryan clutched his pillow to his chest as he watched her. His Teenage Mutant Ninja Turtle pajamas were bunched up around his knees. Annie had to swallow a bitter longing to straighten them, to run a comb through his hair, to smooth the sheets and fluff the pillows. She noticed the odd way Mark was looking at her, so she flashed Ryan an overly bright smile. "Of course I promise. Why would we want to go off and leave you anyway?"

Ryan dropped back against his pillow with a relieved sigh. "I want you to sing to me, Dad."

Mark shook his head. "No singing this morning. You've got to get ready for school."

"Uh-uh." Ryan shook his head. "Sing first."

"Sing first, huh? If I sing, are you going to get moving?"

"Deal."

"What do you want to hear?"

Ryan seemed to consider his choices for a long minute before looking at Annie. "You pick one, Annie."

She looked at Mark in surprise. "Me?"

"Sure," Ryan said. "You're the guest. You pick."

"What nice manners," Mark drawled. "Too bad you can't remember please and thank-you."

Ryan giggled. "Pick one, Annie. He can sing anything you want."

Amused, Annie watched Mark's growing embarrassment. "I had no idea you were such a virtuoso."

"I'm not."

Ryan's face scrunched up into a confused knot. "What's a—a vir . . ."

"Virtuoso," Mark helpfully supplied. "It's a person who knows more about music than they should."

Annie laughed. "No it isn't." She looked at Ryan. "It's a person who knows a lot of songs."

"That's Dad." Ryan stood up and started jumping on his bed. "He knows everything. Even Elvis."

The last was delivered with such awe, Annie was forced to laugh again. "Elvis," she said, doing her best to sound suitably impressed. "Really?"

Mark groaned. Ryan ignored him. "Yeah. Even the hard stuff, where you can't understand the words. Right, Dad?"

Mark rolled his eyes with a reluctant laugh. "I guess."

"I didn't know you had such a passion for singing," Annie remarked.

"Once, a long time ago, I thought I wanted to sing. It didn't take long to put that out of my mind."

"Well," she said, sitting down on the side of Ryan's

bed, "I think I have a hankering to hear 'Wake Up, Little Susie.' It is morning, after all."

Ryan clapped his hands and continued bouncing on the bed. "Yeah, Dad. Do 'Wake Up.' Do 'Wake Up.' "

Mark hesitated only briefly before conceding with a wry smile. "All right, Ry. Put the music on."

Scott stopped his search of the hall table, where Maggie was certain she'd left her keys, and looked up at the ceiling as the first bars of "Wake Up Little Susie" wafted down the stairs. Ryan's voice chimed in on every "oo la la." "I didn't know Ryan did a whole selection of oldies."

Maggie laughed. "You haven't lived until you've heard 'Jailhouse Rock.' " She looked over his shoulder into the drawer. "Any luck?"

"No." He shook his head. "I don't think they're here, Maggie. Where did you have them last?"

"If I knew that, we wouldn't be looking for them."

Scott picked up a catchall basket and began rummaging through the contents. "Did you check your briefcase?"

"Yes." She started up the stairs. "I need to start getting Ryan ready for school. Why don't you try the living room?"

He nodded. "Okay."

Maggie paused, her foot on the top stair. "Scott?"

He looked at her. "Yes?"

"Thank you."

"I haven't found them yet."

Maggie shook her head. "Not for finding the keys. Thank you for understanding. For being you. For everything."

He held her gaze a long moment. "We have a lot to talk about, Maggie."

"I know. When you get back from Dallas. OK?"

He nodded. "OK."

"You remember Scott Bishop, Carl?" Maggie asked, walking into Carl Fortwell's office two hours later. After she'd dropped Ryan at school, she and Scott had picked up his plans from his hotel and spent a productive, if tense, morning inspecting the site of the Cape Hope Resort. Scott had given Maggie significant insight into the layout and structural restraints of the property, making her feel more confident than ever that his plans represented the best possible development of Maxwell Wedgins's investment.

Scott had seemed detached, distracted, but Maggie had been unwilling to tempt the fates by upsetting the mutual truce between them. "I'm taking Scott to the airport," she continued by way of explanation to Carl, "and we wanted to stop off and deliver our proposals."

"Excellent," Carl said, rising from behind his massive cherry desk. He circled it and stopped to kiss Maggie's cheek. "It's always good to see you." He extended his hand to Scott. "Bishop. I hope all this shuttling back and forth from Dallas isn't getting to you. You look a little tired."

Maggie wondered if Carl could see her blush. "I've got my proposal for you," she said, handing Carl the folder. "I hope it's what you were expecting."

Carl smiled at her. "I'm sure it is, Maggie." He indicated the two chairs across from his desk. "Sit down. I'd like to look this over if you don't mind."

She shook her head as she dropped into one of the

chairs. "What do you think of this project, Bishop?" Carl asked, flipping through Maggie's proposal. He leaned back against his desk, still facing them.

Scott shrugged. "Creatively it's great. There are no parameters, a designer's dream. Technically, I'm not sure. I hope the building process will be more centralized once the bid is awarded."

Carl set Maggie's proposal down on his desk before he met Scott's gaze. "It will be. Max Wedgins is, well, different. He's different from anyone I've ever worked with. He knows what he wants, but likes the power of making all of us guess. He's eccentric, but level-headed. A good decision maker, with enough goof-off in him to drive his investors nuts. I think you're going to like working with him."

"Provided that I get the bid," Scott said.

Carl nodded. "Provided."

"Is there something you're not telling me?" Scott asked.

Carl shook his head. "Max is unpredictable even on his best days. He's playing everything close to his chest. Besides, he talks mostly to Pete. I've never even met the guy."

A brief picture of Irene Fussman hanging on Pete Sherban's arm popped into Maggie's head. She frowned. Scott seemed to be following her train of thought. "How much does he talk to Pete?" Scott asked.

"I don't know, twice, maybe three times a week. This is a multibillion-dollar investment. It's only natural he would."

Maggie took a deep breath. "Carl," she said, "do you know any reason why Pete would have been lunching with Irene Fussman yesterday afternoon?"

"No. That would put the entire bid process in jeopardy. There are all kinds of government restrictions on how we do these things, you know. It's not just some haphazard thing."

"I know," Maggie said. "But Scott and I saw Pete and Irene yesterday afternoon at the White Rooster."

Carl shook his head. "That can't be right."

Scott leaned forward in his chair. "It is."

Carl frowned. "Are you sure it was Pete and Irene? The White Rooster is awfully dark." He shot Maggie a knowing look. "Kind of a romantic spot for two business associates."

"We're not talking about Maggie and me," Scott said, his voice sharp.

Maggie felt her skin blush a heated red. "That's not what he meant, Scott."

Carl slanted Maggie a telling look. "No. I just meant that it might be tough to identify someone in there."

"It was definitely Pete and Irene," Maggie said. "I'm sure of it."

Carl exhaled a harsh sigh. "I just can't believe that. Pete and I have been in business together for thirty years. I just can't believe he'd jeopardize a deal like this."

Maggie fingered the carved arm rest of her chair. "Maybe there's a perfectly reasonable explanation."

Scott snorted. "Yeah, sure."

Carl steepled his fingers under his chin, tapping them together in thought. "I don't know. I'll have to look into this."

"I'd appreciate it if you'd look before Max Wedgins awards the bid," Scott said. "I know Challow's got a lot riding on this. So do I. If Pete Sherban is screwing

around, no pun intended, I think Wedgins has a right
to know."

Maggie stood up and extended her hand to Carl.
"I'm sure it's nothing, Carl. If you trust Pete, then
there must be a good reason."

Carl nodded. "Yeah."

Scott frowned. "All the same, you'll check it out?"

"I'll check it out."

Mark paced back and forth in the foyer of Ryan's
school. He rubbed at the tense muscles on the back of
his neck. Scott's plane had left at noon, and Annie had
returned to Dallas with him. Left alone, Mark's
thoughts had been plagued by unpleasant memories
of Pete and Irene, and even worse memories of Scott
and Maggie. His stomach was tied up in knots, and
his head hurt like hell.

To make matters worse, he still hadn't come up
with an effective way to communicate what he knew
about Pete Sherban and Irene Fussman. There was no
way he would tell Ryan, but still, Maggie needed to
know. What's more, Max Wedgins needed to know.

Mark dropped down on a concrete bench. He buried his head in his hands. Maggie had worked so hard
to make it on her own. He knew she was struggling
to make By Design a successful venture, but more
than that, he knew she was struggling to be her own
person. She had been twenty-one when they'd married. Fresh out of college, Maggie hadn't been entirely
sure what she wanted from life.

When she'd married him, she'd married his career.
Being a military wife was no easy task, and Mark had
often thought that as long as the Corps was handing
out medals, they ought to give them to people like

Maggie. The divorce rate among his fellow Marines was astronomically high, but Maggie had made their marriage work through sheer determination and commitment. In the weeks following his death, Mark had watched as Maggie struggled with the new reality of her life. He had never been more impressed than when she'd bundled Ryan into the car and headed for Massachusetts. That had taken more courage than he'd known she possessed.

Every time he watched her lay out a design, or make a proposal, or do something truly ingenius with a room, he felt a twinge of regret that her natural talent had been wasted during the years of their marriage. They had never stayed in one place long enough for Maggie to do more than dabble at her craft. Even then, Mark was forced to admit in hindsight, he hadn't taken her seriously. It hadn't been until he'd seen her on her own that he'd really recognized what a gift she had. Maggie had a way of making a room into a work of art.

And for the first time, Mark was beginning to understand that it wasn't just a hobby for her, or a way to earn a living. For Maggie, it was central to her understanding of herself. If she lost the Cape Hope project, she might be forced to close By Design. If there was one person on the face of the earth whom Mark knew well, it was Maggie. And in the pit of his stomach lurked the knowledge that Maggie would never be able to let go of the past if she didn't prove to herself that she was ready to face the future.

The clanging class bell interrupted his thoughts. Mark leaned against the wall as he watched children fill the corridors. He searched the crowd for a glimpse of Ryan. When he saw him, Ryan was edging his way through his classmates. He smiled brightly at Mark, and stopped to adjust the Batman backpack that was slung casually over his shoulder.

Mark watched his progress through the hallway with something akin to dread. Annie had been right. Maggie and Ryan weren't the only ones refusing to let go. He'd have to give up a lot to give Maggie and Ryan a chance for a future. He didn't know if he could make that choice.

Twelve

*M*aggie turned into the airport parking lot. She pulled into a space, then killed the ignition on the Bronco. "Well, here ya go."

Scott studied her. "You really didn't have to bring me all the way to the airport."

"I wanted to."

He tipped her chin up with his thumb. "What's the matter, Maggie?" She'd been out of sorts since they'd left Carl Fortwell's office that morning.

"Nothing. Just tired." Her smile was sheepish. "I guess I didn't get much sleep last night."

Scott shook his head. "That's not it. Something is wrong. I knew it when we left Carl's office. You just haven't been yourself."

Maggie hesitated before meeting his gaze. "What are we going to do?"

"About what?"

"About us."

"Oh. Us."

Maggie nodded. "Scott, I—"

He pressed his fingers against her mouth. "Maggie, listen to me. I never pretended to have the answers for everything. I'm not even sure I know what all the questions are. I just know that there's something about being with you that feels so right, so complete, that I just can't believe it isn't."

"I feel like I'm shredded up inside."

Scott pulled his gloves off so he could cradle her face in his hands. She looked sad, and vulnerable, and lovely, and he wanted to touch her more than he wanted to keep breathing. "I know this is hard for you. Hell, the timing couldn't be worse. Do you think I don't know what you're feeling right now? All I can think about is that one year ago today I was sitting at Annie's bedside waiting for her to die."

"Scott—"

"No. Listen to me. I know you didn't go through that. I know things were different for you. You weren't prepared, but damn, Maggie, it's time for you to say good-bye."

She enfolded his hands in hers and slowly lowered them from her face. "I'm sorry. Sometimes I forget that I'm not the only person in the world who has suffered through this."

Scott checked his watch. His flight was scheduled to leave in just under half an hour, but Maggie needed him more than he needed to be on that plane. "Who told you Mark had died?" he asked.

She looked at him in surprise. "What?"

"How did you find out?"

"His commanding officer called me. It's standard procedure."

"They didn't send someone by?"

"They did later. Colonel Drake wanted to tell me himself. He called from the base in Saudi Arabia."

"How long were you alone before someone came to be with you?"

"Not long. The colonel had already called the base to make sure an aide was on the way over."

"Was it someone you knew?"

She shook her head. "Not personally, no."

"So you got a phone call in the middle of the day—"

"Night," she said. "It was the middle of the night. Around two in the morning."

He had a sudden vision of Maggie sitting up in her bed, clutching the phone to her ear, weeping. "Oh, Maggie."

"Lieutenant Cross arrived about ten minutes after I got off the phone with the colonel."

"Did you know him?"

"Lieutenant *Marla* Cross. I knew of her. Everyone knew of her. She was the official Marine Corps comforter. You lived in fear of a visit from Marla Cross."

"And you didn't have any close friends, no family you could turn to?"

She looked away. "My parents died in a car accident when I was fourteen. Mark's mother abandoned him when he was five, and he grew up in a series of foster homes. Neither of us had close family, and as for friends, well, Mark's career moved us around a lot. We moved almost once a year, sometimes twice. After a while, it became too painful to make friends and leave them. I knew people, of course, but there was no one I was really close to."

Scott remembered the outpouring of support he'd had from his parents, his two brothers, his sister, and their families. He wasn't sure he could have survived the last three months of Annie's life without them. The thought of Maggie enduring the grief of Mark's death on her own made his heart break. "Maggie, I'm so sorry."

She didn't seem to hear him. She stared at the runway, watching as the planes taxied to the gates. "I didn't tell Ryan until the next morning. I couldn't."

Scott touched her shoulder. "You don't have to do this." God, the pain in her voice was a tangible thing to him. He could feel it vibrating through his bloodstream.

"In a way, I was almost glad that Ryan thought he could see Mark. It kept him from grieving the way I did."

"Maggie—"

"You know what the worst part was?"

He didn't want to know. If it got any worse, he was going to start weeping like a baby. He knew, could feel, the hurt in her. His own memories of that kind of pain were too fresh. He kept them carefully guarded in a locked room where they only occasionally escaped to haunt him.

Even in the brief time he'd been with Maggie, he'd recognized the threat she posed. With Maggie, the pain was always just beneath the surface, waiting to consume him, surging against the boundaries of its cell. And Maggie's quiet words were pounding furiously on the door.

The lines around her mouth, the slight stoop of her shoulders, won out over his urge to flee the car. He couldn't leave her alone to face her demons. Not again. "What was the worst part?" he asked. He wondered if his voice sounded raw to her.

"The worst part was when I saw his body."

"Maggie!" Scott was shocked. "Didn't you tell me he died in a helicopter crash?"

"Yes."

"Then why—"

"At first, Colonel Drake told me they weren't even sure he was dead. They didn't find his body among the wreckage. I spent four days thinking that by some miracle, he could be alive. Then the colonel called and told me they'd identified his body. He was"—her voice cracked—"he was so charred, they hadn't known at first."

Scott reached across the front seat to unbuckle Maggie's seat belt. He didn't wait for her permission to lift her onto his lap. He tucked her head against his shoulder and waited.

Maggie quivered. "They shipped the casket back on military aircraft. Five Marines died in the helicopter crash, including Mark, and I waited while they unloaded the coffins at the airstrip. I . . . I had to see him. I had to." She wiped at the tears that were now falling freely down her face. "Ryan was so sure, and I needed to know."

She wrapped her arms around his waist. She hugged him so tight, he was afraid he wouldn't be able to breathe. He rubbed his hand down her spine. "Just let it out, Maggie."

"It took me forever to get them to open the coffin for me. They didn't want to do it."

Scott privately thought that they shouldn't have done it. He knew what was coming, and the thought of it made sweat break out on his forehead. Maggie's voice broke on a sob. "Finally," she said, "the base's commanding general had to intervene. He agreed that I had a right to see the body. They took me into this little room, and one of the base doctors came in to talk to me. He tried to talk me out of it, but I needed to see him. I had to."

She tipped her head back and looked at Scott. "You understand that, don't you?"

"I know you felt like you needed to at the time."

"I still feel that way. I don't think I could have believed he was dead if I hadn't seen it."

He could feel the tension in her. He remembered the last days of Annie's life, when he'd sat by her bedside, torn between his need for her to keep on living and his desire to end her pain. For days, he'd prayed for each breath she drew. For days, he'd held her cold fingers and willed his life into her body. For days, he'd refused to sleep for fear that he'd miss her last few words, her last breath.

It had taken him months to tell anyone what those days had been like, months before he could bear to face the memories. Something told him that Maggie was facing her memories for the first time. "I know, sweetheart," he whispered. "I know."

She rubbed her face against his shirt. "So they opened it." Her shoulders jerked. "There was nothing, left, Scott. No skin, no features, just . . . just . . ."

"Maggie, don't."

"And he was still wearing his wedding band," she said, collapsing against his chest with a broken sob. "And all the time Ryan kept insisting he could talk to Mark, see him, all I could think of was how he looked lying in that coffin."

Scott felt his heart break in two. "Oh, Maggie."

She ignored him, feeling angry, deceived, cheated. Ryan had seen Mark lurking about in the corners of their home, of their lives, in the year since his death.

But Maggie had been forced to suffer alone. "Ryan kept telling me he was there with us, that he said he loved me and he was sorry. But was he there when I had to stand at the base by myself and wait for them to unload his coffin?" The tears were flowing freely now, and Maggie swiped at them. "Was he there when I looked at his remains?"

"It's all right, sweetheart." Scott hugged her closer. "Just tell me all of it."

"Where was he?" Her voice was hoarse and raw and she looked at Scott as the angry tears streamed down her face. In some corner of her mind, Maggie knew she wasn't being rational, but she couldn't control the surge of anger any more than she could stop the pain. The comfort of Scott's embrace, now, a year too late, had released a torrent of feeling she'd kept carefully guarded beneath the surface. "Why was he there for Ryan and not for me? Why?"

"I'm so sorry."

Scott's words drifted through her like a warm tropical breeze, soothing some of her ragged nerves, but her thoughts still lingered in that sterile office where she'd seen Mark's body. She had been unable to accept that he was really dead, unable to believe he wouldn't come back, unable to believe there hadn't been some horrible mistake.

Marla Cross had argued with her for nearly half an hour before Maggie had threatened to get a court order if necessary. Under strong protest, General Ted Easling had finally agreed to open the casket. Nothing had prepared her for the sight of the charred skeleton. She'd fainted immediately, and told no one afterward. She had been unable to bear the memory.

But now, she was angry that the hurt had been hers

alone to bear. She curled her fingers into a fist and pounded on Scott's chest. "Why did it have to be this way?"

"Shhh, Maggie. Just cry it out. All of it." He reached over and switched on the ignition. He adjusted the heat to take the chill off the air.

Maggie wept for twenty minutes. The windows had long since fogged over, and Scott cradled her on his lap, listening to the sounds of the heater fan and Maggie's muffled sobbing. When she seemed to calm some, he shifted her just enough to slip his hand into his back pocket and produce a handkerchief for her.

She accepted it with a slight hiccup. "Thank you."

Scott waited while she blew her nose. Her eyes were swollen and red, and he brushed her damp hair off her face. "Maggie, I'm so sorry."

She shook her head. "I think I needed that. I never told anyone before, not about the body I mean. I just"—her voice cracked on a sob—"I just kept it all inside of me."

Scott nodded. He pressed a kiss to her forehead. "I know."

She wiped at her eyes with the handkerchief. "I think I made you miss your plane."

"I decided to miss my plane. I don't want you to drive like this."

"I'll be all right," she said, all the while hoping he wouldn't leave. She wasn't ready to be alone again.

"The next flight out doesn't leave until five o'clock. I'll drive you home, and then catch a cab this afternoon."

"It's a whole hour back to Cape Hope."

He gave her a tender smile before shifting her onto the passenger seat. It took him a minute to adjust his long frame into the driver's side. "You're worth an hour, Maggie. You're worth at least an hour."

She leaned back in her seat with an exhausted sense of relief. She needed his tangible physical presence. "Thank you. I . . . I don't want to be alone."

Scott adjusted the heater to defrost before enfolding one of her hands in his. "You don't have to." He raised her gloved hand to his mouth and pressed a kiss on the back. "I'm right here."

Maggie's fingers trembled, and for the first time in nearly a year she felt like the future was not such a frightening thing after all.

From the corner of his eye, Scott studied Maggie as he turned into her driveway. After she'd guided him through the busy airport traffic and onto the main highway, she'd fallen asleep. He'd been relieved when she'd slept through the three times he'd been forced to stop and ask for directions. A man had his pride, after all. "Maggie." He touched her shoulder. "Honey, wake up."

Maggie's eyes drifted open. "Hmmm?"

"We're home."

Maggie blinked. "Home?"

"Your house. We're here."

She rubbed at her eyes. "Oh. I must have fallen asleep."

"Must have."

Maggie still looked disoriented. "What time is it?"

"Just after noon."

"Ryan will be home at two-thirty."

"Why don't you go inside and lie down? I'll wait for Ryan."

Maggie yawned. "Thank you."

Scott pressed a brief kiss to her forehead before opening his door. He rounded the Bronco to open the door for her. "You look a little groggy."

She shook her head. "I feel like my head is stuffed with cotton."

"I'm not surprised," he said. He draped an arm across her shoulders. "That's a lot of emotional stress for you to carry around on your own."

"Did you ever think of going into therapy?"

Scott laughed. "No. I just remembered everything my shrink told me, and then I turned it on you. You needed to cry, Maggie. You were waiting for it." He found the key for the front door on her key ring.

"In the first six weeks after Mark's death, all I did was cry."

"Not that kind of crying," he said, and swung the door open, "the angry kind." Scott let her precede him into the foyer. "You had a right to be angry, Maggie. It doesn't make you a bad person."

"It wasn't Mark's fault that he died. He wasn't trying to leave me alone."

"I know. It doesn't keep you from feeling betrayed, though, does it?"

She shook her head. "No."

Scott saw the fresh tears in her eyes. He caught one with his thumb. Maggie rubbed her face against his hand. "It's okay," he told her. "Everything is going to be okay."

"People used to tell me that all the time right after Mark died, and I never believed them."

"Are you believing it now?"

She hesitated. "I think I am."

There was surprise, even awe, in the words. Scott hugged her close. "Why don't you go upstairs and lie down? Do you want me to bring you some tea, or something?"

She shook her head. "No. I'm all right."

"Sure?"

"Sure." She wrapped her arms around his waist and gave him a tight squeeze. "Scott?"

"Hmmm?"

"Thank you. I'm always thanking you. For everything. You're too good to me."

"You're welcome, Maggie."

Mark narrowed his eyes as the long navy blue Mercedes Benz limousine glided to a stop in front of Ryan's elementary school. He put out his hand to Ryan. "Hold on a minute, Ry."

Ryan stared at the car. "Wow! Who's that?"

"I don't know." But he had his suspicions. Mark had convinced Ryan to call Carl Fortwell earlier that day. The call had been cryptic, as Ryan hadn't known any details, or even the reason for calling his teammate's grandfather. Using the excuse that he wanted to sell Carl a ticket to the father/son game, Ryan had managed to get past the receptionist.

Carl had been patient, benevolent, and Mark had helped Ryan deliver a carefully worded message that cast aspersions on Pete Sherban's objectivity. Ryan had been confused, but Mark felt the message had been adequately delivered.

By the time school let out that afternoon, Ryan seemed to have forgotten the odd conversation. He was telling Mark about his math quiz when the limousine had pulled into the school parking lot. The busses had already departed, and Ryan had just turned onto the path he used to walk home from school. Mark stopped him when he saw the car. He was almost certain it had something to do with Carl Fortwell. Besides, the limousine had silver flames painted on the side. It would take someone eccentric and rich to ride in a car like that. Someone like Maxwell Wedgins.

The rear passenger window slid down. A darkhaired stranger, clad all in black, smiled at Ryan. "Are you Ryan Connell?"

Ryan gave Mark an uncertain look. Mark nodded. "I'm not supposed to talk to strangers," Ryan told the man.

"An excellent rule," he answered. "Your mother probably told you that, and you should listen to her. It simply isn't safe."

Mark tensed. Ryan moved closer to him. "Don't be scared, Ryan," Mark said. "I won't let anything happen to you."

A young woman, blonde and curvaceous and so full of sex appeal that Mark wondered if it was legal for her to be walking the streets, slipped out of the driver's seat and rounded the car. She opened the door for the stranger. He unfolded his six-foot-plus frame from the car, sparing his chauffeur a slight smile. "Thank you, Bobbi. You may wait in the car."

She tipped her hat. "Sure, Max."

Max looked at Ryan. "Would you like something to drink, young man? I have milk, I have soda, I have juice. I've got quite a few other things, but I don't think you'd find them to your taste."

Ryan stared at him. "No?" Max said. "All right, then, that's all, Bobbi." The young woman winked at Ryan, then walked back around the car.

"Allow me to introduce myself," Max said, holding

out a gloved hand to Ryan. "My name is Maxwell Wedgins."

Ryan looked from Mark to the hand, back to Mark. Mark nodded. "It's OK, Ry. Shake his hand."

Ryan took it. "I'm Ryan."

"I'm delighted to meet you." Max indicated a concrete bench with his ebony walking stick. "Shall we sit down? I propose that you sit on one end of the bench, and I shall sit on the other. I'd suggest my car, as it's a good bit warmer, but I'm certain your mother would not approve."

Ryan shook his head. "She wouldn't. No way. She'd kill me if I got in that car."

Max's nod was short, an economy of motion. "Quite right. A smart woman, your mother. Shall we sit?"

Ryan moved to the bench. He sat on one corner and put his backpack between him and Max. Max smiled at him, then sat on the other side of the bench. "There. This is more comfortable, don't you think?"

"Who are you?" Ryan asked.

"I am a friend of Mr. Carl Fortwell's. I believe you spoke with him today?"

"Yeah."

"Mr. Fortwell repeated your concerns to me, and I felt it best for us to discuss the situation man to man." Max looked directly at Mark. "Although now I understand there is more than one party involved."

Mark stared at him. "Can you see me?"

"Of course," Max said.

"Wow!" Ryan looked at Mark. "He sees you, Dad. He really does." He turned back to Max. "No one else can see him except me. Oh, and Annie, but she's not real either."

Mark moved closer to Ryan, never taking his eyes off Max. "Why can you see me?"

Max held out his cane. He waved it through Mark's noncorporeal body. "Probably because I'm insane. I think one has to be very young or insane to believe in ghosts."

Ryan looked at Mark. "What's insane?"

"Crazy," Max answered. "Loony. Whacko."

Ryan's eyes widened. "He's nuts?"

"Completely," Max said.

"Wow!" Ryan turned back to Max. "This is so cool. I never met a crazy person before."

Max propped both hands on the silver head of his walking stick. "Now you have. I have it on very good authority that I am completely nuts."

"What do you want to talk to me for?"

Max looked at Mark. "I believe that your father has something to tell me. Something that is, perhaps, best told while you take a walk with Bobbi." He waited for Mark's confirming nod. Max smiled at Ryan. He pointed to a basketball hoop on the adjacent playground. "Perhaps you and Bobbi would like to play basketball while I speak with your father?"

"She's a girl," Ryan said.

"Nevertheless, I assure you she's quite competent. What good is a chauffeur who cannot beat you at a game of horse?" He looked at the car. "Bobbi?"

She rolled down the window. "Yeah, Max."

"My young friend would like to challenge you to a game of one on one. Bring your ball, would you?"

Bobbi slipped out of the car. She retrieved a basketball from the trunk of the limousine and bounced it twice on the pavement. Ryan's eyes widened. "Wow!"

Mark had to agree. "Wow" more or less summed it up. Max gave him a conspiratorial wink. "I may be crazy, Mr. Connell, but that doesn't have any effect on my eye for, well, shall we say, talent?"

Mark laughed. "No. I guess not." He motioned to Ryan. "It's okay, Ry. Why don't you go with Miss, er . . ."

"Just Bobbi," she said. "I don't like formalities."

Mark nodded. "Go with Bobbi. I'll be right here."

Ryan headed off across the frozen playground, chattering to his curvaceous new friend.

"Now," Max said. "What I heard from Carl Fortwell was that he'd been told twice in the past week that something was amiss between Pete Sherban and Irene Fussman. I believe Ryan's exact words were that Carl should see if Pete and Irene wished to attend the hockey game together as they are such good friends."

Mark felt sheepish. "Ryan wouldn't have understood the details, and I wasn't about to tell him. I knew Fortwell had to be told what was going on. I was hoping he would read between the lines of Ryan's invitation to the game. It would have been a lot easier if I'd just known I could tell you about it directly."

Max nodded. "Indubitably." He cast a quick look at Bobbi and Ryan. "Now that his tender ears are otherwise occupied, perhaps you'd like to tell me precisely what you think I should know."

Mark leaned back against the bench. "I'd love to."

Maggie started awake with a sudden sense of dread. Her eyes darted to the clock—3:16. "Scott?" He didn't answer. She felt disoriented, anxious. She couldn't put her finger on the source of her agitation, but she was certain something was wrong. "Scott?" she said, louder.

Maggie scrambled from the bed. She hadn't bothered to undress when they'd returned from the airport. "Scott, where are you?"

He strolled into her room carrying two mugs of coffee. "Right here. What's wrong?"

Maggie shook her head. "I don't know. Something is. Where's Ryan?" She rubbed her hands up and down her arms for warmth. "It's cold in here."

"He's not home from school yet."

Maggie froze. "What?"

"He's not home from school yet."

"It's after three o'clock."

Scott put the mugs down on the dresser. "I thought he usually got home at two-thirty, but I wasn't sure. I figured I'd wait another fifteen minutes before I woke you up."

"He should be here." She could hear the frantic edge in her own voice.

Scott crossed the room. He clasped her shoulders in his large hands. "Now, Maggie, don't panic. Does he always come home by two-thirty? Could he have stayed after for something? Hockey practice maybe."

She paused, then shook her head. "After-school practice is on Mondays. He should be here."

Scott reached for her discarded jacket. He tossed it to her. "Call the school and check. I'll go start the Bronco."

Maggie lunged for the phone. When a quick call to the school yielded no answer, she jammed her arms into her jacket, as she searched for her shoes. She was nearly in tears by the time she located her left sneaker under the bed.

"Come on, Maggie," Scott yelled from the bottom of the stairs. "Let's go."

She yanked on her gloves and raced down the stairs. "We'll start at the school," she told Scott. "He couldn't have gotten far. They'd have called me if he left early."

"I'm sure he just stayed after," Scott said. He pulled the door shut, then sprinted toward the Bronco. "He probably just forgot to tell you."

Maggie slid into the driver's seat. She jammed the car into reverse and started moving before Scott had his door shut. Her hands were shaking so much, she could hardly handle the steering wheel. Scott gave her leg a reassuring squeeze. "We'll find him, Maggie."

"We have to." She threw the transmission into drive and pressed her foot down on the accelerator. During the five-minute ride to Ryan's school, Maggie suffered the anxieties of hell. She never stopped praying. No sooner did they turn into the small parking lot than she saw the limousine.

Scott let out a shout and pointed to the playground. Ryan was just making a basket. "There he is."

Maggie roared to a stop at the edge of the playground. She threw the door open, then all but leapt from the car. "Ryan!" He waved at her. "Ryan!" Maggie took off running.

Scott's eyes traveled from Ryan to the limousine to the strange man seated on the concrete bench. Anger exploded in his gut. He stalked across the narrow expanse of the parking lot, never taking his eyes off the stranger. Vaguely, he heard Maggie sobbing, from the corner of his eye, saw her fall to her knees and pull Ryan into her arms. Scott's hands curled into fists. He stopped in front of the bench. "Who the hell do you think you are?" he demanded.

Max stood. "I assure you—"

"Oh boy," Mark said.

Scott slugged Max square on the jaw. Max's eyes registered his surprise. He rubbed his jaw. "I regret that I've caused you any anxiety."

"Anxiety?" Scott roared. "I ought to have you arrested."

"Oh boy," Mark said again.

Max held up his hand. "I assure you I meant the boy no harm. Allow me to introduce myself."

"What are you? Some kind of nut who gets his kicks out of terrorizing little boys?"

"Oh boy." Mark buried his face in his hands.

Maggie dragged Ryan up beside Scott. She'd stopped crying and started yelling. "Ryan, you scared us to death. I've told you a hundred times not to talk to strangers. Don't ever do anything like this again."

"But, Mom . . ." Tears were running down his face.

She gave his arm a shake. "Go get in the car."

"Mom—"

"Now, Ryan. We'll talk about it later."

Max gave Ryan a reassuring smile. "Don't worry. I think I can get you out of this."

Scott took a step forward. "You stay out of this."

Max held up his hands. "Now, now. Let's talk about this like adults."

"Mom . . ."

Maggie looked at Ryan. "Get in the car."

Ryan ran toward the Bronco. Scott took a deep breath. He fixed Max with a hard stare. "What the hell is going on?"

"Allow me to introduce myself." He extended his

hand. "I'm Maxwell Wedgins. I had some business to discuss with your son."

Maggie gasped. "Maxwell Wedgins. *You're* Max Wedgins?"

"I am."

"What are you doing with my son? What business do you have terrorizing my family?"

"I assure you I didn't mean to alarm you."

Maggie took a step forward. Scott grabbed her arm. She glared at Max. "You didn't mean to alarm me? You scared me to death. I thought he was lost, or, or worse. Do you know what it did to me when I pulled up here this afternoon and saw him talking to an absolute stranger?"

"I'm afraid I'm beginning to regret my lack of foresight," Max said. "Perhaps I should have contacted you first."

Maggie stared at him. Scott felt the tension begin to drain out of his body in the aftermath of the crisis. Unfortunately, Maggie was suffering no such effects. She was pulling at Scott's restraining hands, and looked for all the world as if she wanted to scratch Max's eyes out. Scott took a deep breath. "Look, Mr. Wedgins—"

"Max."

"Max. I don't know about your experience with children, or children's mothers, but the most powerful force on earth is a mother with an endangered cub. If you had something to discuss with Maggie, you should have called her."

Max gave Maggie a slight bow. "I assure you, Ms. Connell, I deeply regret any anxiety I have caused you, but my business was not with you. It was with Ryan."

Scott felt Maggie tense. He tightened his hold on her shoulders. "What's going on, Wedgins?" she said. "What kind of game are you playing?"

Max leaned on his walking stick. "I needed some information. Ryan was in a position to give it to me. Shall we say that I think it would be violating a gentlemen's agreement were I to relay that information to you."

Maggie sputtered. "A gentlemen's agreement? Have you lost your mind?"

"Absolutely. Haven't you heard?"

Scott looked at the benevolent expression on Max Wedgins's face and knew, somehow, that Ryan had not been in any danger. "In the future," he said, "you'd better make sure you conduct all your conversations with Ryan through Maggie. Do I make myself clear?"

"Completely. I regret any dismay I might have caused."

"Forget it," Scott mumbled.

Maggie stared at him. "I'm not going to forget it. Just because you want the Cape Hope project doesn't mean you have to—"

Scott clamped his fingers tighter on her shoulder. "Stop it, Maggie. It has nothing to do with that."

Max leaned forward. "I meant the boy no harm, Ms. Connell. There must be something I can do to ease your mind."

She turned an icy glare on him. "If Ryan says one thing to make me think that you hurt him, so help me, I'll kill you myself."

"And with good reason," Max said.

Maggie was shaking. Scott was still stinging from her remark about the bid process. He had an acute need to end the conversation and confront Maggie about the charge. "I think we're done. Let's go home, Maggie."

"I'm not done. I—"

"Now." He linked his fingers under her elbow and started toward the Bronco.

"Mr. Bishop," Max called.

Scott spared a glance over his shoulder. "What?"

"I understand you will be skating in the father/son game on Saturday. I wish you the best of luck."

Scott didn't bother to respond.

No one spoke on the short ride back to Maggie's house. Ryan sobbed softly in the backseat while Maggie drove. Scott could feel a slow-burning anger turning to a full-fledged fire in his gut. The more he thought about Maggie's accusation, the angrier he got.

Maggie let them into the house, dropped her keys on the hall table, then turned to Ryan. "Go upstairs, Ryan. I'll be up in a minute."

"But, Mom—"

"Now." Maggie gave him a meaningful glare.

Ryan trudged up the stairs. Scott gave him an encouraging wink, then looked at Maggie. "You were a bit hard on him, don't you think?"

She spun on her heel. "I don't think it's any of your business. He's not your son."

"No, he's not, but there wasn't any harm done, and I think you're coming down on him kind of harshly."

Maggie jerked off her gloves. "Like I said, I don't think it's any of your business."

Scott waited while she shucked her jacket. He felt the slow fury growing, spreading. Maggie looked at him. "Do you want to take your jacket off?" she asked.

Scott shook his head. "Not yet. I want to ask you something first."

"All right."

"Why did you say what you did to Max Wedgins?"

She frowned. "What did I say?"

"About the account. You said that I was brushing over the entire thing because I was worried about landing the account. I want to know why you said that."

"I didn't say that."

"Yes, you did."

Maggie shrugged. "Well, I didn't mean to. I was upset. I was angry. I was scared. If I said something like that, I just wasn't thinking."

"I think you meant it."

"What?"

"I don't think you would have said it if you didn't mean it."

"That's ridiculous. Of course I know you wouldn't do something like that."

"Do you?"

"You're really upset about this, aren't you?"

"Furious."

"Scott, I—"

He held up his hand. "No, Maggie. I have something I want to say. You seem to be having a lot of trouble dealing with our relationship." He noticed her slight wince. "Even the word makes you cringe."

"That's not true."

"Don't lie to yourself, at least."

"It isn't."

"Yeah, right. All I know is, first there was that scene

at Lily and Tom's, then there was the meeting in Pete Sherban's office when you were sure I was cozying up to Irene Fussman—"

"I never thought that."

He ignored her. "And then there was today. My God, Maggie. How could you stand there and accuse me of something like that? What kind of slimeball do you think I am?"

"I don't."

"You know what your problem is? You keep holding me up in comparison to Mark, and I keep falling short. If Mark had been there, he would have creamed the guy, contract or no? Isn't that right?"

"No, I—"

"Well, let me tell you something. Nobody wanted to cream Max Wedgins more than I did. What he did was horrendous, manipulative, hell, maybe even criminal, but I thought it was more important to get Ryan out of there without causing a scene than it was to vent my anger on Wedgins. So sue me."

"Scott, wait. You don't understand."

"I understand all right. I understand that you're scared to death of what's happening between us. I understand that you're terrified that you might actually feel something for me. So you're looking for any flaw you can find in order to keep me at arms' length. The hell of it is, Maggie, I've got plenty of flaws—you just keep finding ones that aren't there."

Maggie shook her head. "I just need time. I'm not trying to push you away."

"Aren't you?"

"No."

"Look. I'm going to get my bag out of your car and walk down the street to find a cab in to town."

"You don't have—"

"I think a long walk in the snow is just what I need about now. Then I'm going to get on a plane tomorrow morning and head back to Dallas. I'll be back on Wednesday. I want you to think real hard about us while I'm gone. I'm going to need some answers when I get back." He walked out the door without sparing her a second glance.

Maggie stared at the front door. She felt cold, bereft, and guilty. As much as she wanted to deny it, there had been truth in Scott's words. He did frighten her, or rather, her feelings for him frightened her.

After she'd told Scott about the days following Mark's death, Maggie had felt purged. Somehow, the telling of it had been as difficult as she'd thought it would be, but the aftermath had been a welcome relief from the oppressive memories. She had never felt closer, more intimate with anyone than she did with Scott Bishop. It had been almost like showing him her soul. When she'd shown him her wounds, he hadn't simply offered comfort. He'd grieved with her. She was certain of it.

She pictured his face, his kind eyes, the easy smile that curved his lips. When she'd fallen in love with Mark, it had been the forever kind of love. Now she felt torn, caught between her memories of the first man she'd ever loved and the very real presence of Scott Bishop in her life.

Maggie walked into the living room. She reached for Mark's picture on the mantel. She trailed a finger across his face. If only she felt like her attraction to Scott was based on more than just a need for his companionship. She had been so alone for so long, it was easy to simply accept what he offered and let it fill that need. But she couldn't. She needed to know that Maggie Connell was her own person apart from anyone and everything else. If she didn't, she'd never be sure she could do it.

When she'd lost Mark, it had been devastating and frightening. When the grief had ebbed, she'd been left with a panicky feeling that she couldn't survive apart from him. She couldn't put herself through that again. To love Scott Bishop, she first needed to believe in Maggie Connell.

Maggie plunked Mark's picture down on the mantel. To love Scott Bishop. Had she really thought the word? Cautiously, Maggie looked at the dark place in her heart where the grief of Mark's death, the fear, the feelings of betrayal and abandonment had once been. In their place, she was surprised to find warm memories of laughter-filled days and the promise of forgiveness.

Thirteen

*M*aggie knocked softly on the door to Ryan's room. She could hear him crying inside. "Ry? Can I come in?"

"Sure," came the muffled reply.

Maggie walked across the room to sit down on the side of Ryan's bed. He was curled up in a ball, clutching his teddy bear. Maggie tweaked the bear's nose. "Elvis looks like he can't breathe you're squeezing him so hard."

Ryan sniffled.

Maggie smoothed a lock of his hair off his flushed face. "I'm sorry I yelled at you, Ryan. I was scared."

He rolled onto his back, and met her gaze. "Why were you scared?"

"I didn't know where you were. I thought you might have been hurt, or lost, or in trouble. It scared me."

"Then why weren't you glad to see me?"

Maggie smiled. "I was. That's why I yelled."

Ryan frowned. "That doesn't make sense."

"I know. It's a mom thing. You know why I was upset don't you?"

221

"I shouldn't have talked to him."

"Honey, I know he seemed like a nice man. Maybe he is, but it's not safe for you to talk to strangers. Do you understand?"

Ryan paused. "But, Mom, Dad was there. That man could see him. He talked to him."

"Oh, Ryan."

"It's true."

"Honey, Daddy is not real. He's not here anymore."

"I know."

"But you can still talk to him."

Ryan nodded. He looked miserable. Maggie looked around the room. "You know what I think we need?"

"What?"

"We need something to liven up this house a little."

"What do you mean?"

"I think we need to decorate for Christmas."

Ryan's eyes widened. "You said we weren't going to decorate this year."

"So maybe I changed my mind."

Ryan propped Elvis Bear back against the pillow and sat up. "Can we get a tree and everything?"

Maggie hesitated. She didn't think she could handle a tree. "Why don't we do the other stuff today, then we'll worry about the tree."

"Can I put the candles in the windows?"

"Yes."

"Are you going to hang that stuff on the stairs?"

"It's called garland, and yes, I'll put it on the banister."

He beamed at her. His red-rimmed eyes were still puffy, and his face was still flushed, but otherwise, the sparkle was back. "Can we make a wreath out of pinecones and stuff? You know, like the one you did last year?"

Maggie nodded. "Yes. We'll go look for the pinecones now if you want to."

Ryan threw his arms around her neck. "I'm sorry about today, Mom."

Maggie hugged him close. She felt a wave of guilt that such simple pleasures would mean so much to him. It hadn't been fair to deprive Ryan of a normal Christmas just because she'd been wallowing in her own self-pity. "I know you are."

"I'll never talk to another stranger ever again."

Maggie smiled into his hair. "Better be careful how you make promises. They aren't always easy to keep."

He rubbed his face against her sweater. "Mom?"

"Hmmm?"

"Can we have pizza for dinner?"

Maggie laughed. She gave his hair a gentle tug. "Don't push your luck, sport."

They spent a pleasant two hours rummaging through boxes in the attic, pulling out the old Christmas decorations. By the time they had found the four boxes Maggie had stuck way in the back of the cramped crawl space, Ryan was covered in dirt. Maggie imagined she probably didn't look much better. "OK, Ry," she said, "let's take these downstairs and see what we've got."

Ryan struggled with one of the larger boxes. Maggie took it from him and pointed to another one. "That one's a little bit lighter. I think it has the garland in it. Can you get it?"

"Sure, Mom."

Maggie shoved the coffee table aside with her foot

and dropped the box in the center of the living room
floor. Ryan dumped his box on the couch. "Wow,"
he said. "This stuff is heavy."

"Yep." Maggie wiped her hands on her flannel
shirt. She was glad she'd changed out of her sweater.
Her shirt was already streaked with dust. "Dirty,
too."

Ryan nodded. He smeared the dirt on his hands
down the front of his sweatshirt. "Let's get the other
two boxes—"

He was interrupted by the ring of the doorbell.
Maggie sucked in a breath, dreading the thought that
Scott might have changed his mind and returned,
hoping that he had. "Will you get that, Ry? I'll go get
the other boxes."

"OK." He shot off toward the door. Maggie was
halfway up the stairs by the time she heard Edith Sophy talking to Ryan. She breathed a sigh of relief.
Edith would be much easier to face.

Maggie carried the last two boxes down from the
attic. She found Edith and Ryan seated on the sofa in
the living room. "Hi, Edith. What brings you here this
afternoon?"

Edith leapt up from the couch and took one of the
boxes from Maggie. "Here, let me help you with
that."

"Thanks." Maggie put the box on the floor. She
stacked the other on top. "What a job," she said, rubbing her dusty hands on the legs of her jeans. "I had
no idea things could get so dirty in the back of your
attic."

Edith laughed. "That's why I always make Roy dig
out the Christmas decorations. The dust makes me
sneeze."

Maggie dropped down on the couch. "Is there something I can do for you, Edith?"

"Well, I was hoping you'd let me borrow Ryan for a few hours."

Ryan hopped onto Maggie's lap. "Mrs. Soph is making cookies for the Church Bizarre—"

"It's a *ba-zaar*, Ryan, not a *bi-zarre*," Maggie said.

"Although," Edith quipped, "some of the things they sell might fall more easily into the latter category."

Maggie laughed. Ryan squirmed on her lap. "Anyway, she's making these cookies, and she says she needs a taster."

Maggie raised her eyebrows and looked at Edith. "A taster?"

Edith fussed with the hem of her skirt. "I'm making my usual four kinds of cookies, and I've tasted so much dough, I'm not sure what's what. I thought Ryan could be of some help to me."

"Edith—"

"Besides"—she waved a hand in Maggie's direction—"I was looking out my kitchen window a few hours or so ago, and it occurred to me that maybe you might have someplace you want to go this afternoon." She paused. "Alone."

Maggie saw the stern look in Edith's eyes and almost started to laugh. She had no doubt that Edith had seen Scott walk down the street and had been wracking her brains for an excuse to come over ever since. "Where would I possibly be wanting to go, Edith?"

"I don't know," Edith said, "but I'm sure you could think of something."

"Can I go with Mrs. Soph, Mom? We can finish the

decorating tonight. Maybe Scott'll come help."

"Yes," Edith said, "maybe he will."

Maggie shook her head. There didn't seem to be any sense in arguing the point. Besides, she couldn't deny she was relieved at the chance to go talk things over with Scott. No matter how much she'd tried to ignore the effect of his words, they continued to nag at her. "All right," she said, "but promise not to be a pest."

"I won't. I promise."

"And don't forget that you have hockey practice tonight."

"Seven o'clock," Ryan said.

"Should you get tied up with . . . things," Edith said, "Roy and I will be glad to see that he makes it to practice."

"Edith!"

Edith made a noise in the back of her throat that sounded suspiciously like a *hrumph.* "Just thought I'd give you the option." She stood up, holding out her hand to Ryan. "Come on, taster, you and I have work to do."

"Don't let him eat too much sugar," Maggie warned.

Edith took Ryan's hand, and led him to the door. "See that you accomplish something while we're gone," Edith shot back. "I'll worry about the sugar."

Maggie spent the next twenty minutes looking for her keys. She glanced at the hall clock on the way out. It was five-forty-five. There was no way she'd have time to talk to Scott and get Ryan to practice on time. She grabbed the phone and punched out Lily's telephone number.

"Hello."

"Lily, hi. It's Maggie."

"Oh, hey, Maggie."

"Listen, I need a favor."

"Does this have something to do with Scott Bishop?"

"Yeah."

"Well, sorry. I gave all my racy lingerie to Good Will last year."

"Shut up, Lily. That's not what I meant."

"Damn."

Maggie ignored her. "I need you to give Ryan a ride home from hockey tonight."

"Oh really?" Lily said.

Maggie wondered how two words could sound so suggestive. "Yes, really. If you don't mind, could you take him to your house and I'll pick him up there?"

"Should I plan on his spending the night?"

"No."

"Maggie—"

Maggie laughed. "Quit being so pushy, Lily. I just need you to help me out."

"Okay, but it's not a problem if he needs to spend the night. All right?"

"All right."

"Good luck, Maggie."

"Thanks. I think I need it."

Maggie hung up the receiver and reached for her coat. She had no idea what kind of mood Scott would be in. He might be mad as a wet hen. She pulled open the front door and shivered. Make that a cold, wet hen. The temperature had dropped again, and his long walk wasn't likely to have put him in a very good temper.

She remembered his deplorable sense of direction

and had a sudden mental image of Scott wading through thigh-deep snow drifts halfway to Connecticut. Maggie pulled the door shut and sprinted for the Bronco. He probably wanted to wring her neck.

Scott wanted to kill her. He pushed through the revolving door of his hotel. His fingers were frozen, his feet stung, and his stomach was growling. The only thing warm was his temper. It didn't help any that Maggie was sitting in the lobby of his hotel, sipping on a cup of hot chocolate, watching him through half-lidded eyes that looked sexy as hell.

"Hi," she said.

He dropped his suitcase on the floor in front of her. Clumps of snow fell to the carpet. "What are you doing here?"

"Waiting for you."

"How long have you been here?"

"Just a few minutes." She wet her lips with the tip of her tongue. Scott's gaze riveted on the tiny motion. "What took you so long?" Maggie asked. "Did you get lost?"

"Yes," he bit out. "I got lost. Satisfied?"

Maggie shook her head as she reached for his suitcase. "Far from it. I—I'm sorry." She picked up his suitcase and started toward the elevator. "You'd better get out of those wet clothes." She dangled a key in front of him. "I took the liberty of checking you back in."

Despite himself, Scott smiled. "Are you trying to proposition me?"

He'd expected her to blush. She didn't. She shot him a sultry glance over her shoulder. "Do you think so?" she asked.

Scott raised his eyebrows, but followed her to the elevator. Maggie punched the button. Scott noticed the way her hand trembled. "So," she said, "what time's your flight tomorrow?"

"Ten. Why?"

"That should give me enough time."

His heart missed a beat. "Enough time for what?"

Maggie met his gaze. His temper cooled at the same instant his body thawed. "To apologize."

"Maggie—"

She shook her head. "I think you should change into something warm first. This could take a while, and I don't want to be responsible for giving you pneumonia."

A fever would be more likely, Scott thought. She looked so incredibly rumpled, and touchable. There was a smudge of dirt on her cheek, her hair was untidy, and he had an almost uncontrollable urge to bury his fingers in it. He forced himself to remember why he'd been angry. It served to cool his ardor a bit, but did nothing for the swelling sense of elation he felt that Maggie was standing in the elevator, staring at him. "I'm glad you came, Maggie." He took his suitcase from her.

She sighed. The elevator door slid open on the fourth floor. "Me too." She led the way to his room.

Maggie unlocked the door, then preceded him into the dim room. She stopped in the center, and faced him. "Look, I—well, why don't you go ahead and change. I'll order some hot chocolate from room service, and then we'll talk."

"Do you mind if I take a shower?"

"A shower?" Maggie's voice cracked.

Scott felt a surge of adrenaline. His ego soared at

the notion that Maggie was disturbed by the thought of him in the shower. He indicated his wet overcoat. "To warm up," he said.

"Oh. Yeah, sure. You take a shower. I'll call room service."

He dropped his suitcase on the bed. From the corner of his eye, he saw Maggie flinch at the sound of the zipper. Scott pulled out his shaving kit and bathrobe before he headed for the bathroom. "Make yourself at home," he said. "Why don't you order us some dinner to go with that hot chocolate? I'm kind of hungry." He shut the bathroom door, then leaned back against it. Kind of hungry. He was kind of hungry, all right. It had taken every ounce of willpower he possessed to keep from tossing Maggie on the bed. What in the hell was the matter with him?

He turned the shower on, hesitated, then turned the knob to cold. He didn't need any more warming up.

Ten minutes later, Scott walked out of the bathroom, toweling his hair. Maggie was sitting in one of the pale green chairs, clutching a mug in her hands. "Better?" she asked.

She'd shed her jacket. The flannel shirt she wore did nothing to disguise the allure of feminine curves underneath. His body tightened. "Sure."

Maggie reached for one of the mugs. "Can I pour you some hot chocolate?"

Scott dropped the towel on the bed. He reached into his suitcase for a pair of jeans, briefs, and a sweatshirt. If he walked around in his flannel bathrobe, he was going to embarrass himself. "Uh, let me just put these on. I'll be right back." He fled into the bathroom. The cold shower had done nothing to ease the effect Maggie was having on him.

Scott stared at himself in the mirror. In the two hours plus it had taken him to get from Maggie's house to his hotel, he'd done nothing but think about Maggie. It was the first time since Annie's death he could remember being able to concentrate on something for that long without the thought of her intruding into his consciousness. He had just come to the startling realization that he couldn't conjure up a clear mental picture of her in his head, when he'd entered the hotel lobby and found Maggie waiting for him.

The effect had been devastating. His senses were still reeling. Surely that was the reason he was having so much trouble getting a grip on himself.

Scott took a deep breath and jerked the sweatshirt over his head. Maggie wasn't ready for a physical relationship with him. Of that he was certain. She wasn't the kind of woman who entered into something like that without an enormously strong emotional bond to precede it. He liked that about her—really, really liked it.

He pulled on his briefs, wincing slightly at the rigid ache in his groin. Maggie wanted to talk, he reminded himself. He pulled on his jeans with unnecessary force. And it was going to be one hell of a long evening if he didn't get his mind off her soft curves and warm body, and find a way to concentrate on what she had to say.

He pulled open the door of the bathroom. Maggie smiled at him. One hell of a long evening.

She handed him a mug of hot chocolate. "Here you go. Mom's surefire remedy for fighting chill."

Like he needed one, he thought. "Thanks." Scott sat down on the bed. "Did you order anything for dinner?"

Maggie shifted in her chair. She tossed him a plum off the food tray. "I thought maybe you'd want to hear what I have to say first. Then if you still want to eat with me, I'll take you dinner." She picked up the other plum and took a bite.

Scott watched as her teeth sank into the firm fruit. He swallowed, suddenly glad she hadn't ordered room service. He wasn't sure he could stay in this room with her much longer and remain sane. A trickle of juice ran down her chin. Maggie swiped at it with her sleeve. Scott took a long, fortifying sip of his hot chocolate. "So what do you want to talk about, Maggie?" he asked, hoping it wouldn't take long, and he could have her seated in a restaurant in less than the twenty minutes he figured he had left.

She swallowed a bite of the plum. "I think I'd better say this before I lose my nerve. So just let me get it out, and then you can start arguing. Okay?"

Scott rubbed his thumb across the surface of his plum. It was soft and cool and felt just like her flesh did under his fingers. He wondered if she'd taste like plum juice if he kissed her. "Okay."

Maggie put her half-eaten fruit down on the tray. "You were right. I mean, some of the things you said. You were right. I have been trying to hold you off, and I'm not sure what I want." She stood, and walked to the window. "Before—before I met you, I knew what I wanted. I wanted to make By Design a healthy business, and I wanted it to be enough to fill up the emptiness. I wanted to believe that Ryan and I could just go on with our lives and never have to face the reality of Mark's death. It was so easy to just pretend he was on a duty assignment. It was so easy to push the grief aside, to believe that he was coming back."

Scott studied her from behind. Her shoulders were tense. Her back straight. He could tell she was struggling. "You can't ignore it forever, Maggie."

She didn't seem to hear him. "Then there was you, and I couldn't pretend anymore. If Mark were still a part of my life, you wouldn't be, and if you are, he can't be." She spun around. "I know this doesn't make any sense. I'm not even sure I understand it, but, well, when you left today, it scared me, Scott. It really, really scared me."

Scott tossed his plum into the trash can. He crossed the room to pull Maggie into his arms. "We're quite a pair you and I."

"What do you mean?"

"I was mad as a hornet this afternoon. It hurt like you wouldn't believe to think that you were pushing me away the whole time I was trying to get close to you."

"I didn't mean to."

"I know." He rubbed his hands down her spine. It felt good, so damned good. "Maggie, I know you're hurting. I have hurts, too. There are days when I miss Annie so much, I feel like I can't breathe." He paused. Maggie wrapped her arms around his waist. Scott continued to rub his hand down her back in soothing strokes. "But she's gone, and I'm not, and life goes on. I also have needs. Man/woman kinds of needs."

"I know."

Scott's hand stilled. "You know?"

Maggie tipped her head back. "I know."

His hand trembled. "Maggie—"

She covered his mouth with her hands. "Shut up and kiss me, Scott. I've been waiting forever."

He pushed her hand away, and groaned. "Lord,

Maggie." He pressed his lips to hers in a hot kiss, full of hunger and desperation.

Maggie clung to him. She twined her hands into his hair, as she leaned into his body. Through her flannel shirt, Scott could feel her soft breasts crushed against his chest. He shifted slightly, cupping her bottom to bring her more fully against him. Maggie moaned.

The sound ignited a fire in his belly that made his hands tremble. He felt like the top of his head was lifting away from his body. He could feel the heat spreading from his groin, shooting sparks through his blood until his pulse pounded. He turned a half-step to topple their linked bodies onto the bed. She squirmed beneath him. An inner voice warned him that they were fast approaching the point of no return. "Maggie?" His voice was a hollow rasp. "Maggie, honey, we have to stop."

She slid her hands under his sweatshirt. "Don't stop. Please, Scott, don't stop."

Her fingernails scored along his chest. His flesh jumped at the feather-light touch. "Maggie," he groaned her name, and captured her lips again, promising himself he would stop after just one more kiss. Her mouth was warm and wet, and she sucked his tongue between her teeth to give him a soft, playful nip. The pressure in his jeans increased tenfold. He shuddered.

Maggie wrapped her leg around one of his, bringing her pelvis into tantalizing alignment with his groin. He sucked in a sharp breath. She rubbed her lips against his, pushed into him, sucked at him. He felt his control slipping away.

"Touch me," Maggie begged. "Please touch me."

Scott's body was shaking so hard, he was surprised

the bed frame didn't rattle. He had to stop. She was vulnerable. He was vulnerable. They'd regret it. Maggie started to unbutton her shirt. His mouth went dry. "Please touch me," she said.

Scott couldn't tear his gaze away from the soft strip of flesh she was slowly, ever so slowly, exposing to him. Three buttons. Four. Somewhere in his brain it registered that she wasn't wearing a bra. Maggie tugged the shirt free from the waistband of her jeans. It gaped open. Scott stared. "Maggie." His voice was barely above a whisper.

"Touch me," she pleaded.

With trembling fingers, he pushed aside the edges of her shirt. Her soft breasts spilled into his waiting palms. He flexed his fingers, and her nipples peaked against his hands. "You're so soft," he whispered. "So soft."

Maggie arched her back. Scott buried his lips in the heated cleft between her breasts. Maggie moaned. Her fingers twined in his hair, and she pressed him closer. Scott couldn't resist the urge to taste her, to feel her. He moved his lips over the generous curve of her breast until he found the turgid peak. Maggie squirmed beneath him.

He felt the heat of her through the straining fabric of his jeans. When he started to suck on her nipple, Maggie's hips bucked. Scott's breath was coming in ragged gasps. He licked and sucked at her breast. When she pulled at his sweatshirt, he lifted his head long enough for her to jerk it free. Maggie curled her fingers into the crisp hair on his chest, giving it a sharp tug.

Scott moved to her other breast, where he lavished the same generous attention on her tight nipple. Maggie's hands flew across his chest in erratic butterfly-light caresses. She shifted beneath him until his thigh was wedged between both of hers. Scott was so absorbed in the intoxicating taste of her, he didn't even realize she was pushing against his leg until her body went taut beneath him. Her hands clutched at his shoulders, and he raised his head, stunned, when he felt her jerk beneath him. Her face, flushed with passion, her eyes clenched tight, was a mask of pleasure so intense, so beautiful, his breath deserted him.

Maggie arched against him and shouted his name as her whole body convulsed in a shuddering climax. Scott stared at her. She sagged back against the pillows. "You're so beautiful," he whispered, ignoring the persistent throbbing ache in his groin. He had never in his life experienced anything quite so satisfying as the sight of Maggie going up in flames. It didn't even matter that he was still hard. He had never been this fulfilled.

Her eyes drifted open. She turned her face away. "I'm sorry."

Scott reached for her chin. He forced her gaze back to his. "You're sorry? Lord, Maggie, I've never experienced anything like that in my life."

She frowned. "But you didn't, I mean . . ."

He shook his head. "It doesn't matter. Sometimes there's as much joy in giving."

She shivered and reached for the edges of her shirt. "I'm embarrassed."

"Don't be. Please don't be." He brushed her hands aside and started doing up the buttons of her shirt. "I kept telling myself you weren't ready. I knew you wanted to wait. I knew you were feeling vulnerable. I shouldn't have pushed you."

"You didn't push. I had to do all the pushing, and then you didn't even—" She broke off the sentence. Her face turned crimson.

Scott pressed a soft kiss to her lips. "No, I didn't, but watching you, I damned near did."

"Scott!"

"You are one hell of a lady, Maggie, and if you'd given me about ten more seconds, I'd have exploded right along with you."

Her eyes widened. "Are you serious?"

Scott moved his still-hardened groin against her thigh. "Do you doubt it?"

"Then why—"

He kissed her again, a long, leisurely kiss. When he raised his head, Maggie's eyes were shut. He pressed a brief kiss to each eyelid. "I wanted to watch you soar, Maggie. I wanted to know I could help you get there." She opened her eyes. He saw the tears in them. "Please don't cry. It rips me apart when you cry."

"I'm not crying."

Scott rubbed his thumb along her eyelid. He showed her the drop of moisture. "What's this?"

"That's not really crying," she said. "Not sad crying." She wrapped her arms around him and hugged him close. "I'm just really glad you're here, and I'm here, and we're here together."

He lay with her for a while, savoring the feel of her warm body pressed against his. But he could already feel the passion building again, and he was unwilling to take advantage of Maggie's vulnerability. Reluctantly, he rolled away. "I think I need another shower."

Maggie laid a hand on his back. "Scott?"

He shook his head. "It will be better for both of us

if I just take the shower, Maggie. Trust me." He shot
her a sheepish grin. "Where's Ryan, by the way?"

She checked the clock on the bedside table. "He's
at hockey practice. Lily and Tom said they'd take him
to their house afterward. I'm not in any hurry."

Scott swung his legs over the side of the bed. "How
about if I take a shower, and you make reservations
for us for dinner somewhere?" He pressed his hand
around the nape of her neck and pulled her forward
for a hard kiss. "Somewhere public and noisy and
bright."

"Like the bowling alley?"

"That's not such a bad idea."

Fourteen

*I*n the days that followed, Scott was given a lot of time to think about his relationship with Maggie. He had returned to Dallas, where he'd tried to settle back into his comfortable routine. Nothing had been able to take his mind off Maggie. Not the strenuous days he spent at the office. Not the two hours each afternoon he spent at the Galleria trying to learn how to ice-skate. Not even the long hours of soul-searching he spent in the living room of his apartment.

After Annie's death, he'd sold their house. In the year following their marriage, he had designed and supervised the construction of the large home with an eye toward the future. Annie had wanted several children, at least four. Scott had found an unparalleled joy in designing the spacious home for his wife and anticipated children.

When Annie died, the memories had been too difficult, too cloying, too persistent. He could no longer stand to walk by the empty playroom, to stand in the solarium and picture Annie curled up in the sun-drenched rocker with a novel on her lap. So he'd sold the house and moved into an apartment in town.

There had been very few pieces of furniture he'd taken with him. A chair, a sofa, the bed, an antique dresser had been the only pieces he'd moved. The rest had been sold with the house, and he'd purchased what odds and ends he did need at inexpensive department stores.

Normally, it didn't bother him. He spent little time in the apartment. He generally slept, showered, and dressed there, before spending the rest of his days at his office. Things were different since Maggie.

Thoughts of her absorbed him, kept him from sleeping. He'd sit in the overstuffed chair in his den and stare out at the stars. He had long since admitted that he was in love with her. It had been easier to accept that than to pretend otherwise. But loving Maggie was a complicated business. The first time he'd fallen in love, it had been an easy thing. He'd wanted to marry Annie, she'd wanted to marry him, he'd placed a ring on her finger, and she'd said yes. Three months later, they were husband and wife. Neither of them had ever considered risks, or dangers, or even the possibility of sorrow in their future. Everything had seemed golden and fated and right.

But loving Maggie, well, there was nothing easy about it. When Annie had died, Scott had known he could never love anyone the way he'd loved her. A person didn't simply grow a new heart when the old one got broken. In a way he'd been right. He didn't love Maggie the way he'd loved Annie. With Annie, it had been a young love, pure and uncomplicated. With Maggie, it was consuming. He desired her physically as much as he desired her spiritually.

The thought of it made him break out in a cold

sweat. How could he risk that much? How could he make himself that vulnerable?

They had talked long into the night the day before he'd returned to Dallas. When he'd boarded the plane the following day, he'd known they couldn't wait much longer to make a decision about their relationship. He'd already invested too much of himself. There was too much at stake.

He'd pulled Maggie to him for a kiss drenched in longing and uncertainty, then met her gaze. "Maggie," he'd said, "when I get back from Dallas, we need to settle some things."

"I know."

"Will you promise to think about us while I'm gone?"

Her smile was sheepish. "I doubt I'll be able to think about much else."

Scott rubbed his thumb over the curve of her upper lip. "It doesn't matter to me anymore that I haven't known you very long."

"Me either," she confessed.

The boarding call for his flight sounded over the airport intercom. Scott lingered a few seconds more.

"We'd better say good-bye," Maggie said. "You're going to miss your flight."

He shook his head. "I told you I don't like good-byes." He gave her another brief kiss. "I'll see you Wednesday?"

Maggie had nodded. "I'll be waiting."

By the time Scott stepped off the plane on Wednesday afternoon, he'd replayed the scene in his mind a dozen times. He'd known Maggie was feeling vulnerable that day, and he wasn't sure what to expect now that he would be seeing her again.

At some time during the last evening they'd spent together, he'd reluctantly agreed not to call her while he was in Dallas. Maggie had wanted time and distance to sort things out in her mind. It went against his better judgment to give her time to brood, but Maggie had been insistent. He hadn't wasted the five days of separation, though. He'd decided that if he couldn't control the way he felt about Maggie, he could at least control what happened to their relationship.

Whether she admitted it or not, he was competing with Mark for Maggie's heart. In his mind, he settled on a plan. He couldn't be Mark Connell, it was true. No one would ever be Mark Connell to Maggie, but then, Mark Connell couldn't be Scott Bishop, either. And that wasn't such a bad thing.

His mind made up, Scott headed back to Cape Hope ready to do battle if necessary. He wasn't going to let Maggie push him away. He wasn't going to let her hide behind the shadow of her dead husband. He wasn't going to let her deny what he knew she felt. He half feared she wouldn't be at the airport to meet him.

He nearly sagged with relief when he saw her standing toward the back of the waiting area. She waved at him over the crowd. Scott shouldered his way through the passengers toward Maggie. He dropped his suitcase in front of her, then held out the lapels of his coat. Maggie walked right into his arms. Scott felt a surge of adrenaline so intense that the blood started to pound in his ears. "I'm really glad you're here, Maggie."

"I told you I would be."

He hugged her close. "I know."

Maggie looked at him curiously. "Are you all right?"

"I'm all right. It's just been a really long time since I've seen you."

She raised her eyebrows. "It was just Saturday, Scott."

"It seemed longer." He picked up his suitcase, then draped an arm over her shoulders. "Where did you park?"

"Short-term lot." Maggie paused. "You're sure you're all right?"

Scott smiled at her. "Maggie, I think I decided while I was in Dallas that I could be anywhere with you and be all right."

"Scott . . ."

He kissed her. "We'll talk about it in the car. Okay?"

Maggie paused, then nodded. "Okay."

She had to steer him toward the door when he got disoriented in the airport. He told her about the meetings he'd conducted his last two days in the office, and Maggie listened, wondering all the while what had brought on his strange mood. No sooner were they settled in her Bronco than Scott pulled her across the console for a hungry, illicit kiss. She was breathless by the time he lifted his head.

"There," he said, "that's a proper hello kiss. I didn't think you'd appreciate it if I did that in the airport."

Maggie moved back into the driver's seat. Her skin was flushed. She could feel it. She fumbled for a minute with the keys. "I hope you didn't forget that Ryan has hockey practice tonight. We won't have much time together."

Scott grabbed her hand. He linked his fingers

through hers and propped their joined hands on his thigh. "We have the trip to the rink, and the hockey practice, and the rest of the week. I'm not going back to Dallas until Sunday."

"Alone," she said. "I meant we wouldn't have much time alone."

Scott raised her hand to rub his lips over her knuckles. "We'll make time."

Maggie stared at him. "You're acting very strange."

"I made some decisions while I was in Dallas."

She wasn't sure she liked the sound of that. "What kind of decisions?"

He shifted in his seat so that he was facing her. "Decisions about you and me. Decisions about what we're going to do."

Maggie felt a brief surge of panic. "Don't you think you should have consulted me?"

"No. These were my decisions to make. You have to make a few of your own, and then we'll make some together."

"I don't think I like the sound of this."

"You will, Maggie." He closed his eyes, then leaned back in his seat. "I haven't felt this good in months."

Maggie decided she wouldn't question his strange mood. Particularly since she wasn't entirely sure she wanted to know what had caused it. Instead, she turned onto the interstate and concentrated on the traffic. Scott seemed to have dropped into a light doze. He hadn't spoken since they'd left the airport. His fingers had loosened on hers, and from the corner of her eye, she could see the relaxed calm of his face.

By the time she reached the Cape Hope exit, her stomach was twisted into knots. She was so tense, she nearly jumped through her skin when an ambulance siren sounded behind her. Maggie guided the Bronco to the shoulder and waited for the emergency vehicle to pass. Only then did she realize that Scott was looking at her.

She reluctantly met his gaze. "Hi."

"Hi. Was I sleeping?"

"I think so. You must have been tired after your flight."

He shrugged. "I guess I was. I didn't mean to flake out on you. I just haven't slept much in the past few days."

"Why not?" she asked, before she thought better of it.

"I was thinking of you."

Maggie took a deep breath. "Oh?"

"Yeah. You were supposed to be thinking about me. Were you?"

She hesitated. She had thought about him and little else during the past five days. Scott affected her in a way Mark never had. It scared her to death. "Yes."

"Reach any decisions?"

"Look, Scott, I don't think—"

He squeezed her hand. "Maggie, this isn't going away."

"I know."

"But you want it to?"

She turned into the parking lot of the ice arena. "No," she admitted. She found a parking space. She killed the ignition before she faced him. "I don't want it to go away. I'm just anxious, I guess, and kind of scared."

"I'm scared, too."

Her eyes widened. "You are?"

"Sure. What I'm feeling for you is some pretty powerful stuff. Forever kind of stuff."

"Scott—"

He held up his hand. "No wait. I know this isn't the best time. We've got Ryan's practice." He looked around the parking lot. "This isn't exactly the most romantic setting in the world, either, but I'm afraid I won't get this said if I don't say it now." He tucked a lock of her hair behind her ear. "You're a little off-balance right now, Maggie, and that's the only way I think I'll ever get you to sit still through this."

Maggie reached for the door handle. "I think we should go inside."

"Maggie," he said, and caught her face between his hands. "What are you afraid of?"

Of loving you. Of losing myself again. Of risking everything and getting hurt the same way I did last time. "I'm not afraid. I just want to see Ryan's practice."

Scott shook his head. "You're shaking like a leaf." He touched his lips to hers in a soft kiss. When he lifted his head, his eyes were a warm, honey-colored hazel. "I love you, Maggie."

How could one simple phrase have such a devastating effect? In the five days since he'd left Cape Hope, Maggie had struggled with her feelings for him. She'd tried, almost succeeded actually, to convince herself it was nothing more than a perfectly normal physical attraction. She was a healthy young woman, after all, and she hadn't been with a man since Mark's death.

But it hadn't worked. She couldn't put aside that, despite the fireworks that went off when Scott touched her, there was something else. Something deeper. Something scary. Something that felt a lot like being absorbed into another person. "I don't think we should talk about this right now," she said.

He shrugged. "OK."

Maggie stared at him. "OK?"

Scott smiled. "There's nothing to talk about. I love you. It's what I've got to work with. I'll admit it's not simple, and it sure as hell isn't easy, but it's all I've got, and I'm through trying to pretend it doesn't exist."

"But Annie . . ."

"I loved Annie. I loved Annie more than I thought it was possible to love anyone, but what I felt for Annie has nothing to do with what I feel for you."

"Scott—"

"I thought you didn't want to talk about this right now."

Maggie wavered on indecision. What was she supposed to say? That she was afraid of him? That she was afraid to let him love her? That she was afraid of the powerful effect it had on her to know that he did? "I don't."

Scott reached past her to push open her door. "Then let's go watch the practice."

Maggie was edgy and disconcerted during the long practice. It didn't help matters any that Lily plopped down next to Scott and started grilling him for information. He seemed relaxed, comfortable, totally at his ease. It didn't seem to bother him at all that he'd just said life-changing stuff to her in the parking lot of the ice rink.

"What about you, Maggie?" she heard Lily ask.

She jumped. "What about me?" she asked. She heard the defensive note in her voice.

Lily's eyebrows lifted a fraction. "I was just asking Scott if he's heard anything about the Cape Hope project."

"I said I hadn't," Scott said.

Maggie sagged in relief. "Oh. Neither have I."

"Weren't you supposed to know something by now?" Lily asked.

"A couple more days, I think," Scott said. He moved his hand from the back of the seat to Maggie's shoulder, where he drew slow, mesmerizing circles against the side of her neck. "Wedgins was supposed to make a preliminary decision first, then ask for changes."

Lily continued to study Maggie. "Did Ryan ever tell you what Wedgins wanted to talk to him about?"

Maggie shook her head. She tried to shift away from Scott's hand, but he countered by moving it to her rib cage. "No. I didn't see the point in pressing him. Ryan seemed to be all right with it, so I let it drop."

"I don't know, Maggie," Lily said. "That situation is really weird."

"I know, but then again, Wedgins is weird. The guy is totally unpredictable. If this weren't such a big job, I doubt many of the bidders would have tolerated such an unorthodox procedure."

"Maggie's right," Scott said. "Wedgins wouldn't be able to pull so many chains if this weren't a multimillion-dollar project."

"Well," Lily said, leaning back in her seat, "I certainly hope he makes a decision soon. We'd love to have you move to Cape Hope, Scott."

Scott pinned Maggie's gaze with his own. "I'd love to move here."

Maggie frowned at him, and whispered, "Stop that," under her breath.

"Stop what?" he asked, his gaze wide-eyed, innocent.

"Stop baiting me in front of Lily."

He rubbed the back of his hand over the outer curve of her breast. Maggie jumped. "Give me a chance, and I'll bait you in private."

Maggie stood up so abruptly, her purse tumbled to the floor. "I have to go to the ladies' room. I'll be right back."

Scott's gaze was knowing. It annoyed her. "I'll be here when you get back," he said.

It sounded more like a threat than a promise. "Fine." She turned and fled the bleachers. Once she reached the dingy bathroom, Maggie sagged back against the wall. "Get a grip," she mumbled.

She moved to the sink and splashed water on her face. What in the world was wrong with her? There was no reason on earth why she should be reacting this way just because Scott Bishop had said he loved her. She looked at her reflection in the mirror. Except that her heart had stopped beating when he'd said it, and she'd immediately tried to summon a clear picture of Mark in her mind.

She hadn't been able to do it. She could see his eyes, clear and blue and full of laughter, but she couldn't bring his face into focus. It was almost as if she was losing him, and with him, herself. In the wake of that realization had come a flood of guilt so overwhelming, she'd nearly stopped breathing.

She had to be out of her mind. It was the only possible explanation. Why on earth should she have such a profound sense of rightness when she was with Scott, only to be followed by an equally devastating sense of sorrow? It was almost as if a part of Mark still existed, as if he were there, watching.

Maggie shivered. That was ridiculous. She didn't believe in ghosts. She'd been listening to too many of Ryan's stories. Mark was dead. She studied her reflection in the mirror. "He's dead," she said out loud, as if to give the words added weight. "He's not here, and he's not trying to keep you from doing what's right for your life."

But in truth, she didn't quite believe it.

Mark paced up and down the ice, oblivious to the small bodies that skated through his elusive figure. "All right," he told Annie. "He's in love with her. He's ready. So what do we do now?"

"Mark," Annie said, trying to gauge his mood, "I don't think we can rush this."

"Rush it?" he said. "What's there to rush? She goes up in flames every time he touches her."

She sighed in exasperation. "There's a lot more to this than just a physical attraction."

"Yeah, right."

She glared at him. "Men are so dense."

Mark stopped pacing to spare her a withering glance. "Don't even think about starting one of these women-are-emotionally-superior-to-men things."

"Well, they are."

"Damn it, Annie—"

"All right. All right. Let's think this through. You've been with Maggie while I was in Dallas. What do you think the problem is?"

"I don't know. She's tense. Jittery. Like she's afraid of something. She used to get like this in the weeks before I left on orders. She'd clean everything in the house, twice, and put so much stuff away she couldn't find anything. It took her almost forty-five minutes to find her boots this morning. If the house gets any cleaner, they could open a hospital in there."

Annie leaned back against the boards. "Hmmm," she mused.

Ryan skated by and waved. "Hi, Dad. Hi, Annie."

She smiled at him. "Hi, Ryan." He got control of the errant puck and took off in the opposite direction. "And she didn't say anything?" Annie asked. "You didn't hear her talk this over with anyone?"

"No one." Mark resumed his pacing. "She didn't call anyone. She didn't have any meetings. She worked on a couple of decorating jobs, but that's all. All I know is, she cried a lot, and picked up the phone to call Scott about twenty-five times."

"This is not good."

"What do you mean it's not good?"

"I mean, things should be progressing now. Look at you. You're almost gone."

Mark looked down at his shadowy body. He had indeed faded to near transparency. Annie, on the other hand, still looked very much the same as the day he'd met her. "Well, maybe it's you." He pointed at her. "You're still a lot more here than I am."

"That really worries me."

"Why?"

"Because, Scott seems to have let go all right." She looked at Scott. He was whispering something in Maggie's ear. "I don't think he's having any trouble putting aside memories of me in order to pursue a relationship with Maggie." She'd come to that realization late one night when Scott had been nursing a beer in the living room of his apartment in Dallas. It had been like tearing her heart out when she'd seen the ragged look on his face and realized it wasn't for her.

That look would never be for her again, yet Mark was right. She had not faded away from reality since the day Scott had first met Maggie. "Maybe we're putting too much emphasis on this fading business. Maybe it doesn't mean anything."

Mark stopped pacing again. "It has to mean something. Why else would it be happening?"

"I don't know; it just can't have anything to do with how much they still need us." She paused. She felt the telltale stinging in her eyes. "Scott doesn't need me anymore."

Mark looked at her in surprise. He brushed an icy flake from her cheek. "Oh, Annie."

Her lower lip trembled. "It's true. I knew it in Dallas. He's in love with her, Mark. The forever kind. He just needs Maggie."

Mark pulled Annie into his arms and guided her off the ice. They sat down next to the rink. "I'm a first-class jerk, you know it?"

She felt a few more tears form on her face. "Why do you say that?"

He smoothed her hair away from her cheek. "Because you have managed to keep everything together during this entire ordeal, and all I can do is complain. I'm sorry this hurts you so much."

"It hurts you, too."

"Yeah," he said with a soft smile, "but men are dense. Remember?"

Fifteen

The following afternoon, Scott straightened his tie and stepped into the receiving area of Carl Fortwell's office. A week before, he would have argued that he'd done everything possible to alert Carl to the probable connection between Pete Sherban and Irene Fussman. But that was before. Before he'd started fighting for a relationship with Maggie.

He favored Carl's receptionist with his best Southern gentleman smile. "Good morning."

She looked up. "Oh, good morning, Mr. Bishop. What can I do for you?"

"I'd like to see Carl if he's in."

"Do you have an appointment?"

Scott shook his head. "No, but I won't need more than a few minutes of his time."

The receptionist looked at him dubiously. "Why don't you have a seat? I'll see if Mr. Fortwell's secretary can work you in."

Scott sat down on the comfortable leather couch. The young woman lifted the receiver and spoke in hushed tones to Carl Fortwell's secretary. "How long did you say you'd need?" she asked Scott.

"About ten minutes."

"Ten minutes," she repeated. "All right. All right, I will." She replaced the receiver, then looked at Scott. "Mr. Fortwell has a meeting in twenty minutes. He can see you now, but only if you're brief."

Scott nodded. "I will be." She started to rise, but he shook his head. "I know the way. Through here, and to the left?" He pointed to the heavy glass doors on the far end of the reception area.

"No. It's to the right."

"Oh, of course. Thank you," he said, and pushed the door open.

Carl met him with a warm handshake and a genuine smile. "Well, Bishop, it's good to see you again."

"Thanks for seeing me on such short notice," Scott said.

Carl motioned to one of the chairs in front of his desk. "Have a seat. I've only got a few minutes, but I wanted to tell you I had a chance to look over your bid plans for the resort. Your work is very impressive."

"Thank you."

"I don't think I'm jumping the gun if I say Max liked what he saw."

Scott was surprised that Carl's words didn't have more of an impact on him. He was almost beyond caring what Max Wedgins thought of his plans. "Actually, I wanted to talk to you about Maggie."

"Maggie?" Carl said. He leaned back in his chair. "What about her?"

"I want to make sure she gets a fair shot at this deal."

Carl picked up a fountain pen and started rolling it

between his fingers. "Do you have any reason to think she wouldn't?"

Scott decided the direct approach would do him the most good. "I do if Pete Sherban is throwing around influence in exchange for a roll in the hay with Irene Fussman."

Carl's expression turned grim. He set the pen down. "That's the third time in two weeks I've heard that accusation, and twice it came from you. I've been in business with Pete for thirty years. I think I know him better than you do."

"You probably do," Scott said, "but I also know I don't like what I see."

"If I recall, you saw Pete and Irene having lunch together at the White Rooster. That's hardly grounds for an accusation like this."

"It wasn't just lunch, Carl. I've had business lunches with female colleagues. They don't entail heavy breathing and butter-melting looks."

Carl steepled his fingers under his chin. "Did you tell anyone else what you saw that day?"

Scott shook his head. "No one."

"Did you and Maggie discuss it in front of her son?"

"Ryan?" Scott said, stunned. "He's seven years old, for God's sake. Do you think I'd say something like that in front of a kid?"

"Then how do you explain the fact that Ryan called me the day you and Maggie dropped off your bids? He wanted to sell me a ticket to the father/son game on Saturday, and suggested that I should ask Pete if he wanted to bring Irene Fussman."

"What?"

"You tell me. I thought it was a little strange coming from a seven-year-old."

Scott searched his brain for any possible reason Ryan might have had for making the strange phone call. He settled on the bizarre encounter with Maxwell Wedgins. "What time on Friday did he call you?"

"I don't know. Around noon."

"Max didn't get to the school until after two-thirty," Scott mumbled, more to himself than to Carl.

"Max?" Carl asked. "What has Max got to do with this?"

"I'm not sure. Friday afternoon, Ryan didn't come home from school on time. Maggie was in a panic. We drove over to the school, and Max was there talking to Ryan." He paused. "Actually, Max was sitting on the playground bench, and Ryan was playing basketball with Max's chauffeur."

"Bobbi?" Carl asked.

"Tall, blond, and leggy?"

"That's the one."

Scott nodded. "It was weird. Really weird. We couldn't get a straight answer out of Max."

"Is that why you hit him on the jaw?"

Scott narrowed his gaze at Carl. "You know about that?"

"Max called me Friday evening. He said he felt really bad about frightening Maggie."

"Hell, he should have felt bad. You don't just detain people's kids and expect them not to get upset."

"Max is a little . . . different."

"You're telling me." Scott shifted in his chair. "So why didn't you tell me you knew about this?"

Carl drew a cigar out of the cherry box on his desk.

He lit it, took several puffs, then leaned back in his chair. "I was curious."

Scott flexed his fingers on the arms of the chair. He liked Carl Fortwell, respected him for his business acumen and his success as an investor. But what he didn't like was feeling like a pawn in some complicated game Max Wedgins was playing with the Cape Hope Resort. "What's going on, Carl?"

"After you and Maggie left on Friday, I talked to Pete. He said he'd had lunch with Irene to talk with her about redoing our office suites. It was plausible enough. I wanted to believe him."

Scott rolled his eyes. Carl flicked the ashes off his cigar, and gave him a quelling look. "Pete Sherban is my partner and my friend. Give me one good reason why I should take your word over his."

"Agreed."

Carl's nod was brief. "But then Ryan called. It was odd. Especially in light of what you and Maggie had told me. There was something that didn't feel right to me, especially since Pete has had almost all the contact with Wedgins. I decided to give Max a call."

"What did you tell him?"

"I told him what you'd told me. I told him what Pete had told me, and then I told him what Ryan had told me. I advised him to look closely at the bids, and make up his own mind what he wanted. He assured me that he might be insane, but he wasn't about to screw around with three and a half billion dollars."

Scott's mouth twitched in amusement. "Well, that's reassuring."

Carl took another puff on the cigar. "Max Wedgins is a lot of things. He likes to tell people he's insane, but I personally think he's just a financial genius.

When that much of your brain is taken up with one thing, it stands to reason that something else is going to suffer. In his case, it's his social skills. He doesn't have any."

"Why do you think he went to see Ryan?"

"I don't know. He didn't tell me when he called on Friday night. He just said he wanted me to convey his apologies to you and to Maggie if I had the chance, and that he wanted me to look into making a purchase on his behalf."

"What kind of purchase?"

"It's an under-the-table deal for right now. Nothing's official. You'll understand I can't give you any details."

It was probably some trifle like IBM, Scott thought. "Of course."

"Anyway, on the heels of that, you come in here today and tell me you're worried about Maggie getting a fair shot at the bid. Hell, after you whacked Max on the jaw, I'd think you'd be a little concerned about your shot."

Scott couldn't stop a grin. "You already told me he liked my stuff."

"Max is weird like that. You hit him, now he thinks you're some kind of architectural whiz kid. I should have beat the shit out of him years ago."

Scott laughed at that. "The truth is, Carl, you'd be right if my only interest in Cape Hope was the resort, but it's not."

Carl stamped out the cigar. He gave Scott a knowing look. "I don't suppose your interest could lie in the direction of a certain blond-haired widow lady."

"Yeah, maybe."

"I thought so. You two looked pretty comfortable when you strolled in here on Friday."

"Maggie's just having a lot of trouble right now. Her business is struggling, and I know she needs this bid."

"All I can do is promise you that I think Max will do whatever he can to be fair."

Scott rubbed his hands on his thighs. "I've worked with Irene Fussman before, Carl. She'll stoop pretty low to get a bid."

"You're pretty sure about this, aren't you?"

"I'd be willing to bet real money that Irene is at least trying if not actively seducing Pete into getting the bid for her."

"I've got to call Max again this afternoon. I have a counteroffer on this purchase I'm negotiating for him. I'll see if he's made any decisions yet."

"What are you going to do if he says he's giving the bid to Irene?"

"It's over three billion dollars. I'm going to believe that Max knows what the hell he's doing."

Scott frowned. "I hope so. There's a lot more riding on this than he thinks."

Maggie put the finishing touches on the garland. She secured a burgundy bow to the banister and looked back to examine the result. "What do you think?" she asked Ryan.

He tipped his head to one side. "It looks crooked."

She adjusted the bow. "Better?"

He nodded. "Better."

Maggie started to scoop up the spare garland and ribbon and dump it back in the box. "I guess we're done then."

"All we need is a tree."

She stopped. "Ryan," she said, shifting so she was seated on the stairs, "I told you we weren't getting a tree."

He frowned. "But, Mom—"

"Honey, we don't need a tree. We don't really have room for it anyway." Maggie doubted he'd believe the rather lame excuse.

"We could get a little one."

"I just don't think it's a good idea this year. It's too late. Most of the trees have been sold." And besides, I couldn't bear to have a tree in this house. Not after last year. Not after I promised your dad that we wouldn't light the tree until he came home. Not after I had to pull those lights off and pack them away in a box, knowing he wasn't coming home. "Maybe we'll get one next year."

"We could go cut one. Dad used to. We don't have to buy one."

"Ryan, I don't think—" She broke off when the doorbell rang. "Could you get that please?" she asked, seizing the excuse to end the conversation.

Ryan set his mouth in a stubborn pout. "But what about the tree?"

"Get the door, Ryan. We'll talk about the tree later." She quelled his pending protest with a sharp look. He trudged off toward the door.

"Oh," she heard him say, "hi, Scott."

Maggie looked up in surprise. "I wasn't expecting you until this evening."

He smiled at her. "I came early." He waved at the taxicab by the curve. He stomped the snow off his boots, then came inside. "I finished up what I was working on and thought I'd come take you guys to lunch."

Ryan rubbed his toe in the carpet. "We were talking about our Christmas tree."

Scott looked into the living room. "What tree?"

"We don't have one," Ryan said miserably.

Maggie dropped the remaining garland in the box. "Ryan, go upstairs and wash your hands, please."

"But—"

"Now, Ryan. I don't want to hear any more about this."

He stomped up the stairs. Maggie closed her eyes and leaned back against the banister. She started when she felt Scott's cool lips on her cheek. "Rough day?" he asked.

She opened her eyes. "Ryan is determined to have a tree."

"So let's get him one."

"It's not that simple. I'm not up to the bother this year."

"Maggie—"

She frowned at him. "It's really none of your business, is it?"

Scott raised his eyebrows. "You're really upset about this, aren't you?"

She exhaled a long breath. "I'm sorry. I'm just— tense. Ryan's off from school today, and he's been cranky since he got up this morning. I guess it's affecting my mood."

Scott placed his hands on her waist. He pulled gently until she leaned against him. "I'd like to affect some of your moods," he said. He bent his head to nuzzle her neck.

"Scott," Maggie protested, "what are you doing?"

"Mood-enhancing exercises."

She swallowed a small laugh. "Well, cut it out."

"See," he nipped her earlobe, "you laughed. It's working."

"It's not—" Maggie gasped when his tongue speared into the sensitive whorl of her ear.

"It's not what?" he asked, his breath a moist caress against her cheek.

"It's not working."

Scott's laugh was warm, and husky. It made her shiver. "Liar." He lifted his head. She could see the laughter in his eyes. "I love you, Maggie," he said.

She cast a quick, anxious glance up the stairs. "Scott, please."

"And it feels just as good to say it today as it did yesterday."

"Ryan will be down in a minute."

"And I think he'd better get used to the idea that I'm in love with his mom."

Maggie pushed at Scott's chest. "He's not ready for this."

"He's not, or you're not?"

"Scott," she said, pushing harder.

He stepped away. "OK, Maggie. I'll back off. For now."

She leaned against the banister. "You're driving me nuts."

"That's the general idea."

Ryan came pounding down the stairs. "I'm ready," he announced. He seemed to have recovered from his earlier pout about the tree, but Maggie knew the issue was far from forgotten. "Where are we going?" he asked.

"I don't know," Scott said. "Where do you want to go?"

"Can we go to the Ice Palace?"

Scott looked at Maggie for clarification. "The Ice Palace," she said, "serves the greasiest hot dogs in town, and has a skating rink in the middle."

"A skating rink?" Scott said.

Maggie looked at him, curious. "Yeah. It's a popular place here in town. People around here do a lot of ice-skating."

"I guess they would."

"Can we go?" Ryan asked.

"I was thinking of some place a little more quiet," Scott hedged.

Maggie studied him for a minute. "This would give you an excellent chance to do some practice skating with Ryan before the game on Saturday. He could teach you a little about hockey."

Scott hesitated. "I guess he could."

"Sure," Ryan said. "I'll show you everything you need to know."

"Well, then," Scott answered, "it sounds like a plan."

Maggie wondered if it was her imagination, or if Scott's face had paled.

Between scolding himself for agreeing to the ridiculous notion of skating with Maggie and Ryan, and reassuring himself that he'd practiced enough in the last week not to make a complete fool of himself, Scott worked himself into a sweat by the time they reached the Ice Palace.

Like it or not, Maggie was going to find out sooner or later that he could barely stand up on a pair of ice

skates. Perhaps sooner was better than later. He had
agreed to skate in the game with Ryan, and if Maggie
could help him even a little, it might keep him from
getting killed by some militant seven-year-old.

They feasted on greasy chili dogs and cheese fries.
Ryan chattered through most of lunch, talking about
the game on Saturday, and how Chuck Bullard was
still trying to get several of the Bruins to officiate.

"Wouldn't it be cool if he could really get Carson
Lipter?"

Maggie smiled at him. "It would be the coolest
thing ever, Ryan."

Ryan nodded. "It would. Coach says Carson is
checking his calendar."

Scott groaned. Maggie gave him a sharp look. "Are
you all right?"

"Sure," he said. "Too much grease I think."

"Can we go get our skates, now, Mom?"

"Okay." She handed Ryan a five-dollar bill from
her pocket. "What size shoe do you wear?" she asked
Scott.

"A nine and a half."

"Get him a ten," she told Ryan.

Ryan bounded off toward the rental window. Maggie looked at Scott. "You've never skated before, have
you?"

"What makes you say that?"

He saw a smile start to twitch at the corner of her
mouth. "Just a hunch. You haven't, have you?"

"Of course I have."

"How many times?"

Scott winced. "You expect me to count them?"

"I bet it wouldn't be too hard."

He paused. He decided he liked the way Maggie's

eyes were shining that afternoon. "Eight," he said.

Maggie groaned. "Oh God. You're going to get killed."

"I will have you know, Ms. Connell, that I spent two hours at the ice rink every day while I was home in Dallas."

"Did you learn anything?"

"I can stand up," he said. Then added, "Most of the time."

Maggie stared at him. "Why on earth did you agree to do this? You've seen a hockey game. You're going to get annihilated."

He thought about telling her he'd promised to do it because it was important to Ryan. He figured that was worth at least a few points in her book, but he took one look at the way her hair lay in rumpled waves around her face, and decided he'd just tell the truth. "I didn't like the way you were looking at Chuck Bullard," he said.

Maggie's mouth dropped open. "What?"

"Chuck Bullard. That night he told you he was worried because Ryan didn't want to skate in the game. You were flirting with him."

"I was not."

"Chuck," Scott said, imitating her tone, "is the Boston area spokesman for the Literacy Council. I have it on good authority he's in line for canonization."

"I did not say that."

"Almost."

"That's ridiculous."

Scott shrugged. "Maybe. Anyway, it made me jealous as hell. I couldn't help it. Next thing I knew I was promising Ryan I'd skate."

Ryan ran up to the table. He had three pairs of

skates slung over his shoulders. He handed the largest pair to Scott. "No tens. I got you a ten and a half."

"It isn't going to make any difference," Maggie muttered.

"What, Mom?"

She shook her head. "Never mind. Sit down and let me help you lace yours up."

Mark leaned back in his chair at the adjacent table and shot Annie a smug look. "I *told* you that's why he agreed to skate."

Annie frowned at him. "It was still a very nice thing to do."

"Maggie's right, you know. He's going to get killed."

"He is not. I've been watching him practice. He's almost got the hang of it."

"It's a hockey game, Annie. The object is for one team to kill the other team."

"They're little boys. How rough can it be?"

Mark shook his head in disbelief. When it came to hockey, Annie was almost as dumb as Scott.

Maggie watched Scott crash into the boards for the third time. She buried her head in her hands and groaned.

"He's bad, Mom," Ryan said. "I mean, he's worse than Oscar Framly."

Scott waved to her from across the rink as he picked himself up. Oscar Framly, she knew, was very, very bad at ice-skating. "He's going to get killed," Maggie told Ryan.

"Yeah." Ryan was staring at Scott. His expression bordered on awe. Maggie figured Ryan was having trouble believing anybody could be that bad on ice skates.

"Do you think we should let him skate?"

"He said he wanted to."

"Maybe we should show him some stuff," Maggie suggested.

Ryan watched Scott from across the rink. "It would help if he bent his knees a little."

"Why don't you go tell him?"

"OK." Ryan took off over the ice.

Maggie leaned back against the dasher boards and watched as Ryan fanned to a stop in front of Scott. Their heads were bent together in conversation. Scott was listening intently to Ryan, even flexed his knees once or twice. In spite of herself, Maggie smiled.

The two of them were so comfortable together. Ryan seemed genuinely to like Scott, and it was evident that the feeling was mutual. It would be easy, too easy, to use that as an excuse to accept the companionship Scott so readily offered. He said he loved her, and Maggie believed him. In the long hours of the night, hours spent alone because Scott had refused to escalate their physical relationship until their emotional relationship was on more solid footing, Maggie had been forced to admit that she loved him, too.

Oh, not the way she'd loved Mark. That was a consuming kind of love. The kind that had required her to forget that Maggie had existed as a person before she'd met him. No, she loved Scott with a deep sense of rightness, of belonging. Why, then, couldn't she just accept him into her life?

Because you could lose him, too, a persistent voice nagged. And the voice wouldn't go away. Maggie had tried, tried hard, to exorcise her fear of the past. She had argued with herself that fear was no good reason to pass up a chance at true happiness. She had convincingly persuaded her subconscious that not everyone got a second chance like she had. But the voice persisted.

When she'd lost Mark, she'd lost everything. It had taken a year before she felt almost whole again. She wasn't ready to surrender any part of that wholeness to Scott Bishop or anyone else. With a heavy sigh, Maggie skated across the ice. She yielded to the very Scarlett O'Hara notion that tomorrow was another day, and besides, if she didn't teach Scott to skate by Saturday, there would be nothing left of him anyway.

Sixteen

Scott propped the ice bag on his knee, leaned his head back against the armrest of the sofa, and groaned. Ryan came running in the living room with a glass of soda. "Here." He pushed the glass into Scott's hand. "It's orange."

"Great."

"How's your knee?"

"Not bad."

"That was really cool when you crashed into the Zamboni."

Scott took a sip of his soda. "Sure was."

"You're going to get killed on Saturday."

"You think so?"

"Yeah. Franklin's probably gonna cream you."

Scott thought about the possibility of getting his bell rung by a seven-year-old. "Franklin wouldn't do something like that, would he?"

Ryan nodded. "He would if you were blocking his shot on goal."

"Well, then maybe I'll just have to get out of the way."

"You're not supposed to get out of the way," Ryan

explained with a patience Scott actually admired. "You're supposed to keep him from shooting. Even if you have to cream him."

"I am not going to cream Franklin."

Ryan shrugged. "He'll get you then."

Scott figured there was probably a lot of truth in that. He was saved a retort when Maggie came into the room carrying a tray. "Okay, invalid, I made you a peanut butter and jelly sandwich. Hope it's okay."

Scott watched her set the tray on the coffee table. She sat in the chair across from him. He reached for the sandwich. "Food of the gods," he said, and took a hefty bite.

"How's your knee?" Maggie asked.

He washed down the sandwich with a sip of orange soda. "Swollen."

"Like your ego?"

He shook his head. "That's deflated."

Maggie laughed. "It serves you right, you know? You should never have agreed to skate in this game."

Ryan was seated on the floor, thumbing through a copy of *Sports Illustrated*. He looked up. "Yeah. That was really dumb."

"Thanks for the support, champ," Scott said, then took another bite of his sandwich.

Maggie shook her head. "Ryan?"

"Yeah, Mom?"

"Why don't you go upstairs and make sure your clothes are ready for school tomorrow?"

"I did already."

"Have you done your homework?"

"Didn't have any."

"Can you find something to do in your room?"

"Why?"

Maggie grimaced. "Because I want to talk to Scott alone for a minute."

"No you don't," Ryan said. He grinned at Scott. "She wants to kiss."

"Ryan!" Maggie stared at him, agape.

Scott choked on his soda. "You think so?"

"Yeah. Why else would I have to go upstairs?"

"Ryan Connell, you do not say things like that in this house."

Maggie looked so outraged that Scott started to laugh. "Maggie, take it easy."

"It's no big deal, Mom. I've seen you do it lots of times."

Maggie covered her face with her hands. "How many times?" she said.

"I don't know. Three maybe."

Maggie groaned. Scott laughed harder. "Well, look, sport," he said to Ryan, "can you give me a break here?"

"Scott!" The look Maggie gave him was censorious.

Ryan looked from Scott to Maggie, then back again. He shrugged. "I guess so. Do I have to go to bed now, Mom?"

She shook her head. "No." Her voice sounded strangled.

"Can I listen to my stereo?"

"Sure."

"Cool." Ryan leapt up and took off for the stairs at a dead run.

Maggie stood without meeting Scott's gaze. She reached for the tray. "I don't know what got into him. I—"

He grabbed her hand. "Maggie, stop."

She tried to pull her hand away. "He never says things like that."

"Maggie." Scott jerked her hand hard enough that she looked at him, startled. "I think it's a very good sign that Ryan's not threatened by our relationship. I've earned his trust."

"What are you talking about?"

"The day we made the cookie tower, Ryan asked me if I was going to marry you."

"He *what*?"

Scott nodded. "He wanted to know if you and I were going to get married."

"What did you tell him?"

"I told him we hadn't talked about it, but when we made a decision, we'd tell him first."

"Oh God."

"Well, wouldn't we?"

"Of course we'd tell him first, but you let him think we were contemplating marriage. He's probably been saying that all over town."

Scott gave Maggie's hand a hard tug. "Sit down, Maggie." She dropped down onto the couch next to him. "I have something to say," he said.

Her expression became guarded. "Now, Scott—"

He shook his head. "No. Listen to me. I love you, Maggie. You know I do."

"Scott—"

He ignored her. "And you love me. Whether you admit it or not, I know you love me. I want to marry you. I want us to raise Ryan. I want us to have babies. I want to build us an enormous house where we can spread out and play with our kids."

He linked his hand behind her nape to pull her toward him. "I want us to teach them how to ice-skate, and play cards, and make root beer."

"Root beer?" she asked.

"Yeah." He rubbed his lips on her throat. "I want to watch you design their bedrooms. I want to see you cheering at hockey games and baseball games and gymnastics meets."

"Scott—"

He kissed her lightly. "And I want to come home at night and know that I get to spend the entire evening with my family."

Maggie felt a sinking sense of dread. "What about me? What am I supposed to do while you're living out this fantasy."

"What do you want to do?" He moved his lips over her cheek.

"What if I don't want more children?"

Scott looked at her in surprise. "Then I guess we'll just have to lavish all our attention on Ryan."

"You'd be content with that?"

"I want children, Maggie, but I want you more. If you're not ready, hell, if you're never ready, I can adjust to that."

"But I'm supposed to stay at home and raise Ryan. Right?"

Scott's gaze narrowed. He sensed danger. "Not necessarily."

She pushed at his hand. "That sounds like the picture you painted to me."

"Maggie, I have no intention of keeping you from doing anything you want to do."

"You're just saying that."

"I'm not. If you want to design, then I want you to."

"If I want to?"

"Well, of course."

"Do you think this is just some hobby for me, something to do while I occupy my time?"

Scott ground his teeth in frustration. "Stop putting words in my mouth. I think you're an incredibly talented designer."

"But you'd expect Ryan and me to leave our home here and move to Dallas with you?"

"Did I say that?"

"You would."

"How do you know?"

"Because your family, your life is in Texas."

"My life *was* in Texas, Maggie. It's not anymore."

She ignored him. "You'd expect me to give up the business I spent a year building just because your job is more important."

"That's not true. If I get the Cape Hope project, I have every—"

"If. That's a big 'if,' Scott. What if you don't get it? You'll go back to Dallas, won't you?"

"I haven't decided. It would depend on what you wanted to do."

"That's not true. You would go back, and you'd expect me to close By Design and go with you."

"Damn it, Maggie, stop telling me what I want and don't want."

"Well, wouldn't you?"

"No, I wouldn't. Why the hell are you so convinced that I'd make you give up your life here?"

"You just would."

"You're being irrational."

"I'm not. I'm trying to protect myself, and Ryan."

"Ryan has nothing to do with this."

"Of course he does."

"No he doesn't." Scott took a deep breath. He waited for his temper to cool. "You're not upset because you think I'd uproot Ryan."

"He's already been through too much. I couldn't make him move again."

"Maggie," he tucked a tendril of hair behind her ear, "Ryan has been through a lot, it's true, but I don't think this is about him."

"It is."

"No. It's about you." He laid his hand on the side of her face. "Tell me the truth, Maggie. Just tell me what you're afraid of."

"I'm not afraid."

"Come on, Maggie, I know you. You're scared to death."

Maggie stared at him for several long seconds. "You'd absorb me," she said.

Scott frowned. "What?"

"I'd become a part of you, just like I became a part of Mark. I'd never know I could make it on my own. I'd never know I could survive apart from you. I didn't think I could survive apart from Mark, and I was right."

"You weren't right." He pushed himself up on his elbow. "Maggie, look at what you've done, at what you've accomplished."

She shook her head. "I couldn't make the business work, I couldn't give Ryan what he needed." Tears started to roll down her cheeks. "I had to tear him away from his friends and his school because I had to run away from the memories."

"Stop," Scott said. "Stop doing this." He wrapped an arm around her shoulders, and guided her down so that she lay beside him on the sofa. "You're beating yourself up over things that aren't even true."

"Yes, they are. Mark became my whole life. When he died, I had nothing left. I can't let you do that to me."

"Honey, listen to me—"

"What if something happened? What if Ryan and I were alone again? What would I do?"

"Maggie," he gave her a quick squeeze, "hush. I want you to listen to me. Just listen. All right?"

She nodded against his chest. Scott stuffed one of the napkins from the coffee table into her hand. He waited while she blew her nose. "Now," he said, shifting her beside him on the sofa, "I want to tell you something."

"What?"

She sounded so miserable, that Scott smiled into her hair. "When I married Annie, I was twenty-two years old. And I loved her the way a twenty-two-year-old boy loves a twenty-one-year-old girl. It was obsessive. Wild, crazy, exciting obsessive. She meant the world to me. My heart didn't beat aside from Annie."

"I felt the same way about Mark."

"I know. When she died, a piece of me died with her. I think it was that piece, the piece that couldn't breathe without her. But another piece lived on. That's the man, Maggie."

He tipped her head back with his thumb so he could see her eyes. "The boy is gone. The man survived. It's the man who is in love with you. And I would never ask you, or expect you, or want you to be anyone other than who you are."

Her mouth trembled. "But—"

He covered her mouth with his hand. "Shhh. Don't

let old demons cloud new joys." He moved his hand to caress her cheek. "Nobody said we had to decide the entire future tonight. We'll take it one thing at a time."

"But what about the Cape Hope project?"

Scott gave her a tender kiss. "What about it?"

"What if you don't get the bid?"

"One problem at a time, Maggie."

She fell silent then. Scott listened to the ticking of the clock on the mantel, and the faint sounds of "All Shook Up," coming from Ryan's stereo. He smiled at the irony.

"Scott?" Maggie said.

"Hmmm?"

"What problem do you want to solve first?"

"Well," he adjusted the ice on his knee, "I think the first thing we should do is help me live through Saturday."

On Friday night, Maggie stared at her reflection in the mirror, wavering on indecision. Scott had insisted that they should have, as he called it, a dress-up-and-impress-each-other date. Maggie had resisted. After their stormy confrontation on Wednesday night, she wasn't sure she was ready for an entire evening alone with him. But Scott had been so insistent that Maggie had finally relented.

She'd been regretting it all day. Lily had picked Ryan up after school, so Maggie had been left with an entire afternoon to worry about the evening. She'd gone through her closet four times. She'd tried on every dress she owned at least twice, and between intermittent scoldings about her ridiculous behavior, and frantic searches for panty hose with no runs, she'd managed to work herself into a first-class swivet.

She was supposed to meet Scott at his hotel at six-thirty. She was dressed and ready forty-five minutes ahead of schedule. Now, standing in front of the mirror, Maggie seriously contemplated changing her dress yet again. She frowned at her reflection.

She'd chosen one of the few dressy outfits she owned. It was a cobalt blue knit chemise. The dress accentuated her figure, and the cowl neckline, which draped provocatively low in the back, added drama to the otherwise simple lines. Matching pumps completed the outfit.

Mark had always liked the dress. Perhaps that was why she hadn't worn it since his death. Somehow, she didn't remember it being so snug. The sweaters and jeans and business suits that now comprised her wardrobe did little to enhance feminine curves. This dress, on the other hand, was meant to entice. To seduce. No wonder Mark had been so fond of it.

She wavered once more, almost opting for the more sedate floral print silk jumper, but something, whether it was the purely feminine pleasure in wearing the alluring dress, or simply the anticipation of Scott's reaction, something made her feel daring. She snapped out the light on her bedside table, scooped up her purse, and headed for the door before she could change her mind.

She arrived at Scott's hotel fifteen minutes early, so she decided to meet him in his room rather than wait for him in the lobby. With her coat draped over her arm, she knocked twice, and waited for him to open the door. His reaction to her appearance was no less powerful than she'd hoped for. He pulled the door open.

And stared.

His tie hung loose around his neck. His fingers were frozen in place on the top button of his shirt. Maggie felt the impact of his appraisal all the way to the tips of her toes. "Hi," she said.

"Hi." He didn't budge.

She pointed to his tie. "Do you need some help with that?"

He gave her a blank look. "What?"

Maggie hid an amused smile. "Your tie," she said. She reached for the top button of his shirt. "Do you need help with your tie?"

Scott looked startled. He stepped hastily away from the door, fiddling with the button. "Oh, uh, no. Do you want to come in?"

Maggie strolled into the room. "I hope it's not a problem that I'm early."

Scott pushed the door shut. In each hand, he held one end of his tie. He leaned back against the wall. His gaze was pinned on Maggie. She looked back over her shoulder. His expression was so heated, his eyes looked like molten gold. "What?" she asked him.

"My God."

She felt a rush of purely feminine satisfaction as she turned to face him. "I guess you like my dress."

Scott's smile was slow, sensuous. He released one end of the tie, then dragged it from his collar with a leisurely tug of his right hand. The soft silk whispered against the starched cotton of his shirt. Maggie stopped breathing.

Scott twined the tie between the fingers of his left hand. His index finger delved into a crevice of the silk. He rubbed it slowly along the length. And took two steps toward Maggie.

She remained, frozen in place, riveted by the look in his eyes. He took one more step. She was simultaneously overwhelmed by the spicy scent of his aftershave and the warmth of his body, so close to hers. In a rapid movement, he looped the tie behind her back. He gave it a gentle tug, and Maggie stumbled the remaining step between them. Her coat fell to the floor.

Scott's mouth was a hairsbreadth from hers. His warm breath fanned over her skin. The scent of him intoxicated her. He rubbed his lips against hers in the merest hint of a kiss. "I guess," he said, then slid his tongue along her bottom lip, "you could say I like your dress."

Maggie pressed her lips to his. Scott's kiss was hungry and hot. He pressed a hand to her bare back. Maggie felt the goose bumps spread down her spine when the end of his tie tickled the sensitive skin at the small of her back. The erotic sensation made her quiver.

Scott groaned and slanted his lips over hers in a possessive kiss so full of desire, of longing, that Maggie feared her knees would buckle. She slid a hand up his chest to clutch his shoulder. She could feel the hard length of him where his groin was pressed against her belly. Scott's hand moved up her spine. He rubbed his hips against hers, then plunged his tongue into her mouth.

The sensation was devastating, consuming. Maggie threaded her fingers through his hair. She raked her nails over his shoulder until her hand closed around the muscled contour of his upper arm. Scott ended the kiss. Maggie dropped her forehead against his shoulder. His heart pounded a heavy rhythm beneath her ear, and he moved his hand down her spine to her lower back, anchoring her against him.

Maggie sucked in a ragged breath. "Well," she said.

Scott's laugh was a husky rasp against her ear. "Yeah. Well."

"I had no idea the sight of me in a dress would have this effect on you."

He slid the tie from her waist. "Yeah, right. You knew exactly what effect it would have on me. Good grief, Maggie, you look like a million bucks in that dress." He scooped up her coat.

Maggie felt the pleasure of his compliment spread through her like heated brandy. She accepted her coat from him, then sat down on the side of the bed. "Thank you. I haven't worn it in a while."

Scott flipped his collar up. He slung the tie around his neck with an efficient flick of his wrist. "Good thing. You'd have had the men of Cape Hope in an uproar."

"You'll have to stop talking like that or my head will swell."

"I'm swelling," he said, his smile wicked. "It's only fair."

Maggie blushed. She decided to ignore the suggestive comment. She leaned back on one hand. "So where are we going for dinner?"

He finished knotting his tie. "It's a surprise."

"There aren't but so many restaurants in Cape Hope. It can't be that much of a surprise."

"This is a surprise. Believe me."

"You're going to have to tell me if you expect me to drive."

"I'm driving."

"Are we going to get lost on the way?" she quipped.

Scott arched an eyebrow. "That wasn't very nice."

"Just checking."

"No," he said, shrugging into his jacket, "we are not going to get lost on the way. I know exactly where I'm going." He paused to press a heated kiss to her lips. "Although, I admit I'm tempted to just stay here."

Maggie shivered. "We could order room service."

Scott straightened. "Not if I want to hold on to my sanity we can't. I've got no business being alone with you in a hotel room while you're wearing that dress."

Maggie slid her arms into her coat. "Scott, we're two perfectly healthy adults, and—"

Scott curved his fingers on her shoulders and interrupted her. "Maggie, you could tempt the pope himself, but I told you how I feel about this. I'm just not prepared to escalate our physical relationship until we work some things out."

She felt the same warm feeling of security he always gave her, coupled with an odd fluttery sensation in her stomach. "You're weird," she said. An amused smile tugged at the corner of her mouth.

Scott rubbed at it with his thumb. "Yeah, probably." He gave her a soft kiss. "I'm also hungry."

"I guess we should eat, then."

Scott reached for his overcoat. "That kind of hungry, too," he said.

Maggie linked her fingers through his. "If you don't stop saying things like that, I might not let you out of this room."

"If you don't stop looking at me with that seductive smile of yours, I might agree to stay."

"Promises, promises."

Scott swatted her on the behind. "You're a wicked woman, Maggie Connell."

She met his gaze, feeling suddenly very serious. "Only with you, Scott. I hope you don't think—"

"I think you're the sexiest woman I've ever known," he said. "And I think when the time is right, we're going to be explosive together, but I need you to understand why I feel this way."

Maggie nodded. "You're right. There are too many things standing in the way of this relationship right now. I don't want either of us to do anything we'll regret later." She gave him a sheepish smile. "No matter what happens, I want us to be friends."

"I want us to be a whole hell of a lot more than friends," Scott said. He led her to the door.

They walked to the parking deck in silence. She showed him where she'd parked, then handed him the keys to the Bronco. "Are you sure you don't want me to drive?"

He unlocked her door. "What's the matter, Maggie? Don't you trust me with your car?"

"I'm just really hungry. I don't want to ride around half the night looking for a place to eat."

Scott waited until she buckled her seat belt. "Oh ye of little faith." He shut her door, then rounded the car to slide into the driver's seat. "Okay," he said, sliding the key into the ignition. "Which way is north?"

"Scott—"

"I'm kidding." He started the engine. "I know where we're going."

Maggie leaned back in her seat. She wondered if he was still talking about their dinner destination, or if he was back to discussing their relationship. "I hope so."

Scott's expression was enigmatic. He backed out of the space before reaching across the console and taking her hand. "You're going to have to learn to trust me, Maggie."

As he drove across town, Maggie thought about the truth in his words. It would be easy to trust Scott. He was so, well, trustworthy. A sudden image of Lassie popped into her head. She hid a smile.

Scott was one of the most sensitive men Maggie had ever known. She remembered his ill-fated attempts at skating. It hadn't seemed to bother him in the least that he looked a little foolish out on the ice. He had known Ryan was having a good time. That had been all the incentive he needed. She cast a sideways glance at Scott's profile. How could she keep from loving a man who cared for her son like that?

Scott turned into the ice-arena parking lot, found a space, then killed the engine. Maggie looked around in surprise. "This is the ice rink."

"Right the first time."

"What are we doing here?"

"Maggie," he said with exaggerated impatience, "I told you that it's a surprise." He got out of the car, then came around to open her door.

"We can't eat at the ice rink."

"Have some faith, my little chickadee," he said, doing a very bad impersonation of W.C. Fields.

Maggie slipped her fingers into his. With all the finesse of a nineteenth-century footman, he helped her alight from the car. He pulled her hand through the bend of his elbow, and led her toward the entrance of the rink.

Wallie Fineman, the night security guard, waved when he saw them approaching. "Evening, Mr. Bishop. Everything's ready."

Maggie looked at Scott. "Everything's ready?"

Scott's only answer was a slight smile. He handed Wallie what looked like a very sizable tip. "Thanks, Wallie. I hope it was no trouble."

"No sir. Mr. Bullard cleared everything with the owner. Edith Sophy just left about ten minutes ago." He tipped his hat at Maggie. "Evening, Maggie."

Maggie was sure he blushed. "Hello, Wallie."

Wallie unlocked the door. "Now don't you worry about a thing. Just take all the time you need."

Maggie waited until the door clanged shut behind them. "Scott Bishop, what are you up to?"

It was dark inside the arena. Only the dim lights from the exit signs illuminated the small hallway. Scott bent his head and gave her a brief kiss. "It's magic, Maggie," he said when he lifted his head. "Just you and me and no one else. I want us to put everything else aside. No worries, no memories, no sorrow. Just tonight." He swept her hair back from her face with his hand. "Can we?"

Maggie met his gaze. "I'd like that."

Scott's smile sent a rush of flutters running through her bloodstream. "Thank you." He took her hand, and led her down the dim corridor.

When he pushed open the door to the rink itself, Maggie gasped in surprised delight. A single spotlight illuminated a silvery circle on the newly cleaned ice. Like a deserted island in a frozen sea, a midnight blue velvet spread lay in the center of the ice. Cushions and pillows, a lone picnic basket, and a bottle of champagne on ice awaited them.

"Wait," Scott said, "they forgot something." He hurried over to the audio pit, where the master controls for the rink were housed. She heard him throw two switches. The soft sounds of Nat King Cole's romantic voice filled the chilled air, and immediately, a pale light touched the spinning mirrored ball in the ceiling. Maggie stifled a giggle. The ball, usually so garish, so tacky, added just the right touch of drama to the stillness of the deserted ice rink. The tiny flashes of light were like stars against the darkened backdrop of the arena's domed ceiling.

"Very impressive," she told Scott, when he returned to her side. He wrapped his arms around her waist from behind, then bent his head to nuzzle her neck.

"You think so?"

"Um-hmm."

"I hope Edith remembered to put the foam under the velvet. I don't want our butts to freeze."

Maggie did laugh then. "And so romantic. You really know how to sweet-talk a girl, don't you?"

Scott turned her in his arms. His expression was serious. "No more kidding around, Maggie. I really wanted this to be like running away from home for us. If I could have, I would have taken you into Boston, but I knew you wouldn't want to leave Ryan. This was the best thing I could think of."

Her heart flooded with a sudden warmth that had nothing at all to do with her heavy wool coat. She laid her palm against his cheek. "I can't think of anywhere I'd rather be right now than alone on that island with you."

Scott turned his face to kiss her palm. "Thank you, Maggie," he said, then swept her up in his arms.

She gasped. "What are you doing?"

"I didn't think you'd want to walk across the ice on high heels."

"You're never going to keep your balance if you try and carry me."

"I think I'll do a lot better in shoes than I do on skates."

Maggie held as still as she could as Scott started to work his way across the ice. "Maybe I should just sit down, and you can slide me out there on my rear end."

"Now who's being romantic?"

She laughed. "There isn't going to be anything romantic about this if we both end up in the emergency room."

"Maybe if I fall and break my arm, I won't have to humiliate myself tomorrow night at the game."

But he didn't fall. He reached the velvet oasis with astonishing ease, and set Maggie down amidst the cushions. She reached for the buttons of her coat. "I'm quite impressed, Mr. Bishop."

He dropped down beside her. "You haven't even begun to be impressed." He helped her remove her coat. "Are you sure you'll be warm enough? I asked Chuck to turn up the heat as high as possible."

Maggie nodded. "I'll be fine. It's not too bad in here."

Scott shrugged out of his overcoat. "Okay, but tell me if you get cold." He reached for the picnic basket. "Edith promised me a feast."

Maggie leaned back against one of the cushions. "I'll bet she did. This is right up Edith's alley. You've made a friend for life in that woman."

Scott flipped back the lid of the picnic basket. He

sniffed appreciatively. "A fellow can't go wrong with a friend for life who cooks like this."

"Knowing Edith, it's probably pheasant under glass."

He pulled out a glass dish. "Close." Steam rose from the delicious-smelling casserole when he lifted the lid.

While the music played and the mirrored "stars" twinkled overhead, they dined on Edith's sumptuous feast, finishing off with the most decadent white-chocolate cheesecake Maggie had ever tasted. It really was like being alone in the world. Maggie had never felt more pampered in her life.

Scott served her from the endless supply of food in the hamper, kept her champagne glass filled, entertained her with stories about his large family and his childhood. As she finished the last of her cheesecake, he found a thermal carafe of coffee in the bottom of the hamper, along with two china cups and saucers. He poured them each a cup, then hastily replaced the used dishes in the picnic basket before setting it aside.

Maggie leaned back against the cushions and watched the mirrored ball turn in slow, hypnotizing circles. Scott put his arm around her shoulders. He pulled his overcoat over their legs, then settled back with his coffee in his hand. "Are you warm enough?" he asked.

"Um-hmm," she said, feeling blissfully content. Her head fit very nicely in the curve of his neck.

"Full enough?"

"Stuffed."

He trailed his fingers up her arm. "Feeling romantic?"

Maggie smiled. "Decadent is more like it."

For several long minutes, they lay in companionable silence. When Scott finally kissed her, it was as if they'd just melted together. She leaned into him. "I love the way you touch me," she said.

"I love touching you." He slid his hand up her rib cage to cup her breast. "You make me feel so good, Maggie."

She rubbed her mouth against his. "I know."

Scott took her mouth in a long, leisurely, thorough kiss. The contrast of his heated hands and heated mouth and heated breath against her cool skin was startlingly, amazingly erotic. Maggie was sure they were going to melt a hole in the ice rink. She slid her hands inside Scott's suit jacket to caress him through the crisp fabric of his shirt.

He tore his mouth from hers. "Ah, Maggie. Do you know what you're doing to me?"

"The same thing you're doing to me, I hope."

"Is this a good time for me to ask—" He broke off the question with a groan when the lights in the arena suddenly flared to life.

Seventeen

"**O**h crud," Scott muttered.

Maggie sat up. "What's going on?"

"I don't know." He looked around the arena. "Who's there?" he yelled.

Maggie shielded her eyes against the glare of the fluorescent lighting. "I don't see anyone. Maybe it's a timer or something."

"Maggie?" Chuck Bullard's voice came from the far end of the rink.

"Chuck?"

"Hell," Scott muttered.

Maggie punched him lightly in the ribs. Chuck was picking his way across the ice toward them. "Chuck, what are you doing here?"

He gave Scott an apologetic look. "I'm sorry to, er, interrupt."

"Then why did you?" Scott asked, irritated.

Chuck looked embarrassed. "This is really important. Just give me five minutes, then I promise I'll get out of your way."

"No problem," Maggie assured him. "What's wrong, Chuck?"

"I don't know that anything's wrong."

"Something better be wrong," Scott said.

Maggie poked him in the ribs again with her elbow, harder this time. "Scott," she said, a warning note in her voice. "I'm sure Chuck wouldn't be here if it weren't important."

Chuck gave her a grateful look. "It's about the game tomorrow."

Scott closed his eyes and leaned back against one of the cushions. "What about it?"

"Maggie," Chuck said, "do you know anything about Max Wedgins buying the Bruins?"

Scott's eyes popped open. "*Buying* the Bruins?"

"Contracts and all," Chuck said.

Maggie stared at him. "Max Wedgins bought the entire team?"

"The deal went down today."

Scott let out a low whistle. "That must have been the purchase Carl was talking about."

"What purchase?" Maggie asked him.

Scott shrugged. "I saw Carl earlier this week. He told me he was negotiating a major purchase for Wedgins."

Chuck nodded. "This would definitely constitute a major purchase."

"Can you do that?" Maggie asked. "I mean, can you just go out and buy a team like you'd buy a new pair of shoes?"

"Well," Chuck stuck his hands in his jacket pockets, "normally it's not that easy. Somebody has to want to sell first."

"Did anyone know Bill Harrison wanted to sell the Bruins?"

"There have been some rumors," Chuck said. "He's not in the best of health, you know."

Maggie put her coffee cup down. "So Max Wedgins just walked in and bought the team?"

"It's not all that bizarre," Chuck assured her. "I mean, Wedgins already owned the ice arena. It's not so weird that he wanted to own the team."

"But this is a little sudden. Isn't it?" she asked.

"Well, yeah, but that's kind of what I wanted to talk to you about." Chuck pulled a folded piece of paper out of his pocket. "I got a visit from Carl Fortwell tonight. He brought me this."

Maggie opened the piece of paper. "Oh my God! This is a check from Max Wedgins to the Boston Literacy Council for forty-five thousand dollars."

"That's not all," Chuck said.

Maggie looked at him in amazement. "There's more?"

Chuck nodded. "Fortwell said there would be announcements on television and radio, and in all the major papers tomorrow that the game was going to feature most of the Bruins."

Scott frowned. "But you only have confirmations from Polokov and Turson."

"Not anymore. I don't know what Wedgins did, but my phone's been ringing off the hook. I got eight players who suddenly think playing in this game is the hottest thing that ever happened to their careers."

"This is incredible, Chuck," Maggie said, still looking at the check.

"It's incredible, all right. Thing is, I asked Fortwell what brought all this on, and he said I'd better ask Ryan. I knew you guys were here, and I figured I'd talk to you about it first."

"Ryan?" Maggie said. She looked at Scott.

"Don't look at me. I'm as much in the dark as you are."

"You don't think this has anything to do with what happened the other day, do you?"

Chuck looked baffled. "What happened the other day?"

Scott wiped a hand over his face. "We had a little run-in with Wedgins. It seems Ryan called Carl to invite him to the father/son game—"

"Carl's grandson is playing," Chuck said. "Of course he's coming."

Scott nodded. "But Ryan said something to him that made him call Wedgins."

Maggie laid her hand on Scott's thigh. "You didn't tell me this."

He shrugged. "I didn't think anything about it at the time." He looked back at Chuck. "Long story short, Max showed up at Ryan's school to talk to him."

"You mean you've actually seen this guy? I thought he lived in hiding."

"He does," Scott said. "Sort of."

Maggie handed the check back to Chuck. "But he did show up that day to talk to Ryan. Come to think of it, I remember him saying something about the game as we left."

Chuck slid the check back into his pocket. "So whatever Ryan told him, Wedgins decided to buy the team and make this into some enormous event. Don't you think that's a little weird?"

Scott shook his head. "Not for Max Wedgins it's not. It's just the kind of thing he'd do."

"But why?" Maggie asked.

"Think about it. He's getting ready to plunk a three-and-a-half-billion-dollar resort down in the middle of Cape Hope. The town council's giving him hell. The zoning board is giving him hell. The environmentalists are giving him hell. What better opportunity for him to stir up a little goodwill than by doing something like this?"

Chuck exhaled a deep breath. "Whatever his reasons, it's a done deal now. I'd be lying if I didn't say I was ecstatic over it. There's no way we could have ever raised this kind of money."

Scott threw his arm across his eyes with an exultant whoop.

"What's your problem?" Maggie asked.

Scott rolled his arm back so he could look at her. "If Chuck's got all these Bruins coming, what kind of bastard would I be to insist on skating? They're the real crowd pleasers."

Chuck shifted uncomfortably. "If you really want to skate, Scott—"

Maggie started to laugh. "He doesn't want to skate. He can't skate."

"Did you have to tell him," Scott asked.

Chuck looked at him, dumbfounded. "You can't skate?"

"It's not a federal offense, you know."

"But why did you volunteer to play?"

"It's a long story," Scott answered before Maggie could tell him the real reason.

"You'd have gotten killed," Chuck said.

"It's starting to irritate me that everyone's so sure of that."

"Trust him," Maggie said. "You'd have gotten killed." She looked around the ice arena. "If Max is going to do all that advertising tomorrow, there's a pretty good chance we'll sell this place out."

"Or at least come close," Chuck said. "Especially with so many of the Bruins playing."

A giggle escaped Maggie's lips. She clamped her hand over her mouth. Scott looked at her. "What's so funny?"

Maggie's eyes were brimming with laughter. She lowered her hand. "I'm supposed to be in charge of the hot dogs and soda."

"So?" Chuck said.

"So I was planning on three hundred people."

Scott started to laugh. "How many people does this place seat, Chuck?"

Chuck looked around. "It's pretty big because the Bruins used to use it for a practice arena. I'd say it seats about three thousand."

Maggie fell back against the cushions with a shout of laughter. "Where on earth are we going to get five thousand hot dogs between now and tomorrow night?"

Annie swung her legs back and forth under the bleacher seat. She studied Mark's back. He was leaning against the dasher boards, watching Maggie and Scott and Chuck collect the picnic supplies. "Don't you think this is great, Mark?" she asked.

He gave her a quick look over his shoulder. "Yeah. It's great."

"If they sell out the arena, think of all the money they'll raise."

He looked back at the ice. "A lot."

"You don't sound very happy about it."

"This is weird."

"What do you mean by weird?"

"I want to know what kind of game Max Wedgins is playing."

"Maybe he's just a nice man."

"Men like Wedgins aren't nice. They're shrewd, generous maybe, but not nice. They don't do anything without a motive."

"You heard what Scott said. Maybe he's doing it for publicity."

"I don't think so."

She rubbed her hands together. She was starting to feel chilled. "Why not?"

"It's hard to explain." Mark walked over to where she was sitting. He dropped down onto the bleachers next to her. "I just think he's up to something."

"Is it a good something?"

"I'm not sure."

"But you're worried?"

"Yeah. I'm worried."

Annie put her hand on his forearm. "Why?"

Mark met her gaze. "Maggie needs this job. Not because of the business, although it would help, but because she needs to know she can do it."

"What do you mean?"

He propped his elbows on his knees. "I don't think I realized, not until recently anyway, how much Maggie gave up when she married me."

"Mark—"

He shook his head. "No, really. You don't understand what it was like for her. We moved something like six times in the first two years of our marriage. She never had time to make friends, or develop interests, or be her own person. Maggie had to become an extension of my career. That was the way it worked."

He glanced back at the ice where Maggie was leaning against Scott as they walked toward the exit. "That's why she's so scared."

"She thinks she'll become a part of Scott just like she became a part of you."

"Yeah."

Annie nodded. "She told him that, or something like it, the other day."

"If she gets this bid, it will really prove to her that she's capable of making it on her own." Mark looked down at his hands. "That's why we're still here. I'm sure of it."

"But there's nothing we can do to help her get the bid."

"I could talk to Max Wedgins again."

"I don't think that's a good idea."

"Why not?"

"Because you've already alerted him to the situation between Pete and what's-her-name. If you do anything else, then Maggie still won't have achieved what she wants. If you get the job for her, she won't have done it on her own."

"But she won't know."

Annie shook her head. "Men really are dense."

"What's that supposed to mean?"

"It doesn't matter whether or not she knows, Mark. It matters that she went after the job and got it. That's what counts."

"That's ridiculous."

"You're just going to have to trust me on this."

Mark reached for her hand. "I'm just afraid that I'm running out of time. Look at me. I'm almost gone."

Annie looked at their joined hands. His was nearly invisible, while hers was still stubbornly present. "I know."

Mark seemed to read her mind. "There has to be some reason why you're still here, Annie. Maybe they need you more than they need me."

She shook her head. "No. That's not it. Scott is ready to move on. He's completely ready."

"Then what's going on?"

She gave Mark's hand a squeeze. "It has to be something else. I just hope we figure it out before it's too late."

With a conspiratorial smile at Maggie, Scott carried another armful of hot dog buns into the concession stand on Saturday night. She wiped a latex-gloved hand over her brow. "Thanks," she said.

"That's the last of 'em. I checked with the other stands. They're almost out, too."

"When we sell out, we sell out." She fitted a hot dog into a bun and dropped it down into its cardboard container. She handed it to Tom Webb. "There you go, Tom. Enjoy."

"Great event, huh, Mag?"

"Yeah, great."

Scott dumped what remained of the frozen hot dogs into the steamer. The father/son hockey game had indeed been a smashing success. They were late into the third period, with a capacity crowd and a tie game on their hands.

Scott started filling cups with soda. To say the afternoon had been hectic was the understatement of the year. He and Maggie had traveled to six different food wholesalers trying to scrounge together five thousand hot dogs, five thousand buns, fifty gross of cased potato chips, and enough soda to satisfy the enormous crowd. The event had been sold out by two o'clock that afternoon.

Chuck had been shuttling players from Boston all day. When the kids had heard that Carson Lipter and the other five starting members of the Boston Bruins were coming in to play, they'd gone nuts. Scott and Chuck had started crunching numbers over dinner, and, including Wedgins's check, they figured they were going to raise about seventy thousand dollars.

Maggie grabbed two of the cups. "Are we out of Sprite?"

He nodded. "Yeah."

She plunked the two cups down on the table. "Give me root beer then."

Within twenty minutes, Maggie had finished selling what remained of the hot dogs. She waved the remaining customers toward other concession windows, then jerked down the metal door. She sagged back against the counter. "Whew."

Scott pressed a cup full of soda into her hand. "No kidding."

"I'm exhausted."

"Yeah. It's a good exhausted though."

"I wish we had been able to see the game."

Scott glanced at the clock. "There should be about seven minutes left in the period. Let's go watch."

Maggie followed him into the bleachers. He was glad to see that Ryan was on the ice. "Look," he pointed to the ice. "There he is."

Maggie found their seats next to Lily and Tom Webb. "How's he doing, Lil?"

"He's doing great. He scored a goal."

Maggie glanced at the opposing team's goalie. "Who's in goal?"

"George Framly. Oscar's dad," Lily said.

"That explains that," Maggie said.

Tom pointed at the kids' goal. "Yeah, but look who's in our goal."

Maggie recognized Ray Phillipi, first-string goalie for the Boston Bruins, by the number on his jersey. "That explains why the score is tied, and the kids aren't getting creamed."

"They're doing pretty well," Lily said. "Look, Ryan's got the puck."

Ryan was skating down the ice. One of the Bruins took a rather unconvincing fall, and Ryan broke free. Only Carson Lipter and George Framly stood between him and another goal. Despite the all-in-fun tone of the game, Maggie felt herself grow tense. "Come on, Ry," she yelled.

Ryan dodged left. Carson countered. Ryan faked right. Carson didn't budge. The crowd was on its feet. Maggie handed her cup to Scott as she jumped up. He had to juggle it a minute to keep from spilling it, but he finally got it settled on the floor. He stood next to Maggie. Everyone was glued to the drama unfolding on the ice. Even using a short stick, Carson Lipter was intimidating. Ryan concentrated on the puck. He eased left, then right again. Carson cast a quick glance at the goal.

Scott thought George Framly was starting to look panicky. Carson tried to wrest the puck away from Ryan, but Ryan countered by flipping it out of reach. Carson shot his stick forward. Then Ryan, with a finesse that had the crowd holding its breath, knocked the puck between Carson's legs. He grabbed Carson's thigh with one hand and swung around him like a fireman on a pole. The crowd roared. Ryan landed safely on the other side, skated forward, and flipped the puck right over George Framly's glove, straight into the goal.

The goal siren went off. Maggie threw her hands up with a whoop. The crowd started yelling. Scott was laughing so hard his stomach hurt. Even Carson Lipter looked impressed. He skated over to Ryan and lifted him off the ice. With Ryan squirming on his shoulder, Carson flipped the puck up to him. Ryan waved it at the crowd. Nobody even thought about playing the remaining minute and a half of the game. There wasn't a soul in the arena who wasn't content to let the kids have the win.

George Framly, at least, looked relieved. Ryan spotted Maggie in the crowd. He held the puck up for her inspection. Maggie grabbed Scott's hand, then waved back at Ryan.

And in that moment, Scott knew they could make it as a family. He just had to convince Maggie.

By the time the hollering was over, and they were all in the Bronco headed for Maggie's house, it was after eleven o'clock. Ryan was asleep in the backseat. He was still holding the puck and the jersey Carson Lipter had autographed for him.

Maggie leaned back in the passenger seat with a heavy sigh. "I'm bone-tired."

Scott shot her a wry look. "I'll bet. I've never known anyone who cooked five thousand hot dogs in one day."

"You helped," she said, smiling at him. "I don't think I had a chance to say thank you for everything you did."

"Just don't try and sucker me into this next year."

She laughed at that. "If there is a next year, Chuck's going to have to find more than one person to organize his concessions."

Scott liked the way Maggie had slipped so easily into his reference about the future. He reached for her hand. "It felt good, Maggie. It felt good to do this with you. It felt good to watch Ryan shoot that goal and know I was a part of it."

Her fingers tightened on his. "It did, didn't it?"

Scott looked at her in surprise. "Do I detect a slight warming trend to my way of thinking?"

She closed her eyes. "You detect a lady too tired to discuss this right now."

Scott rubbed his thumb against her palm. "I love you, Maggie."

She yawned. And if he hadn't known better, he'd have sworn she did it to hide the fact that she said, "I love you, too."

Maggie drove Scott to the airport, early the next morning, for his last trip to Dallas before the holidays. "Are you sure," she said, pulling into the airport parking lot, "that you want to come back to Cape Hope for Christmas?"

"Maggie," he gave her an exasperated look, "I'm sure."

"But your family—"

"My family is spread out all over the country. Mom and Dad don't expect everyone to be there."

"Still, I think they'd want you home. I mean, why would you want to spend Christmas with me and Ryan when you could be with your family?"

"Because I love you. Because Christmas is going to

be as hard for me this year as it's going to be for you, and I think we ought to get through it together."

She switched off the ignition. "I just don't see that—"

Scott kissed her. It was a warm, generous kiss that made her skin tingle. He dropped a brief kiss on the tip of her nose before lifting his head. "Give up, Maggie. You're stuck with me."

"It's not that I don't want you to spend the holiday with us, it's just that I'm sure your family would want you at home. Annie's death was hard on them in their own way."

"My family wants me to be happy. You," he said, "make me happy."

Maggie studied him for several long seconds. "When will you be back?"

He smiled at her. "Wednesday. Pick me up at the airport?"

Maggie mentally calculated the date. Wednesday was the twenty-second, the day after Annie's death. She wondered if he was deliberately delaying his arrival, but didn't feel like she could ask. She nodded instead. "I'll be here."

Eighteen

*I*rene Fussman drummed her fingers on Pete Sherban's desk. "What do you mean he hasn't made a decision yet?"

Pete shrugged. "It's like I said. Max is temperamental. He says he needs a few more days."

Irene pushed aside a flash of irritation. She slipped from her chair to walk around Pete's desk. She saw his skin flush. He pulled at his tie. "But you do have everything under control?" she asked, sitting on the edge of his desk.

Pete nodded. "Sure, sure. I told you, Babe, I've got Wedgins eating out of my hand."

Irene put her hands on his shoulders. "I wanted to be back in New York with a contract by now."

"I know." His gaze was riveted on her breasts. Irene arched forward. Pete cleared his throat. "I don't want to push him." He started to unbutton her blouse. "Besides, is it so bad spending a few more days here with me?"

She hastened to reassure him. "It's not that, lover," she said. "You know it's not. I just don't want that nasty business between us anymore."

304

Pete thrust his hand inside her blouse and roughly palmed her breast. Irene moaned for his benefit.

"What do you want between us?" he asked.

Irene stifled a groan. She reached for his tie. "Nothing."

Pete shoved her skirt up, then buried his face between her thighs. Irene squirmed against him. She barely stifled a relieved sigh when his intercom buzzed. "Pete," she said.

He nipped the inside of her thigh. "Ignore it."

She pulled on his thinning hair. "Pete, I think you should get that." He licked her panties. Irene pushed at his shoulders. "Baby, your secretary knows we're in here."

"Shit," he said, and raised his head. He stood up, then reached for the receiver. "What is it, Connie? I'm in a meeting."

Irene straightened her skirt. She could hear Connie talking in agitated tones, but couldn't understand what she was saying.

"Tonight?" Pete said, sounding outraged. "What the hell does he want to meet tonight for?"

Irene's interest peaked. Intuition told her that Pete was talking about Max Wedgins. "Fine," Pete said. "What line?"

He covered the receiver. "Wedgins wants to meet tonight," he told Irene.

She felt a tingle of excitement. "When?"

"Eight."

"I want to be there."

Pete shook his head. "No way. I told you, the guy's a recluse. He won't see anyone but me."

Irene laid her hand against the straining fabric of his fly. "You'd better take his call, lover."

Pete groaned, then punched the button. "Max, hi."

Irene opened Pete's fly. He tried to push her hand away. She could hear Max Wedgins talking on the other end of the phone. He told Pete he wanted to see him and Carl at eight o'clock.

"Does it have to be tonight?" Pete asked.

Irene slid off the desk and knelt in front of him.

"Shit," Pete said. He took a hasty step back. "What, oh, nothing, Max. Yeah. Eight o'clock. I got it." He tried to take another step back, but backed into his chair. He tumbled into it. Irene pushed his knees apart. "Did you—" Pete's breath came out on a hiss. "Did you tell Carl? Fine. Good. OK." Pete leaned his head back against his chair. "Bye, Max."

He dropped the receiver as he reached for the back of Irene's head.

Mark looked from one to the other in disgust. He willed himself back to Maggie. Pete's conversation with Irene, coupled with the odd phone call, had confirmed his worst suspicions about Max Wedgins. He was playing some kind of game.

Mark found himself in the Bronco, studying Maggie's profile as she drove back to Cape Hope from Logan Airport. Christmas carols were playing on the radio. Maggie was wiping the tears from her face. He wondered why he'd never noticed before what a determined face it was.

He'd always thought of Maggie as being a little on the fragile side. When he'd first met her, he'd been attracted to the fact that she made him feel so powerful. He'd wanted Maggie to need him. At the time, she had. But the woman she was today was a different person. She might not realize it yet, but as a mother, as a woman, Maggie had become so much more than she'd ever thought she would.

He felt a rush of love so intense, it made his eyes sting. He stared at her. "Maggie," he said, "I know you can't hear me."

"Jingle Bell Rock" was on the radio. Maggie turned it up. Mark ran his hand over the outline of her face. "I love you, Maggie. I will always love you, but I can't hold on to you anymore." He closed his eyes on a shuddering sigh. "It's time for you to fly on your own."

Scott took another sip of his beer. He was seated on the couch in his apartment, with his long legs stretched out in front of him, listening to the clock tick. It was raining, not so common a thing in Dallas, but highly appropriate for his mood.

For the hundredth time that day, he questioned the wisdom of his decision to spend this day, the anniversary of Annie's death, alone in Dallas. He could have flown back to Cape Hope. He could have gone to visit his parents. They'd practically begged him to come. He could have gone to the office and tried to concentrate on his clients. But he hadn't.

He'd sat down on the sofa and replayed in his mind every second of every minute he'd spent with Annie on this day one year before. The clock chimed twelve. Three hours, forty-two minutes to go.

The phone rang, and, as he had all day, he ignored it. On the third ring, the answering machine picked up. He waited for the outgoing message to play through, then heard the tape click on. "Scott, Scott, are you there? It's Maggie."

Maggie. He closed his eyes. He couldn't talk to her.

"Scott, I called your office. They said you weren't in. I—you don't have to talk about it if you don't want to. I just thought you might like to talk to someone about, well, anything but that."

Scott's stomach twisted. Trust Maggie to know the reason he had been unable to face the world today. Every other day since Annie's death, he'd dealt with the sympathy, with the questions, with the prying. Today, he couldn't. He couldn't talk about it, but he couldn't *not* talk about it. The wounds were too raw.

Maggie kept talking to him through the answering machine. "I talked with Chuck," she said. "He said we raised seventy-one thousand and some change with the hockey game. He wanted you to know how much he appreciated everything you did.

"Ryan says hi, and Edith Sophy said to let you know she'll be glad to give you the recipe for that cheesecake. I . . ." Her voice trailed off. Scott was almost afraid the answering machine would hang up on her. "I . . . if you want to talk, about anything, I'm—"

Scott grabbed the receiver like it was a lifeline. "Maggie, don't hang up."

She sighed. "Hi."

"Hi."

"I didn't know if you were there."

"Yes, you did," he said. "You knew I was sitting here in the dark feeling sorry for myself."

"Scott, you don't have to talk about it if you don't want to."

"I don't know what I want. I just don't want you to quit talking."

"OK. What do you want to know?"

"Anything. How's the weather?"

"Snowing again. We're going to have three feet on the ground by Christmas."

"Am I going to have any trouble flying in?"

"I don't think so. We're pretty good at handling this kind of thing. It's only a problem when it all comes at once."

Scott leaned back against the sofa. "My plane's scheduled to land at eleven-thirty. Are you going to meet me?"

"I said I would. Today is Ryan's last day of school until after the first. I'll bring him with me."

"Great. How's he doing?" He was finding an odd kind of fortitude in the mundane conversation.

"He's fine. He's been strutting like a peacock ever since the game. Carson Lipter sent him a Christmas card."

Scott had a sudden memory of the way he'd felt, standing in the bleachers, holding Maggie's hand during that game. "I'll bet he's beside himself."

"Pretty much." She paused. "How are *you* doing?"

"Okay," he lied.

"Scott," she said, "it's *Maggie*. Tell me how you're doing."

He paused. He stared at the clock, and listened to Maggie breathe on the other end of the phone. "I'm splitting apart," he finally said.

"Oh, Scott."

Scott clutched the receiver tighter against his ear. "Maggie, I think I want to tell you about this."

"I'm listening."

"Where do I start?"

"Why don't you tell me what you miss most about Annie, and we'll go from there."

He stretched out on the couch. "You know what I

miss most? This is going to sound really dumb."

"No it isn't."

"I miss her hair. She had the most incredible hair. It was kind of honey-colored, with these red highlights. I could spot her all the way across a room just by looking for her hair. It kind of shone around her face like a halo. It was so soft, like silk. I remember one day after she'd started having chemo, I found her in the bathroom sobbing."

"Her hair was falling out?"

"Yeah. She was holding this brush and it was full of her hair. I kept telling her it didn't matter, and she kept crying." He rolled to his side. "I even bought her a Dolly Parton wig. I thought if we laughed about it, it would help."

"Did it?'

Scott drew a shuddering breath. "For a while. I don't think either of us thought she was going to die at that point."

"When did you know?"

He swallowed. "She knew first. She kind of started to prepare me for it. She would try and talk about what it would be like for me when she was gone. I didn't want to listen. Then," he stopped and cleared his throat, "then one day around the middle of September, we were on a walk. I looked at her, and I just knew. God, I almost fell to pieces right there on the sidewalk."

"Did you tell her?"

He shook his head. "I never admitted it to her. I couldn't. During the next two months, things got really bad. She was so weak, so sick. I can remember waking up in the night and hearing her vomiting in the bathroom. She never wanted me to help her."

"When did you have to put her in the hospital?"

"December fifth," he said. He'd broken into a cold sweat. He started to shiver. "After that, it happened really fast. I stayed there as much as I could, just holding her hand and talking to her."

"I'm sure it helped, Scott."

"It helped me. I felt like I had a million things to tell her. I was terrified to sleep or leave the room. I was so afraid I'd miss something if I wasn't there."

"Scott, you couldn't have been there twenty-four hours a day."

"Part of me knew that, but God, Maggie, I was petrified. I've never been that scared in my life. Every night she made me kiss her good night before she went to sleep. She always said the same thing. Always."

He thought he heard Maggie crying on the other end of the phone. When she spoke, her voice sounded shaky. "What?"

"She always said, 'see you in the morning.' " He felt a sad smile ghost across his lips. "I clung to that. I was like a drowning man holding on to a thread. As long as she said 'see you in the morning,' I could believe everything was going to be all right."

"Oh, Scott."

He heard Maggie's voice break. "It wasn't until the day she died, today, that she started losing consciousness a lot. I remember just sitting by her bedside and praying for every breath. I remember what I was doing every minute of that whole damned day."

Maggie sniffled. "What time did she go?"

"Three-forty-two. She opened her eyes for the last time around three-thirty. She was pulling on my hand. I leaned over the bed so I could hear her. Her voice was so faint by then, it was barely above a whisper." He could feel the tears rolling down his face now. He wiped at them with his cuff. "She looked right at me, and she said 'Kiss me good-bye, Cowboy.' "

"Scott," Maggie's voice broke on a sob.

"Did I tell you that Annie never liked to say good-bye?"

"Yes."

"She knew. I knew. She closed her eyes, and she slipped away twelve minutes later."

"Scott—" Maggie's voice cracked. "Scott, I wish I was there with you."

"I wish you were, too."

"I don't think you should be alone this afternoon."

He shifted on the sofa, pausing to wipe away the lingering tears. "I needed to think. I couldn't face the questions."

"I know, but, I don't like to think of you going through this alone."

"I'm not alone anymore," he said. "I have you."

"I love you, Scott."

He closed his eyes. A simple admission, so simply made, so joyously received. "Thank you, Maggie."

"I—are you sure you're all right?"

"For the first time today, I feel like I'm going to make it to sundown."

"Do you want to keep talking?"

He shook his head. "No. I just want to be alone for a while."

"All right. If you need me, I'll be home all afternoon."

"I'll remember."

"Can you at least consider yourself hugged until tomorrow?"

"Do I get the real thing at the airport?"

"Guaranteed."

"I'll make it."

There was a long pause. "Scott?"

"Yeah, Maggie?"

"We're going to be okay."

"I know we are. I'll be there tomorrow, and we'll get through the twenty-third together. All right?"

"All right."

"I love you, Maggie."

"I love you, too."

He waited until he heard the dial tone before he hung up the receiver.

Annie pulled her knees against her chest and rocked quietly back and forth, her eyes burning with unshed tears.

"Annie?" Mark said.

She looked at him in surprise. "What are you doing here?"

"I heard Maggie talking to Scott. I thought you might need me."

The breath squeezed out of her. "Shouldn't you— shouldn't you be with Maggie?"

Mark shrugged. "Maggie's okay. Besides, I can't do anything for her."

"Isn't it difficult for you to be apart from her?"

Mark squatted down in front of her chair. He laid his palm against her face. "I'll be all right. I just wanted to be here for you."

Annie threw herself against his chest. Mark shifted

so that he was sitting in the chair, holding her on his lap. "I'm so sorry, Annie."

"I can't even touch him. I can't talk to him. I just have to sit and watch him hurt," she said.

"I know." He ran his hand down her back. "I know."

She was silent for a long time. "You know what?"

"What?" he asked.

"I know for sure now that this isn't Heaven."

Maggie buried her face in her hands as soon as she hung up the phone. There had been so much pain in his voice. She couldn't believe how easily she had concentrated on her own grief during the past few weeks and completely ignored his. It hadn't been until she'd phoned his office that morning and found he wasn't in that she'd begun to realize how much pain he was in.

She felt selfish. And shallow. And childish. She cried into her hands until the tears ran down her wrists. How could she have done this to him? How could she have allowed herself to lose sight of the fact that his pain was no less than her own?

She lifted her head. Her gaze found Mark's picture on her dresser. She got up and crossed the room. Holding the picture in her hands, she thought about the last time she'd seen him alive. He'd been so confident about his mission, so sure. She couldn't even imagine what it must have been like for Scott to see Annie suffer over the long months of her illness.

She thought about Scott's kind eyes, the way his gaze softened when he looked at her. She thought about the way he made her feel, how she believed, really believed, she could do anything she set her mind to when she was with Scott. Resolutely, she set Mark's picture down on the dresser.

She opened her jewelry chest, then stared down at the wedding band on the third finger of her left hand. With a gentle tug, she removed it. She laid it carefully on the top shelf of the jewelry box before quietly closing the lid.

And she wondered where she and Ryan could find a Christmas tree.

When Scott stepped off the plane the next day, he looked worn-out, and wonderful. Maggie walked straight into his arms.

"Scott, guess what?" Ryan was tugging on his coat.

Scott's gaze locked with Maggie's for a few seconds. The look he gave her said, "I love you, I missed you, I'm glad you're here," all in an instant, before he shifted his focus to Ryan. He scooped him up in his arms. "What, sport?"

"We got a Christmas tree. A big, huge one. Mom cut it herself."

Scott glanced at Maggie. "Really?"

She nodded. "It was no big deal. I've cut a tree before."

He pressed a kiss to her lips. "That's not what I meant."

"I know."

"How are you, Maggie?"

"I'm OK."

He grabbed her hand. "Let's get out of here. I want a real answer to that question."

Scott had checked his luggage, and they had to wait by the turnstile until he collected his bags. Maggie left Ryan with him, and went to drive the car around. By the time he tossed his bags in the back, and climbed into the passenger seat, Ryan was talking a mile a minute. "Did Mom tell you I got a card from Carson Lipter?"

"She sure did." Scott turned in his seat to adjust Ryan's seat belt for him. "Did he offer you a contract with the Bruins?"

Ryan giggled. "No. It just said, 'Merry Christmas.' "

"I guess Mr. Wedgins would have to offer you the contract."

Maggie could feel Scott's gaze resting on her face. She concentrated on the traffic. "Yeah," Ryan was saying. "He's the new owner. Coach Bullard says he gave all the guys Christmas bonuses if they played in the game. He said it was a lot of money. I told Franklin it was probably like a whole hundred dollars or something."

"Probably," Scott agreed. He reached for Maggie's hand. "Where are we going?" he asked.

Ryan didn't seem to notice the very adult tension in the car. "Mom said we could go Christmas shopping. I haven't finished yet."

"Oh yeah?" Scott said, turning to look at Ryan. "What have you got left to buy?"

"I gotta get something for Franklin and something for Miss Price."

"His Sunday school teacher," Maggie supplied helpfully.

Scott nodded. "Your teacher, hmm? That could be tough."

"Yeah, 'cause, I want to get her something she likes."

"What are you getting Franklin?"

"A Bruins jersey," he said. "Just like mine."

Scott glanced back at Maggie. "Like the one your mom has?"

She blushed. Ryan frowned. "What one?"

"The one she sleeps in."

"Oh," Ryan said. "No, that one's old. It's really worn-out. I want to get Franklin one of the yellow ones."

Maggie shot Scott a knowing look. She could tell by the expression on his face that he'd been trapped by his own game. He'd been trying to embarrass her by talking about her nightshirt, but Ryan's innocent description had taken him by surprise. She turned onto the interstate with a wry smile. "If it's all right with everyone," she said, "I thought we'd have lunch at the Ice Palace."

Nineteen

*B*y that evening, Maggie was exhausted. They'd spent the entire afternoon Christmas shopping in Cape Hope. Scott had seemed to recognize her need for the distraction of bustling activity. He'd helped her concentrate on Ryan, and she'd been surprised to find that the afternoon had quickly passed.

She'd left the two of them the task of setting the tree in its stand, and decorating while she prepared dinner. Scott had trailed after her into the kitchen. "Maggie, wait."

"What?"

"About the tree. I know that was hard for you."

She shrugged. "It didn't seem fair to Ryan not to have one."

"When did you decide?"

She paused in the process of rummaging through the pantry. She met Scott's gaze. "Yesterday. After I got off the phone with you."

Scott crossed the kitchen in two quick strides. He raised her left hand to his lips to kiss her now bare ring finger. "Don't think I didn't notice this," he said.

Maggie hesitated. She felt the same nagging sense

of discomfort that had plagued her since she'd removed her wedding ring. "Scott, I—"

He pressed a brief kiss to her lips. "Let's just make it through tomorrow, honey. We'll worry about the rest later. OK?"

She nodded. "OK."

Standing in the kitchen twenty minutes later, Maggie heard Scott and Ryan laughing in the living room as they decorated the tree. She lifted the lid off a pot to stir the beef Stroganoff. The spicy scent of onions and black pepper rose in a swirl of steam. Maggie sniffed appreciatively. Edith Sophy would be proud.

She pulled plates and silverware from the cabinets and put them on the counter so Ryan could set the table. The sound of "Blue Christmas" wafted in from the other room. Maggie was sure Ryan was doing his Elvis impersonation for Scott.

She was stirring a gallon of iced tea when the phone rang. "I got it," she yelled, reaching for the receiver. "Hello?"

"Maggie?"

"Yes."

"It's Carl Fortwell."

Her heart leapt into her throat. "Oh, Carl. Hi." Maggie propped the receiver against her shoulder. She started separating the rolls. "What can I do for you?"

"It's about the bid, Maggie," he said.

He sounded grim. Maggie set aside the rolls. "What about it, Carl?"

"I think Max is going to give it to you."

She was almost afraid to believe him. "What?"

"I think Max is going to award you the bid."

"Carl, I—I don't know what to say."

"Nothing is final yet. We had a meeting with him the other day, and he said he'd make a definite decision by Monday. He sounded really positive about your designs, though. I thought you'd like to know."

Maggie cast a quick glance at the door. "Carl, what about the structural design?"

There was a long pause on the other end of the phone. "I don't know."

Maggie's heart started pounding. "He didn't give you any indication at all?"

"No. He's playing this really close to his chest. I don't know what Pete has told him, and I'm not sure what Max is thinking. He did say something about wanting to keep the bid local."

"Local?"

"Yeah, you know, use an in-state company."

"But, Carl—"

"Look, Maggie, Max is leaning on Pete for this. I don't know what else to tell you. I don't have much influence."

"Scott's designs are perfect for the tone of the resort."

"Maybe Max thinks awarding the bid in-state will save him grief with the zoning commission."

"That's not fair."

"It's business. It's not supposed to be fair."

"Is there anything I can do?"

"Just sit and wait. Max is so unpredictable, I hesitated to even call you tonight. I just figured things were a little rough on you right now, and some good news might help."

Maggie realized with something of a shock that it almost seemed unimportant to her whether By Design was awarded the bid or not. Scott had invested so much of himself, staked his career, possibly his future on the Cape Hope Resort. If Max Wedgins awarded it to another firm simply because of some stupid advice from Pete Sherban, it would be disastrous.

"Maggie?"

She started. She had all but forgotten that Carl was on the other end of the phone. "I'm still here, Carl. I was just thinking."

"Listen, you and Ryan have a good Christmas. I just wanted to call and let you know things look good for you."

"Thanks. Merry Christmas to you, too."

"I'll talk to you as soon as I know something definite."

"OK. Bye, Carl."

"Bye, Maggie."

Maggie dropped the receiver back in its cradle. She stared at it, frowning.

"Who was that?"

She jumped at the sound of Scott's voice. She hoped she didn't look guilty. Somehow, she didn't want to talk about the bid, or Carl, or Max Wedgins. Not tonight. "Lily," she said. "She called for a recipe."

Scott slipped his arms around her from behind. "Why are you frowning at the phone like it's going to bite you?"

"I—I think I told her the wrong amount of flour."

He nuzzled her neck. "Call her back."

Maggie tipped her head to the side. "No. I'm pretty sure it was right. It won't matter that much anyway."

He turned her around in his arms to give her a lingering kiss. "Come see the tree. It looks good."

Maggie hedged. "Dinner's ready. Why don't you guys come eat first."

"You can't put this off forever, Maggie. Come on. It's just a tree."

"You know why I don't want to do this."

He nodded. "Yeah, I know. It's important to Ryan, Honey." He laced his fingers through hers.

"Scott, I—"

"Maggie." He gave her hand a gentle pull. "It's going to be all right. I promise."

She dropped the dish towel she was holding onto the counter. "All right. Let's go."

Scott ushered her through the swinging door. The tree that had seemed so short and fat when she'd cut it looked massive now that it was inside the house. The lace angel tree-topper scraped the ceiling, and the boughs spread well into the living room.

"What do you think, Mom?" Ryan asked, pointing proudly to the tree. "See what we did. We put all the ornaments on by color. The blue ones are on the bottom, then green, then red, then gold, then mixed-up."

"Very impressive," Maggie said, staring at the white lights. "I see you found the lights."

"Yeah." Ryan adjusted an ornament to a lower limb. "They were crammed in a box way in the back of the attic. I had to use the flashlight."

Scott's fingers tightened on her hand. "It wouldn't have been a tree without lights," he said.

"No." She felt her throat tighten. "No, I guess it wouldn't."

"Don't you like it, Mom?"

Ryan was looking at her with obvious concern. She managed a weak smile. "It's wonderful, Ry." She jerked her hand from Scott's. "I, um, I need to wash up before dinner. Can you guys set the table?" She fled the room without waiting for an answer.

She sat down on the side of her bed and stared at Mark's picture on the dresser. "You're being ridiculous," she scolded herself. "You're being totally ridiculous. It's just a tree. What's the big deal?" She pressed her lips together, determined not to cry.

"Maggie?" Scott said from the doorway.

She didn't look around. "I'm fine. I'll be down in a minute."

He shut the door behind him. He crossed the room to sit down next to her on the bed. "Maggie, it's okay."

"This is so silly," she said. She wondered if he could hear the slightly hysterical note in her voice. "It's just a tree. There's no reason why I should be acting like this. You think I'm acting silly, don't you?" She blinked several times to keep tears from falling.

Scott put his arm around her shoulders. "I'm the one who sat in my apartment all day yesterday and stared at the walls. I'm not going to tell you you're acting silly."

"Well, I am," she said. "Why should I be so upset over a tree?"

"It was the lights, wasn't it?"

Maggie choked back a sob. "Yes."

"Tell me about the lights, Maggie," he said quietly.

She kept staring at Mark's picture. "He was supposed to be home the week after Christmas. Ryan and I promised him we'd wait. I told him I wouldn't light the tree until after he got home. The day"—she gulped back a sob—"the day his body arrived, I came home and tore the lights off the tree."

"Oh, Maggie," Scott pulled her against his chest. "Honey, it's all right."

"I don't want to cry over this. I don't. It's silly."

"It's not silly."

She pushed at his chest. "Stop being so nice. I'm going to start bawling. I don't want Ryan to see me like this."

He gave her hair a gentle tug. "What do you say I go and tell Ryan to unplug the tree? You can meet us downstairs in a couple of minutes, and we'll eat."

"Okay." She sniffed.

"Then after Ryan's in bed, you and I will sit on the sofa, and you can cry all over me."

Maggie choked out a slight laugh. "You have no idea what you've let yourself in for."

"I think I can handle it." He rubbed his hand over the soft fabric of his shirt. "See. Flannel. High-absorbency."

She sat back, wiping her eyes. "I'll be down in a minute."

"We'll be waiting," he said.

Maggie entered the kitchen five minutes later to find Scott and Ryan making a miniature teepee out of spoons. "That's some centerpiece," she said.

Scott flashed her a smile. "Yeah, well, it was either this or a clown made out of oranges, strawberries, and toothpicks. My repertoire is sort of limited."

"Good choice."

Ryan balanced a fork on top of the teepee. "That is so cool."

Maggie carried the Stroganoff to the table. "Okay, Ry, wash your hands so we can eat."

He climbed down from his chair. "Can I have tea instead of milk?"

"I guess it's all right," she said.

Scott took the pot from her. "All right?" he asked, his hazel eyes filled with concern.

Maggie nodded. "All right."

* * *

It was after ten o'clock when Ryan finally wound down enough to go to bed. Maggie finally had to bargain with him by agreeing to let him listen to Christmas carols for another thirty minutes as long as he stayed in bed. She switched out the light. "Good night, Ryan."

"Good night, Mom."

She trudged down the stairs, bone-tired. Scott had built a fire in the living room, and the orange glow of the flames cast dancing shadows on the walls. The scent of the Christmas tree, coupled with the spicy woodsmoke, made the house feel particularly cozy. Maggie sank down onto the soft couch with a tired sigh.

Scott slipped his arm around her shoulders. "Tired?"

"Exhausted."

"I'll bet. It's been a rough day for you."

She momentarily thought of her conversation with Carl, but thrust it aside. "I'm sorry I got so emotional over the tree."

He rubbed his knuckles on her arm. "No apology necessary."

"I don't know what's wrong with me."

"Maggie," he said, "you're overwrought. Who wouldn't be in your shoes?"

She curled her fingers into his shirt. "I think Mark would expect me to be taking this better."

"Mark's not here," Scott said. Maggie noticed a slight edge to his voice. "I am, and I don't expect you to be taking this any differently than you are."

"I'm so tired," she said. "It's like it never goes

away. Every time you think you have it under control, something else sneaks up on you."

"Do you want to talk about it?" he asked.

"No," she said, realizing she didn't. "I don't. I've done all the talking I can. I just want to sit here for a while and be close to you. All right?"

Scott shifted so they were stretched out on the couch. "I'll be right here if you need me."

As Maggie dressed the following morning, she thought about the wisdom of what she was about to do. Scott had never returned to his hotel last night. Instead, he had stayed on the couch with her, and sometime, late in the night, she'd managed to talk about Mark's death and what it had done to her.

She had been surprised that she had not been more emotional. Perhaps she owed that to the fact that she'd already told Scott so many of the things she'd been through. Persistently, though, her thoughts had returned to her conversation with Carl. The longer she talked with Scott about Mark, the more she thought about how long she'd dwelled on the past. That, in turn, made her think about the future, which naturally led to thoughts about Cape Hope.

During the night, Scott's touch had been comforting, rather than passionate. He had seemed to realize that what she needed was his companionship. Unselfishly, he had given it. Even his kisses had been soft and compassionate. He didn't push. He gave instead. Maggie had felt cherished. Loved. Valued.

Shortly before dawn, they'd fallen asleep. When Maggie woke, Scott was in the kitchen fixing breakfast for three. She had stretched like a languorous cat, enjoying the unique feel of being pampered. Scott had carried a cup of coffee to her. "You keep this up, and I'll get spoiled," she said.

"You mean after all the trouble I went to arranging dinner at the ice arena, all that was really needed was a cup of coffee on the couch?"

Maggie smiled slightly at the memory as she tied a silk scarf into a loose bow. She had reached her decision to pay a visit to Max Wedgins while she was drinking that cup of coffee. She didn't know exactly what was going on, or what kind of game Max was playing with the bidders, but she did know that Scott Bishop deserved a whole hell of a lot more than a brush-off from Pete Sherban.

She had told Scott that she had to drop some things off for a client, then finish up her Christmas shopping for Ryan. Scott had volunteered to keep Ryan with him that morning, which gave Maggie the perfect opportunity to call on Wedgins. The trick would be getting in to see him.

She eyed her reflection once more. The forest green suit was flattering and professional. It was also the most expensive outfit she owned. It had seemed outrageously extravagant when she'd bought it, but now, she was glad she had splurged. She figured she would need every confidence booster she could get, and every little bit would help, even if it was just a two-hundred-dollar suit.

She walked down the hall to Ryan's room. She could hear him singing "Rockin' around the Christmas Tree" at the top of his lungs. She rapped on the door. "Ryan?" He didn't answer. Maggie pushed open the door to find Ryan dancing on his bed. "Ryan," she said, louder.

He bounced around. He gave her a toothless grin. "Hi, Mom."

Maggie switched off the stereo. "I have to go out for a couple of hours. Scott's going to stay here with you." Ryan's hair was standing straight up on his head. She tried to smooth down a particularly untidy cowlick.

"Where ya' going?"

"To see a client."

"You look good," he said. He sounded quite matter-of-fact.

"Thanks."

Ryan bounced twice on the bed. "When will you be back?"

"Before lunch."

"Oh."

"Why?"

"Can Scott and me do something while you're gone?"

"I guess you can do whatever you can talk Scott into."

His eyes widened. "Wow."

Maggie kissed his forehead. "Be nice to him, Ryan. He's new at this."

"Okay, Mom."

Scott was waiting for her at the bottom of the stairs. He was holding her briefcase and keys. "You look great."

She smiled at him. "I try."

He handed her the briefcase. "Have a nice day at the office."

"This is terribly domestic."

He swept her into a dramatic embrace, dipped her, and gave her a sound kiss. "Better?"

Maggie laughed. "Yeah. Better."

"Do I get any last-minute instructions for the kid?" he asked.

Maggie pulled her coat from the closet. "Don't let him railroad you into anything."

Scott looked outraged. "Madam, I am perfectly capable of controlling a seven-year-old."

"Um-hmm." She tossed the muffler around her neck. "I can't wait to see what condition my kitchen is in when I get back."

"That's not fair. He snuck up on me last time."

"Just watch your back, Cowboy."

On the long drive to Max's estate, Maggie intermittently rehearsed what she was going to say and choked on panic. Mark watched her from the passenger seat. "I don't know if this is such a good idea, Maggie," he warned.

She turned down the volume on the radio. "And another thing, Mr. Wedgins," she said, "I don't think this process has been in the best interest of all parties involved. If you truly wished to plan a resort that would serve this community as well as utilize our best resources, you should have used a more open-ended bid process."

Mark rolled his eyes. She was in her "avenging angel" mode. "Now, Maggie, listen to me. You heard what Fortwell said. You practically have this in the bag. What are you trying to do to yourself by going up here to see Wedgins?"

Maggie exited off the highway. "If you would be inclined to award the bid to an architect for any reason other than the viability of the project, then you have no business undertaking a project of these proportions."

"This is really dumb."

She muttered something beneath her breath. "That was dumb. Who am I to tell Max Wedgins what kind of projects he can undertake? The man has more money than God."

She parked in front of the steel gates of Wedgins's estate. She tipped her head forward to rest it against the steering wheel. "I cannot believe I'm doing this."

"I can't believe you are either," Mark said. If he hadn't been sure it was his imagination, he'd have sworn that Maggie frowned at him.

A buxom redhead dressed in a well-tailored uniform, exited the security post to walk over to the Bronco. Maggie rolled down the window. "Can I help you, ma'am?" the young woman asked.

Maggie looked at her name tag. "Connie. Yes, Connie, you can help me. I would like to see Mr. Wedgins."

She checked his clipboard. "Do you have an appointment?"

"No. I just want to see him."

"Well, I'm sorry, ma'am, but Mr. Wedgins doesn't—"

"Look," she paused, "Connie, I don't want to cause any trouble, and I certainly don't want to ruin your day, but it's imperative that I see Mr. Wedgins. Would you just let him know that Maggie Connell is here, and she wants an appointment."

Connie shifted from one foot to the other. "Ms. Connell, I can't—"

"Connie, are you married?" Maggie asked suddenly.

"Yes, ma'am. Got two kids."

"I'll bet they're girls. They're girls, aren't they?"

"Yes, ma'am." She was starting to look wary.

"Maggie, you're scaring her," Mark said. "She's going to think you're psychotic or something."

Maggie continued to look at Connie. "If something was so important to them and your husband that you were willing to drive all the way up here two days before Christmas to try and get an appointment with Mr. Wedgins, wouldn't you be terribly upset if the security guard wouldn't even ask?"

She looked unsure. "But, ma'am—"

"Are you going to get in trouble if you ask?"

Connie shook her head. "I guess not."

"Okay then. I'll make a deal with you. You ask, and if he says 'no,' I'll leave. How's that?"

Connie gave her a reluctant smile. "All right, Ms. Connell. You wait right here." Connie bounded off toward the security office. Through the tiny window, Mark could see her talking on the phone. After several long seconds, she leaned out the door and gave Maggie a broad smile. "He said 'yes.' " Connie sounded shocked.

Maggie waved at her. "Thanks, Connie."

The young woman pushed a button and the gates began to slide open. "Good luck, Ms. Connell," she said as Maggie drove past her.

Maggie clutched at the steering wheel. Mark's head started to pound. "Maggie, what have I got to say to get you to turn around?"

"I've got to go through with this."

"No," he said. "No you don't."

"I'll just go in there, and I'll tell him he's a fool if he doesn't give Scott's designs a chance."

"You're going to lose the bid if you hack this man off, Maggie."

"What's the worst thing he can do?"

Mark groaned. Maggie turned the last corner of the long drive. She stopped to stare at Max Wedgins's house. "Wow," she said, at the same instant Mark said, "Damn."

"Who lives in a house like this?" she asked, opening the door to the Bronco. "It looks like some castle straight from Europe."

Mark scrambled out of the car. "It probably is. He probably had it flown in brick by brick and resurrected right in the middle of Massachusetts." Maggie was walking up the wide stairs that led to the front door. Mark hurried after her. "Look, Maggie. You know how this guy is. I don't think he's going to appreciate it if you just barge in on him."

Maggie stopped in front of the twelve-foot-plus wooden doors. She looked first at one, then at the other. She giggled. "I don't think places like this have doorbells. What am I supposed to do, bang on the door?"

The door opened. A tall, curvaceous brunette, dressed in a black cutaway coat and gray pin-striped trousers, greeted Maggie. "Hello, Ms. Connell. I'm Anita, the butler. Mr. Wedgins is expecting you."

Mark watched the butler lead Maggie through the enormous foyer. He had a brief memory of Bobbi the chauffeur and Connie the security guard. His opinion of Max Wedgins rose a few notches. The man certainly knew how to pick a staff. He'd give him that.

Maggie followed Anita down a long corridor. The butler indicated a comfortable-looking sofa. "If you'll wait right here, Ms. Connell, I'll let Mr. Wedgins know you're here." She opened an impressive mahogany door and disappeared.

Maggie sat down on the sofa. She was gripping the handle of her briefcase so tightly, Mark thought the handle might snap off. "It's not too late, Maggie," he said.

Anita stepped back into the corridor. "All right, Ms. Connell. Max is with some people right now, but he said he'd see you."

Maggie took a deep breath, then stood up. "Thank you."

Anita pushed the door open for her. The room was so large, it took Mark a few minutes to locate the cluster of people at the other end. The black-and-white marble floor seemed to stretch an eternity between the door and Max's desk. It was the most enormous desk Mark had ever seen. It looked more like a yacht than a desk. Particularly since it was purple.

Max was dressed in all black, but the various paintings and tapestries and furnishings in the room were all brightly colored. It looked like a giant crayon box gone amuck. Max was seated behind the desk. He smiled at Maggie. To his left was a young African-American woman. She wore wire-frame glasses that did nothing to detract from the classic beauty of her face, and wore a blue business suit that didn't even begin to hide the curves underneath. Mark grinned.

Max stood up. "Do come in, Maggie. We were just discussing you." For the first time, Mark noticed the two people to Max's right. He frowned. "I believe you know Pete and Irene," Max said, indicating the couple with a sweep of his hand.

Maggie nodded. "Yes. Yes, I do."

Pete tugged at his tie. "It's, ah, good to see you Maggie."

Maggie glared at him. "I'll bet it is." She started across the long room.

Max looked from Maggie to Pete to Irene, then back to Maggie, with an expression Mark could only call predatory. "This," he said, indicating the young woman to his left, "is my lawyer, Daphne."

Daphne nodded at Maggie. Max's gaze connected with Mark's. Mark stalked forward to the desk. Max, he knew, was the only one in the room who could see him. He planted his fists on the edge of the purple desk, and leaned forward. "Look, Wedgins, I don't know what kind of game you're playing, but I don't like it."

"Won't you sit down, Maggie," Max said, indicating the chair in front of his desk. Maggie dropped into it. Max's eyes never left Mark's. "Perhaps," he continued, "you're here for some reassurances?"

Mark glared at him. "You bet I am."

Maggie opened her briefcase. She removed a binder. "Actually, no I'm not."

Mark ignored her. "This bid is damned important to Maggie, Max. You'd better not be screwing around with it."

"I assure you," Max told Mark, "my judgment is sound."

"I'm sure it is," Maggie said, "but there's something I want you to consider."

Max shifted his gaze to Maggie. "Would you like some refreshment? I'll have Ellen bring you some coffee." He reached for a button on his phone.

Maggie shook her head. "No thank you."

Mark sat down on the edge of the desk. "I'd like to

get a look at Ellen. Does she fit the description of the rest of the staff?"

"Quite right," Max said. "Very well, Ms. Connell, what can I do for you?"

Mark couldn't help but notice that Pete was starting to look extremely uncomfortable. The look Irene gave Max was nothing short of lascivious. "Max," she said, laying a red-tipped hand on his knee, "perhaps you'd like us to step outside so you can speak with Maggie in private. I wouldn't want us to intrude on your conversation."

"Yeah, sure," Pete said, "we could just go wait in the library."

Max leaned back in his chair. He stroked his chin. "I believe Helen"—he paused to look at Mark—"that's my librarian," he looked back at Pete, "is in the process of a rather extensive recataloging. I fear you'd be in her way."

"Well," Irene said, "we could go into the garden, then."

"What's the gardener's name?" Mark drawled.

"Francine," Max answered.

"What?" Pete asked.

"Francine," Max said again, "my gardener. She informed me this morning that the walks are iced over." He looked at Irene's three-inch heels. "I don't think you'd be very comfortable."

Irene muttered something beneath her breath. "Wherever. It doesn't matter."

Max shook his head. "No, I think you'd be better off here. I'd like you to hear what Maggie has to say."

Pete coughed. "How do you know what she has to say?"

"Call it a hunch."

Maggie shifted in her chair. "Look, this isn't some game we're playing, and I don't have all day. I just want to get this over with."

"You're right," Max said. He pushed a button on his intercom. A door to his right opened, and a woman with platinum blond hair, as tall and attractive as the rest of Max's staff, entered the room. "What do you need, Max?"

"Georgette," he said. He looked at Mark again. "Georgette is my housekeeper." He glanced back at the young woman. "Georgette, would you please ask Iris to check the thermostat? It's grown cold in here, and I don't want my guests to be uncomfortable."

"Sure, Max." She turned to leave.

Mark gave Max a wry look. "They seem happy enough working for you."

"I compensate my staff extremely well," Max said to the group at large. "It's no wonder I receive such excellent service." He leaned back in his chair. "Daphne, I have a feeling this is going to be rather important. We might need to analyze its legal ramifications later. I'd like the whole meeting transcribed rather than the usual summary. Do you want me to get my secretary?"

"No need to bother Janet, Max." Daphne punched a couple of keys on her laptop computer. "I'll do it. Ready."

"All right, Maggie," Max said. "What brings you here?" He looked at Mark. "I'm sure it wasn't an easy decision."

"No. It wasn't," Mark said.

Maggie looked first at Max, then at Pete and Irene. "Actually, it was an easy decision. I made it when I got off the phone with Carl Fortwell last night."

"Carl?" Pete said. "What were you doing talking to Carl?"

"Carl and I are friends," Maggie answered. "We have been for quite some time." She gave Pete a dry look. "Why wouldn't he call me?"

Pete blanched. "No reason."

Irene was studying Maggie with a dark look in her eyes. "Maggie, Mr. Wedgins is extremely busy, and—"

Max waved his hand. "Not that busy. I also consider Maggie to be my friend. I had time for your impromptu visit," he said, sliding an icy look at Irene. "I certainly have time for Maggie's."

Mark grinned at Max. "Nice move, Max."

Max looked at Maggie. "What can I do for you, Maggie?"

Maggie handed him the binder. "This is a complete study on vacation resorts in the surrounding area. I did it when I was trying to put my bid together."

Max laid the binder on this desk and began idly flipping through it. "There's a lot of background work in this."

"I'd never done a proposal of this scope before, and I—"

"All the more reason you shouldn't worry about it, Maggie," Irene said.

Max gave her a glacial look. "This shows very good business sense. No one should go into a large project without sufficient background research."

"I thought you would feel that way," Maggie said. "That's why I wanted to show you the numbers on the resorts in Connecticut, Massachusetts, northern New York, and Rhode Island. I think we can safely say that the demographic profiles of those areas are most like the profiles of Cape Hope."

"I'd agree," Max said.

Pete shifted in his chair. "I don't see what this has—"

Maggie glared at him. "Be quiet, Pete. This is my meeting."

Max glanced at Mark. "Very impressive," he said.

Maggie obviously misunderstood him. "It's just simple background research," she said. "I wanted to know how similar resorts were faring."

Max took a few minutes to study the data. "According to this, only the Burlington project is in the black."

"That's right." Maggie leaned across the desk and pointed to a row of figures. "The others are having trouble attracting a consistent repeat clientele. That's the lifeblood of modern hotel facilities."

Max shut the binder. "You have a theory on this, I suppose."

"I do." Maggie reopened her briefcase. She pulled five hotel brochures and handed them to Max. "These are the brochures of the hotels I studied. Look at the Burlington resort compared to the other four."

Max flipped through the brochures. "The Burlington is smaller."

Maggie shook her head. "No, I mean, look at the structure. Only the Burlington fits the historic and cultural profile of the surrounding area. The others have more of an Atlantic City look. This one," she said, pointing to a particularly glossy brochure, "is one of Jason Challow's projects. It looks like it should be called the Soap-a-rama."

Max looked over his shoulder at Daphne. "Make

sure you get 'Soap-a-rama' in the notes."

"Got it, Max."

Maggie tapped the Burlington brochure with her index finger. "All I'm saying is, if I were you, and I was planning to invest over three billion dollars on a project, I'd think long and hard about what forces I let influence my decision." She looked meaningfully at Pete and Irene.

Irene glared at her. "That's a very simplistic approach, Maggie. You must know that Max would have considered all the options before making an investment of this size. He has been rather successful so far. I'm sure he's not in need of your business acumen."

Max frowned at Pete. "I don't like rude people," he said.

Pete flinched. "Now, Max, I'm sure—"

Max held up his hand. "Save it." He looked first at Mark, then at Maggie. "So what you're saying, Maggie, is that you think perhaps I'm not considering certain external circumstances in awarding the structural bid for this project?"

"That's right."

"Aren't you worried about the interior bid?"

Maggie paused. "I'd be lying if I didn't say I'd like the chance to work on this project. My business could use the work, and I could use the opportunity, but frankly, that has nothing to do with why I'm here this morning."

Max steepled his fingers under his chin. "Then why are you here?"

"Because even if you awarded me the bid, I wouldn't do it unless Scott Bishop was the architect."

Irene smirked. Max didn't take his eyes off Maggie.

"That's a rather large sacrifice on your part, isn't it?"

"Scott believes in this project. I've seen his work. His designs are brilliant."

"Are you threatening me, Maggie?"

"Hardly," she said. "It isn't as if you couldn't get another decorator at the drop of a hat." She indicated Irene with a wave of her hand. "I'm sure Irene would be delighted to work on the project with any architect you choose."

"Undoubtedly," Max said.

Mark nodded his agreement. "This is a selfless thing for Maggie, Max. Don't hold it against her."

"But you really need this bid, don't you?" Max asked.

"Without it, I'll have to give up By Design."

Mark was starting to feel desperate. "She needs it for personal reasons, too, Max. She's got to know she can make it. When we were married, I never gave her the chance to stand on her own."

Irene drummed her nails on Max's desk. "I think you'd have to think twice about giving a project this large to someone with so little experience, Max. She can hardly make a go of her business."

Max ignored her. "So why are you doing this, Maggie?"

"Because Scott Bishop deserves this project. He at least deserves to be considered fairly, without outside influences driven by greed and"—she looked meaningfully at Pete and Irene—"whatever else."

Max nodded. "Duly noted. Did Carl tell you last night that I've decided to postpone my final decision until after the holidays?"

Mark leaned over the desk. "Scott wants Maggie to

marry him, Max. She's not going to unless she gets this bid."

"He did," Maggie said. "I just wanted to make sure you'd heard at least one more side of the argument."

"Even if it meant that you had to risk losing the bid?"

"Even that."

Max stared at the brochures on his desk, his expression pensive. The only sound in the room was the ticking of the red lacquer clock on his desk. Finally, he extended a hand to Maggie. "Thank you for coming, Maggie."

She hesitated before taking his hand. "Am I dismissed?"

"You all are," Max said.

Maggie shook his hand. Pete leapt out of his chair. "Now see here, Max—"

Max stood up. "I've plenty of things to consider. You've overextended your time, Pete." He looked at Irene. "Good of you to come, Irene. I'll consider your proposal."

She slid her hand into Max's. "I hope you will, Max."

Mark frowned at Max. "Don't tell me you can't recognize a viper when you see one?"

"If you will see yourselves out, I'm sure my footman, Kara, will help you to your cars. Thank you for coming."

Maggie scooped up her briefcase. "Thank you for seeing me, Max."

He smiled at her. "Do tell that young son of yours I said hello."

"Max—" Mark said.

Max shook his head. "I wish to be alone, now. I can't think around people."

"I'm not a person," Mark insisted. "I'm a ghost."

"Go."

Twenty

*M*aggie made three more stops before returning home. She hadn't lied when she'd told Scott she needed to finish her Christmas shopping. She turned into the driveway, feeling surprisingly lighthearted considering the events of the morning. At the sight that greeted her, she started to laugh.

A full-size, genuine igloo had been erected in her front yard. Ryan was crawling out the tiny front door. "Hi, Mom," he yelled when she got out of the car.

"Hi, Ry," Maggie said.

Scott was smoothing a trowel over the side of the igloo. He smiled at her. "Did you get everything done?"

She nodded. "Yep." She crunched through the snow toward the igloo.

"Look it," Ryan said. "Scott put a hole in the top so I can light a fire inside."

"Won't the igloo melt if you put a fire inside?"

"No, Mom," he said, looking disgusted. "The Eskimos have fires. How else would they cook stuff?"

Maggie couldn't argue with that. "No fire without my help, okay?"

"Okay." Ryan disappeared back into the igloo.

Maggie looked at Scott. "I see he kept you busy."

Scott kissed her. "Yeah. We missed you."

"It took a little longer than I thought it would."

"How was your client meeting?"

She felt a twinge of guilt for not telling him the truth. "It went OK." Not really wanting to discuss it, she decided to change the subject. "Have you guys decided what you want to do for lunch?"

Scott shook his head. "I was just starting to get hungry."

"Can we really light a fire in that thing?" Maggie asked, pointing to the igloo.

Scott raised his eyebrows. "In theory we can."

"So how about if we sit around and roast hot dogs."

"I'm game if you are."

Maggie laughed. "Let me go change, and I'll be right out with the feast."

They huddled inside the igloo, eating roasted hot dogs and potato chips, until it became apparent it was going to cave in on them. Ryan was the last to leave. Maggie had to practically drag him through the door. The igloo collapsed with a loud *whump*.

"Ah, Mom," Ryan said. "It would have stayed up if we'd kept banking the walls."

Scott shook his head. " 'Fraid not, Ry. I think it was doomed. We shouldn't have lit the fire."

"But the real Eskimos do it."

"It's also a lot colder north of the Arctic Circle than it is in Massachusetts," Maggie said.

Scott rubbed his hands together. "Wanna bet?"

Maggie gave Ryan a gentle push toward the house.

"Come on, Ry. Scott's not used to roughing it in the cold."

"It was fifty-seven degrees when I left Dallas," Scott said, "and they were talking about record lows."

"What a wimp," Maggie said over her shoulder.

A snowball connected with the back of her head. She squealed. "Hey!"

Ryan dived for Scott's legs. "I got him, Mom."

Maggie picked up a clump of snow and hurled it at Scott. It hit him between the eyes just as he toppled to the ground. With Ryan on top of him, he tried to squirm away through the snow. Maggie pelted him with another snowball.

By the time Scott finally surrendered the fight, the three of them were soaked and shivering. Amid much laughter and good-natured teasing, Maggie hurried Ryan into the house for a hot bath. "And don't come out until you're pink," she said, shutting the bathroom door.

Scott was standing right behind her. He pinned her to the wall. "I'm cold, too, Ms. Connell."

"Hah!" she said. "I can tell by the look in your eyes that you're not one bit cold."

He nuzzled her neck. His lips were cool from the snow. Maggie felt a curl of heat work its way down to her toes. "How long do you reckon we have before Ryan gets tired of playing with his rubber ducky?"

"Not long enough for what you have in mind," she said.

"How about a few kisses just to steam me up, then?"

Maggie curled her fingers around the back of his neck. "Is that all it takes?"

"Did I happen to tell you that you look incredibly sexy when you're wet?"

Maggie shook her head. "No. You didn't."

Scott kissed her nose. "Well, you do. It kind of has me wondering what you'd look like in the shower."

"Scott!"

He tipped her head back. "I'm cold, Maggie. Heat me up." His lips came down on hers in a hot kiss that did indeed make her feel steamy. Her cold clothes felt almost soothing against her scorching-hot skin. Scott worked his way through the layers of her coat and sweater until his frigid fingers found the bare flesh of her stomach. Maggie gasped.

Scott slid his tongue between her lips. She sucked at it. "Ah, Maggie," he said. "You feel so good. I want you so much."

"Scott," Maggie pressed against his hand. "Scott, I—"

A sudden light spilled into the hallway. Scott lifted his head to see Ryan, stark-naked, standing in the door of the bathroom, watching them. "I need some shampoo," he said.

Maggie jumped. Scott eased her coat back into place. "Shampoo," he said. "Where's the shampoo, Maggie?" He wondered if his voice really did sound ragged.

"Hall closet," Maggie choked out. She wrenched away from Scott, walked to the closet, and grabbed a bottle from the top shelf. She handed it to Ryan. "Here ya go, sweetie."

Ryan tipped his head to look at her. "Were you guys kissing?"

Scott nodded. "Uh-huh."

"How come?"

Maggie closed her eyes. Scott felt some of his equilibrium return. "Because it's fun."

Ryan frowned. "But you had your tongue in her mouth."

Maggie groaned. Scott smiled at Ryan. "Sure did."

"That's gross."

"You won't think so when you're older."

Ryan shrugged. "I'd never do that. It's disgusting."

Scott gave Ryan a gentle push back into the bathroom. "Finish your bath, sport. You're not supposed to come out until you're pink, remember?"

Ryan wrinkled his nose, then closed the door. Scott looked at Maggie. "Mood broken?"

She opened her eyes. Her lips twitched in amusement. "You could say that."

"Just for the record, Maggie," he said, "there is nothing disgusting about having my tongue in your mouth."

Maggie laughed. She pushed at his shoulders. "I'm going to change into something dry. I'll meet you downstairs."

"Sure you don't need help?" he asked. He bent his head and gave her a soft kiss.

"Don't start that again. No, I don't need help."

"Darn."

"What I do need is for you to unload the stuff out of my car."

"Okay."

"Do you think you can put a bike together before tomorrow morning?"

He looked offended. "I'm an architect. I build things for a living. How hard can it be?"

* * *

"Famous last words," Scott muttered two hours later as he sat amid a pile of nuts, bolts, and bike parts.

Annie leaned back on Maggie's bed, watching him. "If you read the directions, it wouldn't be so hard."

Scott picked up the handlebars. "I wonder if I'm supposed to connect these first."

"I'm sure it's in the directions."

"Don't be silly, Annie," Mark said, walking into the room. "The directions are nothing more than the manufacturer's suggestion on how to assemble something." He looked at Scott. "How's he doing?"

"Not so good. He already had to take the chain assembly apart."

Scott swore softly when he banged his knuckles on the sharp edge of a bolt. Mark shook his head. "He's never going to finish that by Christmas morning."

"Yes, he is," Annie assured him. "He once put together an entire go-cart for his nephew in one night. It took until four in the morning, but he finished it." She paused to study the strained lines of Mark's face. "How's Maggie doing?"

He shrugged. "Okay. She's in the kitchen with Ryan. They're making gingerbread men."

"How are you doing?" Annie asked.

Mark let out a shuddering sigh. "Hanging in there. She scared me to death this morning. I wish to hell I knew what Max was thinking."

"Me too, but that's not what I meant."

Mark met her gaze. "You mean this being the day I died. Don't you?"

Annie nodded. "Yes."

"I'm glad Maggie's not hurting too much. She's staying too busy to dwell on things."

Annie hesitated. She remembered Maggie's conversation in the Bronco with Scott the day she'd told him about seeing the remains of Mark's body. Mark had been with Ryan that day, and he hadn't heard it. Somehow, she'd known that Mark had no idea Maggie had seen his remains. "Mark," she said, cautious.

He was watching Scott struggle with the bike. "Yeah?"

"There's something I have to tell you."

He looked at her. "What?"

"I think I figured out why we're still here."

Mark's eyebrows rose. "I thought you already figured that out. We're supposed to help Scott and Maggie get together."

She shook her head. "That's just part of it."

"What do you mean?"

Annie took a deep breath. "Remember when we talked about how you're disappearing, and I'm not."

"Sure," he said. He held up his hands for her inspection.

Annie laced her fingers through his. "The first time we talked about this, you told me you thought Maggie was having trouble letting go of you because she hadn't been given the chance to say good-bye. Remember?"

"Uh-huh. It was different for you and Scott. He was with you when you died."

"Maggie did have a chance, Mark."

He frowned. "What do you mean?"

"The day she drove Scott to the airport—the day Max showed up at Ryan's school—remember?"

"Yeah."

"I was in the car with them. Do you know why Scott didn't leave for Dallas that day?"

"I thought it was because Ryan was missing."

Annie shook her head. "That happened later. It was because Maggie told him about the last time she'd seen you."

"The day I left for Saudi."

"No. That was the last time she'd seen you alive."

Mark looked confused. "I don't understand."

"Mark, Maggie went to the airstrip the day your remains arrived back in the States."

"I expected that she would," he said. "I was with Ryan that day."

"Did you know that she convinced them to open your casket?"

"What?" He looked appalled.

"It's true. She demanded to see your body."

"But—" He paused. "Oh my God. I died in a helicopter crash. I must have been—"

"She said it was really bad. You were almost completely burned. The only way she recognized you was from your wedding band."

Mark dropped down on the side of the bed. "Oh my God."

"Maggie said good-bye a long time ago, Mark."

"They had no business letting her see that."

"She needed to. She needed to know you were really gone."

He shook his head. "I had no idea."

"Mark," Annie laid her hand on his shoulder, "listen to me."

"I can't imagine what that must have been like for her."

"It was like saying good-bye, Mark. It was awful and terrible and rotten."

He looked up. "Why didn't you tell me?"

"I've been thinking about this ever since. I couldn't figure out why you were slowly disappearing, and I was still here. I think I know now."

"What's that got to do with it?"

"Mark, Scott never needed me here in order to say good-bye. We already did that. We did it the day I died. Maggie never needed you here to say good-bye. She did that the day she looked into your coffin."

"What are you saying, Annie?"

"It was you, Mark," she said. "I let go of Scott a long time ago. That day in the hospital when I told him to kiss me good-bye, I let him go. But you, you never let go of Maggie. I'm not here because of Scott. I'm here because of you."

"What's that supposed to mean?"

Annie wrapped her arms around his waist. "You told me once that Maggie wasn't going to be able to let you go until she knew she could stand on her own. Didn't today prove anything to you?"

"I think she blew the account, Annie. I don't think Max is going to give it to her."

"It's not about the account, Mark."

"Sure it is."

She shook her head. "Men really are dense, you know that?"

"What are you talking about?"

"Maggie confronted Max Wedgins on behalf of Scott. Even if it meant giving up the account that could make or break her business, she stood up for herself and for him. She did it, Mark. She won."

"But if she doesn't get the account, she'll lose By Design."

Annie smiled at him. "But she got what she really needed. She was her own person today. She made a

decision about the future of her business, about her
future, and she stuck by it. She flew, Mark. She really
did."

He stared at Annie for several long seconds. Somehow, he knew she was right. It hadn't been about the
business. It hadn't been about Maggie getting the bid.
It had been about Maggie feeling good enough about
herself to do what she'd done that morning. Maggie
had chosen to stand up to Max Wedgins. Knowing
she was risking the future of her business, and quite
possibly her future with Scott, Maggie had done what
she thought was right. Mark had known it from the
moment she'd walked into Max's house. He just
hadn't been ready to let go. He wanted to believe that
Maggie still needed him.

He thought about Ryan, about what it was going
to be like to say good-bye. A picture of Ryan rolling
in the snow with Scott popped into his mind. He
looked at Scott struggling to put the bike together and
thought of all the things he was going to miss by leaving Ryan. He wasn't sure he could give that up. It
would be like dying again, only worse.

But Annie was right. His conscience told him so.
Ryan needed security, a real family. Maggie needed
to be free of the past. Neither of them could have that
unless Mark let go. "Well, then," he said, his voice
sounding raw, "I guess maybe it is time to say good-
bye."

And Annie started to disappear.

Christmas Eve passed in a flurry of activity. Ryan
spent the morning with Franklin, while Maggie and
Scott completed some last-minute shopping. By late
afternoon, Maggie had almost managed to believe

everything was going to be all right. She'd enjoyed a strange sense of well-being since her meeting with Max Wedgins the day before.

Somehow, the strain of the bid process had passed, and having Scott with her had helped her get through the more painful memories of Mark. For reasons she couldn't quite discern, she had decided not to tell Scott about her meeting with Max. It had seemed best to enjoy the simple pleasures of Christmas without worrying about the resort or its affiliated problems.

She'd helped Scott pick out presents for his family, wrapped gifts with him, laughed with him. By the time Lily dropped Ryan off at the house, he was practically climbing the walls he was so wrapped up in Christmas excitement. Scott took him outside to play in the snow, leaving Maggie free to finish stuffing Ryan's stocking and wrapping the last of his presents.

Alone, in the quiet of her room, she felt a strange sense of Mark's presence. She looked at his picture on the dresser. "Mark," she said, "I don't know if you're here. I don't know if you can hear me, but I . . ."

Mark held his breath. Annie slipped from the room. "Go on, Maggie," he said.

"I want you to know that I never stopped loving you. A part of me will always love you." She taped a bow on top of a package.

"I know that," he said.

"It's time for me to move on now," she continued. She cut paper for another box. "And wherever you are, I hope you'll understand that. I'm in love with Scott Bishop. I just hope you approve."

Mark felt a tremendous weight slip from his shoulders. He sagged back on the bed. "Oh, Maggie. All I ever wanted was for you to be happy."

"He wants me to marry him," Maggie said.

"You'd better."

"I don't know if I can do that."

"No, Maggie—"

"But I can't stop loving him either. At first, I felt like I was being unfaithful to you. He's a good man, Mark. He's a really good man."

"Then why the hell aren't you going to marry him?"

"I'm just afraid that if I marry him, I'll lose myself again. Without you, I wasn't me. I don't want that to happen all over again. I'd be afraid to do that to Ryan. He needs more stability."

"He's got stability. He's got you."

"You know, I envy him sometimes. I wish I could see you, talk to you like he does. It helps him."

"No, it doesn't," Mark said. "It helps me. It's selfish. I'm selfish. I just didn't want to let go."

"If I could talk to you, maybe I'd know what to do. Maybe I'd feel like I knew who I am."

"Maggie, you're an incredible person. You've grown so much. Don't let fear stop you from getting what you want."

"I guess I'll just have to wait and see."

"Don't push him away, honey. You'll lose him."

She tied a ribbon into a neat bow. "But I want you to know that I'll never forget everything you meant to me." She trimmed the edges of the ribbon. "And I'll always be glad for the years we had together, and especially for Ryan."

"Oh, Maggie." Mark buried his face in his hands.

Maggie set the package aside. She started to tidy up the leftover bows and ribbons.

"Maggie, listen to me," Mark said. "Just listen to

me. You can't throw this away. He loves you. In some ways, he loves you more than I did. Scott loves *you*, the real Maggie. I loved the way you were when you were with me. You're a different person now, Maggie, a better person. I don't think I really fell in love with that person until the past few weeks. There's nothing in the world I want more than for you to be happy."

Maggie picked up the wrapped packages. She headed for the door.

"Maggie, wait," Mark said.

She looked around the room, then switched off the light. Mark scrambled from the bed and went after her. "You've got to listen to me."

Maggie went downstairs and set the packages under the tree. For a moment, she fingered the plug for the lights. Mark held his breath. "Do it, Maggie," he whispered. "Turn them on. Say good-bye."

She dropped the plug and left the room.

He groaned. "Damn it."

Annie walked up behind him. "We're running out of time, Mark."

"I know."

"What do you want to do?"

He took a deep breath. "Ryan," he said. "He's the only tangible link I have to Maggie anymore. I think I've got to get out of the way."

"You want to disappear completely? Leave them before we have to?"

"You're the one who said I had to let go."

"Do you think you should do it on Christmas eve?"

Mark wiped a hand over his face. "I have this sick feeling that it's a now-or-never kind of thing. I don't think I have much of a choice. Maggie's still unsure about Scott because she's afraid for Ryan."

Annie slipped her hand into his. "When do you want to do it?"

"Tonight. I'll do it while he's asleep."

Mark stood by Ryan's bed and watched him, reposed in sleep. The afternoon and evening had been bittersweet. He'd listened to every word, memorized every motion, every step, knowing they would be the last hours he'd ever spend with his son. Maggie, Scott, and Ryan had gone to church for the Christmas Eve service, and Mark had stood in the aisle, listening to Ryan sing Christmas carols. Ryan had grinned at him.

Through the course of the afternoon, Annie had been fading steadily. She was almost as transparent as he by late evening. Maggie had sent Ryan to bed shortly after they returned from the church, and Mark had spent long hours telling him stories and singing to him. Ryan had seemed to sense that something was wrong. He'd refused to go to sleep, asking for one more story, one more song, until finally, his eyelids had grown heavy and he'd sagged into the pillows.

Mark watched him for a long time. Annie sat quietly in the corner of the room, rocking back and forth in the rocking chair. "It's time, Mark," she said softly.

"I know."

"Are you going to wake him up?"

"I can't just leave him. I have to say good-bye."

"Are you sure that's best?"

Mark nodded. "He wouldn't understand if I just disappeared."

"What are you going to say?"

"I don't know." Mark kept staring at Ryan.

"Are you sure you want to go through with this? We could just leave."

Mark shook his head. "I've been a coward about this all along. If I hadn't been, I would have done this a long time ago. I owe him this."

"All right." She continued to rock.

Mark sat down on the side of the bed. "Ryan," he said. "Ryan, wake up."

Ryan moaned in his sleep.

"Come on, buddy, wake up."

Ryan's eyes drifted open. "Is Santa here?"

Mark smiled. "No. It's not Santa. It's me."

"Dad?"

"Uh-huh."

"Is it morning?"

"No, it's not morning."

"I'm tired."

"I know you are, son. I just have something I want to tell you."

Ryan rubbed his fists in his eyes. "What?"

"I love you, Ryan."

He yawned. "I love you, too, Dad."

Mark swallowed. "Do you remember how I told you one time that I wasn't sure I'd be here forever?"

"Yeah."

"It's time for me to go, Ryan."

Ryan frowned. "Go where?"

"Away."

Ryan sat up in bed. "You're leaving?"

"I'm leaving."

"For how long?"

"Forever."

"No!" Ryan looked at Annie. "Tell him he can't." He looked back at Mark. "You can't leave me. Why are you leaving?"

"Ryan, listen to me. Don't you want to have a real

dad? Someone who can hold you, and play with you, and comfort you?"

"No." He was sobbing now.

Mark felt like his heart had been ripped out. "I think you do, son. I think you need a real father, and not just one you imagined."

"Don't you love me anymore?"

Mark clenched his eyes shut. "I'll never stop loving you, Ryan. Not ever." He felt tears start to stream down his face.

"Stay with me," Ryan started to sob. "Don't leave me alone, Dad."

Mark stood up. He reached for Annie's hand. "I have to, Ryan. I love you. That's why I have to say good-bye."

"I'm scared," Ryan said.

"Don't be scared. Nothing is going to hurt you. Mom's going to look after you."

"Don't leave me." Ryan's voice sounded hoarse.

Mark felt the force of the broken plea like a knife thrust through his heart. Annie's fingers tightened on his. He looked at her. He saw the tears, real tears, spilling from her eyes. "You're crying?" he said. He wiped her cheeks with his hand. "I thought you couldn't cry real tears."

Annie leaned against his shoulder. "I guess it took both of us to make it happen."

And together, they disappeared into the night.

Scott was leaning back on the couch, staring at the fire, when he heard Ryan's sob. He plunked his coffee cup down on the table. "It's Ryan," he told Maggie.

She tipped her head. "Are you sure?"

The muffled noise sounded again. Scott shot off the

couch and headed for the stairs. "I'm sure."

He took the stairs two at a time. He shoved open the door to Ryan's room. "Ryan? Are you all right?"

Ryan was sitting in the middle of his bed, clutching his pillow. "He's gone," he said, his voice muffled by the pillow. "He's gone."

Scott crossed the room. He sat down on the bed, then lifted Ryan onto his lap. "Shh. It's a dream, Ryan."

Ryan shook his head. "Daddy left. He isn't coming back." He leaned against Scott's chest. His little body shook with heartbroken sobs.

Scott felt his chest constrict. "Ryan, it's OK. Nothing's going to happen."

"Why did he leave?"

Scott rocked him back and forth. "How do you know he's gone?" he asked.

Ryan hiccuped. "He told me he was leaving. He said he wasn't coming back."

"Did he say why?

"Because he wants me to have a real dad."

Maggie appeared in the doorway. Scott cautioned her with a brief shake of his head. "You know, Ryan," he said, "did I ever tell you about the day Annie died?"

"No," Ryan said, still crying.

"I didn't want her to die. I knew I'd miss her a lot, but there wasn't anything I could do about it." He rubbed his hand down Ryan's back. "For a while I tried to pretend she was still alive."

Ryan tipped his head back to look at Scott. His face was streaked with tears. "Really?"

Scott nodded. "Really. But one day, I just had to admit to myself that she was gone."

"Were you sad when you said good-bye to Annie?"

"Uh-huh."

"Did you cry?"

"I cried for a long time. I think sometimes, it takes a very long time before sadness goes away." He met Maggie's tearful gaze across the room. "Sometimes, it doesn't ever completely go away."

"I miss Dad."

"I know you do."

Ryan was quiet for a long time. His tears were hot through the fabric of Scott's shirt. "Scott?" he asked.

"Yes?"

"I'm scared. Don't leave me alone."

Scott stretched out on the bed, still holding Ryan. "I'm not going anywhere."

"Don't leave me." His voice was a muffled sob against Scott's shirt.

Scott hugged him closer. "I won't. I'm not going to leave you. I promise."

Twenty-one

Maggie looked out the window at the fresh Christmas snow that had fallen during the night. Scott was still asleep in Ryan's room.

After Scott had stretched out on the bed with Ryan, Maggie had fled to her own room, where she'd spent the better part of the night searching her heart. The image of Scott, rocking Ryan against his chest, of him comforting her son, had been enough to make her own tears start to flow. Sometime, just before dawn, she'd finally fallen into a fitful sleep. She'd dreamed of Max Wedgins.

In her dream, he'd been standing alone on the site of the Cape Hope Resort, laughing, laughing like he knew something the rest of them didn't. She awakened feeling fitful, and on edge.

She was jerked from her reverie when the door flew open, and Ryan came racing into her room. He wrapped his arms around her legs. "It's Christmas," he said.

"Sure is," she said, ruffling his hair. "I imagine you've been downstairs already?"

"Yeah. Santa left me a bike. It's really cool. It's just like Franklin's."

"Where's Scott?"

"Sleepin'."

Maggie nodded. "Well, what do you say you and I go make some breakfast, then we'll wake him up."

"Can't we open presents before we eat?"

"Ryan," she said, smiling, "you ask me that every year. You know we're not going to open presents until after breakfast."

"Can I eat the chocolate out of my stocking?"

Maggie had long ago decided that Christmas was as good an excuse as any for breaking a few household rules. "Yes," she said. "You may eat the chocolate out of your stocking."

Ryan shot out of the room. Maggie changed from her bathrobe to jeans and a green sweater. She stopped by Ryan's room to look in on Scott. He was, indeed, sprawled across the bed. She shook her head and pulled the door shut.

Downstairs, Ryan chattered while she made French toast. "Mom," he said, "can I call Franklin and ask what Santa left him?"

She glanced at the clock. She could just imagine Lily's reaction if Ryan called her house at 7:00 A.M. "You have to wait until eight-thirty."

"But, Mom, I'm sure he's up."

"Who's up?" Scott asked, walking into the kitchen.

Maggie smiled at him. "Good morning."

"Franklin," Ryan said. "I want to call Franklin and tell him about my bike."

Scott sat down on one of the kitchen stools. "I think your mom is right. You'd better wait until eight-thirty."

Ryan frowned. "OK, I guess." He looked at Scott.

"Will you come help me build something with my new Legos?"

Scott grinned at Maggie. "This, I can handle. I happen to be an expert at Legos."

"I'm scared," she said.

Scott wriggled his fingers like a mad scientist. "Are you kidding? We'll have a replica of the Eiffel Tower in no time."

"I'll go dump 'em out," Ryan said. He dashed from the kitchen into the living room.

"How's he doing?" Scott asked Maggie.

"Recovered," she said. She dropped four pieces of bread into the French toast batter. "How are you?"

"Nothing more than a crick in my neck from sleeping in that short bed. He kicks a lot."

"Scott, I—" She paused in the process of flipping toast. "I don't know how to thank you for what you did last night."

He rounded the counter in two quick strides. He grasped Maggie's shoulders. "You don't have to thank me, Maggie. I was here. He needed to know someone understood what he was going through. I was glad I could be that person."

She went up on her tiptoes to kiss him. "You're a good man, Scott Bishop."

He put his arms around her and held her close. "Good enough for you?" he asked. He kissed her then, a long, lingering, morning-kind of kiss full of promise, and far too short.

"Scott," Ryan called from the living room, "are you coming?"

Scott lifted his head. "Duty calls," he said.

Maggie laughed. "Get used to it."

When they finally sat down to breakfast, it was a

boisterous affair, with Ryan trying to eat as fast as he could and Maggie trying to slow him down. Scott studied Maggie from across the table with a look she found all too disconcerting.

Ryan was fidgeting so much, she was afraid he'd tip his chair over, so she finally decreed breakfast was finished. Ryan was back in the living room in a matter of seconds. Scott reached for Maggie's hand. "Maggie, I want to ask you something."

"Hurry up," Ryan called from the other room.

"Not now, Scott."

"Yes, now."

"But Ryan—"

"It won't take long, Maggie. You know what I want."

"Scott, I can't—"

"I want to marry you."

Maggie took a deep breath. There it was. She'd been dreading it. "Do you want an answer right now?"

"Yes would have been nice, but I guess that's better than a flat-out no."

"I'm just not ready for—"

"Mom," Ryan called. "Come on."

Scott held Maggie's gaze. "I want to know by the end of the day, Maggie."

"But what about Cape Hope?"

"Cape Hope's got nothing to do with whether or not you're going to marry me. You're just using that as an excuse."

She shook her head. "I'm not."

Ryan crashed through the door. "Are you guys coming?"

Scott pushed his chair back. "By the end of the day,

Maggie," he said, then followed Ryan back into the living room.

Maggie was on edge the rest of the morning. Ryan tore into his packages with typical seven-year-old zeal. When he got to the cowboy hat Scott had brought him from Dallas, he nearly went beserk. "Oh, cool! It's a real one, Mom. Look"—he pointed to the feather on the hat band—"it has a feather and everything."

Scott plunked the hat down on Ryan's head. "You look just like a genuine cowboy, sport. The real thing."

"This is so cool. I'll bet Franklin doesn't have anything like this."

Maggie fidgeted. Scott draped his arm across the back of the sofa. "I have something from Dallas for you, too," he whispered in her ear, "but I figured I'd give it to you in private."

Ryan set the hat box aside and reached under the tree for another present. He pulled out a small box wrapped in newspaper. Maggie frowned. She didn't recognize it. "What's that?"

Ryan stared down at the box. "It's for Scott."

Scott sat up on the couch. "For me?"

Ryan nodded. "Yeah. I'm sorry it's not wrapped better."

Scott shook his head. "There's nothing wrong with the way it's wrapped."

"Ryan," Maggie said, "I didn't know you'd bought a present for Scott."

"I didn't."

"Then what is it?"

"Maggie." Scott gave her a censorious look. "Don't I get to open it first?"

Ryan thrust the package into his hand. "Here. I hope you don't think it's dumb."

Scott peeled back the newspaper to reveal a shiny red box. He looked first at Maggie, then at Ryan, then back at the box. He lifted the lid to reveal a green pocketknife. Ryan scrambled over on his knees to point at the knife. "It has six blades," he told Scott. "Even scissors."

"Ryan," Maggie said, "where did you get that?"

Ryan stroked the green enamel casing of the knife. "I bought it last year for Dad," he said quietly. "I"— he looked at Scott—"I just thought you might want it."

Scott closed his eyes. Maggie could see the pulse working at the base of his throat. When he opened his eyes again, they were shiny. "It's a great knife, Ryan. I've never had a better knife."

Ryan's face brightened. "Really?"

"Really." Scott tipped the box to drop the knife into his palm. He opened each blade with the proper amount of reverence, and allowed Ryan to explain all the possible uses to him.

Maggie felt the tears sliding down her cheeks as she watched them. It looked so right. It just looked so right. Somehow, all the fears, all the worries, started to dissolve. It didn't matter anymore that the Cape Hope project was unresolved. It didn't matter whether they lived in Dallas or Massachusetts or Timbuktu. It didn't matter that she wasn't sure she could make a go of By Design.

What mattered was that Scott Bishop believed in her. He believed in them.

She glanced at Mark's picture on the mantel. In that instant, she knew. She knew she'd never lose herself to Scott Bishop the way she'd been lost with Mark. No, she'd loved Mark the way a child loves a child. It had been complete and unconditional. No sacrifice had been a burden. No obstacle had seemed insurmountable. But with Scott, it was a deeper, firmer, more consuming kind of love. The kind that only two people whose hearts have been broken can find when they help heal each other.

She slipped from the couch to walk to the window. The snow was still falling. She heard it whispering its quiet cadence against the windows. Maggie leaned down and reached for the plug to the Christmas tree lights. Suddenly, she was aware that Scott was watching her.

"Maggie?" he asked. His gaze was intense as he searched her face.

She stared at the plug. Her fingers started to tremble. There was an eerie tension in the room, like time had stopped. The clock on the mantel ticked. The sound of the snow seemed to roar in her ears. And that was when she heard it.

The wind began to whistle under the eaves of the house, and it was as if she heard Mark's voice telling her to let go.

"Maggie?" Scott said again.

She looked at him. Mark's voice prompted her. She looked at the plug. Such a simple thing to carry such a dramatic meaning.

"Mom," Ryan said, walking over to wrap his arms around her legs. "I think Dad wants you to."

Maggie looked down at his blond head. "When did you get so smart?" she asked.

He tipped his face back to look at her with a toothless grin. "When you weren't lookin'."

Maggie felt her eyes brim with tears. She looked at Mark's picture on the mantel once again. It was out of focus. It must be the tears, she thought.

"Go ahead, Mom," Ryan said.

Maggie leaned down and plugged in the tree. The white lights flared to life. Scott crossed the room to pull her into his arms. A brisk wind started to rattle the windowpanes.

"Does this mean what I think it means?" Scott asked.

Maggie wiped the tears from her face. "If you still want us."

"What are you talking about?" Ryan asked.

Scott sat on the couch and pulled Maggie onto his lap. He patted the seat next to him. "Sit down, Ryan. I gotta ask you something."

Ryan climbed onto the couch. "Yeah?"

"How would it be if I married your mom?"

Ryan seemed to consider it. "Would we have to move again?"

"I don't know," Scott said. "It depends on whether or not Max Wedgins likes my drawing for the Cape Hope project."

"If he does, do we stay here?"

"Yes."

"But if he doesn't, we'd have to move?"

"Probably."

Ryan looked at Maggie. "Do you want to move to Dallas?"

"I want us to be a family, Ryan."

Ryan shrugged. "I guess it's okay."

Maggie tucked her head against Scott's shoulder with a small laugh. "Well, there you go. We both accept."

Scott hugged her close. "A man couldn't ask for anything more than that. We'll work it out, Maggie. No matter what Wedgins decides, we'll work it out."

Maggie decided it was time to tell him about her meeting with Max when the doorbell rang. She frowned. "Who on earth?"

"I'll get it," Ryan said. He bolted off the couch.

Scott took the opportunity to topple Maggie back on the sofa for a kiss. "God, I love you," he said, and slanted his mouth over hers.

She pushed at his shoulders. "Scott—"

He stopped her protest by sweeping his tongue into her mouth.

"Ahem. I see I'm obviously interrupting something." The voice sounded from the doorway.

"Oh, they do that all the time," Ryan said. "It's OK. They're going to get married. I said they could."

Scott seriously considered ignoring the intrusion, but he could feel Maggie pushing at his chest. Reluctantly, he lifted his head. Max Wedgins was standing in the middle of Maggie's living room. He was dressed in black evening clothes, complete with a heavy wool cape and top hat. "Max," he said.

Max's lips turned into a smile. "Sorry to interrupt, Bishop."

Maggie scrambled up from the couch. "What are you doing here?" she asked Max.

Max tipped his black top hat to her. "Madam, that is no way to speak to your future employer."

"Future employer?" Maggie said.

"Yes." Max reached into his pocket and removed three envelopes. "I was going to forestall this announcement until Monday, but your rather passionate argument changed my mind."

Scott stood up. He frowned at Max. "What argument?"

Maggie poked him in the ribs. "I'll tell you later. Max," she said, "I hope you know I meant what I said."

"Of course," he said. He handed her the first envelope. "There is an advance for your expenses. I shall expect you to coordinate with the architect on any changes."

"Max—" she tried again.

He handed the second envelope to Scott. "I trust, Bishop, there is enough there to cover the expense of your relocation to Cape Hope. I can't have you coordinating this project all the way from Dallas."

Maggie's mouth dropped open. "You're giving the bid to Scott?"

Max gave her a wry look. "I had already decided to do so. You don't think I was taken in by the rather dubious charms of Irene Fussman, do you?"

"I—Carl said that you—"

Max fingered the third envelope. "I was curious about you, Maggie. I'll admit to doing a bit of manipulative matchmaking. I wanted to see just how important the bid was to you. When you showed up at my house to argue on Scott's behalf, I knew that was the kind of passion I wanted on this project. I was also fairly certain you were having a good bit of difficulty with your relationship with poor Mr. Bishop. Your former husband and I discussed it at length."

"You talked to Mark?" Maggie asked.

"See, Mom. I told you." Ryan slid his hand into Maggie's.

Scott was staring at Maggie. "When did you go see Max?"

"Later," she told him. "How could you have talked with Mark?" she asked Max.

Max pushed his hat back on his head with the tip of his walking stick. "You know, of course, that I'm insane? Everyone says so. It does have certain advantages, being out of one's mind, that is. I could see him all along."

"Is he here now?" Scott asked.

"Oh no. He's gone. I believe he was waiting for the two of you to get things straightened out." He looked at Scott. "Your Annie is gone, too. I assure you, they're quite pleased with the whole business."

"This is unbelievable," Maggie muttered.

"I hope you'll forgive an eccentric man's irresistible impulse to meddle, and accept my sincere congratulations."

Scott nodded. "Sure."

Max looked at Ryan. "And lest you think I've forgotten your part in this, young man"—he handed the last envelope to Ryan—"this is for you."

"What is it?" Ryan stared at the envelope.

"Four season tickets and two locker-room passes for the Boston Bruins. I confess, I don't know a thing about hockey, and now that I own the team, I'll expect you to keep me well informed about their doings." He gave Ryan a conspiratorial wink. "Perhaps you'd better call me from time to time and give me an update."

Ryan tore open the envelope. "Oh, cool! Mom, I gotta call Franklin." He raced out of the room.

Max spun his walking stick between his fingers. "Now that we have that settled, I'll expect to see you both in Carl Fortwell's office the Monday following the new year. We have a resort to build." He turned toward the door.

"Max," Maggie said, "you're welcome to stay for lunch. That is, if you don't have other plans."

"Alas," he said, indicating the limousine parked at the curb, "I have already made arrangements for my holiday celebration."

Bobbi leaned against the limousine. Through the open door, a pair of shapely legs, complete with Christmas red high heels were visible. Maggie giggled. Max brushed the snow from his cape with a dramatic sigh. "Perhaps I shall accept that invitation at another time."

"The door's always open," Scott said.

Max nodded. "I'll remember." He regarded the two of them carefully. "I suppose I will have to delay building long enough to allow you a proper honeymoon. Ah well, a month should do it. With all this snow we've had, there's no doubt our groundbreaking will be put off any way." He tipped his hat. "Merry Christmas. Tell Ryan I'll be expecting his call."

He walked out the front door, closing it quietly behind him. Scott looked at Maggie. Maggie looked at Scott. They both started to laugh. Scott grabbed her around the waist and spun her in a circle. "If I hadn't seen it myself, I never would have believed it."

Maggie framed his face in her hands and kissed him. "I love you, Scott."

"I love you, back," he said.

She shook her head. "You don't think he really talked to Mark, do you?"

"Who knows?"

Maggie looked at the tree. "I can't deny that I felt

like I could hear him talking to me this morning."

"Do you think they were here all along?" Scott asked.

"I don't know. It seems incredible."

"Ryan was so sure."

"So was Max."

They stared at each other. Maggie listened to the wind in the eaves. "It couldn't be. Could it?"

Scott opened his mouth to answer when a sudden draft wafted across the room. The bells on the Christmas tree jingled. The tinsel shimmered in the slight breeze. He felt the faint gust of air brush against his face.

"Scott," Maggie said.

"Yeah?"

"I think Mark's picture just winked at me."

Epilogue

One year later

Mark dug his toes into the sand, with a loud, lusty yawn. A man could get used to this. After he and Annie had left Cape Hope, they'd decided they had seen enough of snow and ice for a while. Except for the occasional visits they made back to Massachusetts, they spent their days on this tropical island. Mark had begun to see Annie in a whole new light after they'd left Cape Hope, and lately he was beginning to see signs that maybe she wasn't oblivious to him either. It was looking eminently possible that this life after death wasn't as bleak as he'd first thought.

He was suddenly aware of Annie's presence beside him. He opened one eye. "Where have you been?"

"Around," she said.

He gave her a knowing look. "You were in Cape Hope, weren't you?"

"I just wanted to see how they were spending Christmas this year," she said. She looked defensive. "Yeah, right."

She poked him in the ribs. "You're the one who

sneaked back on Thanksgiving so you could smell Maggie's sweet-potato casserole."

"Well, at least I didn't cry myself silly when Amy was born."

"It was sweet," Annie said.

"I don't see what was sweet about Scott passing out."

"He was moved by the moment."

"He was sick as a dog."

Annie flung a handful of seawater at him. "You're hideous."

He grabbed her hand. "That was cold."

She splashed him with her foot. The spray hit him square in the face. At his startled yelp, she tugged her hand free. She began running down the beach. "Bet you can't catch me, Romeo."

Mark took off after her.

Maggie rubbed her foot against Scott's bare leg. "How much longer do you think we have?" she asked.

He craned his neck to look at the clock. "It's five-thirty. Ryan should be begging to get under the tree in about ten more minutes."

Maggie traced a lazy pattern on his chest. "Do you want your Christmas present now?"

He arched an eyebrow. "Can I have it in ten minutes or less?"

She tweaked one of his curling hairs. "You're rotten."

"What am I supposed to think when you ask me a question like that while you're draped all over me?"

"I should have known."

Scott heard a slight sound from the nursery adjacent to the bedroom. "Make that five minutes," he said. "She's gonna be squalling for breakfast any second now."

Maggie stretched, wondering how it was possible to feel so content. She could hear the wind whistling through the eaves of the house. They had never bothered to have the draft fixed. It meant too much to them both. Maggie propped her head on Scott's chest. "Do you think they're arguing?" she asked.

He knew right away she was referring to Mark and Annie. "Who knows. They sure do make enough noise up there."

"I think they're really happy, Scott."

"I know they are."

She kissed him. "I'm really happy."

"I didn't think it was possible to be this happy," he confessed.

Maggie glanced at the family portrait now prominently displayed on their dresser. "Scott?"

"Hmmm?"

"What would you say if I told you that by this time next year, we'd have to have a new portrait made?"

He looked at the picture. "Don't you like that one?"

"I love that one. It's just that it'll be incomplete by next Christmas."

"Incom—" He stopped. "Maggie, are you saying what I think you're saying?"

"How do you feel about adding another room onto the house?"

Scott laughed as he rolled her beneath him. "Really?"

"Really. I'm due the end of September."

"You don't mind do you? I mean, it's so soon after Amy."

She shrugged. "I would have liked to have waited a little while longer, but we're so, well, compatible. I guess it was kind of inevitable."

Scott kissed her soundly. "I have never felt this good in my whole life."

She wrapped her arms around his neck. "Merry Christmas, darling."

"Merry Christmas," he said, bending to kiss her again.

The shutters began to rattle, and the windows to squeak. The sun glistened on a fresh Christmas snow. And the wind blew through the frost-laden pines of the quiet corner of paradise in a place called Hope.

Dear Reader,

Sexy Scottish heroes, tantalizingly long nights spent mesmerizing a man, love stories that won't be forgotten...all this—and more—awaits you next month from Avon romance!

Linda Needham is fast becoming a rising star of romance, and her latest, *The Wedding Night*, is a wonderful, sensuous love story filled with all the power and passion of her earlier books. When a young woman is forced to marry a dark and dashing nobleman she expects to do her duty...but she never dreams she's also lost her heart to the one man capable of breaking it.

Lois Greiman's *Highland Brides* series is at the top of many readers' list of favorites. Her latest sweeping, sexy love story *Highland Enchantment* is sure to please anyone looking for a thrilling hero...and a powerful love story. If you haven't read the earlier books in the series, don't worry! This title is supremely entertaining romance for you, too.

Susan Sizemore is a name many of you recognize, and her Avon debut, *The Price of Innocence* is filled with the lush sensuality and powerful emotion that her fans have come to expect. When Sherry Hamilton looks across a crowded ballroom, she never expects to meet the eyes of the man who once took away her innocence. Can she now face a man she has never stopped hating—and loving?

Mary Alice Kruesi's *Second Star to the Right* is a must read for lovers of contemporary romance. It's tender, poignant, and one of the most magical love stories I've read in years. A single mother comes to London to escape her past, and finds her heart stolen by a man who makes her once again believe that dreams can come true.

It's all here at Avon romance! Enjoy,

Lucia Macro

Lucia Macro
Senior Editor

AEL 0499